SI
SLICING

TONY J FORDER

A DI Bliss Novel

Also by Tony J Forder

The DI Bliss Series
Bad to the Bone
The Scent of Guilt
If Fear Wins
The Reach of Shadows
The Death of Justice
Endless Silent Scream

The Mike Lynch Series
Scream Blue Murder
Cold Winter Sun

Standalone
Degrees of Darkness

To all our key workers…

ONE

I T WAS IMPOSSIBLE FOR him to decide which he feared most of all: enduring the constant pain gnawing its way through to the centre of his being, or the stomach-convulsing dread of how the man in the ragged mask would inflict it upon him next time.

For the most part, his current existence was intolerable – a raging miasma of terror and suffering no sentient being should ever have to withstand. Squirts of adrenaline coursing through his system no longer held any positive effect, his shredded nerve endings responding as if shards of glass raced through his bloodstream, nicking vital veins and arteries as they decimated him from the inside out. The agonising intensity of the pain wore away at him, physically and emotionally, worsening his decline and devouring what little reservoir of strength remained.

Arguably, the worst aspect of each passing intolerable minute was having no option but to tolerate it.

Merely thinking about the persistent discomfort somehow led to a resurgence of physical sensation, and though by no means as sharp or penetrating, the violent throbbing caused a variety of muscles to spasm. His jaw clenched and both rows of teeth clashed against each other, adding to his overall suffering. In these moments, his head flew back as far as it was able, the cords in his neck extended, eventually becoming so taut he imagined they were about to snap. The expectation of further misery tore gaping wounds inside his mind, as if burrowing into his brain in an effort to conceal itself from what lay ahead.

Contemplating the next dose of unrelenting torment and despair left him drooling and gibbering like an asylum patient after a round of electroconvulsive treatment.

It was not only the awful, gut-wrenching dread of the blade causing him to react this way, nor the horror associated with the attention his fresh wounds would receive immediately afterwards. For by now, even the subtlest whisper of dry leaves, a rustle of undergrowth, or the skittering of claws on hard-baked soil made him writhe and weep in fearful anticipation of the creatures whose thirst for blood and appetite for warm meat marked him down as easy prey.

He did not know for certain how long he had been naked and exposed to the elements, strung up between wooden posts driven deep into the earth, lengths of twine binding him by his neck, chest, waist, thighs, shins and ankles. The design of the structure to which he was bound left him angled forward, and he constantly felt as if he were on the point of tipping over onto his face. It left him in a permanent state of disequilibrium, which he had swiftly come to appreciate was the least of his concerns.

His bindings forced his naked body into a human X shape, the vulnerability of which became apparent to him early on. When rodents came calling, they did so via every soft, exposed route giving off heat, and the horrific nature of their initial penetrations had left him begging for swift release.

A number of days and nights had passed since he'd been strung up this way; were it not for the sultry weather, his exposure might already have cost him his life. Not a moment in recent memory had slipped by without him longing to welcome the cold embrace of death. During rare moments of lucidity, he assessed his deterioration, and believed himself to be clinging to life by the faintest of threads.

The torturous existence he had experienced was enough to break him, psychologically and physically – but not spiritually. Quite the opposite, in fact. He was not a man of God, yet still he prayed for blissful release, the severing of that mortal strand currently preventing him from moving into the great unknown. How he had not succumbed to his multiple wounds was a mystery he had no inclination to solve; how he had withstood it mentally was incomprehensible to him.

Torture, he now knew with absolute certainty, broke the psyche along with the mind and body, overcoming the most basic human will to survive. Yet his was by no means the classic method of destroying a person's resolve, because for many the end could be bought with a confession, with information. For him there was no price to pay, because so far none had been sought. For him the nightmare continued unabated, a ritual of punishment meting out unimaginable cruelty upon him.

His left eye hung heavy in its socket, compressed by the weight of the scab-encrusted lid. It oozed, stung like paper cuts, and itched so badly he wanted to scratch at it until it was as raw as the lid had been. The scratches and bite marks that had torn into the cornea now hampered his vision through the gelatinous leakage.

Only it still saw things.

Terrible things.

Things approaching noisily through the undergrowth in a swarm of matted hair and grim determination; grey and vague in shape, but seen for all that. When he snapped his eye shut, his mind continued to recreate the images for him, and the horror of imagination was almost always worse than the reality, resulting in him opening it back up again.

But what it saw terrified him.

Every. Single. Time.

So much so, it practically came as a relief when his tormentor happened to return before the hungry scavengers had scampered up his legs in search of any nourishment unleashed by the previous visit. The sound of an approach lacking stealth in dense woodland caused the creatures to scatter in all directions, for which he was so thankful it forced a fresh welling of scalding hot tears to pulse from his eye. The bloody pulp of socket no longer encasing his right eye seemed to weep in sympathy, yet all it did was dribble pus onto his cheek.

It did not matter if pain was approaching in the form of a demented mind and a sharpened blade. Because at least this time he would not feel the warm breath of vermin – made fetid by the rotting particles of his own tissue caught between their teeth – upon his flesh. For the moment, the gnawing mouths and lapping tongues as rough as sandpaper would be denied.

He looked up as the man moved to stand before him. As usual he had a rucksack over one shoulder, inside which he carried fresh water and food. And, of course, a variety of tools and devices. Behind the terrifying figure, a sturdy thicket of trees coalesced into an amorphous blur; a solid and impenetrable wall barring his escape. A wall with skeletal limbs reaching out to either fend him off or wrap him up in their unforgiving embrace, prolonging his captivity either way.

'Kill me,' he pleaded for what must have been the dozenth time, his eye now focussed on the man whose most awful trait appeared to be his merciless patience.

As on every previous occasion, the man remained silent. His face unrecognisable behind a mask of thick material with holes allowing him to both see and speak if he chose, the figure regarded his captive without a flicker of sympathy or regret in those dull, emotionless eyes.

After allowing him to hungrily devour a tasteless turkey sandwich and gulp down half a bottle of tepid water, the man in the mask reached out to pinch the flesh of his shrinking stomach and raised a sharpened steel blade. His prey submitted this time with little more than a whimper. Today the surrounding woods would not echo with the sound of his cries for help or pleas for mercy. Today, they would reverberate to his agony and horror being given voice.

TWO

THE BISTRO OFFERED STUNNING views overlooking Torquay Marina on the beautiful English Riviera. At a table for two out on the patio, Bliss leaned back in his chair, basking beneath glorious sunshine in eighty-degree heat. The polo shirt and light grey chinos he wore made him comfortable and relaxed. His eyes, however, were fixed in a tight squint, since he had chosen not to wear sunglasses. Every so often he took a sip of lager from his pint glass, reminding himself to eke it out as he had a long drive ahead of him later in the afternoon.

Boats bobbed gently on the water within the compound of the sea walls, tugging at their moorings; bowriders, motor yachts, sailing boats, and skiffs. Nothing as ramshackle as his cruiser back home in Peterborough, but still Bliss found pleasure in their rhythmic fall and rise. Beyond the curving grey wall of the marina, the sea out in the bay was calm, deep blue, glittering as if strewn with shards of broken mirror.

'Hey, where'd you go to, Jimbo?'

His wandering gaze shifted across to the owner of the voice and fingers snapping him from his contemplation. 'You remember what I once said I'd do to you if you called me Jimbo again?' Bliss asked, smiling as he shook his head.

Her eyes sparkled. 'You said you'd throw me off the roof. I wouldn't mind, but I was already about to jump. You won't be threatening me with that this time, I don't suppose.'

'Don't tempt me.'

'Aw, you'd never have done such a horrible thing to little old me. Spanked me, maybe. I can imagine you doing that.'

'At the time, yeah, so could I.'

Molly laughed and clapped her hands together. 'I was only a kid. Now I'm seventeen, so it'd be, like, assault or something.'

'Rather than the child abuse it would've been.'

'Yeah.' She paused to take a hit of her lemonade. Belched out loud. Giggled as she used the back of her hand to wipe her lips. 'We've come a long way since then.' She sounded wistful.

'*You* certainly have,' Bliss said. The many years of abuse she had suffered seemed not to register any longer, and he was glad of it. 'You're looking great, Molly. You've put on a bit of weight – believe me, you needed to. But you also look toned, and your skin has a healthy glow to it.'

'What are you doing checking out my skin, you perv?'

He groaned and rolled his eyes. 'You're relentless. Tell me again why I drove all the way down here to see you?'

'Because you loooove me,' she said in a sing-song voice, hugging herself as she twisted from side to side in her seat.

Her laughter was infectious; Bliss couldn't be happier to hear it, despite bearing the brunt of her childishly humorous remarks. It was all a far cry from the first time he'd laid eyes on her one bitterly cold, wet December morning, a few minutes before he'd pulled her back from the edge of the roof she was about to jump from. Molly's involvement as a county lines drugs courier had later led Bliss and his Major Crimes team to protect her from a pair of ruthless men – one a supplier, the other a dealer. Eventually, with his help and encouragement, she had been sent around the country to couples offering emergency foster care, until she wound up in Torquay with a family by the name of Berry, who had decided they wanted her to remain with them provided she was happy to stay.

By this stage, Molly had revealed her full name and family details to the authorities, having initially refused to do so. Following a thorough investigation, social services decided she should remain in their care until she turned sixteen, at which point she'd be able to choose to leave the system or continue to live with Adam and Fiona Berry and their own eight-year-old daughter. Molly opted to stay, and her documented pathway plan meant she could do so now until her eighteenth birthday, with the possibility of extending her care order until she reached twenty-one.

But Bliss had come bearing news he knew would change everything, and he was becoming increasingly concerned about how Molly would take it. The changes he saw in her were dramatic and positive, but no matter how deep a person buried fifteen years' worth of memories, preventing them from ever resurfacing was an impossible task.

For security reasons, Bliss hadn't been able to see Molly after she left his reach until a couple of months ago, by which time her transformation had astonished him. From her carefree attitude to the way she carried herself with a straight back and firm shoulders, he guessed her life was better now than she had ever dreamed was possible. Her taking up the option to remain with her foster parents until she turned eighteen reinforced his opinion. Curiously, she looked younger today than she had when he'd first encountered her. She had worn her situation like a second, thicker skin, impervious to the mistreatment she suffered at the hands of wicked men. Having successfully sloughed it off, a new and shiny version of Molly had emerged.

'How are things at home?' he asked.

'Brilliant,' she replied quickly, turning her head to face the sea beyond the marina walls. 'Couldn't be better.'

From her physical reaction and the way she answered him, Bliss knew the girl still feared having her happiness snatched away at any moment. Only, he knew something Molly did not; something Fiona Berry had asked him to share with the girl during his visit. The request had taken him by surprise, but it was Fiona who had reminded him how close he and Molly had become during the short time they were thrust together. Apparently, barely a day went by when she did not mention him, and the Berrys insisted he should be the one to tell her what they hoped would be welcome news.

Bliss drained his glass and cleared his throat before launching into his prepared speech. 'Molly, how would you feel about being adopted by Adam and Fiona?'

The girl turned to face him, a puzzled frown creasing her forehead. 'For real?' she asked.

Bliss nodded. 'It came up a while ago, and social services have since cleared the way with your biological mother. The men who were after you are no longer interested in either you or those taking care of you. With the sheer volume of people willing to make statements against them, and prison sentences handed down to all the main players, you are well and truly off their radar. You'd be wise to steer clear of London and Peterborough for the time being, but otherwise you're safe and not considered a threat to their organisations – which means your foster parents are also safe. With no possibility of you being ripped from their care and placed elsewhere, they broached the subject of adoption with social care. When they got the go-ahead, I was given the honour of discussing it with you first. Testing the water, if you like. So… what do you think?'

For a second or two, Molly failed to react. Bliss watched her process everything he'd told her. Her shoulder-length, dark brown hair flapped with abandon in the breeze that whipped in off the sea. With the added weight filling out hollows in her cheeks, she was a great-looking kid, who wore surprisingly little makeup. She blinked rapidly, and Bliss thought maybe the wind wasn't the only thing bringing tears to her eyes. When she finally spoke, her features became a curious mask of both delight and bewilderment.

'You mean they want me to carry on living with them? Even after they stop getting paid to keep me?'

Bliss shoved his glass to one side and leaned forward, resting his elbows on the beaten copper tabletop. 'Molly, I'm saying they want to adopt you now. I'm telling you the money means nothing to them, but you do. Adam and Fiona don't want to be your foster parents any longer. They want to be your parents. They want you to be their child.'

'Seriously?' The girl was incredulous. Bliss understood all she had endured at the hands of her mother, the only parent she had ever known. The thought of somebody else wanting her in their life was something she was having difficulty with.

'Molly, it's been almost twenty months since I found you on that rooftop, but things have changed for you so dramatically that it might as well be decades. You've been fortunate enough to find a couple who love you so much they want to give up fostering you and legally make you their own child. In turn, they have been fortunate enough to find a vulnerable girl who just needed somebody to care for her and make her realise she was no longer on her own. Now you have the opportunity to become the woman you were always destined to be.'

Molly dipped her head. Bliss suspected she was finding it difficult to imagine all of the many possibilities and consequences. The girl's hard life was behind her now, but its painful legacy could be summoned up in an instant. He gave her the time and space she needed to work through it. When she regarded him once more,

Molly was smiling. 'Is it all right by you if I say yes to them?' Her voice quivered.

'By me? Of course it is. Why on earth wouldn't it be?'

'Because back in Peterborough when you saved me, I made such a big deal about coming to live with you. I thought you might think badly of me if I agreed to stay with them, to be adopted by them.'

Bliss shook his head. 'Not at all. I couldn't be happier for you, Molly.'

Through the tears spilling onto her cheeks, she laughed and said, 'So is it all right by you if I still have a bit of a crush on you instead?'

'I'd be disappointed if you didn't.'

Bliss was thrilled. When he first met her, Molly had been used and abused by suppliers, dealers, and their friends since she was barely into her teens. Nobody would have blamed her if she had been mentally destroyed by everything life had thrown at her. Yet he had taken to her immediately, such was the spirit and wit and temperament she had displayed when confronting such adversity. He believed she would have stopped herself from jumping off the hotel roof at the last second, but was nevertheless so glad he hadn't allowed her to put his theory to the test.

The first time she thanked him for saving her life, Bliss had pointed out that for him to have succeeded, she would have to go on and live her life to its utmost, to become the best version of herself she could possibly be. He had given her a second chance, no more. What followed was all down to her. Molly had grasped the opportunity with both hands.

'You'll have a great life,' he said. 'And you deserve to. Don't ever think otherwise. New parents, new little sister, new home. I hear you're doing well in school, so you have everything going for you now.'

Molly's smile faltered. 'Does this all mean we won't see each other again?'

Bliss narrowed his gaze, reprimanding her with a fierce look. 'Don't be so bloody ridiculous. Your new mum and dad are terrific people, and they are perfectly happy for us to spend time together as and when we can. And, in case I have to add this for your benefit, so am I.'

He was touched by the way her smile broadened and weight appeared to lift from her shoulders. Two vertical indents between her eyes also looked to have filled out. The conversation had gone remarkably well, and Molly seemed delighted by the thought of being adopted into the Berry family. He felt happiness radiate off her, and he warmed himself in its fierce glow.

When his phone rang, Bliss groaned, thinking it would be HQ back in Peterborough; a job for him to pick up and run with, no doubt, despite being off duty. The number he read on the screen of his work mobile was not one he recognised, however. For a second he debated whether to answer it, but then he asked Molly if it was okay. She shrugged as if questioning why he would bother asking. In her previous life, a phone could never remain unanswered.

'DI Bliss,' he said as he hit the green accept button.

'Jimmy Bliss. I'm glad I managed to get hold of you. I don't know if you remember me, but this is Pete Conway. DI Conway as was, back in the day.'

Bliss recognised the name. Conway had joined the Serious and Organised Crime Agency the year after Bliss had taken up a post at the new unit. A couple of years later he'd transferred out again, and Bliss hadn't thought about the man since. The call intrigued him.

'Yeah,' he said. 'Of course. How's it going, Pete?'

'Not so bad, Jimmy. I'm a Superintendent these days, down in Wiltshire. I contacted Thorpe Wood a few minutes ago, and they gave me your number.'

'Should I be concerned?' Bliss could not imagine why Conway would be calling him all these years on, and he had no cases running with any connection to the Wiltshire constabulary.

'To be honest with you, Jimmy, I'm not sure. It's just – we've got a peculiar one on the boil, and when we ran the details through HOLMES, your name popped up.'

Swallowing thickly, Bliss said, 'Okay. What are the circumstances, Pe… Superintendent Conway?'

'Pete is fine. Anyhow, we can't make much sense of it right now. But the gist is, a bunch of tourists came across a discarded carrier bag at one of our tourist spots. Inside it they found a reasonably large slice of human flesh. About the size and heft of a chicken breast fillet.'

Bliss closed his eyes for a moment. Nine days ago, a significant chunk of meat later identified as human was discovered inside a white plastic bag placed in the stone fireplace of the Knights' Chamber, above the gateway to the Bishop's Palace at Peterborough Cathedral. So far no identification had proven possible, and no accompanying body had been found; neither had the hospital or walk-in clinic reported any relevant injuries. Despite the two incidents being over a hundred miles apart, he wondered if this was the break his team had been looking for.

'Was there anything carved into your find?' Bliss asked. With Molly sitting across the table, he deliberately avoided using the words 'piece of flesh'.

'Regrettably, there was. That's one of the reasons why HOLMES made the connection between the two cases.'

The Home Office Large Major Enquiry System was into its second version, which was proving far superior to its predecessor. Bliss thought this kind of specific detail would have been a cinch for the data system to have spat out within seconds.

'Does the detail of the carving mean anything to you?' he asked.

'No. It's a series of letters and numbers, none of which suggest a thing to us. And before you ask, no, it's not the same as in your own case.'

Bliss cursed silently. 'Have you had a chance to check blood type?' he asked.

'I know what you're getting at, Jimmy. No, we haven't yet processed blood type because we've had this case for just a few hours. But in response to your unasked question, this cut of flesh is not from the same person as the one you have up there.'

'Shit!' Bliss said. This drew a disapproving look from a couple two tables down, causing him to lower his voice. 'How do you know that?'

'Because yours is listed as IC1. And I'm pretty sure we'll be reporting ours as IC3.'

Until formal identification was made, IC codes determined the perceived ethnicity of a person. Bliss assumed somebody was in the room with Conway, which explained why he had elected to use official terminology. The bloody chunk of flesh found in the bag at the Knights' Chamber had white skin. Caucasian. Conway was telling him the flesh in their case was black. Afro-Caribbean.

'Yeah, believe me, I realise how that sounds and what it means,' Conway continued. 'This whole bastard thing just took a turn for the worse.'

Bliss was inclined to agree. This was more than he had initially imagined. 'Are you in your office?' he asked, checking his wristwatch.

'That's where I'm calling from.'

Reluctant as he was to leave Molly earlier than intended, he'd said everything he'd needed to say. The girl was happy. They'd spent time together, and he'd be bailing out on no more than a couple of hours with her. His glance caught her own. She grinned and gave a shy nod, wiser than her years. Molly knew what he wanted from her, and she had willingly acquiesced.

'Wait right there,' Bliss told Conway. 'I'm on my way.'

As he pocketed his phone, Bliss looked across the table. He found it difficult to describe his relationship with Molly. Not father and daughter, nor brother and sister. Closer to uncle and niece, perhaps, or even friends. What he did know was that she was now an indelible part of not only his past and present, but also, he hoped, his future. Though he had only met with her on three occasions since she left Peterborough on the outward journey to the rest of her life, a special bond and closeness had developed between them. It defied everything that had brought them together in the first place.

'I'm sorry to put the kibosh on our day, but I have to go.'

'I know. Duty calls, and all that heroic stuff.'

He smiled. 'I'm no hero, Molly. Believe me.'

'You are to me, Jimbo.' Molly shrugged. 'But then, so was Spongebob.'

THREE

B LISS ARRIVED AT THE Swindon Gablecross headquarters thirty minutes later than he had intended, having got snarled up in roadworks on the way. What he saw as he pulled up was impressive. The exterior of the fifteen-year-old building was significantly more welcoming than the dour edifice of the Thorpe Wood police station back in Peterborough. It looked like a school or a hospital, its top-to-bottom glass central atrium and surrounding cream walls portraying a corporate facade. Bliss parked up and announced himself to the civilian receptionist, from whom he received a visitor card and lanyard. Shortly afterwards, he was escorted up a naturally lit flight of stairs and along a narrow corridor to the detective superintendent's office.

Peter Conway had gained pounds in addition to years, seemingly on a two-for-one basis. The crisp white shirt he wore stretched tight across his stomach, a tribute to the quality of the stitching holding the buttons in place as they strained to break free. His blotchy cheeks and jowls suggested a man out of condition and struggling to cope with the hot weather despite the air-conditioned room. The two shook hands and exchanged the usual pleasantries as Bliss took a seat.

Conway had provided a few basic facts over the phone, but now announced that he was already late for an important meeting and had little time to elaborate. 'You ever heard of West Kennet Long Barrow?' he asked, mopping his forehead with a balled-up wad of tissue paper. 'I've been living here for donkey's years and I hadn't. Evidently it's a minor tourist attraction, especially for those into ancient landmarks.'

Bliss was already nodding. 'As it happens, I not only know the place, I've also visited it. My parents loved Wiltshire, and my mother was into mythology and the mysteries of the past. Probably her Celtic heritage breaking through. I got into the whole thing as well, though. We did the tour of those ancient sites several times when I was a nipper. Come to think of it, I may still have a cousin living in nearby Calne.'

Conway rearranged himself in his chair, fingers interlaced across the bulge of his belly. 'You have me at an advantage. I'll be honest, when I visited the scene this morning, I couldn't see what all the fuss was about. An ancient burial chamber marked by standing stones – as if this area doesn't have enough of those. An odd place for somebody to dump an excised portion of human flesh, wouldn't you say?'

'I would. Only, I'm sure you realise it almost certainly wasn't dumped.'

'What do you mean?' Conway's eyebrows angled down towards the bridge of his nose.

'Leaving the carrier bag where it's bound to be discovered, in an iconic spot… that smacks of deliberate placement to me.'

'Yes, of course. Makes sense. More so since I became aware of the case you have running in Peterborough.'

'Have you had any luck in identifying who…?'

The superintendent shook his head. 'Still too soon. Blood testing and DNA analysis will take time. And so far, nobody has strolled into A&E with a chunk of their body missing.'

'I wouldn't hold my breath on the DNA if I were you,' Bliss said. 'There was no match in our own case.'

'I noticed that on the report HOLMES spewed out. Our own forensic results won't be available for a day or two. I doubt we've had time to gather the swabs and send them off to the lab as yet. We've only been on the case for a few hours, Jimmy. I was hoping you might be able to steer us in the right direction.'

'In what way?'

'You've been living with this for over a week now. You have the advantage over us.'

'Not necessarily. As of today we're nowhere, it's a stalled case, and it's caused a lot of frustration among my happy campers. If anything, I'm hoping your find will restore some enthusiasm back home. Let's hope whoever did this made a mistake this time.'

'Interesting. Shame you don't have more to go on.' Conway nodded, pursing his lips and gazing upwards, as if digesting the information.

Bliss smiled but shook his head. 'No, it's not. I can tell you already reached the same conclusion. Sir, forgive me, but why are you sitting there stroking my ego? You called me, you clearly wanted me to make myself available for a consultation. Only, you're off to a meeting and I get the impression I'm being courted for something.'

Conway chuckled. 'You always did have a way with words, from what I remember. Blunt to the point of insubordination. Okay, it's a fair cop. My feeble attempts at making you feel immediately useful have bitten me on the arse, and I apologise. The truth is, I'd like you to stick around. Visit the site and get a smell of it, draw it into your lungs. Check out the evidence exhibits, sit in on a briefing or two. That way we pool and double our knowledge.'

Bliss ran a hand across his face. 'To what end?' he asked. 'You want me involved because you think there's more to it?'

Conway blew out a puff of air. 'I have questions, Jimmy. It's early days, but my people are already scratching their heads. You're heading up an identical case, so in effect we're both hunting the same person. Rather than leave the fate of this op to my superiors, who'd probably fanny about in numerous meetings before taking the most politically prudent course of action, I'd like to hand operational leadership over to you.'

'Why me, sir?'

'Because despite what you say, you're over a week further down the line on this. I also know you to be scrupulously fair, so you'll make sure we get credit for whatever work we do to support you. Plus, you already have a major stake in whatever this turns out to be.'

Bliss nodded. Now wasn't the time for humility. 'Running side-by-side operations with my unit taking the lead isn't a bad idea. I had a similar role in a case with the Lincolnshire force a while back. We pulled that one off successfully, but it relied on a lot of goodwill. You think your bosses will go for it?'

'I don't see why not. It makes no sense trying to force it the other way round, and working two entirely separate cases isn't in the best interests of solving the bloody thing.'

'Then how about your team? How happy will they be playing second fiddle?'

'They won't be. As you would expect. But if I make it clear this is what's best for our victim, they'll have no choice but to get over it.'

Bliss liked what he heard in the other man's earnestness. Unmistakably, Conway's main concern was for the investigation and not his personal glory. The stamp of a decent copper. About to reply, Bliss was struck by a moment of realisation, which prompted a question. 'The excised flesh,' he said. 'Ours was removed from somebody who had a pulse at the time – not a corpse. How about yours?'

Conway nodded. 'Same. As far as I know.'

'You working on the assumption they may still be alive?'

'We are. The physical evidence is pretty much secondary, because we think there's a victim out there somewhere bleeding to death. Pathology will need to confirm, but the crime scene manager was adamant: the flesh was removed from a living person. A man, in this case.'

'Hence the urgency.' Bliss did not have to deliberate. 'Okay, I'm on board for the time being. Let's skip back to the flesh engravings for a moment. Any clue as to their importance?'

'None whatsoever. There's something about them, though. I feel as if I should know what they mean, but I don't. None of us do.'

'So what does yours say? The carving?'

'Two letters followed by two numbers. *PC94*.'

Bliss thought about it for a few seconds. The inclusion of two numbers this time was different. The carvings his team had identified read either *WSHO* or *OHSM*, depending on which way around the section of flesh was read. The disparity gave him a queasy feeling; it suggested this case was going in the direction he feared most.

He quickly switched his mind to other matters. 'Does the geography concern you at all?' he said. 'If our victim in Peterborough was the first to have flesh sliced from his body, why not remove another piece and leave us that instead? Why move down here and risk going for a second victim when you already have one? In fact, why leave anything here at all?'

'I had the same concern while you were driving over here. I did wonder if it was simply a question of logistics: your victim is somewhere in or around Peterborough, mine is in or around Swindon.'

It made sense to Bliss. You wouldn't want to drive far with chunks of human meat about your person. Unease bumped up against him once again, disparate thoughts jostling for attention. Two victims plus the engravings in their flesh suggested to him there was more to come. And a fresh victim indicated the first was already dead.

Conway finished drumming fingers against his stomach and got to his feet with a less than subtle groan. 'Anyhow, Jimmy, I genuinely have a meeting to attend. I thought you'd want to visit the location while there's daylight left. I realise now you're already familiar with the place, but given the head start from your own discovery, I thought maybe you'd spot something we've overlooked. Something you might recognise meaning in.'

Bliss stood. He had fallen into line, but he wanted to make his feelings known. 'You know I'm going to agree simply because there's the possibility of the victim still being alive, but you have to know it's a long shot. Your man may well have been living and breathing when a decent-sized section of his flesh was removed from his body, but the chances of him showing up now are remote.'

They started walking out of the office and back along the corridor with its deep blue flooring and pale walls. 'I realise that,' Conway said softly. 'But if you're going to lead this case, I have to assume you're itching to get out there to take a look at the scene for yourself. In all honesty, I don't remember a great deal about your work with SOCA during my time there, but I do know you have a reputation for being hands-on and thorough.'

The Superintendent accompanied him back down the stairs, while Bliss contemplated in silence. 'You want me to send a gatepost with you?' Conway asked.

Bliss almost smiled. It was common to refer to officers at the rank of sergeant as gatekeepers, and when their colleagues were feeling particularly droll they'd use the derogatory term instead. Bliss had known officers who became slow and lazy after their promotion to DS; no longer in the frontline when the grunt work was being handed out, and not high enough up the greasy pole to slide back down again if they chose to sit behind a desk. He thought of Chandler and Bishop and knew there was no way either of them would ever be compared to a gatepost.

He shook his head. 'No, I'll be fine on my own, thanks.'

Conway did not argue. 'Fair enough. Take a ride over, have a look around. There's a team briefing here at six. Come back, listen to what we have, study the evidence, share your thoughts with us. I'll put you up in a nice hotel for the night, then you can choose to either drive home in the morning or give us a day of your time tomorrow as well.'

Bliss took a breath. He did not enjoy being painted into corners, but he also recognised the position Conway was in. If there was the slightest chance of their victim still being alive, he would take help where he could find it. Realising he would have done precisely the same thing had he been the superintendent, he dipped his head in acknowledgement and said, 'I'll stick around for now, sir. No promises, though. Those carvings mean absolutely nothing to me, but I can't deny I'm both intrigued and excited by this second find.'

'Excellent. Give us the rest of today and tomorrow, Jimmy. That's all I ask.'

'Sure. But I think we both know your victim won't be found alive. Neither of them will be, in my opinion.'

FOUR

A CCORDING TO THE ROADSIDE signage, the city centre was straight ahead, but Bliss knew the route meant encountering the Magic Roundabout, a notorious abomination consisting of five mini roundabouts surrounding a larger sixth. After a brief holdup, he eventually turned left and headed towards the M4, though his tyres would not be touching the motorway itself.

Bliss sat back and allowed the drive to flush irrelevant thoughts from his system. Ignoring the racial discrepancy between the two slices of flesh, he kept returning to the carvings. If they were meant to be a clue, why had the combined intelligence and imagination of two entire teams of detectives been unable to decipher them? Something was off. But what? What were they all overlooking? Were the figures deliberately vague? Were the individual carvings making their own unique statement, or was the person responsible feeding them information in stages? Neither *OHSM* nor *WSHO* had triggered anything substantive in him or his colleagues, and Conway's team had got no hits from their *PC94*. Put them together in either combination and they still amounted to nothing, as far as Bliss could tell. So the obvious question now was: what if the message was incomplete?

The thought chilled him, physically causing hair to stand erect on his arms and at the base of his neck. It made him shudder, because it suggested whoever was responsible was set on playing a long game. A second find of human flesh showing up less than ten days after the first seemed to confirm the theory. It implied something about their quarry: the person responsible was thinking several steps ahead, like a chess player. This type of personality was the most terrifying of all opponents, and Bliss felt his stomach clench.

There were also the victims to consider. Were he and his colleagues looking for two men minus a considerable chunk of flesh each, living in agony beyond all imagination, or should they be searching for two dead bodies? Bliss leaned towards the idea that the Peterborough victim was dead; the only reason to suspect otherwise was that no remains had been discovered – so far. Nor had there been any other grotesque surprises left for the police in plastic bags.

Bliss adjusted the direction of his thoughts. Why remove the portions of flesh? Perhaps the perpetrator thought of himself as a man to be feared, teasing it out by depositing his victims piece by piece, and this was his way of revealing his proclivities to the police and the public at large. Did these findings imply both current victims were dead, and this nutjob was out there waiting to choose his next? Bliss was having trouble getting a handle on it, not seeing the ultimate goal. It felt like some outlandish twist on Schrödinger's cat – except that in reality nothing was ever both dead and alive.

His mind reached out to DS Chandler, his partner. He imagined what she would say to him questioning their offender's endgame.

'Perhaps he doesn't have one.'

'Oh, they all have one,' Bliss would scoff in reply. He shook his head bitterly. Mundane or twisted, sordid or run-of-the-mill, they all have a goal. They don't always know what it is themselves, but it's there, lurking in the absence of light at the back of their minds.

Bliss's pool Ford Mondeo ate up the miles. He put his foot down when gaps opened up, blowing past slow-moving vehicles as he approached Avebury, before turning west on the A4. Conway had told him his team and the forensic unit were gathered together at the scene.

'Much media up there?' Bliss had asked as he'd been about to head out the door.

'Enough. They've been drifting in throughout the day. We've set them well back, but you know what they're like.'

Bliss pictured the scene. He didn't relish the thought of getting caught up in all the official hoopla, so continued further along on the A4. He drove past the entrance to West Kennet Long Barrow, before pulling into a lay-by which had been designated a visitors' car park. He realised it would be a harder slog trudging uphill to the scene, but he also knew he needed the exercise.

As he got out of his car, Bliss glanced along and across the road to a large mound that looked like an enormous upturned bowl covered by grass. He recognised Silbury Hill, though it had been many years since he had visited the area. He remembered a lot of its history still: the largest artificial mound in Europe, over four thousand years old. Built during a time of great change in and around Britain, but especially in this particular region. As he'd breezed through the winding roads of Avebury, he'd admired the village's remarkable standing stones, which were erected during the same Neolithic period – as was the Long Barrow he now approached.

At the gated entrance to the burial site, a lone uniformed constable barred his way. The PC's cheeks were glowing red and the overbearing heat looked to be taking its toll on him. He wore a short-sleeved shirt and his arms were turning a deep shade of pink. 'Sorry,' he said cheerfully, 'the Long Barrow site is closed for the rest of the weekend at least. There's been an incident up there and I'm afraid I can't allow you entry.'

Bliss flashed his warrant card. The officer began feeding him directions to the spot where the official vehicles were parked, but Bliss insisted on entering through the kissing gate. One quick check on the officer's two-way communications device and he was allowed through.

As the sun descended over to his right, its heat gradually dissipated. A procession of wispy clouds appeared to be following it into the far horizon, spectators on the trail of a major celebrity. Out on the exposed hillside a faint breeze stirred the tall grass, but it was cooling and welcome. As he made his way up towards the site, Bliss continued to dredge his memory regarding the historical significance of the burial chamber he was climbing towards. Its construction had begun four hundred years before that of Stonehenge. Forty-six bodies, from children to elders, were believed to have been entombed inside it, all seemingly within three decades of each other, though the Long Barrow had remained open for over a thousand years. The side chambers were arranged inside a precise isosceles triangle, drawing admiration from historians and geometrists alike.

Once again, Bliss heard Chandler's voice grating inside his head. *'How do you know all this shit?'*

He leaned into the climb; the chambers themselves were half a mile from the road and all of it on a steep incline. 'It's not "shit",' he would have replied, with no small measure of exasperation. 'It's our nation's history, our heritage. I happen to be fascinated by it, and have been since my parents brought me here. After that, I wanted to know more, so I borrowed books from the library.'

Yet none of what he had learned from his studies was going to help him explain why somebody would leave a bag of human meat up there now. Given its remote location, he and his team would have to ask themselves why anyone would go to such lengths to deposit the product of their insanity there. Maybe the site was chosen deliberately, something symbolic, at least to whoever had taken the time to leave the macabre item.

Nudging the thought aside, Bliss worried about his state of mind. Chandler wasn't in her usual spot beside him, yet still he was conversing with her. It was taking place inside his head, but the discussion reminded him of how inseparable they had become. He had long considered her to be the Yin to his Yang. Chandler had once told him she thought of herself as the Jiminy Cricket character, whispering words of advice in his ear. After Bliss had told her that Pinocchio kills the talking cricket in the original version of the story, she never mentioned it again.

Feeling the pinch in his calf muscles and along the backs of his thighs, Bliss was relieved when he reached the long mound. An outcrop of large standing stones, several of them ten or twelve feet high, concealed the entrance. The place was swarming with forensic techs, uniformed officers and a few suits standing in the background, each of them in animated discussion.

Bliss took a moment to gather his breath. Hands on hips, he sucked air in and blew it out in a steady stream. He was parched and felt the nagging twinge of a stitch in his side. He also needed to prepare himself mentally for what lay ahead, because from the moment he'd heard from Conway, he had been unable to shake one thought in particular. The kind of person who went around slicing flesh off living men and creating a puzzle for the police from the pieces, was the kind of person who would eventually kill and kill again. Because by the time they had reached such an extreme, theirs was an existence of escalation and experimentation wrapped around a central core of intent.

It was simple: there was every chance the police were witnessing either the birth or rebirth of a serial killer.

FIVE

A UNIFORM WITH THREE CHEVRONS on his shirt sleeves spotted Bliss approaching, broke away from the group he'd been in deep conversation with, and introduced himself as Sergeant Malcolm Talbot. In his role of duty officer, he had attended the scene after the first responding PCs reported in. Having examined the slab of flesh and declared it real rather than a latex prop from a horror movie, Talbot had set about securing the entire site, summoning both CID and the CSI team, as well as informing the police surgeon. He also arranged for the family of Welsh tourists who had discovered the bag to be interviewed and provide statements.

'The poor sods were keen to get an early start because they wanted to visit both here and Avebury today, and figured they'd kick off with the site most liable to be quiet first thing in the morning.' Talbot, sweating in his hi-vis vest, raised his eyebrows. 'Not their day, I guess.'

'Any idea what time window we're working with?' Bliss asked.

'Not as such. Mr Lewis says they arrived shortly after eight. We can't know for certain when the last visitor was here yesterday, however. Or an earlier one today, for that matter. It's mostly a tourist spot, but it's also used by pagans for ritualistic worship. People are expected to visit during reasonable hours of daylight – but given the site is wide open, there's no way of officially recording how many come to the Long Barrow, nor precisely when.'

'Did you say pagans?'

'Yes.' Despite the affirmative, Talbot shook his head. 'And I can imagine where your thoughts are leading, so let me stop you right there. No, this would not be part of their ritual worship. Around the time this place was built, maybe. But not now.'

Bliss nodded. He knew something about pagans. 'As I understand it, they have closer ties to Wicca than Satanism. Earth worshipper types. Quite peaceful in this modern age.'

'So far as we're aware, yes. Apparently they prefer… intimacy, rather than bloodshed, if you know what I mean.' Talbot waggled his eyebrows and allowed himself a smirk. He had angular features, and red hair which extended to a light dusting of trimmed beard. His skin tone did not cope well beneath a burning sun.

'The condition of the flesh may provide us with a clue in regard to timing,' Bliss suggested, steering them back on course. 'I've not been told of any blood being discovered here, so any body the slice was removed from has to be elsewhere, but possibly close by. If pathology and forensics can tell us how much time passed between the loss of blood flow and the discovery, then we get our window. Any thoughts on how whoever left the bag for us got here?'

Talbot shrugged. 'Impossible to say at this point. There are any number of ways to approach the site, and plenty of spots where he could've parked up. We're searching for fresh tyre marks and footprints, but it's not the cleanest of locations. It's too well-travelled, so I wouldn't bank on us identifying the method of access.'

As they talked, the two men were ambling around the perimeter of the site itself, keeping outside the blue and white ribbon of tape erected by the first responders. Talbot stopped opposite the entrance to one of the chambers. A ring of stones, several of which towered over the rest, protected the aperture. He pointed at a gap between the largest boulder and one of its lesser brethren.

'They discovered the carrier bag in there. About two or three paces in. Mr Lewis said they thought perhaps another visitor had dropped it accidentally, so they were keen to return its contents to whoever had misplaced it. You can imagine his reaction when he opened it up.'

Bliss could. Vividly. As a police officer, you got to see up close an awful lot of things nobody was ever supposed to encounter. The human form was designed to remain intact, but the bloody mess of those times when its internal composition was uncovered revealed stark imagery of an intense, graphic nature; few who were exposed ever forgot their first time. Unless he worked for the emergency services or had served in the military, Mr Lewis was unlikely ever to have encountered fragments of human flesh before today.

'I take it you've checked out their story?' Bliss asked.

'As far as possible. Their B&B landlady in Marlborough confirms they left immediately after breakfast, shortly before seven-thirty. It's a fifteen-minute drive and a ten-minute hike up here from the main road. So unless they brought the bag with them, I think we can safely rule them out.'

Bliss already had, but he'd hate anything to slip through the net. Opening his mouth to suck down a decent lungful of warm air, he looked around. It wasn't far off fifty years since he had last visited the Long Barrow, but it didn't look to have changed a great deal compared with the images bubbling out of his memory like an unwatched pot boiling over. He didn't recall the path across the burial mound, nor the wooden fencing along its edges, but everything else was familiar. He spotted no other markers that could have been intended for his eyes only.

'Is it okay if I go inside?'

Talbot nodded. 'The crime scene manager has cleared the area. You need to follow the designated pathway in and out. It's tight in there, so you go on your own. Yellow marker number one indicates the original location of the bag, according to the Lewis family. Have a look around. Any questions, I'll be waiting right here for you.'

Beyond the protective upright boulders, a supporting structure of smaller rocks and stones led into the entrance on a slight decline, above which a huge stone lintel had been mounted. Battery-powered Nomad LED floodlights illuminated the tunnel. The densely compacted, flinty tunnel floor was solid underfoot, and levelled out once inside the chamber. Bliss found uneven surfaces hard going due to his Ménière's disease; the condition often triggered vertigo attacks, so he was grateful to re-establish some equilibrium after the vagaries of the climb and the undulating terrain outside the burial site.

The marker showing the precise location of the carrier bag was, as described, between two and three paces into the chamber. Not immediately visible from the outside, but not so far in that a casual observer would miss it. *I'd have to know what was inside the bag if I saw it lying on the floor*, Bliss thought. *Most people would.*

Three further markers stood on the floor of the chamber. He made a mental note to ask the crime scene manager for a list of items found during the forensic sweep. Whatever they collected might still be in their van; if not, Bliss would need to check with the exhibits officer when he got back to Gablecross.

Recalling his conversation with Conway, Bliss scoured both the ground beneath his feet and the rocks and stones used to create the chamber. He walked further in, looking for any sign left expressly for the police by the perpetrator. He was amazed to find the pale grey stones – now stained a light shade of green – unblemished by graffiti; the place was a paradise for would-be taggers, he imagined.

But neither could he see any mark, symbol or message carved or painted for his attention.

When Bliss emerged back into daylight, Sergeant Talbot was talking to another man, whose white protective suit had been pulled down around his waist. 'You the crime scene manager?' Bliss asked, walking up to the two men, his hand already extended.

'That I am,' the forensics investigator said. He removed a glove and they shook. 'Damien Hawthorne.'

The man cut a slight figure. His narrow face appeared gaunt, and he wore thick glasses with a heavy tortoiseshell frame. Bliss thought the man looked undernourished, as though the bottle of water in his hand might be the only thing to pass his lips all day. 'Good to meet you, Damien. Tell me, there are four evidence markers inside the chamber. I understand the first indicates the location of the bag, but what other items did you find?'

'Most likely nothing of value to the investigation, but bagged and tagged all the same. We collected a metal eyelet from a boot or walking shoe, an ice lolly stick, and a discarded sticking plaster. A greater number of shoeprints than you can possibly imagine, of course, but the bag and its contents was the real prize.'

Bliss rubbed the back of his neck, still feeling a prickling heat upon his skin. 'I take it you examined the item in question before sending it off?'

'As far as I was able. Human, male, IC3, and in my opinion the victim was almost certainly alive when sections of his flesh were removed. I got them biked over to our lab immediately afterwards.'

'Male because of body hair?'

'Precisely.'

Bliss had picked up on something the crime scene manager had said. 'You mentioned sections of flesh. Plural. What else was inside the bag?'

Hawthorne's face betrayed the first sign of hesitation as he glanced at Talbot. 'It's all right, Damien,' the sergeant said amiably. 'DI Bliss is on board.'

The man exhaled his relief. 'Of course. Apologies, Inspector. In addition to the obvious main cut of flesh, there were also several finer, smaller strands. Offcuts of tissue and gristle, I suppose you might say.'

'Bugger,' Bliss said on a sigh. 'I was hoping it would be something different, but we had the exact same thing in our own case.'

'Your own case?'

The police officer and crime scene manager were both frowning at him. Bliss winced and shook his head. 'Sorry, I thought you knew. The reason Superintendent Conway asked me to take a look at the scene is because we had our own bag of ugliness on my patch in Peterborough, the week before last.'

'Now that is interesting,' Hawthorne said, immediately enthusiastic. He took a swig of water before pressing on. 'Mind you, I'm not sure how it affects my own musings.'

'Your own musings?' As the outsider of the three, Bliss played along.

'Yes. Any thoughts about *The Merchant of Venice* in relation to your crime?'

'I'm not up on my Shakespeare,' Bliss confessed. In truth, he wasn't a fan at all, but he quickly identified the forensic man's line of thinking. 'Isn't there something about a pound of flesh?'

'Indeed. Shylock demands it as security on a loan.'

'It hasn't featured in our thinking so far, no, but I'll bear it in mind.'

'Well, it was just a thought. Any other evidence, as far as you're aware?'

'Other than the bag and its contents, no.' Bliss asked for a sip of water, and gratefully slaked his thirst.

'Just one whole section and a few strips of straggly flesh and gristle,' the CSI manager said as Bliss handed back the bottle.

Bliss nodded. 'Ours was also from a male, but a different person entirely, it seems. Different race, in fact, which is unusual.'

'Oh, Jesus.' Talbot threw back his head. 'So there are two victims out there, two virtually identical finds?'

Something else struck Bliss for the first time. 'Yes, there are. But there's another similarity: ours was also left for anyone to find, and at a historical monument, of sorts.' He explained about the Bishop's Palace and its attachment to the cathedral.

'Doesn't sound entirely coincidental,' Talbot said. He stood with both hands clasped at his waist, one thumb moving animatedly over the other. 'As for the find itself, I wondered why the Super had asked us to extend you every courtesy. He did mention you two had worked together.'

'Not exactly. We both worked for the NCA at the same time.'

'Ah, I see. The UK's very own FBI. I'm impressed.'

Bliss had heard the same observation many times, and always refuted it. 'Don't be,' he said, shaking his head. 'That may be the media's view of the agency, but it's mostly incorrect. They do a lot of important work, though.'

'Either way, you've had a lot longer with your evidence than we have with ours, so what can you tell us about it, Inspector?'

Bliss grunted. 'I'm afraid all we have are questions – minus answers. Our single large cut of flesh was in a similar condition to the one found here this morning; relatively fresh, minimal decomposition. No other body parts or the body itself, dead or alive, to go along with it.'

'How about the carvings on the back of the flesh?' Hawthorne asked.

'Ours was different, but definitely intended to tell us something.' He didn't know how much Conway had revealed, so kept the precise details to himself. Talbot was sharp, however, and his eyes narrowed.

'So, you're busy working on your op, and along comes another which fits precisely, and it just so happens that you and Superintendent Conway both worked for the NCA at the exact same time.'

'As it happens, I misspoke earlier. It's the NCA now, of course, but back then it was SOCA.'

'Still, you'd have considered the connection, yes? Between the excised flesh, the victims, whoever sliced off the flesh and left it for us to find, the carvings, plus you and the Super. Has to all tie together somehow, wouldn't you say?'

Bliss rolled with it. It was hard to argue with the train of logic, but he disputed it anyway. 'It's certainly possible, and I'm not ruling it out, by any means. However, I do see it as coincidental at the moment. Superintendent Conway and I never even worked a case together. He asked me to take a look at the scene in case there was something else out here, something I'd perhaps notice as a result of our own investigation. If there is, I'm not seeing it. Nothing beyond the obvious.'

Talbot gestured towards the scene. 'Well, we'll be around for a while yet. If we come across anything unusual, I'll make sure you're notified. That's if you don't see it on the news first. Bloody media people are already asking about your presence here.'

'What did you tell them?'

'I didn't. They exchanged words with a couple of my officers. Neither man knew who you were or why you were here, so they weren't able to answer any questions.'

'Probably for the best,' Bliss said.

'That's what I thought. We could do without the distraction.'

Looking around the hillside, the A4 running like a black river below, Bliss did not like the odds. 'You've got a tough job on your hands with a scene this size.'

'You're not wrong,' Talbot said, grimacing. 'I have help coming over from Oxford, though, which should speed things up.'

Bliss understood the man's lethargy. Even the smallest scenes of crime could be extremely demanding; something on this scale was as close to unmanageable as you could get. He was unable to think of anything else he needed, either from Hawthorne or the duty officer. He said his goodbyes and started walking back down the hill towards his car.

The scene had told him nothing he didn't already know. He'd hoped to gain a greater insight from his visit, but without any genuine expectation. As with his own case, the scene he'd visited was not the scene of crime; there, he would expect to find a wealth of evidence. Given the distance between the finds, he had to assume a similar distance existed between the crime scenes. He was beginning to consider narrowing the focus and concentrating on the carvings and their possible significance.

Bliss let all speculation fall away as his eyes took in the landscape and terrain. Somewhere out there lurked a madman playing games. Also out of sight, two men either in utmost terror or no longer breathing. Fear thrived in the unknown and the unseen. The thought took up residence in the darker regions of his mind.

SIX

SINCE MOVING BACK TO the city of Peterborough in the autumn of 2017, Bliss had given no thought to living elsewhere, and the Thorpe Wood Major Crimes unit would undoubtedly be his final posting. Although recent changes to the retirement age would allow him to extend his service for a further seven years if he wanted to – or didn't screw up – he had no desire to see out his days in some quiet backwoods where nothing of consequence ever happened. He had an exceptional team around him who followed his methodology; if he moved on, he would be unlikely to find the kind of understanding he now enjoyed with senior management. He saw no reason to consider leaving his present home. Not until after retirement, at least.

Bliss thought Swindon was similar to Peterborough if you drilled down deep enough. Both were typical built-up cities, yet each had wide open spaces surrounding them. But whereas the flatlands around his home were often bleak and desolate, especially during the winter months, he found the sweeping Wiltshire hillsides inspirational. They offered an abundance of scenery to capture the imagination, heart and soul – if such a thing existed. Until now, he had given little thought to what he would do with himself after he retired, but having been reminded of this county's glorious landscape, Bliss could imagine himself settling down in these parts. He liked the idea enough to give it serious consideration.

A nice quiet country cottage next to a nice quiet country pub in a nice quiet country village. Provided the pub sold Guinness on draught, it sounded like a marriage made in heaven.

Even the area station was a major improvement on the sullen, faded brickwork of Thorpe Wood. As for its interior, the plumbing and air conditioning appeared to work, the vinyl flooring retained its sheen, carpets felt springy beneath his feet, walls reflected light rather than capturing it without ever letting go, and his money was on the heating actually delivering the ideal temperature when needed.

Superintendent Conway had allocated Major Incident Room Two at Gablecross to the investigation. As Bliss had expected, it was airy and bright and seemed not to carry the stale odour of food or people in its paintwork or soft furnishings. In his role as Senior Investigating Officer, Conway had been hard at work since the two had last spoken. When Bliss entered the room five minutes before the evening briefing, the Super had already pulled in an office manager and a finance manager to take the administrative burden – actioning, analysis, HOLMES support, documentation, intelligence, and exhibits – leaving him to concentrate on the investigation itself. A major incident was a beast of many moving parts, and it was Conway's job to ensure the beast did not become an overbearing, unwieldy monster. Especially one that consumed budget as if it were going out of style.

In Bliss's experience, the SIO typically took a hands-off approach, retaining an overall perspective of the case and attending briefings as required, but mainly acting as the figurehead. Usually it was those of his own rank – and, more often than not, the sergeants and constables beneath – who did the spade work. He knew of many inspectors content to lead from the rear, though he had never understood why. Whether his desire to immerse himself in an investigation implied he was a control freak or simply a man who liked to be involved rather than a sidelined observer, Bliss neither knew nor cared. Either way, he had been unable to detach himself from the daily grind. Which was what most cases were.

Conway kicked off the meeting with a statement outlining the progress made so far. He confirmed the discovery of a substantial chunk of flesh together with several finer strands of tissue. The male victim had been alive when brutalised, and forensic and pathological examinations were underway. When he turned his attention to the similar case in Peterborough, all eyes turned to Bliss.

'Inspector,' Conway said, 'perhaps this is the perfect time to introduce yourself.'

Bliss groaned inwardly. There was never a good time to be thrust into the spotlight, so he got through it quickly. 'Hello, everyone. I'm DI Jimmy Bliss, currently stationed at Thorpe Wood in Peterborough. I wish I had more to tell you after working the case for nine days, but so far what we have amounts to what you have: bugger all. But this additional piece of human flesh should eventually give us something to work with, and the figures carved out of it are clearly significant. In my view, that's where we should be concentrating our focus.'

'What about the two victims? Surely all of our efforts ought to be steered towards finding them?' The question came from a man seated to Conway's left. He was older than the others, and Bliss guessed he was the DI on whose shoulders the investigation would inevitably fall. He didn't look Bliss squarely in the eyes, preferring instead to aim the question at his own DSI.

'Normally I would agree,' Bliss said, fixing his attention on the detective who had spoken. 'And of course, you and your colleagues are free to investigate your own crime as you see fit. Superintendent Conway asked me to take a look and offer my opinion, which is what I'm doing right now. In addition, as we have already identified a direct connection between your fresh case and our ongoing one, he has also suggested I take the lead here for the time being. So I'll tell you how I see things. In my view, if either of these two vics is still alive, the best way we have of tracking them down is if we solve the mystery of the carvings.'

His challenger gestured towards the interactive whiteboard, on which the case was broken down into neat tables. 'And with respect, I'd disagree. You've had the Peterborough case running for, what, nine or ten days now, and you and your team are still drawing a blank on the figures carved into that piece of flesh. I doubt we have greater minds here, so it's not hard to see it panning out the same way for us. I'm not sure where following the exact same lead gets us. All I'm saying is, I'd rather not waste time trying to decipher these figures, which may mean nothing to anyone but the demented bastard who carved them.'

'I take your point, Inspector…?' Bliss let it hang there.

Curiosity lit a flame in the man's eyes, as if he were wondering how Bliss had known his rank. 'Paston,' he said.

'Okay, DI Paston. I understand what you're getting at. If we find the perpetrator, it may lead us to his victims. But tell me, where would you start? You have no witnesses, no forensics, no physical evidence apart from the human flesh our culprit deigned to leave you. Exactly where would you begin your manhunt?'

'I haven't had this op for long,' Paston said, becoming hesitant. 'It's going to take me a while to form a strategy.'

'Okay. Let me save you some time. There is no strategy for this. Sure, you can appeal for witnesses, go door-to-door locally – if you can find any doors out there, that is – and I urge you to do it all so you can say you've ticked off the necessary investigative boxes. You don't know me, DI Paston, so you may think I'm being arrogant in assuming you won't hit on something we failed to consider. That's not the case. If you or any members of your team can jump in right now and tell me you have a bright idea how to proceed, I'm all ears. Until then, I firmly believe these carvings were made for the specific reason of telling us something.'

'If that's the case, why can't we understand it?' someone else asked – a female detective this time. 'Why haven't you been able to understand yours?'

Bliss spread his hands. 'I don't know. As I have freely admitted, I don't have all the answers. But I suspect the reason is because we don't have the entire message as yet.'

'Would you explain your thinking on that specific issue, please, Jimmy,' Conway said.

Bliss guessed the DSI had taken the room's temperature and not liked what he'd found. His team were unhappy at having somebody from a different area trampling all over their investigation – especially one who had so far not been able to gain traction with his own case.

'Of course, sir. Let's take a look at the elephant in the room, shall we?' he said. 'Two substantial slices of flesh from two different men, left in similar ways for us to find, and marked as they are, tells me this is the beginning of something, not the end. Irrespective of any obscure connections, we have at least two victims out there. If they're not dead, then they're badly disfigured and, we must assume, in a terrible state. Our case in Peterborough is stalled. No DNA, no victim ID, no apparent matching missing persons report. Same here, as far as we know, although obviously it's early days and it could all change rapidly. However, two men go missing and nobody reports either? How's that possible? Were they chosen at random, are they vagrants plucked off the street? It would explain why they're not on our radar. Are they even missing? Were these punishments doled out to two men who were sent on their way afterwards, minus significant chunks of their own bodies? If so, then they have to be villains themselves – why else would they not report their ordeal to us?'

Another of Conway's team was shaking his head. 'If you don't mind my saying so, DI Bliss, you just talked your way out of what you initially mentioned. You began by saying this wasn't over. Yet now you're telling us these two men might have been punished for some sort of gangland transgression, which would suggest we're not looking at a serial in the making.'

'I don't mind you saying so at all,' Bliss replied, keeping his composure. 'And if I believed that had happened, then I would agree with you. But I don't believe it. I was merely providing alternatives to save you time in coming up with them yourselves.'

'They sound like acceptable leads to me.'

'They do. But none of them bear closer scrutiny, in my view. Because the last theory only works if we disregard the chunks of flesh themselves.'

Conway stood and walked across to the board. 'How so?' he asked, studying the details closely.

'No gangland criminal, no matter how outrageous they are, is going to stage the exhibits the way these two were.'

'That seems a reasonable assessment.'

'Coming back to the figures carved out of them – in my opinion, they are a crucial component. There's a relevance there, but we also have to ask ourselves if our victims' identities are significant, as well. What if they were neither homeless nor chosen at random? What if they were targeted family men? Which brings us full circle to why we've had no reports of hospitalisation or men being reported missing.'

This elicited a range of audible sighs from inside the room. 'That's an awful lot for us to take on board, Inspector,' Conway said, coming back to the table. 'All ifs, buts and maybes.'

Bliss nodded, casting a glance around the room. 'Which is precisely what my team and I are still working with more than a week later. And from what I'm seeing here, it's all you'll have by next weekend as well. With no obvious way of tracing our victims, we're reduced to waiting for something else to happen.'

'Such as?' DI Paston leaned back in his chair, hands clasped behind his head.

'Either another scrap is left from a different body, or we receive additional pieces from the same two victims. If one of them provides us with another carving, it may make sense of the previous two. Or somebody reports their husband, boyfriend, son, brother or mate missing. Or somebody walks into A&E and offers up a bloody body to be sewn up.' Bliss let out a breath and hiked his shoulders. 'Tell me I'm wrong,' he said. 'Please do. I'll be happy to buy the first round if you can prove it.'

The female detective who had spoken previously shuffled in her seat and offered up a sigh of resignation. 'To be fair to us, and as the boss has already made clear, we've been working this for a few hours, compared to your many days. And to be fair to you, the picture you just painted doesn't seem to have any faults.'

'Look, I share your sense of disappointment,' Bliss told her. 'I've lived with it longer than I care to admit. My only suggestion right now is to look harder at these carvings. After all, other than the locations where they were dropped – plus the obvious fact that we're dealing with two different vics – the next major difference between the finds is those two engraved markings.'

'And do you have any other thoughts on those, Inspector?'

Bliss rubbed the pad of his left thumb across a tiny scar on his forehead. 'I do, but they're not positive ones,' he said. 'Are you sure you want to hear them?'

'Let's have it.' Superintendent Conway leaned towards him. 'That's what you're here for.'

'Okay. Let me make it clear to you all that the moment I saw those figures carved out of the flesh found in Peterborough, my immediate thought was to wonder if this was the first of many such finds. A chunk of flesh without the carving tells a different story. With it, we're talking about intent, above and beyond the mutilation itself. It also occurred to me from the moment I saw what had been done that we might have to wait for further finds to show up before we'd be able to make any progress. Of course, at the time I was thinking of *our* next find and assuming it would be from the same victim. Now I've had time to reflect on today's discovery, and the additional confusion it's caused, I have to say that in my view we may not get anywhere until there's a third find. Maybe even a fourth.'

A ripple of disquiet spread throughout the room. Bliss held up a hand and raised his voice above the clamour. 'Listen, I'm not suggesting we pull back on the reins, or that we don't put everything into this that we possibly can. But I've been here before, and I'm seeing the exact same frustrating lack of worthwhile evidence or information. You asked what I think, so I'll tell you. Whoever's behind this is playing a game. He wants our interest, but he also wants to string it out. There will be another bag left for us, and it wouldn't surprise me if what we found inside that one was worse still. Either way, there will be a string of carved figures, because that is our man's real focal point. Perhaps adding the next engraving to those we already have will trigger a spark in somebody's head. And, like I say, it may require a fourth or more for it all to make sense.'

'That's a somewhat dispiriting notion,' Conway said. His face was a study in anxiety, beads of sweat collecting at his hairline. He didn't appear to know what to do with his hands.

Bliss nodded. 'I agree, sir. But when you slot all the pieces together, it's what we're left with. The carvings are the key, and because the ones we have so far don't make any sense, my instinct says there are more to come.'

SEVEN

THE BARN WAS A wreck, dilapidated by age and decades of neglect. For every half-intact board remaining, another was either absent or perished beyond saving. The surviving planks hung perilously, often by a single rusty nail. Buckled and bleached, most leaned to one side or the other. Parts of the roof offered colander-like protection from the elements, rods of bright light spearing through minor fissures; others were missing entirely, having blown away or collapsed. In a number of repaired areas, corrugated tin strips rattled and emitted mournful groans each time the barn shifted on its weak foundations. One vicious squall and the structure would no longer be standing.

The man lashed to the X-shaped crucifix positioned in the centre of the barn was beyond caring about his exposure, and longed for the storm to come and take him with it. His mind had shut down in protest against the vermin crawling all over him, satiating their hunger by consuming him little by little. Nutritional deprivation and thirst had left him weak and helpless, his flesh toasted from the sun whose light and burning heat streamed in through the jagged openings in the shattered roof. All of this misery he was able to withstand – not that he had any alternative – but every time he heard the approach of the vehicle bumping over the dirt track towards the barn, his entire body began to tremble until convulsions set in.

With the masked man came sustenance. A sandwich of some description. Fresh water. It wasn't a lot, but it kept him alive. And though he no longer wanted to live, baser instincts kicked in when food and drink was offered. He rationalised his capitulation by telling himself if he did not slake his hunger and thirst willingly, the masked man would surely force it down him. But there was no comfort at all in knowing that the prolonging of his existence also extended his capacity to be tortured.

The slow and deliberate slicing of his flesh with a variety of sharp objects flushed his system with adrenaline, yet its numbing effects lasted mere moments before raw nerve endings reacted, sending massive surges of pain ripping through his weakening body. His torturer had initially begun with minor cuts and lacerations, before moving on to the meat packed around the waistline, pinching bountiful love handles between the fingers of his left hand and using the right to carve off three-inch slabs. Buttocks and thighs came next, the masked man continuing to seek the chunkier areas of flesh.

All of which was horrifying beyond belief. Yet what followed each slice was infinitely worse. The man's blowtorch spat blue flame, and as its heat cauterised the bloody wounds, the same exposed nerve endings erupted in the excruciating grip of utmost agony. As the flame seared him, he smelled the vile stench of his own skin roasting. He heard his blood bubbling and popping as it turned black and hard. He had often pleaded with the man in the raggedy mask to get it over with, to end the torture, but this only seemed to fuel his tormentor's lust for inflicting pain.

During those moments when he was entirely alone in the barn, with not even a passing fox taking an interest in him, he hallucinated. Colours altered – at first the world became monochrome and two-dimensional, then brightly garish. People from his past dropped by to pass the time of day with him, and at one point the soil beneath his feet began to shift before erupting; myriad creatures emerged from the bowels of the earth to prod and poke at him, swarming all over his flailing body. None of it daunted him nearly as much as the hooded man, though. For when he came, he brought all kinds of real agony and misery along with him.

As the memories of previously endured horrors galvanised his torment, he suddenly jerked his head up as far as it would strain on tendons weakened through lack of use. An engine. A vehicle approaching. He steeled himself for what was to come, braced against the vicious brutality about to be inflicted upon him. But the moment he tried to make a steel trap of his jaw, determined not to play the masked man's game this time around, fresh floods of tears streamed down his cheeks. Snot bubbled from his nose, thick mucus leaking from each nostril to mix with his salty, hot tears. Were it not for the dehydration, his bladder would surely have voided itself.

What was it going to be this time, he wondered? His fevered mind could scarcely bear the uncertainty as the engine died. Moments later the man appeared inside the barn, his backpack of nightmares hanging easily over one shoulder.

For the steady and patient slicing, the man used one of three different knives he kept wrapped in a roll of cloth from which he'd also fashioned the ugly mask. For broader sections requiring greater depth, a cleaver had been his weapon of choice; the production of an axe this time caused the crucified man's eyes to bulge and strain, his body lurching into spasm. But his bonds allowed only small, ineffective movements. The masked man had been efficient.

Approaching with the same sense of unhurried ease as he had on each previous occasion, his tormentor first untied the thick cord from around his left wrist before sliding it up onto the forearm and retying, pulling it tighter until it became a tourniquet. The tortured man's hand lay against the sturdy wooden post to which it was tethered, fingers splayed, and as his peripheral vision caught sight of it he knew what was going to happen next. Without word or pause or emotion, the man swung the axe hard. Its sharpened steel edge chopped deep into the left arm at the wrist, where the harsh binding cord had already eaten into the flesh. The axe initially withdrew with difficulty, before falling again. After a third and final blow, the hand came away as the blade retracted. Blood spurted from the vast open wound. The masked man picked up his prize and placed it inside a white carrier bag, together with the scraps of tissue and bone that had fallen into the dust.

He was without a care in the world, or so it seemed; indifferent to both his grotesque actions and the terror and agony being exacted.

Gasping as he attempted to suck in air and cry out at the same time, the victim glanced sidelong at a wrist gushing blood, the jagged ulna and radius spearing skywards like driftwood caught on a beach. The cloth wedged between his teeth and fastened behind his neck dulled the mighty roar of suffering, but the electric sluice of razor-sharp pain ripped through his bloodstream and caused a writhing twist of panic to spear vertically along his spinal cord. He yelled to no effect, wept as if fountains had erupted from both eyes, gagged on harsh breaths behind a cloth that was damp with sputum. His tiny world collapsed deeper into itself, and pinpoints of light danced like a cloud of fireflies around his head.

'No more,' he gasped; a faint whisper. 'No more.'

The masked man ignored him. He returned to his toolkit, and took out the butane blowtorch.

EIGHT

O N MONDAY MORNING, BLISS had Chandler collect him from home.
She was dressed in her usual style – halfway between formal and
casual, but tasteful and appropriate for the weather. She wore her
hair differently every day; today's choice was a single braid, which
meant she'd risen early and had time to spend on her appearance.
Astonished at being asked to chauffeur him around for the day, his
DS was not slow in relaying her shock the moment he slid into the
passenger seat of her Ford Focus.

'You have a perfectly adequate pool car sitting right outside your
house,' Chandler said, jabbing a finger towards the grey Mondeo
parked up on his narrow driveway.

The last vehicle he'd owned had been written off by his insur-
ers following a chase incident; it was the second such car he'd
destroyed in the same year. Given the quotes he'd obtained for
insuring another car, he had decided to stick with pool cars for
the foreseeable future, though he intensely disliked having to share
with others. This was his third Mondeo, and he'd managed to secure
this one on a semipermanent basis.

'Just get us to HQ and stop being such a harpy,' Bliss said, dis-
missing the half-hearted complaint with a flap of his hand. 'I put

in a lot of miles over the weekend. I ache like a bugger, and I need a break from driving.'

'Even at the risk of having to endure mine?'

'Evidently so.'

Chandler rolled her eyes and groaned. 'Well, you're in a pleasant mood, I see. What's up – did it not go well with Molly?'

'No, my trip went swimmingly. She's loving life, and it shows. I'd say she's blossoming into a fine young woman, and I could not be more pleased about that if I tried.'

'That's lovely to hear. So she obviously settled in with her foster parents all right?'

'Better than we ever imagined. They want to adopt.'

'Molly?'

'No, me. They finally realised the one thing lacking in their life was a curmudgeonly geriatric. Yes, of course Molly. Why say it like that?'

'No reason. She's just… troubled, is all.'

'Which is something her foster parents see beyond. Anyhow, she's a different kid to the one who gave us all that grief. Like I said, she's becoming a stable young lady, and a very pleasant one as well.'

'So what's with the attitude this morning?'

Bliss drew in a deep breath and told his partner about the rest of his weekend, including how on Sunday he and Superintendent Conway had continued to draw blanks. With no additional information coming through from either the scene or the investigation team, they had decided there was little point in Bliss hanging around after lunch.

'I'm knackered,' he explained. 'Too much driving, too much yomping up and down hillsides, too much lousy police station coffee.'

'Did your friend at least treat you to dinner on Saturday night?'

'No. He had to get home to his family – and I'd hardly describe him as a friend. He fobbed me off with a female DS who'd spoken up at the briefing. Or fobbed her off with me, more like. I'm not quite sure how she felt having to give up her Saturday night for me, but at least she got a free meal out of it.'

'Was she working with you yesterday as well?'

'She was. Came across well, actually. Quite a laugh – in your face, a bit hard to read at times, but knew her job and stayed tight-lipped when she had nothing to add. You might consider taking a leaf out of her book on that score, Pen.'

Chandler gave him two fingers and threw in a blown raspberry for good measure. 'Don't call me Pen. So, the upshot is you spent your weekend off working and it took our own case no further? You'd think that would be impossible with a whole new crime scene and fresh evidence.'

Nodding, Bliss said, 'My thoughts precisely. Except it isn't really a crime scene, although of course they treated it as such – same as we did with our own discovery. Still, whoever did this came and went at two sites without being observed, leaving no trace of themselves, and no evidence other than what they wanted us to find.'

'They always leave some kind of trace, boss. And take it away with them.'

'Yes, thank you, Penny. I'm well aware of Locard's principle. What I'm saying is that we've turned up nothing obvious. Nothing to point us in a particular direction.'

'I suppose if the second find does anything, it at least confirms our own impression: the carvings are a crucial element. Even though we've not been able to decipher their meaning so far.'

'If there's a connection between our victims, I'm baffled as to what it could be.'

'You're not the only one.'

Chandler took the first junction moments after crossing the river, and at the roundabout hung a left onto Thorpe Wood road. As they approached the station, she asked if his time in Swindon had given him any novel ideas regarding how to handle their own case.

'Nothing at all,' he answered. 'It's frustrating – but today I'm expecting Conway to officially approve a joint task force.'

She glanced across at him. 'I hope you insisted on us running it.'

Bliss smiled, delighted by her eagerness. 'I didn't have to. Conway approached me with the idea. He figures an ex-SOCA colleague won't leave him out in the cold, so it made a lot of sense for him to step back and push us forward at the same time.'

Chandler snorted. 'Yeah, but that's him. Will his boss feel the same way?'

'Pete thinks he'll go for it. As he said at the time, this is a case we're bound to get exasperated with, but it's also one we'll work our nuts off to resolve. The brass will see it differently: a troubling case consuming budget and time and lingering like a stain on their records.'

'When you put it like that, why would we want it?'

'We already have it – our own operation, at least. Pete says he'll attempt to ease it through by implying that half the resources equals half the costs and sharing the stain around. We will lead, but it'll be a joint op. In reality, not just in theory.'

Chandler nodded, accepting the logic. Bliss knew she would be keen to make progress on an investigation that was rapidly running out of steam. Their team was most effective when it had momentum, and being stalled was beginning to wear on them all. She was also experienced with joint task force operations, especially when the Thorpe Wood Major Crimes unit was in charge.

After Chandler had found a parking spot and killed the engine, Bliss remained in his seat. When she asked him what was up, his thoughts turned to a disturbing incident the previous afternoon. It had left him feeling rattled, and he found himself telling the story. 'Curious thing,' he said softly. 'When I got home yesterday, there was a dog curled up on the little open porch outside my house. I saw its ear twitch, and it opened one eye, but other than that it didn't stir. Not even when I went to the front door. It was an old lab, and it reminded me of my two towards the end. But this one was so thin its bones protruded through its pelt. It didn't have a collar on, but you don't usually see stray labradors. Anyway, I tried to coax the poor thing indoors, but it just lay there. So I brought it out a plate of food and a saucer of warm tea and left the door open in case it decided to follow me inside.'

'And did it?'

'No.'

'What did you feed it? I've been to your house, Jimmy, and it's usually a toss-up between you and Old Mother Hubbard as to who has the barest cupboards.'

'I had half a loaf of stale bread left over, so I made a couple of slices of toast. Bonnie and Clyde used to love a bit of hot buttered toast.'

'Yeah, but to be fair, they would have wolfed down anything you gave them.'

He smiled at the memory. 'That's true. Anyhow, when I went back outside half an hour later the plate was empty, the tea was all gone. But so was the dog.'

'Maybe it wasn't a stray, after all. Maybe it was just hungry.'

Bliss nodded, reaching for the handle to open his door. 'I suppose. The thing is, the bloody image of it stuck in my mind all night. The dog was old and tired, looked as if it had no place to go, and I couldn't shake the idea that it was going through the final motions. Winding down its clock.'

Chandler's gaze across the roof of her car was shrewd as she locked up. 'Don't worry about it, Jimmy. It was a hungry animal.

No more, no less. It didn't represent anything greater. You didn't see yourself in dog form.'

Bliss laughed the suggestion off as the pair headed into the station; outwardly, at least. Inwardly, he wondered why Chandler's mind had taken her to precisely the same place as his own. From the moment he first laid eyes on the dog until the point at which sleep eventually claimed him, he'd accorded the animal greater significance than a mere stray happening to have settled on a patch of ground outside his house to grab a nap.

Throughout the night, his sleep had been uneasy. He worried about where the dog was. Had it gone off somewhere to die? All alone. Nobody to care for it, nobody to provide it one last night of shelter. Was it out there now, wandering lonely streets as its wearied body began to break down?

The first thing Bliss had done after waking was to check outside. The water he'd left beside the doorstep was gone, but any passing animal might have lapped it up. As he showered and dressed, he fretted, asking himself why he was associating the dog so closely with himself. They were not at all the same; he had choices, but the lab did not have free will. The whole thing was ridiculous, yet it clung to him like a second skin.

Shrugging all thoughts of the dog aside as he and Chandler made their way into the building, Bliss got his head back on straight. A tough few days lay ahead, and he needed all of his wits about him. As soon as he was safely ensconced behind his desk, he entered his credentials into the computer system and caught up on the weekend jobs.

Uniform had been busy with the usual nightclub fallout, Traffic equally so in separate vehicle thefts and chases across the city, while the drugs squad had been called out to the same address twice in one night. A single major crime had occurred when a teenage boy was stabbed by a girl also in her teens, thought to be earning her stripes with an all-female gang whose territory stretched from the Dogsthorpe area to New England. The young lad was recovering in intensive care, having required surgery after a kitchen knife penetrated his spleen. The girl had been arrested by officers following up on a witness statement, and removed from her mother's home. She was charged at 1.37am with wounding with intent to cause grievous bodily harm. A Section 18 offence was a serious one, and if found guilty the girl's gang entrance fee might cost her the rest of her life behind bars. If legal aid pleaded it down to an assault without intent, the maximum sentence reduced accordingly to five years. Her solicitor would fight for the reduction, but going by the report Bliss was currently reading, the CPS were hot for this one.

Knife crimes were never anything less than tragic and wasteful, in his opinion – a view he often extended to the perpetrators as well as the victims. His thoughts drifted back to the first time he had set eyes on Molly, standing on a hotel rooftop in the icy winter rain, clutching the knife with which she had stabbed a drug dealer by the name of Ryan Endicott. So long ago, yet it felt like yesterday to Bliss. How close had Molly come to ruining her own life only hours before he met her when she was a mere step away from certain death?

Not wishing to dwell on the awfulness of such a possibility, Bliss logged out. He'd follow up on the stabbing later on, but he thought right now it would be best to get a head start on the joint task force by running the situation past his own boss. He sent a text message to DCI Warburton, requesting a meeting as soon as it was convenient, then went in search of his team.

Chandler was chatting with her fellow sergeant Olly Bishop, and DC Gul Ansari. There was no sign of his valuable DCs Hunt and Gratton. When Bliss questioned their absence, Bishop reminded him that Hunt was on annual leave, while Gratton was tied up in court all day. He and Hunt had made an arrest following a series of armed robberies in which a pair of crowbar-wielding thugs on a motorcycle had attacked the windows of small jewellery stores. Turned out to be brother and sister, keeping it in the family after their father had been sent down on his fourth stretch for burglary. With the more experienced detective expected to be away on holiday, Gratton had volunteered to work with the CPS and give evidence.

'Has Penny filled you in regarding my little jaunt to Wiltshire?' Bliss asked the remaining two detectives. He already knew the answer, but wanted to give the impression of being charitable to his DS. In reality, he had no doubt Chandler had recounted his news the moment she'd laid eyes on her colleagues.

Bishop nodded. He was a bull of a man, and already looked uncomfortable in his ill-fitting navy Cambridgeshire Police T-shirt. Bliss always thought it looked as if it had been designed to be worn by a Yeti. 'Sounds as if they had about as much luck as us – amounting to zilch. This second carving sounds interesting, though.'

'Yeah, maybe.' Bliss still believed there would be further figures on additional slices of flesh, which explained his lack of enthusiasm. 'Once we can make sense of them, it'll open up an avenue for us to explore. Right now, I'm pissed off again. Our wheels were stuck in the mud and we were going nowhere fast, so when I heard about the second chunk of flesh, it got my hopes up.'

'And we all know how you feel about hope, boss,' Ansari said, raising her eyebrows.

Bliss was not a fan, and those who worked closely with him knew better than to express their own blind optimism in his presence. He cleared his throat and said, 'I don't feel as if we're going to be moving forward any time soon. If this is a game, I'm convinced our man still has several pieces of the puzzle for us yet.'

'So how do you think this JTFO will work?' Chandler asked. 'We stick to our own areas of investigation and link with Swindon online and through records?'

Bliss had worked on many joint task force operations. The largest ops tended to have too many moving parts to work cohesively, invariably leading to confusion and territorial disagreement. Those with two, three, or a maximum of four separate units involved in a single operation were big enough to make a difference, yet small enough to be effective without unduly ruffling feathers.

'It depends,' he replied. 'I suspect it'll be a mixture, doing pretty much as you suggest on a daily basis, but with some face-to-face meetings and briefings thrown in. Most of them we can do online, but others we may need to drive down for. It's a five-hour round trip, so there are likely to be some overnighters involved. That going to be okay with Shrek, DS Chandler?'

Matching his leery smile, Chandler fluttered her eyelashes and said, 'I'm sure Graham will understand. His own job requires him to travel extensively, remember?'

Bliss did. At the start of the year, Chandler had flown out to Turkey to spend a week with her daughter who lived on the south coast. On the flight home, she'd sat next to a chatty man who happened to live in Huntingdon. They got on well during the journey, and as they headed to passport control, the man – Graham – took a shot and asked her out on a date. Chandler had accepted, and the pair were now a steady item. He was built like an oak wardrobe, bald with curiously twisted ears, and Bliss had immediately christened him 'Shrek' following their first meeting.

Ignoring the numerous possibilities for humorous quips, Bliss was delighted for his colleague and friend. Chandler had endured a lot of pain and ugliness in her life, especially after her Turkish boyfriend had abducted their two-year-old daughter and taken her back to his homeland, where she had remained without word for almost seventeen years. By the time Chandler got to see her own daughter again, Anna was a young woman herself – not far off the age Chandler had been when the girl was so abruptly removed from her life. Two weeks ago, Anna had come over to the UK on a student visa to prepare for her linguistics PhD at Cambridge University, having been accepted into Churchill College. Already buzzing with her new relationship, Chandler found it hard to believe her change in fortune at having her daughter now living an hour's drive away as well, their close relationship restored.

About to get deeper into the conversation about the JTFO, Bliss's attention was diverted by his mobile telling him a text message had come in. It was from DCI Warburton, instructing him to meet her in the conference room in five minutes.

He glanced up to see three expectant faces. 'The boss,' he said, jiggling the phone. 'I thought I'd get in first on the whole joint task force angle.'

'You think they'll go for it?' Ansari asked.

Bliss pocketed his mobile and spread his hands. 'I don't see why not, Gul. A nice big win for Major Crimes is precisely what the doctor ordered.'

'You're assuming it's a case we can win, boss.'

He teetered in place, about to leave but forced to stop by her apparent doubt. 'I don't like to assume anything,' he said. 'However, I do have faith in this team. Even with doubters like you in it, Gul.'

He winked at the horrified expression on her face and left the room, laughing to himself.

NINE

THE CANTEEN WAS STILL open by the time Bliss's meeting with his boss was over. The room was heaving, leaving not a single spare chair available, so he bought himself a coffee and took his drink back upstairs. A small partitioned room at the back of the Major Crimes area had once been used for breaks and minor meetings, but had since been commandeered by DCI Warburton for use as an office. She had eschewed the larger, grander room on the floor above to be closer to the team. The concept was fine by Bliss, but it had robbed the squad of their own area in which to snatch a drink together away from their desks. Bliss brought the coffee into his office and shut himself away.

Moments later there was a knock on the door. He closed his eyes and blew out a long, irritated breath. This was precisely why he preferred to take breaks elsewhere; if you were in your office, people considered you available. The door opened without him having uttered a word. His exasperation increased – until he saw DCI Warburton's head peek around. Seeing him at his desk, she came all the way in.

The meeting had gone about as well as he had expected, after a surprise beginning. Bliss had wondered why the DCI had chosen the conference room to meet in – a puzzle solved the moment he entered to find Superintendent Fletcher waiting for him as well.

'I thought you were on annual leave, ma'am,' Bliss said as he took his own seat at the table. 'Otherwise I would have come to you directly with this.'

'I was. We were only in the Peak District, and when I heard about the find down in Swindon, I thought I'd better get back here.'

Bliss liked that about the DSI. She allowed her team to carry out their duties without micromanaging, but she believed in making herself available throughout the more serious crimes. Having gone on to discuss the second find in more detail, Warburton and Fletcher agreed it made sense for Bliss and his team to lead a joint task force with Gablecross. Fletcher said she would call her counterpart in Wiltshire to suggest they combine efforts and budgets, and to draw up specific protocols for the operation. Bliss had left the DCI and Super to it afterwards, so Warburton must have come to his office to discuss something further.

'Happy with the arrangements?' she asked, remaining on her feet but leaning back against the wall. As a rule she'd always worn trouser suits, but he'd noticed a shift towards long, flowing dresses lately. Today's was sleeveless, with a faint butterfly pattern on the sky-blue material.

'I was,' he replied carefully. 'Whether I still will be after you've said your piece is a different matter.' He took a long draw from his coffee, the hot liquid spiking his system.

'It's nothing you haven't already realised, judging by what you said upstairs,' Warburton said. 'The DSI made the call while I was with her. She asked for, and received, full cooperation. However, Gablecross mentioned their concerns over the possibility of DSI Conway being compromised by a potential prior association to the case and to you, though they are no further along in understanding exactly why or how that might occur.'

Bliss brushed it aside. 'So these crimes have ended up being investigated by two people whose careers crossed many years back. And now they're projecting further down the line and seeing problems where none exist.'

'It's called anticipation, Jimmy. You have no idea precisely what kind of case you have on your hands, and DSI Conway has admitted the same thing. Neither of you know what these weird flesh carvings mean. But you did work for the same unit at the same time many years ago, and now the connection between your two individual cases is clear. I'm not suggesting they're right to have concerns, but they are absolutely right to consider the potential and anticipate problems arising from it.'

'And I still say there's nothing to it, boss. This kind of chance encounter happens all the time. Take that fraud case we ran with Leicestershire a few months ago, for instance; I happened to have worked a couple of cases with their SIO when I was based in Bedford. Nobody imagined that investigation was personal to us, and of course it never was. Also, as I've been at pains to point out, Conway and I never worked the same case together. There is no connection between me and him, other than a passing one.'

'I understand, and I agree with you – it's extremely unlikely, because the association between the two of you is so tenuous. However, Gablecross are already imagining the headlines once these two crimes are officially linked and the media's FOI requests confirm the SOCA association.'

Bliss threw himself back in his chair and groaned. 'Bloody Freedom of Information requests. The bane of our existence.'

'I thought the bane of our existence was policy and procedure, according to you?' Warburton's lips thinned, hinting at banter rather than complaint.

'Yes, well… those as well.' His brief amusement faded. 'If it becomes a sideshow to the investigation, though, it's a pain in the arse. Conway's bosses are just worried that he may be compromised by media speculation. They need to get over it.'

'They're being proactive, Jimmy. It's a watching brief for now, that's all.'

'Leaving you with the small matter of whether I end up in the same boat.'

Bliss saw by the change in Warburton's expression that he had guessed right.

'Look,' he said, taking the edge off his voice. 'If I'm wrong and somehow we're linked to these crimes in a way we can't yet see, then we'll deal with it at the appropriate time.'

'Of course,' Warburton said. 'But we both know there's a difference between how you currently regard the issue – before you've got the bit between your teeth – and how you'll feel further down the track if you have to be removed from the case when you're into the final straight.'

Bliss raised a feeble smile. 'You did well to keep the horse racing analogy going there, boss.'

Warburton inclined her head and pushed her mass of wavy auburn hair to one side. 'I thought so. I almost lost the reins halfway through, but I whipped myself back into line just in time.'

He nodded his appreciation this time. 'Smoothly done.'

'Thank you. Listen, we've worked together long enough now for you to understand the way I do things.'

'And vice versa.'

'I'm not sure I'd go that far. I think even if I had a dozen more years under my belt I'd still not fully get to grips with the way your mind works. However, we have reached an understanding. I also think we get along pretty well. Unlike Alicia Edwards who claimed to be giving you enough rope to hang yourself with, I think of it more as one of those extendable dog leads. I want you out there doing your thing and sniffing out clues, but I also need to know you'll come to heel when I call.'

Bliss set his coffee down on the desk harder than he'd intended. The mention of him and a dog in the same sentence so soon after his conversation with Chandler was unnerving, but he shut it down before it caused his mind to race. He liked and admired the DCI, and was keen for them to continue working closely together. 'With respect, boss, I see no issue here. There's no current evidence to suggest a personal or professional prior connection to this case, and I don't foresee any. Admittedly, there are a couple of minor coincidences in play, but I've already considered and dismissed them. And unless circumstances change, I see no reason why I should not run the JTFO.'

'And I'm saying I agree, Jimmy. For now. You've already said you expect further bags to be left for us to find. So, go ahead and get this show on the road, but if or when another chunk of flesh, or whatever else, eventually turns up, we speak again and we pay particular attention to any conceivable link to you as well. Agreed?'

'Agreed.' His smile this time was fulsome. 'Boss, if you're looking for me to fight you on this, you'll be disappointed. We're on the same side.'

Warburton nodded. 'Good. What's your immediate plan of action?'

'I want to draw Pen, Bish and Gul into the task force. John and Phil can come aboard when they're available. I'd also like to co-opt two civilian staff to represent us and liaise with Gablecross. Access to uniforms, too, as and when this thing takes off. Especially when it comes to interviews. The initial find was here in Peterborough, so ours was the original op, but as yet I see no reason to have a single case manager, nor exhibits and finance officer. I think those aspects can stay as they are, each of us working on our own, but providing full documentation and records to the other. It's too fussy and too busy regards physical resources to work it any other way.'

'Sounds like a plan to me. It will also make Gablecross feel valued, which in turn might promote a greater determination to make a success of the task force. I assume you'll request four of their investigating team plus two civilians to form the JTFO so we have even numbers?'

'Of course.'

After a slight pause, Warburton pushed herself away from the wall and said, 'Do you have any idea at all where to start?'

Bliss was ready for the question. 'The carvings, for me at least, are still the most crucial factor. The slices of flesh are critical items of evidence, of course, and those engraved figures are a signature of sorts. We just have to work out what they mean.'

'I agree. The… interracial element is unexpected, wouldn't you say?'

'It is. Took me by surprise.'

'Any significance?'

'None apparent, boss.'

'Okay. Well, keep me informed, Jimmy.'

When the DCI left to return to her own office, Bliss finished off his drink before going back out to chat with his colleagues. Each was as eager as they had been earlier to take part in the joint task force operation, perhaps more so following his confirmation they were leading it.

'I'll call Pete Conway shortly,' he told them. 'Have him choose his best foursome. Like us, their sole focus will become this case, and they'll liaise with us every step of the way. No jurisdictional nonsense, either. You trust them as if they were part of this unit, and I'll make sure the DSI passes on the same message to his troops. I got a bit of pushback on Saturday when I attended their briefing, but you'd expect that when we're on their turf and looking to take over their case. I'm sure Conway will fix it. I never knew the man at SOCA, but my impressions were favourable when we met over the weekend. He has an outstanding record, from what I could gather.'

'Boss, I have to ask,' Chandler said, looking apprehensive. 'But did you believe him when he said the figures meant nothing to him? Do you think he told you everything? Held nothing back?'

Bliss understood the point she was making, and why she had asked the question. 'In my opinion, he was genuinely bemused. The look on his face told me he knows of no possible significance to those figures. Plus, the man is putting the investigation ahead of himself, the need to resolve the case above any desire he has to be the one who solves it. That's good enough for me.'

'Sounds like he made the right calls,' Bishop said.

'I believe so. Anyhow, I'll have a word with him and we can get this thing started. Until I have something better to offer, I'd like you three to start from scratch on our own case. Go through it all again – everything we have. I don't think you'll find anything we missed, but we have to start somewhere, right?'

'I realise it'd be a bit contentious, boss,' DC Ansari said, 'but do you see any merit in us swapping case files with Gablecross? They work our find, we work theirs. Fresh eyes on both?'

'You know, that's not an awful idea,' Bliss said, wagging his fore-finger at her. Ansari was a star in the making. 'I'm happy for others to study our work and go at it their own way. And if they find something we overlooked and it gives us a new lead, I'll be even happier. I'll suggest it to Pete when I talk to him. Well done, Gul.'

'You're not convinced, though, are you, boss?' Chandler said.

'About what?' he asked.

'You think no matter which of us looks at whatever evidence is available, none of us will find anything new.'

Chandler's insight delighted Bliss; it meant she was on her game. 'Not entirely, Pen. But not far off, either. I'm satisfied with how we ran our case. We did our due diligence, and from what I've seen, Conway has his people doing theirs. Unless they happen to get a DNA hit on their slice of flesh, then no, I don't see us moving forward yet.'

Chandler held him with her perceptive gaze. 'Until?'

'Like I said before. Until carrier bag number three turns up.'

TEN

THOUGH HE HAD SEEN it many times, Bliss still did not understand the attraction of the Emperor Trajan statue on Tower Hill.
The London Wall itself stood as a vestige of Roman architecture
opposite the Tower of London, but the bronze statue in front of it
was an enigma. Legend suggested the head did not match the body,
so Bliss had always been fascinated as to which section featured
Trajan and which did not. Also, it was historically unconvincing
as a reminder of Roman rule, given the Emperor never visited
Britain. Bliss also wondered why anybody should want to remind
themselves of living under occupation.

He knew the area well, having briefly been posted to Tower
Bridge station on the other side of the Thames in Bermondsey.
During his rare breaks, he had often escaped the confines of the old
building to walk across the bridge, and had eaten many a sandwich
on the exact bench beneath which a third white carrier bag had
now been discovered.

Earlier in the day, Bliss had taken a trip over to Peterborough's
NHS hospital at Bretton Gate. Upon entering the mortuary, Bliss
immediately noticed Nancy Drinkwater's absence from her office at
the far end of the corridor. He hoped she wasn't carrying out a post

mortem, as he was looking to re-examine the original slice of flesh and would require her authority. He walked past the procedure and examination rooms, relieved not to find her leaning over a corpse inside one of them. Whatever noxious combination of chemicals and body secretions was polluting the air particles around him, at least he knew it was not from a fresh corpse. He pushed open the penultimate door along the passageway and stepped inside.

The pathologist was getting changed, and let out a loud yelp of surprise as he barged in. The sight of Drinkwater yanking up a pair of trousers, having not yet slipped a top on over her bra, caused Bliss to swivel on his heels and turn away.

'I'm so sorry, Nancy,' he said, his back to her now. 'I should have called out before blundering in like an idiot… But if it's any consolation, you're in decent nick for a woman your age.'

'And screw you too, Ray,' she replied, no malice in her voice. He heard the whisper of clothing hurriedly being pulled on, and chuckled to himself.

Drinkwater had once told him he reminded her of the actor Ray Winstone, and she seldom referred to him by any other name now. Neither the nickname nor the reference bothered him. Continuing to face the door he had come through, Bliss said, 'Any danger of me taking a look at our chunk of flesh, Nancy?'

The rustling behind him grew louder, and he heard a zip being pulled. 'You mean you didn't get enough of an eyeful just now?'

'Well, I wouldn't go that far. I did see more than I would ever have been invited to appreciate, though – and jolly pleasant it was too. Everything seemed to be in good order. And I do so admire matching underwear, by the way. But there are some days when only a slice of male flesh will do.'

'I'm in full agreement there,' she said, brushing past him and heading for the door.

They examined the flesh together. Bliss explained that he was looking for any sign of other engravings, be it another figure or some other kind of marking or design.

'Don't you think I would have included it in my PM report had that been the case?' Drinkwater said curtly. 'Or are you suggesting I missed something?'

'Not at all. I would never do something so crass. You're a scary woman at the best of times. But I'm sure these engravings mean something, and I needed to see them again. just to satisfy my curiosity.'

It was still impossible to tell which way around the figures were meant to be read: *WSHO* or *OHSM*. And Drinkwater had been right – there were no other clear markings in the flesh. It was while he and the pathologist discussed the findings that he received the phone call telling him there had been another find.

Less than forty minutes after the call came in, Bliss and Chandler were on a train to King's Cross, after which they tubed it to Tower Hill, where a uniform met them. Bliss knew the way: exit into Trinity Square, turn left, walk past the famous sundial and continue along the concourse towards the wall, and finally down a slope into the small garden area where the statue stood on a plinth so small it seemed to detract from the figure's significance. The entire square was now sealed off by flapping tape and uniforms wearing short-sleeved shirts but still baking and sweating beneath the weight of their stab vests.

The pair signed in. As they entered the garden, a strikingly tall beanpole of a suit broke away from a small group of fellow detectives and forensic techs who were gathered in conversation. Despite the heat of the day, the man looked pale and unflustered as he extended his right hand. They exchanged shakes and Mr Tall-and-Skinny introduced himself as Detective Inspector Max Riseborough from the City of London police.

'I gather you have recent experience of this,' he said, nodding in the direction of the bench upon which sat the white plastic bag.

'Various cuts of human fillet, yes,' Bliss replied. 'But not the entire severed hand you've landed.'

Riseborough grimaced. 'Ugly business. Seen worse, of course, but from what I hear this catch is bigger than we originally imagined. A serial, no less.'

While the DI spoke, Bliss regarded the scene investigation going on behind him. The forensic techs seemed to be going about their business in a calm and orderly manner, which was always a good sign. 'That's certainly possible,' he said. 'Though as yet we don't quite know what kind of serial. We have no remains to go with our bits of body, so we can't be certain at this stage if we're even searching for a killer at all. Gablecross are still waiting for DNA results on their victim, but with a bit of luck we can get a decent set of prints off this hand. If fortune is favouring us today, we may get a match.'

'Hmm,' Riseborough said, bowing his head. 'That remains to be seen. From what we were able to ascertain upon first examination, the fingertips had been sliced off and cauterised.'

Bliss sighed. Precisely what they didn't need. 'That'd be a ballache, for sure. But from everything we learned during our journey down here, there's every possibility of us having three separate victims out there somewhere.'

'Yes. I had a quick word with Pete Conway after making contact with you. He's on his way over from Swindon. He tells me you'd just agreed upon a JTFO when our call came in to rock the boat.'

Bliss caught something in the DI's tone and manner. 'You know DSI Conway?' He feared he already knew the answer.

'I do. We spent some time working together. Pete was based at Wood Street nick, over by the Barbican. I was working out of Islington.'

'That rambling old brick fortress on Tolpuddle Street?'

Riseborough gave a wide, toothy grin. 'The same. There was always a prodigious amount of overlap between his nick and mine, and me and Pete collaborated on all the serious stuff. The whole area was a cesspit of crime and criminals, and we spent far too much of our time jumping all over them from a great height.'

This third professional connection troubled Bliss, but he took it in his stride. 'Small world. I was stationed right here for a short while, too – south of the river at Tower Bridge.'

'Just for the record,' Chandler piped up, 'I've also worked in this part of London, during my stint on Operation Sapphire. Though I'm sure it's not at all relevant.'

Riseborough arched his eyebrows. 'Working rape and sexual assault must be a drain on the emotions.'

'It was. I did over ten months of my secondment here. I worked a lot of sickening cases. But this one is shaping up to be something unique.'

If it were possible, Riseborough had paled further still. He turned to glance over his shoulder at the bag now lying open on the bench. When he shifted his attention back to Bliss and Chandler, his mouth had thinned and a heavy frown sagged on his brow. 'I think you may be right, Sergeant. Pete said the figures on the hand meant nothing to him. They're not ringing any bells for me, either. How about you, Jimmy?'

A description of the engraved figures had been one of the first things Bliss had asked for when he took the call from Conway. Two letters and two numbers again: *FE04*. Nothing about it spoke to him, other than wondering if it suggested a date. He shook his head. 'I've racked my brains – thought about little else all the way down here – but I'm coming up empty. Given the first two…'

Bliss's voice trailed away. Riseborough's mouth had fallen open and his face was now a vacant mask turning rapidly from white to grey.

'You all right there, Max? You're starting to look a little peaky.' Bliss put a hand on the man's arm, searching for signs of alarm in his eyes. He'd once worked alongside a DC, a decent detective with a big family and a loyal and loving wife, whose heart gave out on him as the two of them chased down a burglar on foot. Bliss had administered CPR, breathed into his colleague's mouth while covering his nose, just as he had been trained to do. All to no avail. Bliss got him back, but the heart attack killed the man before the ambulance had taken off with him inside it.

Riseborough had wide eyes on him now, thin creases lining his forehead. He swallowed with obvious discomfort. 'Shit. I fucked up.'

Bliss looked anxiously around to see if anybody else had over-heard. 'You may want to think more clearly before you start putting words to it, Max.'

'No, it wasn't a costly oversight. Or at least, I don't think it was. Not when it comes to the big picture. The thing is, though, I saw it. Saw it right there in front of me, written out on one of my DC's notepads. We got *WSHO* from your scene, Jimmy. Pete's gave up *PC94*. The carving into the back of my guy's hand reads *FE04*. Broken down into three sections, they're pretty meaningless, though I'm annoyed I didn't pick up earlier on the letters from the first scene. That's possibly because when I initially saw them they were in reverse order. But now it's registering. When you piece them together, in order of find, they do mean something. Something important. *WS* gives us the nick, which is Wood Street. *HO*...?' he offered.

Chandler snatched at it. 'First two letters of homicide?'

Riseborough was slowly nodding his head and sighing gently. 'Precisely how we were taught to describe it back in the day. Hom-icide, not murder or suspicious death. Then came the year, and here we're going back to 1994. So station handling, crime type, year, followed by SIO's initials: *PC*, in this case. Final characters give us the month and day of month. Put it all together and it becomes a case file number. An old one, telling us that on the fourth of February 1994, a murder was recorded at Wood Street police station and assigned to Pete Conway. If I'd seen the whole thing from the beginning I would've got there a lot sooner.'

Bliss was relieved to have had the mystery solved, but disconcerted by the meaning. The current three cases referred back to a twenty-six-year-old murder. Given its location, it was not an investigation he had ever worked on, but it clearly had a significant connection to Conway. Not a coincidence, after all. His mind slid sideways to the man or men responsible for the severed hand and the slices of flesh.

'Whoever's doing this is biding their time,' Bliss said. 'Taking it at their own pace. They want to be recognised for what's being done, but they're not coming quietly or easily.'

'Or without more victims, potentially,' Chandler pointed out.

Riseborough offered to call Conway. 'I expect he'll give it some thought during the remainder of his journey. Hopefully he'll be here soon enough, by which time something will surely have dislodged somewhere in his memory.'

Bliss accepted this observation with a grunt. He did not like the direction in which this case was leading them. The past was capable of taking you unawares, and he'd bathed himself in its dusky light far longer than necessary. Memories often led you astray; hindsight was seldom favourable.

'He's having a think about it,' Riseborough said when he'd finished his call to Conway. 'But he's just around the corner, so he'll be joining us in a minute or two.'

Bliss decided to switch focus and bring them back into the moment. 'Who discovered the bag?'

'Local worker. Fancied a break on a bench by the wall. Saw the bag lying underneath. He says he'd intended handing it in if he'd found ID, but who knows? Anyway, he got more than he bargained for when he opened it up. One of my team is interviewing him now, back at Bishopsgate.'

Bliss knew the DI was referring to the principal City of London police station. He turned a full circle, surveying the background. The garden was enclosed, caught in a wedge between the London Wall, Tower Hill underground station and Tower Hill Road. A stream of cars, vans, black cabs, and red buses flowed by in a dull roar of engines, punctuated every now and then by a squeal of brakes or someone jabbing their horn.

'There are traffic cameras out there on the street,' Bliss said, pointing towards the tower itself. 'Plus a surveillance camera across to the left. Looks to me as if it's facing this way. What with those and whatever we have up by the station, I'm thinking we have a great chance of spotting whoever left the bag, and tracking where they came from and where they went afterwards.'

'Yes, we'd already clocked those ourselves,' Riseborough said – a little defensively, Bliss thought. 'And you cannot believe what a quagmire it led us into. We operate the road safety cameras, obviously, but the surveillance camera is the responsibility of the local borough council, Tower Hamlets. Throw into the mix the London Transport Police and we have three separate surveillance systems, none of them talking to each other. I already have a member of my team chasing up the critical footage from the council – if they can pinpoint the person dropping the bag, it will establish a specific time period for the others to check. Should make life a bit easier.'

'If it had been a bomb instead of a hand, they'd make it work like clockwork,' Bliss grumbled. 'But this is just some poor sod's appendage, so why pull out all the stops?'

Riseborough smiled for the first time. 'Things are not quite as cut and dried as they were in your time here,' he said. 'The effect of counterterrorism has meant far greater levels of cooperation between all parties. It's a bind because we have to pull three different surveillance systems together, but we'll get what we need from them. I'm quietly confident of that.'

'I hope you're right, sir,' Chandler chimed in. 'This may be our most important breakthrough yet.'

'Don't go getting your hopes up, DS Chandler. There is one camera for roughly every fourteen people in London, and given we have both the Tower and the bridge within yards of us, I'd assume the average decreases right here. But there are gaps, and while I'm certain we'll have footage before the end of the day, I wouldn't be betting anything on it leading us to our man's front door.'

Before either Chandler or Bliss had a chance to respond, Pete Conway arrived. 'This damned case file,' he said, slapping a hand against his thigh after brief introductions were made. His face was as red as a tomato. 'The bloody thing eluded me entirely at first. But the moment it clicked into place, the whole torrid episode came flooding back.'

Bliss took one rapid glance at the investigation scene, still in full flow. 'Something important?'

Conway nodded. 'And not to me alone, Jimmy. Not just to this particular find, either. I think it explains everything.'

ELEVEN

'You remember the Islington crime syndicate?' Conway said. The four detectives sat in Riseborough's favoured incident room at Bishopsgate. Its interior was shabby, a coat of paint long overdue, but the room was a decent size and benefitted from large sash windows that overlooked the street. Natural light flooded in, and the windows were raised to create a flow of fresh air. DSI Conway was taking them through what he believed to be a significant investigation connected to the current joint task force operation.

'The Doyle family,' Bliss replied immediately. 'Irish mob. Into just about every despicable racket you can think of.'

Conway nodded. 'That's them. They kicked off in the eighties. What with them and the various faces from Hoxton to the east of our manor, Islington and Wood Street nicks were the busiest stations for serious and organised crime in the whole of London. And not a lot went on without the Doyle family either having a slice of the pie, giving their blessing to it, or at least knowing everything about it.'

'Those were the days,' Riseborough said. His voice was soft. Reflective. He sat with one arm resting on the other, stroking his chin. 'It was like the bloody Wild West out there. You name it, they organised it. Serious, vicious crime – so bad the Met convinced the CPS to bring in the security services towards the end of their reign. At least twenty-five murders to their name, and countless violent and armed attacks.'

'So how do they feature in all this?' Bliss wanted to know.

'Indirectly,' Conway said. 'Maybe. Maybe not. I'll tell you the story and you can make up your own minds. On the fourth of February 1994, the body of Geraldine Price was discovered in scrubland close to Wenlock Basin, just off the Regent's canal. She'd long been food for rats, and plenty of them had paid her a visit. We identified her from dental records, but we had a good idea who she was from the moment she was first spotted; Mrs Price had been reported missing by her husband ten days earlier, and the search was widespread. According to her employers, Geraldine left work in Holborn on time, but Mr Price said she failed to arrive home. We looked hard at him, of course. We traced her route home, and we know she got off the bus at her usual stop on City Road. Somewhere between there and her home in Murray Grove, Hoxton, she disappeared. The husband was at home with their two children and Mrs Price's parents who had come for dinner, so he had a perfect alibi.'

'And you fancied one of the Doyle brothers for it?' Riseborough asked. He seemed surprised.

'No. Not at first. She didn't fit in with their racket, and never had any dealings with them as far as we knew. But our DCI got so desperate that he contacted the brothers to see if they knew anything about it. He offered them a deal in exchange for information, and Mrs Price turned up a couple of days later. The post mortem told us she had been sexually assaulted on multiple occasions. Objects were used, and there was anal penetration in addition to oral and vaginal. Many of her bones were broken – ribs, jaw, eye socket – so she was heavily brutalised throughout her ordeal.'

Conway paused, took a breath, and sipped water from a bottle Riseborough had pulled from a small fridge before they had taken their seats. He shook his head and exhaled before continuing. 'I've seen sadder and more deranged things in my time, especially cases where kids were involved. But this was one of the most sickening things of my entire career. At the time she disappeared, Geraldine Price was a real looker. Blonde, busty, leggy, gorgeous, she had the lot. Initially we thought she'd been spotted walking home after getting off the bus, most likely by a couple of chancers who liked what they saw as they drove by, and who then snatched her off the street. According to official TOD, she had been dead for two or three days when she was found, which meant she had been kept somewhere for about a week while she was repeatedly assaulted.'

'You said you didn't like these brothers for it at first,' Chandler pointed out. 'That suggests you did at some point afterwards.'

'As it happens, Geraldine's father, Robert Naylor, was a car dealer. He had minor connections to a few of the villains in Hoxton, though was not believed to be one himself. When somebody from the Islington syndicate came calling for protection money, Naylor considered himself already protected by the Hoxton mob and sent the bloke off with a flea in his ear. That same night, his lot was firebombed. There were one or two mid-level reprisals, but the Hoxton faces weren't one single gang, certainly not on a par with the sizeable outfit the Doyles were running. So Naylor soon found himself adrift. A stubborn man, by all accounts. When the Islington thug approached him again, Naylor refused and set two dogs on the man. We reckoned the brothers might have given permission for a couple of their less empathetic scumbags to pick up Geraldine and have their way with her, showing Mr Naylor how badly they took his refusal to do business with them.'

'Jesus,' Chandler breathed. She sat next to Bliss, her jacket removed, hair still braided to keep her neck cool. The beads of sweat on her brow were caused by the heat, but could just as easily have been prompted by the picture Conway was painting of life under the rule of a criminal family.

'I only ever heard the stories about them,' Bliss said. 'Never encountered them, thankfully. Their reach didn't extend as far east as Bethnal Green or Mile End. But we all took them seriously. "The Krays on steroids" was how we referred to them.'

'Anyhow, the murder of Geraldine Price remains unsolved to this day,' Conway finished. 'Naylor never believed the Doyle family were involved. He told us he was badly beaten and had a few fingers broken in response to his refusal to pay for protection, after which he shelled out every week. He saw no reason for them to involve Geraldine too, and the case went cold on us.'

'Any other suspects?' Riseborough asked.

'A number of leads, but none we pursued for too long. Going back to the Doyles, we considered it to be more than an odd occurrence when Geraldine's body turned up a couple of days after our boss had spoken with them. We did a bit of digging along those lines, but got nowhere fast. We had no information coming in off the street, despite offering decent money for it. I was surprised we never made more ground. I always believed it had to be locals.'

'Because where they dumped her was half a mile or so from where they must have picked her up,' Bliss said.

'Precisely. In the end, we came to the conclusion that whoever did it was passing through. Perhaps stayed with relatives for a week or so. Geraldine Price happened to stray across their orbit at the wrong time. Anyhow, that's where the carved figures tie things up.'

'Which is good to know.' Bliss shrugged. 'But where do we come in – me and Max?' He used his thumb to indicate them both. 'Judging by his lack of input during your story, I'm guessing Max wasn't involved in the Price case. And I certainly wasn't.'

Conway reached into his trouser pocket and took out his phone. 'When the date and case clicked, I did a Google search to refresh my memory. I doubt if any newspapers had an online presence in 1994, although there are archives scanned in now. I found nothing of relevance to us as a group. The three of us, I mean.'

Chandler leaned forward, fanning her neck. 'So you're saying there is no connection, other than a natural one?'

'That's my guess, for what it's worth. The way I see it, if we look back over our careers, there are only so many degrees of separation between most coppers.'

'I've heard people talk about six degrees of separation,' Riseborough said. 'I've never known what it means or how true it is.'

He was an unruffled character, Bliss thought. Seemingly unimpressed by anything he had heard so far, and sceptical of anything he did not understand. But Bliss had read an article on the subject, and thought he could shed light on it. 'The premise suggests all people are six or fewer social connections away from each other. Globally, I don't see how it stacks up, but I can easily see it being the case in the narrow confines of our job. So, to answer my own question, I don't think you or I enter into this equation, Max. Its roots begin with one specific crime. As for our connecting lines, I'm all for putting them down to chance unless something convinces me otherwise.'

'I think we can agree this is primarily aimed at me,' Conway said. There was a hint of reluctance in his voice, but he embraced the theory anyway. 'The Price murder, certainly. The case file reference tells us as much.'

Bliss stood up from the table and stretched out his arms, rolling his neck. All the recent hours of travel and sitting in unfamiliar chairs had left him feeling stiff and sore. 'My gut tells me I agree with you, Pete. But having links to all three locations myself is disturbing.'

'I'd argue two of those are indirect,' Conway said. 'My case at the Long Barrow has a tentative connection to your childhood at best – and anyway, who would know about that? Your posting to Tower Hill all those years ago is hardly a major leap, considering the number of us who have been through the doors of multiple stations over the years.'

Bliss angled his head, squinting at the DSI. 'That's true enough. You hadn't arrived at the scene when I mentioned being stationed nearby, though. For you to know I worked there means you checked out my history.'

Conway didn't so much as blink. 'Naturally. You and Max both.'

Bliss wasn't entirely happy about Conway prying into his records, but he accepted that he would have done the same thing had the roles been reversed. He decided not to take the matter further, or register his displeasure.

Riseborough cleared his throat. 'I suggest we put it all behind us now and maintain our focus on the specific case itself, which it seems may well have its origins in organised crime.'

Chandler leaned back in her chair and crossed her legs. 'I don't think you can necessarily draw that conclusion,' she argued. 'Just because it was gangland territory doesn't prove the Doyle family, nor any other gangs, had any involvement in what happened to Geraldine Price.'

'I have a similar opinion,' Bliss said, glad to hear his DS expressing the same view. 'The murder doesn't have the feel of an organised hit. Price herself doesn't fit, as far as I can tell, and the sexual component feels all wrong. In my view, the next move is to prioritise the three findings we have so far and the men they have been taken from.'

Riseborough shrugged. 'I agree with your final statement. However, if we concentrate our efforts on the original case, I think answers may come more readily than if we spend time trying to work out who these sliced and severed items belong to.'

'Max does have a point,' Conway said, looking at Bliss. 'We got nowhere with the contents of our two carrier bags, and there's no reason to suspect the hand will provide us with any form of identity.'

Bliss did not respond immediately. Something the Super had said was nudging him, but he couldn't quite put his finger on it. He stared off into the distance for a moment before it came to him.

'This isn't just about items left for us,' he said finally. 'What I mean by that is – our man is not simply slicing off slabs of meat and chopping off hands and offering them to us. We're forgetting the tiny slivers of tissue he leaves us, too.'

Conway jerked upright in his seat as if he'd touched a live wire. 'Of course,' he muttered distantly, snapping his fingers. 'Of course. The slices.' Silence followed, but when he spoke again his eyes were gleaming and concentrated on all three colleagues in the room. 'I told you how, when Geraldine Price's body was eventually found, it was bitten and chewed to buggery by rats – but I completely forgot about her other wounds. The pathologist's report mentioned there were sections of flesh excised from the body, around the midriff and thighs.'

Despite his repugnance at the act itself, Bliss felt energised by Conway's admission. 'Sliced off, in other words,' he said.

'Yes. They were assumed to be part of whatever torture the woman had undergone. Excised or sliced, it all amounts to the same thing.'

'I don't suppose she was also missing a hand?' Chandler asked.

Conway shook his head brusquely.

'Possibly because she died before they had a chance to remove it,' Bliss suggested.

All eyes turned to him. Nobody spoke.

He continued, nodding. 'I think I know what this is. And if I'm right, the removal of body parts only counts for something if the body is alive when it's done. It's part of the art.'

'The art?' Conway blurted out. 'What the hell are you talking about, Jimmy?'

'The cutting. Slowly slicing off chunks of human meat. The removal of hands, feet… parts in general. It's why scraps of tissue were also placed into the bags with the hand and the other slices. He wants us to know what he's doing.'

'And what exactly is he doing, boss?' Chandler asked. Her cheeks were flushed, the day's heat coating her skin in a glossy sheen.

Looking up, Bliss blinked a couple of times before forcing himself to reply. 'It's called Lingchi. Often referred to as slow slicing or lingering death. It's an ancient Chinese form of torture and eventual execution. You probably know it by its incorrect Western name: death by a thousand cuts.'

TWELVE

RESPONSIBLE FOR OVER FOUR hundred thousand residents, workers, visitors and commuters on a daily basis, the City of London Police understandably took a major interest in both financial crime and fraud. Although the administrative headquarters were at the Guildhall in the Moorgate district, the force's operational functions took place behind the stained grey edifice of its Bishopsgate station in which Bliss, Conway, Riseborough and Chandler now sat grouped around the incident room table.

The four attempted to make sense of their findings. What they had so far was based almost entirely on supposition and speculation, intelligent guesswork – driven by experience and logic, but guesswork all the same. Yet no matter where their discussions took them, invariably they eventually returned to Bliss's theory.

'How is it you know so much about this sort of thing?' Riseborough asked, distaste obvious in his tone and manner.

'Mostly by chance,' Bliss replied. 'Many years ago I had one or two issues with anger management, and somebody suggested I look to meditation and relaxation, which led me to Zen and other eastern philosophies. During my research I strayed into reading about Chinese mysticism, and I caught the tail end of a link that eventually took me to Lingchi. The word has many translations, the best of which defines it as a slow process. We've come to regard it as "death by a thousand cuts", which it isn't, but I'm convinced it's what we're facing here.'

'If so, then it's monstrous,' Conway said. The room was doing him no favours, despite the flow of air. His entire face was red and turning a darker shade every few minutes. The man had removed his jacket and tie and unbuttoned his shirt collar, but he was struggling in the stifling room. At one point he had asked for an electric fan, but although Riseborough had requested one, it had yet to arrive.

'You okay, sir?' Bliss asked him.

Conway huffed his concern aside. 'Not so's you'd notice. But let's get on with it.'

'All right. So, we're all agreed. It *is* monstrous. But it also tells us a lot about our perpetrator. First, he has to have room for this. A place that's easy to bring men into and, perhaps, out of again. Somewhere quiet and unobserved. But mainly it tells us this man is extraordinarily patient. So far, he's managed to take at least two, probably three, separate men through however many cuts and slices he deems sufficient before severing an appendage. Removal of an entire body part should occur at the point at which death is inevitable. The idea of Lingchi is to keep the victims alive for as long as possible, and the mastery of the art stems from removing enough flesh and parts to inflict enormous pain over an extended period, but without causing death. Although the victim's death is ultimately unavoidable, the actual skill is in prolonging life while carrying out numerous atrocities.'

Chandler winced and swallowed. Her face creased as she shuddered and said, 'If that's what's happening to these victims, it's barbaric.'

'It is.' Bliss nodded, thinning his lips.

'But if so, then why?' Conway asked again, bringing them another full circle. 'I know we keep coming back to the same question, but we're no closer to answering it.'

Bliss had formed a theory, and was happy to share it. 'I'm seeing two paths crossing here. First, to spend this amount of time and have such incredible patience, but also to inflict physical and emotional torture on a person, you have to have a personal grievance against them. Second, whoever is doing this is either seeking to punish you, Pete, or they want you involved in this investigation.'

Around the table there was mutual consent to pursuing this theory as a backdrop to the three cases. It was Conway who broached the subject of extending the existing joint task force operation to include Riseborough's team.

'I'm happy for DI Bliss and his Major Crimes unit to continue taking the lead,' Conway said. He looked across at Riseborough, raising his eyebrows. 'How about you, Max? You'd have to agree in principle and run it by your senior leadership team.'

Riseborough took a while to compose his response, and when he spoke it was clear he did so grudgingly. 'I have to say, it feels wrong to turn over an incident of this magnitude to someone else. Investigations like this don't come along too often. However, it would be the most logical thing to do. This entire current case seems to have kicked off in Peterborough, after all.'

'How about the Met?' Chandler asked. 'Would you need their agreement?'

Riseborough shook his head in answer. 'No. They're a separate entity, because the Square Mile isn't one of the thirty-two boroughs. And be glad of it, because there is no way they would be agreeing to pass up a case like this.'

'You wouldn't be passing it up,' Bliss corrected him. 'And certainly don't put it that way to your top brass. The Super and I were all set to handle it by utilising our own teams, focussing primarily on the contents of the bags found in our own areas. Only, instead of isolating those investigations, we intended to share them. As with any JTFO, however, it required one person to head it up. I'm happy to continue in the role, but I'm open to alternatives if you have suggestions of your own.'

'I've run a few JTFOs with the Met, county police services, even the security services and of course counterterrorism, and I've had many positive experiences. I've yet to lead one, but I've never minded being a part of the overall solution. Personally, I'm game if you two are, and I have no objections to Jimmy here taking the reins. Whether senior leadership agrees, I can't say.'

'As Jimmy suggested when he and I discussed it,' Conway said, 'tell them we'll be sharing all costs and they'll start thinking about their budgets instead of media appearances.'

Riseborough chuckled. 'That will definitely work with my lot.'

'We all want the same thing,' Chandler said, rising from the table and moving across to stand by one of the open windows. A sweat stain spread between her shoulder blades. 'And when we nail the bastard, we each get a share of the limelight. And by that I mean our units, not individuals. You'd struggle to find a more camera-shy boss than mine.' She turned to smile at Bliss, who winked back.

'The best way to approach the top brass is with a feasible plan of action,' Conway suggested. 'At this juncture, any mention of this slow slicing behaviour is liable to fry their brains rather than convince them of anything. I'm all for keeping the theory under wraps for the time being. I'm not suggesting I don't believe it, but our leadership teams are bound to want hard evidence at this stage.'

Nodding, Bliss said, 'I agree with you, sir. But unfortunately, we still have so little concrete evidence to go on.'

Conway put his head back and blew out his frustration in one steady stream of air. 'And why do you think that is, Jimmy? Is this man taunting us? Is he initiating a chase? Why not just kill and be done with it if murder is his end goal? Why all the drama?'

'I think for him it's part of the ritual. The method, I mean. Offering us evidence of his horrific acts is something else entirely. It's his adrenaline rush. Murdering these men in this particular fashion is clearly something he feels passionate about, and there will be a reason for it – in his mind, at least. By leaving the finds, I think he's letting us know he thinks of himself as better than we are. He's saying we will never find these men unless he decides otherwise.'

'You don't think he's taking chances because he wants to be caught?' Riseborough asked.

'You mean because he has a deep desire to pay for his crimes?' It was a decent thought, but Bliss shook his head. He took a gulp of water before continuing. 'No, I don't believe that's the case here. Quite the reverse, in fact: I reckon he does it to show us he's in control.'

'Which he is,' Chandler pointed out. She propped herself up on the windowsill, one toe still in touch with the floor. 'Can you imagine the patience, organisation, and sheer will it must take to keep this up with three different victims?'

Her words hung in the air between them. Seconds later, the meeting was abruptly interrupted by Riseborough's ringtone. He checked the caller ID. 'Sorry, I have to take this.'

Riseborough spoke for a couple of minutes. From his end of the conversation, it seemed to Bliss as if something had finally swung their way.

When he was finished with the call, Riseborough placed his phone on the desk and surveyed each of them in turn, wearing a triumphant smile. 'You wanted evidence,' he said. 'I think we've just landed a vital piece.'

'Something to do with the hand at Tower Hill, right?' Bliss said, going with his instincts.

'Oh, yes. The pathologist says four fingers were sliced deep enough to remove their prints. Which means he left us one. Not only untouched, but unblemished.'

'From which your people got a match,' Bliss whispered, barely able to breathe.

Riseborough sat back in his chair and folded his arms. His wide grin became one of satisfaction. 'Yes. We got a match.'

THIRTEEN

CHANDLER HAD LEFT HER vehicle at the railway station. It was shortly after 9.00pm when they arrived back in the city, and although she lived close by, she insisted on driving Bliss home rather than allow him to take a cab. They continued to discuss the operation, galvanised by the change in fortune and its possible implications. Bliss became so embroiled in the possibilities opening up in front of them that he took no notice of where they were until Chandler's Focus hit the first speed bump on the curving drive leading into the car park of the Windmill pub in Orton Waterville.

Bliss groaned as he sank down into his seat. 'Not tonight, Pen,' he said. 'It's been a bloody long day and I've still got plenty to do before I turn in.'

Chandler parked, put on the handbrake and killed the engine. 'Such as?'

'I want to check the logs to see what came in after we left HQ. I also need to prepare for tomorrow's early briefing. You know as well as I do the ground we have to cover.'

'So, nothing important. Nothing whose wheels couldn't be oiled by a pint or two of the black stuff. Nothing you couldn't put off until morning.'

Bliss relented with a sigh. 'If I said you had me at "a pint or two" would it be an awful cliché?'

'It would. But when did the fear of regurgitating an old chestnut ever stop you?'

The last of the early-evening family punters had fled, leaving serious drinkers to their solitude, by the time Bliss and Chandler walked down towards the pub. As the pair made their way down a path of stone steps, Chandler suggested they sit outside to soak up what little light and heat remained of the day. 'I'll get the first round in,' she said. 'Find us a seat up on the deck.'

It was rare for Bliss to do as he was told, but he tended to capitulate whenever a drink was on offer. Alcohol helped him think. His mind was brimming over with the events of the past few days. Most investigations were laboured, a process of routine traces, interviews and eliminations while building a sturdy framework upon which to hang the case. The better investigators learned to spot momentum the way a surfer observes spume and the peak of a wave, giving them the best opportunity to ride it all the way in. Bliss felt as if he was on the shoulder of one now, searching for a way of breaking into the pocket and riding the tube. It was both exhilarating and terrifying at the same time. The former because he felt they had taken a giant stride towards their perpetrator, the latter because there was now the overwhelming and occasionally paralysing fear of letting them get away.

In his early days in the job, Bliss had been too eager and fearless. He had yet to realise that fear was good, something you needed to balance out the adrenaline bursts, a lack of trepidation carrying with it the genuine possibility of hurting both you and your case. These days, he pushed any excitement down as he felt it mounting, allowing a certain calm to settle over him. Emotions swirled around inside his head like frail autumn leaves caught in a warm updraft, but he had long since learned to maintain dominion over them.

He looked up as the pub door creaked open and Chandler stepped out, carrying his glass of Guinness. He started to smile, but his face quickly became a mask of confusion. His partner stood with a foot jammed against the door to prevent it swinging shut behind her, and his was the only drink she carried. A moment later a second figure appeared in the doorway, and Bliss realised his colleague had deceived him.

He kept his gaze on Chandler as the two women made their way over to the raised decking. His eyes never left her face, but she never once looked at him. Bliss shifted uneasily in his seat, tension working its way through his muscles. He did not appreciate being played like this, and he had to fight the urge to stand up and march off. By the time the pair arrived at the table, he had no choice but to turn his eyes towards Chandler's companion.

'Good evening, Emily,' he said, immediately realising the tone he had used was as formal as the words he had chosen. He forced a smile and softened his gaze. 'Fancy seeing you here.'

Emily Grant pulled out a chair and sat down, setting her own glass of white wine on the table. Chandler remained standing, and Bliss now fought against acknowledging her at all.

'I'll leave you two to catch up,' she said. 'See you at briefing, boss. Text me if you want a lift in.'

Bliss muttered something unintelligible. Heat rushed to his chest and neck. It was unforgivable of her to have put him in this awkward situation.

'You're going to have to let it go,' Emily said a moment later. 'I imagine you're angry with her right now, but you'll get over it. This is Penny we're talking about. She's all yours during working hours, Jimmy. Outside of that, she's her own woman.'

'Was this her idea or yours?' Bliss asked.

'A collaboration. Penny and I have been in contact for a while now. I talk, she listens; she talks, I listen. Mostly we talk and listen about you.'

Realising he was overreacting and behaving like an idiot, Bliss nonetheless felt as if his skull was being crushed beneath the powerful grip of something unseen. A bright flare of pain took off and danced before his eyes. He cursed himself for being so ridiculous, but having first accepted and eventually embraced a life of solitude, this setup felt like a violation of his trust by both women.

Currently working as a forensic anthropologist, Emily Grant had entered his life as a lecturer running a course he and Chandler had signed up to during his first posting to Peterborough, and for a second time when he'd called her to the scene of what turned out to be a body dumping rather than a murder. All they had at the time were bones, and Bliss had thought Emily's expertise would be useful. He'd also wanted to see her again. The two had dated for a short while afterwards, before Bliss was uprooted and posted back down to London at the end of the investigation which had led him and his team to expose corruption and murder within the city police force.

Many years later, Emily had approached him to discover the truth about her husband's death. In an ugly crime mixed up with an uglier set of circumstances, Bliss uncovered a murder made to look like a suicide. This discovery soothed Emily's tortured soul, though it did nothing to ease her pain or overcome her grief. His part in her discovery that her husband was anything but what he claimed to be was something which, to this day, troubled Bliss immeasurably.

Later that same year, left stricken by a tough investigation, his raw emotions exposed by Molly, Bliss had closed the door firmly on two potential relationships. The first was with a local journalist, Sandra Bannister. Their relationship had yet to get off the ground, but the pair had been skirting around a first date. The second was a rekindling of his earlier relationship with Emily, with whom he and Chandler had worked again, albeit briefly. Bliss had found himself drawn to her as strongly as he had been the first time around, yet he had pulled back from the brink and never taken the step necessary to encourage a renewed interest.

'So what exactly do you two find to say in these chats about me?' he asked now. He took two long swallows of his drink, observing Emily over the rim of his glass. The years had intensified her natural attractiveness. Fine lines around her eyes and mouth accentuated the graceful ageing process she was going through, adding character and depth to a ready smile.

'You ask your questions as if they're accusations, Jimmy. I realise you feel like we ambushed you, but if both Penny and I thought this was the right thing to do, we can't both be wrong, surely?'

Bliss felt trapped by the clever phrasing. To argue now would cast him in a negative role, rather than the person being taken advantage of. 'That may depend on why we're both here and she's buggering off.' He was aware of Chandler's Focus bumping back down the drive behind him, but he ignored it. By contrast, Emily smiled broadly and waved.

'We decided you and I needed to talk,' she said. Another wave, then she picked up her drink to take a sip.

'About?'

'Us.'

'There is no us, Emily.' Bliss shifted in his chair again; after a moment, he looked directly at her. 'I don't mean to sound harsh or cruel, but there just isn't.'

To his surprise, she chuckled. 'You fidget like an anxious school-boy when you're uncomfortable. I've seen great change in you since we were first together, Jimmy, but you're still a child at times. A little boy trapped in a man's body. It's an endearing quality.'

'Well, it's an old man's body now, so maybe I ought to do some growing up.'

Emily pursed her lips in a way he had always found alluring. 'Older, shall we say? And don't give up that childlike side of your nature too easily, Jimmy. Being mature and responsible is overrated.'

Bliss took another long swallow from his glass, letting go a deep sigh as he set it down again. 'I don't know what we're doing here, Emily. I don't know what you expect to achieve.'

'I told you. I want to talk about us. And I don't need you to tell me there is no us again. Your absence from my life tells me that. What I mean is, I want to see if we can find a way for us to be… well, us again.'

'What makes you think anything has changed?' he asked.

'Because things do change. They change every day. When we met up again at the find out by Flag Fen, there was an undeniable spark between us. You acknowledged as much yourself at the time, but you killed it stone dead because of your condition. You cut me out of your life because you didn't want to inflict your illness on me. I'm sure you believed your decision was noble, and in some ways it may have been, but you did so without ever asking how I felt or what I wanted.'

'Because I didn't want you to be with me out of pity.'

Shaking her head, Emily said, 'You can be so damned infuriating at times, Jimmy Bliss. Tell me, why do you alone get to make that decision?'

He was ready for the question. 'Because it's my illness. I have no choice but to live with it. Nobody else needs to.'

'Nobody? Doesn't Penny have to live with it five, six, sometimes seven days a week? Don't the rest of your team?'

'When they see me, when I'm working, I'm managing my symptoms as best I can. But there always has to be a period of release, some down time. Time when I sleep or lie still and recuperate. Do you want that to be all you get, Emily? The tired, worn out, frazzled and unstable me?'

This time it was Emily who was prepared. 'What I would have liked was you doing me the courtesy of letting me make the decision for myself.'

Bliss watched the sky change colour behind her, pastel oranges becoming dusky, reds slowly turning purple. Thin clouds straggled along the skyline like the contrails of unseen airliners. He used the pause to gather his thoughts before speaking.

'I understand. But you have no idea what you'd be getting into. Emily, my condition isn't one of the illnesses people create ribbons for. Ménière's disease robs me of my balance and my confidence. Yes, at the moment I'm able to work – though I'd argue, less effectively as time goes by. But I can physically make it in most days, provided I also rest and take care of myself. That won't always be the case. I'm going deaf, slowly but surely, and one day I may lose my hearing altogether. My episodes of vertigo have increased, and the duration of each attack is a little longer. The effects are both lasting and severe. And the main reason why I stepped back from us – from any kind of long-term relationship – is because I don't know how much worse it's going to be in five years or a decade from now. Like I said, I have no option but to accept uncertainty as my future. And I know you, Emily. If you started a journey with me again, you would stay with me all the way to the end. You'd never consider walking away, no matter how awful it got.'

Emily's face crumpled and her shoulders sagged. 'So when did loyalty and integrity become such a terrible thing?' The mounting frustration in her voice added an edge to it. 'Isn't it something we ought to have discussed? Instead, you told me why we weren't able to see each other any more and then walked out of my life. I tried talking to you as a friend afterwards, but you always resisted.'

'Because it's hard for me,' Bliss snapped back. He checked the tables close by, making sure they could not be overheard. There was nobody else around, but he lowered his voice anyway. 'You're not the only one who thought there was something between us, Emily. You're not the only one who wanted more.'

'But I'm the only one who didn't get a say in our futures, Jimmy. You didn't just decide what yours would be – you took mine and tossed it away at the same time.'

Shoving his glass to one side, Bliss rested his arms on the table and said, 'Because I wanted you to move on. We went through it all once before, all those years ago, remember? You moved on. You found somebody else, married him. Carved out a life for yourself. I wanted you to do it again.'

Emily regarded him coldly for a few moments. 'Is all this because of what happened between us the first time around? Because I walked away from what we had?'

'Do you think so little of me?' Bliss asked softly. 'Am I really so small and petty in your mind?'

Again she seemed to shrink into herself. 'No. No, and I'm sorry for suggesting it. Look, I understand why you chose to push me away. Of course I do. I'm not insensitive to how you see yourself and your rotten condition. You picture a life of misery for me, only ever getting the dregs of you, the part of you worn down by the daily grind and your illness.'

He nodded. 'And it's not just about my disease. There's my job to consider, too. You know the kind of hours I do, the pressure I work under at times. You also know how little I focus on other things when I'm in the zone. You can't possibly want any of that for your future, Emily. You just can't.'

When the resulting silence threatened to go on too long, Emily took a sip from her glass and said, 'Jimmy, as I've told you already and I will tell you again now, what I wanted was to be asked. To be able to choose for myself. To have been granted the opportunity to have a conversation like the one we're having now. I don't know if you realise, but not allowing me to talk about it with you at the time hurt me. It hurt to know you didn't trust me enough to make my own decision.' She shrugged and her narrowed eyes met his. 'It hurt me so badly.'

Bliss closed his eyes, wanting to block out the sound of her pain in the same way. In all his soul-searching prior to his decision to step away from forging a relationship with anybody, he had only ever considered the ache and discomfort his situation was sure to cause in the future. Now he realised how foolish and disrespectful he had been – and, to a large degree, how naïve.

'I'm so sorry,' he said. He reached a hand across the table and held it there, palm up. After a brief hesitation, Emily grasped his fingers in hers. 'Sorrier than you'll ever know. I'm a bloody fool. There's no denying it. But you always knew that about me. And of course, you're right and I was wrong. As I so often am when it comes to this sort of thing. Sometimes I think I'm far more comfortable confronting a seven-foot bruiser armed with a chainsaw than I am a gentle soul like yourself. I should have had this discussion with you a long time ago. Explained myself, listened to you. I'm a berk, Emily. In many ways, I always have been.'

She smiled, and he could see the weight lifting. 'You can't excel at everything, Jimmy. You're great at your job, you're wonderful with your colleagues, and especially with your team. If there's not enough of you to go around outside of work, then those of us who take an interest in you and your life will have to decide if what remains is going to be enough.'

'And would it have been?' Bliss asked tentatively. All at once, her answer was important to him.

Her hand squeezed his. 'It would. And in truth, it still could be.'

FOURTEEN

HE MAJOR INCIDENT ROOM beat like a healthy heart. Exactly how Bliss liked it. During the previous week, the room had taken on a forlorn and sombre atmosphere as the exemplary efforts of the team led them nowhere. He had worked hard to keep their spirits up, but as experienced detectives each of them had endured investigations which for one reason or another never quite got off the ground. There were always a few that ran their course but stalled and fizzled out as the pressure of other cases pushed them further and further down the pecking order.

Before leaving London the previous evening, Bliss had sent out a text alert to his entire team, advising them of the 8.00am briefing. The forensic investigation following the find at Tower Hill had provided all the momentum he and Chandler had needed to reinvigorate them. A grounded op had found its wings at last.

Bliss began by outlining the broad details surrounding the discovery of the hand in the carrier bag, then covered the subsequent conversations and discoveries in depth. When he felt his team were sufficiently on board with the development of a three-way joint task force operation led by Thorpe Wood, he moved on to the call DI Riseborough had received from his crime scene manager.

'The fingerprint belongs to a man who was once a major thorn in the side of police in the Islington, Clerkenwell and Hoxton areas of London. Tommy Harrison was a Class A villain back in the day. According to intelligence, he lives well off his reputation, but no longer carries the threat he once had.'

'Did you know him, boss?' DC Ansari asked.

The team were aware of Bliss's background in the Met, so the question was not unexpected. After Riseborough had mentioned it the previous day, his mind had immediately sought to dredge up some kind of memory.

'The name rings a bell,' he said. 'I'm pretty sure he and I never bumped into each other, though.'

Ansari's face shone with anticipation. 'Still, it's a major breakthrough for us.'

'You're right, Gul. However, the true significance emerges when we consider the case file reference carved into his hand. Earlier in the briefing, I told you about the awful Geraldine Price murder. Well, it turns out, the investigating team at the time interviewed Harrison as a suspect. He was bailed, but upon presenting himself to police thirty days later, he was released without charge. According to DSI Conway, they liked him for it but were unable to break his alibi. Conway suggested Harrison might not have been one of the men who picked up Price on the night she went missing, but had been involved in her subsequent rape and abuse, and possibly even her murder.'

'Where does the removal of his hand and the disposal of it fit in, boss?' DS Bishop asked.

'Conway said the team running the case always believed several men were responsible. It wasn't unusual for gang members to hold women somewhere and use them for whatever purposes they chose. As sickening as it sounds, most of these women were also tricked out and forced to endure a steady flow of "customers" to make money for the gang. But I don't recall any of them ending up like Geraldine Price.'

Bliss broke off there, letting his statement linger for a few seconds. He expected the same rising tide of anger in the others that he himself had felt after hearing about the woman's horrific ordeal. He wanted to extract every drop of sympathy for Price, because he sensed it would be in short supply for their current victims once the team understood his line of thinking.

'Pen and I went over it with both Conway and Riseborough, and we settled on two particular lines of inquiry: first, was Tommy Harrison's hand removed by one of his fellow gang members from back in the day? And second, are our other two victims part of the same gang?'

DCI Warburton had stood at the back of the room in silence until this point. Now, arms folded across her chest, she strode down the short aisle between the desks to join him at the front. 'So you think these men are being silenced one by one by whoever actually murdered the poor Price woman? A member of the same gang?'

Bliss nodded. 'It's certainly one of the key questions we have to answer.'

'But why? I'm not sure I understand.'

'Because of the method being used. Geraldine Price's body was left for the vermin to feast on, but before being killed she'd been sliced up so badly her entire torso was disfigured from the neck down. She may have been alive but on her way out when she was dumped, meaning she wasn't quite dead when the rats came sniffing around. Our three current victims have been sliced up in one way or another, and what you wouldn't be aware of until now is that there are clear signs of vermin activity on all the pieces we've been left so far. Forensics called to confirm as I was leaving my office for the briefing. Needless to say, we don't regard these similarities as coincidental.'

'Boss, have you not considered a revenge motive?' DC Ansari asked. She sat alongside Bishop, her usual partner, in the centre of the room. 'Someone who was close to Geraldine Price?'

Bliss dug a hand into his jacket pocket and pulled out a Twix. He tossed it underarm to the detective constable, whose catch earned a round of applause and a murmur of light-hearted banter from the rest of the team.

'It was the first thing I thought of, Gul,' Bliss said. 'And you earn your treat for the best question of the day so far. But DS Chandler said much the same thing during yesterday's meeting, and Conway wasn't having any of it. And after hearing him out, Pen and I agreed he was probably right. The reason he's convinced it has to be somebody who was involved is because of those details I just spoke about. Neither the flesh slicing nor the rodent activity was ever mentioned in public, and the media certainly never got to report on that aspect.'

'Which is why you shifted focus to this Harrison's gangster friends from back in the day,' Bishop said. The burly sergeant reposed in his usual languid style, but not missing a thing.

'Precisely.'

'So you're certain there's no way the family learned the details? We're ruling out a revenge motive entirely?'

Bliss looked around the room. He and Chandler had spent more time with all this information, apart from the forensic breakthrough about vermin contact with the three recent victims. And although he didn't want to get sidetracked, he owed it to his team to cover every avenue that had been discussed in London. He spared a sidelong glance out of the window, its tinted glass reflecting away the worst of the sun's glare. It was going to be another scorcher of a day, and he envied those who were busy enjoying it.

His eyes travelled back to the team. 'DSI Conway did spare a thought briefly for Geraldine's father, because Robert Naylor was a bit of a mad sod and something like this wouldn't be entirely out of his comfort zone. Conway said he'd follow it up today, but in addition to the fact that Naylor couldn't possibly have found out about the details I just mentioned, he is also an old man now – more than twenty years older than our three victims, at least.'

'Which does leave Price's husband and son, boss,' Bishop said.

'True. But we have the same issue with them. Neither was made aware of those specific facts, so how could they use them against anyone?'

'Okay, yes, I see that. But slicing people up is far from unusual, and any dumped body will encourage vermin activity. It may still be pure coincidence.'

Bliss ran a hand over his face. He glanced up at the whiteboard before replying. 'Absolutely. I agree. I don't think any of us were convinced one way or the other yesterday, and in answer to your original question, the revenge motive is not being ruled out. But we have to start somewhere, and we needed a focal point.'

'So what are the specific plans?' Warburton wanted to know. 'Did you reach any form of agreement with Superintendent Conway and DI Riseborough?'

'Yes, boss. The Super suggested we extend the JTFO to include the City of London force. Max Riseborough was reluctant, but he settled for going along with the idea provided he got the okay from his bosses. We should hopefully have confirmation soon.'

'With you continuing to take the lead?'

'Yep. We have the last word on any course of action. We work separately but also as a single unit, run out of Thorpe Wood. We decided to each return to our own areas and operate from there, but coordinate liaison and full cooperation between all three as soon as we get the word from Max.'

'I haven't spent a great deal of time with them,' Chandler interjected, 'but both the Superintendent and DI Riseborough came across as genuine men. We all want the same thing here. As far as we can tell, it's the Super alone who has a connection to this, with the boss and the DI from Tower Hill being drawn into it by chance.'

'I don't get that part of it,' Ansari said, cupping her face in both hands, elbows planted on the desk. 'Why pull this Superintendent Conway into it at all? Why all the theatrics? Why not take these men out and dump them where nobody will ever find them?'

'Because, irrespective of motive, it's a game to them, Gul. And most games are no fun if you play them on your own.'

'Oh, I don't know about that,' Bishop said, a big grin on his face. 'I can think of one or two.'

Chandler chuckled. 'I bet you can, big boy. You've been married so long now I'm sure you have to.'

Bliss joined in with the laughter. It helped break the tension, and although the jokes made at times like this were usually feeble, they always met with his approval. There was a time when he had hated having his briefings interrupted, but he had come around to accepting the benefits of an open forum.

'Leaving aside Bish's penchant for pocket billiards,' he said, shaking his head in mock admonishment at his DS, 'if we're right, and this is a fellow gang member silencing everybody else involved, then we're looking at a solid enough motive. As for their choice of method, I'm thinking it speaks to their psychology. If they got a kick out of slicing up Geraldine Price – and perhaps others before and since – and leaving her for the rats, it would be natural for them to do these latest victims the same way. It may even be a signature of sorts. Taunting the SIO from Price's murder may be the cherry on top – he's not only reminding Conway that the police didn't solve Price's murder, he's also telling him he won't get a result this time, either.'

Ansari nodded as if accepting the premise, but continued to look pensive. 'But the... death by a thousand cuts, this slow slicing stuff, it's all a bit contrived, isn't it?'

'Of course,' Bliss said. 'But it's precisely the sort of thing this kind of personality enjoys most of all. Killing these men is clearly the ultimate goal. Taking his sweet time about it is the gravy – not the end result, not the killing. In fact, for all we know, he hasn't yet killed any of the three victims, which is something we all need to keep in mind. As for why he chose to lure the Superintendent in, I reckon it's his way of giving Conway the finger. He wants to remind him he's still out there, with all the same tastes and desires. And he's telling us all that he's smarter than we are.'

'Although the boss and I do have an alternative strategy,' Chandler said. 'Well, it's his strategy, really, and I'm going along with it right up until it fails to pan out.'

This resulted in a wave of casual laughter before Bliss filled them in. 'As Gul rightly pointed out earlier, we do also have to consider revenge as a motive. Just because we're aiming our beady eyes and ears at the "fellow gangster" scenario, doesn't mean we intend to ignore any other reasonable possibilities. An act of revenge would also explain why Conway has been drawn into it, because in the eyes of the family he will have failed Geraldine Price. So yes, we will also take a long, hard look at her family. In fact, I'm seriously considering going all the way back to the original investigation and taking it on with a fresh eye. The way I see it, if we solve the Price case, we might just go a long way to solving our current one.'

Bliss allowed a minute or so of lively discussion before cutting through it to speak again. He explained the agreements that had been reached the previous evening. Conway and Riseborough had fresh crime scenes to pursue, whereas his own had run dry. The Wiltshire-based DSI was now almost certainly compromised by his connection to the case, so Bliss assigned Bishop and Ansari to work closely with the Gablecross team and make decisions on their behalf. DC Gratton was due back into the fold later that morning after his day in court, but still minus Hunt, so Bliss decided to assign him the task of liaison between the three areas.

They still had Tommy Harrison to follow up on – provided they got the nod from the City of London police. Bliss accepted the task on behalf of himself and Chandler. He also took on responsibility for delving back into case reference *WS-HO-PC-94-04-02.*

When he was finished, he stood to one side and handed the briefing over to DCI Warburton. As the formal SIO, if she had issues with his case management, now was the time to raise them. Instead, she wished the team well and assured them of her best efforts in talking DI Riseborough's bosses around if they balked at the idea of handing over their one genuine lead.

As the briefing broke up, Bishop cornered Bliss and asked for a quick word in private. Bliss had an idea what it was about, but he remained tight-lipped until the two were sitting at his desk, the office door closed.

'I'm struggling, boss,' Bishop said, getting straight to the point as usual. He moistened his lips and puffed out a long stream of air. 'With the job, and with my home life. Struggling to cope. Two years on, and I still see her face everywhere I look.'

Bliss knew without asking who he meant: DS Mia Short. Shot dead as Bishop knelt beside her, his colleague's blood and body matter strewn across his own face. Bliss bit into his bottom lip before responding, getting a grip on his own emotions. 'Struggling with what, exactly, Bish? I've been keeping a close eye on my team – and you in particular – since Mia was killed. Granted, your overall demeanour has changed, but other than a couple of blow-ups, I've not seen any sign of you being unable to do your job. You don't crack as many jokes as you used to, but still you raise the occasional laugh. How are things at home, between you and Kathy?'

The big man's face crumpled, his bottom lip quivering. 'Not great. I mean, it's not as if she keeps telling me to snap out of it or anything. She'd never be so insensitive. She sympathises as best she can, but she's not alone in thinking I should be over it by now.'

'Who else does?'

'Me. I do. I try, believe me. I had my sessions with the shrink, I did my mental exercises. And, yeah, there are days when I don't allow myself to get despondent. But I come in here every morning and I see the desk where she should be sitting, and it slaps me around the face as if it's the first day without her all over again.'

Bliss took a breath. He felt Mia's loss acutely, of course but he had not been the one by her side when she lost her life. He would not be the one to forever remember scrubbing himself raw to cleanse himself of her blood and tissue and brain matter. Nor did he regard it as something you got over, not entirely. Yet not moving on from it gnawed away at your insides until they became raw all over again.

'Do you need some time off?' he asked. 'I'll sign on the dotted line right now if you want me to, Bish. Paid leave, trauma conditions. You took hardly any when it first happened. You're due some on compassionate grounds. Overdue, if anything.'

His sergeant nodded, eyelids heavy and shoulders stooped. 'I've thought about it. Perhaps getting away for a couple of weeks. But I wonder what I'm going to do with myself. If I'm not working, I'm just left with more time on my hands to think about her. So I come to work and I think about her anyway. And when I do consider going away with Kath and the kids, I wonder how that will make things better, because Mia is always with me no matter where I go or what I do. I feel trapped, boss. Am I making any sense?'

Bliss had reacted the same way following the murder of his wife, Hazel. Like Bishop, he had flared up on occasion afterwards, taking his misery out on others. His escape truly had been the job, whereas his colleague was reminded of his loss every working day. It made perfect sense.

'You need a break, Olly – not just a leave of absence during which you sit and stare at the same four walls, but a genuine holiday. You and the family. Go somewhere you've never been before. Let your mind focus on something entirely new. Explore, walk, swim, ride a bike… anything but sit and dwell. Repair yourself, and do the same thing for your marriage while you're at it. I think you need it, mate. I really do.'

Bishop nodded, blinking rapidly. 'You can swing that for me, boss? The time off, I mean.'

'Absolutely. Whatever you need.'

'Is it okay by you if I see this case out first?'

'No problem. Be glad to have you on board.'

The two men shook hands and regarded each other awkwardly before Bishop put his arms around Bliss and pulled him into a hug. 'You're a diamond, Jimmy Bliss,' he whispered. When he stepped back, his eyes were moist.

Bliss slapped his sergeant's arm. 'Whatever you need, whenever you need it, Olly. I mean it. You don't have to wait until we're in the squad together. Call me, knock on my front door. I'm not being altruistic. You're a decent man and a bloody great copper, and I don't want to lose you.'

He waited ten minutes, composing himself, knowing Mia's desk would draw his eyes the moment he walked back outside into the squad room. When it came to having a tough time moving on, Bishop was not alone.

'So where do you and I start?' Chandler asked him as he appeared, the room empty for the time being. She grinned. 'I'm assuming you won't be waiting for the go-ahead to trickle down from Bishopsgate before getting stuck in.'

Pleased to be thrown back in at the deep end, Bliss nodded. 'You assume correctly. But we start with you telling me what the hell you thought you were doing last night.'

Chandler's eyes brightened. 'How did it go? Did you talk for long?'

'I asked first, and I'd like an answer.'

'Are you serious? What I did was a good thing.'

'What you did was trample all over my personal life. Same thing you've been doing as long as I've known you. Pen, the conversations you and I have every so often are strictly confidential. You can't go around using that information to set traps for me.'

Slumping into her chair, Chandler frowned and said, 'How is it any different from what you do? I never asked you to get involved in my search for Anna, yet somehow you went as far as arranging for the security services to make enquiries with their Turkish counterparts.'

'That was different,' he insisted.

'How so?'

'Because it was impossible for you to resolve the situation on your own. It needed a nudge in the right direction. I was owed a favour, so I used it. And you certainly can't complain about the outcome.'

'No, and I'm nothing but grateful to you. But it's not the outcome we're talking about here. You're having a pop at me for sticking my nose into your private life, but you did precisely the same thing to mine. The ends justify the means.'

Bliss let the silence hang between them. Chandler was right – yet again. 'I was mortified when Emily came out of that pub door with you last night,' he said finally. 'I felt sick to my stomach. Do you have any idea what kind of position you put me in, Pen? I nearly walked away before you even reached our table.'

'But you didn't.'

'No.'

'And did things go better than you'd anticipated?'

His head became crammed with images and memories of the conversation he and Emily had enjoyed. At times it had been tough on him. Talking about his feelings was never something he enjoyed doing. But he knew Emily had cajoled Chandler into arranging the setup for a reason. She was determined to establish where their relationship might go provided they both wanted it enough.

'It went well,' he acknowledged grudgingly. 'But it could so easily have gone the other way.'

'But it didn't, did it? And even if it had, at least you'd have known. You wouldn't still be wondering if you'd done the right thing.'

Bliss smiled. 'That's exactly what Emily said.'

Chandler leaned forward, looking up at him expectantly, arms folded. 'So, go on. Tell me every little detail, no matter how insignificant.'

'Do I need to remind you this is a place of work, and we have plenty to do?'

'If you happen to be a stuffed shirt in need of a personality bypass, then yes. Go ahead.'

He drew in a deep breath. 'Look, when we're next on a break I'll give you the broad strokes. They'll have to do you.'

Chandler smirked. 'There were broad strokes, were there?'

'Not funny,' he said, though he was struggling not to laugh.

'Just tell me one thing.'

'Okay. One.'

'Are you seeing her again?'

Bliss gave it enough of a pause to infuriate her. 'Emily and I are having a meal on Saturday evening.'

Chandler slapped her hands together and began rubbing them. Her face beamed. 'Just call me Cupid,' she said, unable to contain her joy.

As he calmed her down with hand gestures, Bliss tried to remind Chandler he was still angry with her for having sandbagged him. But his heart was no longer in it, and he could tell she knew. 'Let's forget about it for now,' he said. 'Serious faces on, Pen. It's time we got cracking on Tommy Harrison.'

FIFTEEN

AN ILLEGITIMATE SON OF a copper so bent he was called the 'Fish-hook', Thomas Harrison was the result of a brief assignation with a good-time girl from Hoxton. After spending his first year in care, Tommy eventually grew up on the same estate where the Price family lived. He was known to adore his mother, for all her many deficiencies, and he was fiercely protective of the woman and her reputation. The regular teasing he endured as a child helped forge his ability with both fists – and his forehead, whenever it was needed.

Not an exceptionally big lad, he was nonetheless a scrapper with a temper and a chip on each shoulder. Those who elected to torment him with disparaging remarks about his mother's way of earning a living seldom did so twice. Occasionally, Tommy took things too far; the beatings he administered went on too long, their results far more catastrophic than strictly necessary. Many observers believed he enjoyed inflicting pain, which served to enhance his reputation. To goad the man he became was to invite punishment of the kind that often resulted in a lengthy hospital stay, eating liquefied food through a straw.

Bliss had gleaned the details from the records he'd printed out before leaving the office, and filled out the rest using his imagination. He read them as Chandler drove south, relaying relevant snippets to her while she tutted about his continued reliance on hard copies rather than technology. An hour and forty minutes after leaving HQ, they pulled up outside Tommy Harrison's sprawling mock-Tudor pile, which backed on to a golf course. Alongside a shiny new Range Rover stood an Essex police Volvo. Bliss had called ahead to have a patrol crew make the first knock and to keep whoever answered on site until he and Chandler arrived.

One crew member exited the patrol vehicle as the two detectives piled out of the Focus. He nodded and smiled by way of a greeting, using a hand to shield his eyes from the sun. 'My sergeant is inside the house,' he told them. 'Tommy's wife answered our knock. She called in her daughter and son-in-law for backup.'

'That their Range Rover?' Bliss asked, cocking a thumb in its direction.

'Yes, sir. The wife's motor is in the garage. No sign of Tommy's.'

Bliss appraised the young officer, picking up on something. 'You keep referring to him by his first name. You were familiar with the man, I take it.'

'Were?' The officer's squint narrowed further.

'Slip of the tongue. But you do know him, yes?'

'We all do in this neck of the woods. If you don't get to encounter the man in person at some point, you certainly get to hear about him.'

'Bit of a wild one, is he?'

'Mad as a box of frogs, sir. One of the few men I've ever met who truly does not give a shit.'

Chandler chuckled. 'Now's your chance to meet another one,' she said, inclining her head towards her boss.

Bliss ignored her, and the junior constable's choice use of language. 'So, what does the family think is going on?'

'They're used to it, sir. Our presence, I mean. All the wife keeps asking is what her old man is supposed to have done now.'

Intrigued, Bliss thought about the possibilities. They had no idea when Tommy Harrison was taken, but his hand had been removed from its wrist sometime early on Monday morning. At least one night away from home therefore seemed likely. Yet his wife was apparently unconcerned by his absence.

Inside the large house, the patrol sergeant had a quick word with them both. He had been unable to answer the family's many questions, his instructions having been merely to keep Mrs Harrison indoors awaiting two detectives from Peterborough, with no additional explanation. His sense of the situation was that none of them were hiding anything, nor were they overly concerned by Harrison's absence.

Bliss offered his thanks and asked him to wait outside the house as backup. He entered the living room and introduced himself and Chandler to the family. Tommy's wife, Vicki, was a blowsy woman whose unkempt appearance was at odds with her pristine and luxurious home. Everything inside looked as if it were glowing, radiating cleanliness, with a showroom sheen to it all. It smelled fresh, too. Bliss wondered if the Harrisons employed a housekeeper, but thought it best not to enquire.

'Mrs Harrison,' he began. 'When did you last see your husband?'

'Saturday evening,' she replied smartly. 'And don't ask me where he was going, because I don't know.'

'That's true,' the daughter chimed in. 'I was here when Dad went out, and Mum gave him pelters.'

Bliss knew she meant her mother and father had argued, and that her mother had been verbally abusive towards him. 'So why did he go out?' he asked, looking back at Mrs Harrison.

She wore a grey lounge suit, at least one size too small and bearing stains suggesting it hadn't been washed for a while. 'I assumed he was on a job with that bunch of lunatics he still hangs around with.'

'A job?' Chandler said, her head popping up.

'Yeah. Look, the local filth know who and what Tommy is. Me and him have a don't ask, don't tell policy. As long as he provides, I don't need to know where the dosh comes from. I gave him earache about it this time because we'd agreed he was out of the game and was going to spend more time with me.'

Poor sod, Bliss thought. 'So you suspected Tommy was up to no good. Yet you weren't concerned when he failed to come home for the past three nights.'

She shrugged and her face became a petulant scowl. 'It goes like that sometimes. If they were planning something heavy, they'd often take off together for days at a time.'

'Without telling you where?'

'Well, dur. Defeats the object when you lot come calling to ask about him if I know where he is, don't it?'

Nobody offered them a seat, but Bliss took one anyway. Chandler remained standing by his side. He worked his way past Mrs Harrison's innate dislike of the police and began to probe into her husband's background and recent activity. The defensive wall she threw up was impressive. Bliss figured he'd penetrate it in time, but he moved on to asking about Tommy's acquaintances. Her earlier outburst had felt sincere, and he sensed a genuine antipathy towards her husband's friends. It felt like easier ground to cover, and might be more productive.

As it proved to be. She willingly produced a list of names and contact details. In her words, if any of the men she had named were also missing from home, they were bound to be with her husband. Bliss was pleased to have moved things forward, but decided to take a chance on Mrs Harrison being loose-lipped about the past.

'Tell me,' he said, 'does the name Doyle ring any bells with you? I'm talking about your time back in Hoxton, where you and Tommy first got together.'

'The Doyle family? Of course. Who hasn't heard of those sick bastards?'

'You weren't a fan, I take it?'

'You can say that again. It was them who forced us all out of there in the first place. Whole load of us came out here to Essex, mainly to get away from the Doyle mob. They weren't happy to stick to their own patch in Islington, so they muscled in on Hoxton, too. They didn't ask politely, either, if you know what I mean.'

Bliss did. 'I assume they used violence and intimidation as opposed to chocolates and flowers.' The caustic tone came easily to him. If this woman sought sympathy for her plight, she would have to look elsewhere. Villains shitting all over other villains was not something high on the list of things he cared about – unless innocents got caught in the middle, as was so often the case.

'It was like some kind of ethnic cleansing,' she said, shaking her head at the memory. 'Only it weren't the ethnics being cleansed, it was them doing the cleansing. Fucking Irish!'

Bliss noticed the son-in-law turn his head away. He put it on the back burner to return to later. 'So there is absolutely no chance your husband ever did any work for the Doyle family?'

The woman stared at him as if he were insane. 'What the... are you serious? Do you have any idea what it was like between rival gangs in London, especially in the seventies and eighties?'

'As it happens, I do. I was born and raised in Bethnal Green. I worked the area, both as a uniform and as a detective. So yes, I have a pretty firm grasp on what gangland wars were like.'

'Why ask bloody stupid questions, then?'

Tired of the attitude, Bliss gave a loud sigh. 'I just wondered if Tommy did anything with them in the early days. Before they looked to take over the manor. Your old man knew the Doyle brothers, so he could have done a job or two with them before they established their reputation.'

Her scowl deepened, and her mouth twisted as she spoke. 'There is no bloody way. Tommy knew all about the Doyles right from the off. Steering clear of them was an unspoken rule.'

'But if nobody spoke about it, how can you be sure he didn't wander?' Chandler asked.

Harrison turned her pained expression towards the DS. 'Because I know my husband, love. We met when we were sixteen. He was solid and he stayed that way. We all kept our distance from the Doyles. It was them what came the other way, and my Tommy was as angry as anybody when they did. I'm not denying he knew them. All I'm saying is, he wouldn't have worked with any family from the outside.'

The man's wife was certainly confident of her husband's fidelity when it came to the crews he worked with. It didn't surprise Bliss, but he was disappointed by it, nonetheless. He had hoped to tie Tommy Harrison in with the Doyles, because he suspected the family had more to do with Geraldine Price's murder than they'd let on during the original investigation – or at least, one or more of them had knowledge of it and knew who was directly involved. Bliss had also asked himself whether Tommy and Geraldine living on the same estate was significant, or just a twist of fate. Putting it to one side, he turned his attention back to the daughter's husband.

'Hope you don't mind my asking,' he said, 'but a few moments ago when Mrs Harrison cast aspersions on the Irish, you flinched. Was that a direct response to her slating the Irish people as a whole, or the Doyle family in particular?'

Bliss saw Vicki's face cloud over as she turned to look at her son-in-law. The daughter, meanwhile, sat facing forward, both cheeks turning pink. As for the man himself, he glared at Bliss, a tic pulsing beneath his left eye.

'Sir?' Bliss prompted, not about to let him off the hook.

'I'm half-Irish. Vicki knows but doesn't seem to care. I'm used to her ranting when she's fuelled up on vodka, but even when she's sober it seems like she wants to blame us all for what a single family did.'

'You can always fuck off out of my house if you don't like it,' Harrison barked. She pointed towards the door as if he might have forgotten the way during the time he had been in the living room with her.

'You think I'd be here if it weren't for Phoebe?' He gave his wife's arm a squeeze, but refused to look at her mother.

'You'd have no bloody reason to be, you doughnut.'

Wedged between the squabbling pair, the daughter closed her eyes and appeared to shrivel into herself.

Bliss glanced up at Chandler. Her focus was on the three people sitting on the large expensive-looking sofa. He jabbed an elbow into her side, and asked the question with his eyes and an almost imperceptible hike of his shoulders.

Do you have anything more to ask?

Chandler shook her head. The look she gave him suggested she was as sick of these people as he was. As the family argument continued to rage back and forth, Bliss worked through what he had learned. He believed Vicki Harrison when she claimed her husband had never had anything to do with the Doyle brothers. But what he wondered now was why none of them had asked why he and Chandler were there.

'I don't mean to interrupt this latest edition of Happy Families,' he said, punching the words out to cut across the raised voices. 'But I'm finished asking questions, so I need you all to calm down and listen to what I have to say.'

Something about his tone or manner snagged Vicki's attention. She stopped mid-tirade and looked directly at Bliss. In her eyes, he saw the first dim light of fear dawning.

'My Tommy is all right, isn't he?' she said, a pleading edge to her question.

'No, he's not,' Bliss replied after a momentary pause. 'I can't tell you exactly how he is, because the truth is – we don't yet know. We don't have a clue where he is, either. But there is one thing I can tell you with absolute certainty, Mrs Harrison: your husband is far from all right.'

SIXTEEN

ON THE DRIVE TO Theydon Bois, Bliss had noticed a mobile café in a lay-by just after the M11 slip road. Heading back the same way, he now saw a Transit van and two heavy goods vehicles parked up beside it, which implied the food was fit for human consumption. He told Chandler to stop and offered to buy them both lunch.

At the long white trailer's counter, Bliss asked the man behind it if he sold Earl Grey tea. The look he received in return was withering. 'Not unless he's the Earl of Lidl, mate,' the café owner said, cackling at his own dry wit.

Bliss responded with a lukewarm smile to match the quality of the joke – and the tea, no doubt. 'I hope it's not too late for you to ask for a refund,' he said.

The man's eyebrows converged. 'Who from?'

'The customer services training camp. I reckon you're about to get the lowest mark ever recorded.'

The owner said nothing, responding instead with a wide grin as Bliss ordered two coffees and two bacon rolls. He waited close by to make sure none of it received a phlegm topping.

While they consumed their lunch in the car, he and Chandler explored in greater detail the list of names Vicki Harrison had provided. Shortly after Tommy had been exposed as the man to whom the severed hand had once been attached, his entire criminal record had been made available to the joint task force, and the records included known accomplices. Chandler accessed the information on her phone and compared the list with the one Mrs Harrison had given them. Of the six names she had written down, only one did not match those on the police database: Phillip Walker.

'We should start with him,' Bliss suggested. He dabbed a fingertip on the sheet of notepaper Chandler had propped up against the steering wheel. He left behind a blob of tomato ketchup, but made no move to wipe it away. 'In case either of us gets hungry later,' he explained.

Chandler stopped chewing her roll for long enough to say, 'Makes sense. Paying this man a visit, I mean. Not the "saving ketchup for later" nonsense, which is straight out of Jimmy Bliss's Culinary Tips for the Insane. He's in North Weald, which isn't too far from here.'

'Precisely. We get him over with on the way home. I want to run the other names by Conway and Riseborough before we look into them. This one doesn't seem to be on our radar, though.'

'Which makes him even more interesting.'

Bliss liked the way his partner thought. In his experience, the higher you looked up the criminal ladder, the less likely it was to find somebody with a record or featuring in any police intelligence data whatsoever. These men – and the occasional woman – were generally the brains of the outfit, people who kept to the shadows and out of the spotlight. They led from a distance, keeping their muscle at arm's length. If he and Chandler were right, this detour on their way home might prove invaluable.

'You were quiet back there,' he said, mopping his lips with a paper serviette. He also checked the mirror to make sure there was no sauce smudged around his mouth. 'At Harrison's drum. You usually have one or two insightful questions, but… nothing.'

Chandler finished eating and wrapped everything up in the grease-stained bag her roll had come in. 'To tell you the truth, I felt a little bit out of my depth. You know the Harrisons of this world from your time in London – and working for the NCA, I suppose. I meet organised criminals on the odd occasion, but these old-time villains seem to be a different breed altogether.'

'For the most part, their reputations are well-earned, and they did live the life. I knew many of them, and even regarded a few as friends at the time. But there were also some real scary bastards out there.'

'Like this Doyle family, yeah?'

'Them, and many others like them. Psychopaths, Pen. Pure and simple.'

'Makes you wonder how they ever get someone remotely normal to share their life. Look at Vicki earlier. The woman was inconsolable – her daughter, too. They don't even know if the man is dead, but their grief was genuine. They have hearts, they have compassion. How does that stack up with what they know about his past?'

Bliss understood what his partner meant. The incongruence had always baffled him as well. 'I think if you tell yourself something long enough, you end up believing it. In all likelihood, Vicki Harrison may have told herself a thousand times that her old man couldn't possibly have been responsible for all the things he's meant to have done.'

'You think the three of them will keep the news to themselves, as we asked?'

'I reckon so. I think you made yourself perfectly clear. If they think there's the slightest chance of him still being alive, and that by spilling their guts they'd risk putting him in greater danger, then yes, they'll keep schtum.'

It was barely a fifteen-minute drive from the lay-by to their destination, during which Chandler did her best to tease information out of Bliss about Emily Grant. He was equally determined not to give too much away, other than suggesting he was looking forward to their meal over the coming weekend.

'So, no intention of backing out due to work commitments?' Chandler said.

She dropped the remark in casually, though he sensed it was anything but. Bliss had asked himself the same question. The months had flown by since he had last considered dating Emily. At the time, he had also been growing increasingly fond of Sandra Bannister from the *Peterborough Telegraph*. Following a particularly gruelling few days working the case in which he had met Molly, he finally made up his mind which path he wanted to take. He and Sandra had not been on a single date, although they were all set to make it work. But Bliss had realised two things as he sat at home contemplating his future: first, they were from different and radically opposed worlds, and their jobs would have them butting heads all the time. The thought of being with her was a pleasant one, but he saw no future beyond a few brief assignations. And second, he had never entirely shaken Emily from his mind, often yearning for what might have been, and mourning lost opportunities.

His decision made, Bliss had succumbed to a vertigo rush which all but wiped him out for the best part of two hours. While he recovered, with a drink in one hand and a heavy weight lodged inside his chest, he realised he couldn't inflict his illness on Emily. It wouldn't be fair to her, even though the two had met around the same time as he had received his diagnosis. She knew more about his condition than most but, like him, it had also altered during the intervening years. His disease was chronic and would now never leave him. It was a progressive one, too, his ultimate prognosis unknown. He was happy they had spoken since, but looked no further ahead than their next meeting.

He didn't answer Chandler's question directly, and they rode in silence until they reached the home of Phillip Walker. When Chandler pulled up outside the man's residence and killed the engine, Bliss surveyed their surroundings. The apartment complex stood on an estate not far from the North Weald airfield, around the corner from a large industrial park. Peering up at the stained exterior of the building, he gave a low grunt.

'What?' Chandler asked, following his gaze. 'You asking yourself if this is the home of a criminal mastermind?'

'That's exactly what I was doing,' Bliss said. 'But you know something, Pen, I can see the brains of a criminal enterprise living in a humdrum gaff like this. Who would suspect them of having untold wealth stashed away in an offshore bank account?'

Nodding, Chandler said, 'Or this could be his crash pad – his proper home elsewhere, perhaps registered to a partner or his business.'

'The thought never occurred to me. You may well be right.'

They had to walk around the other side of the complex, through a maze of passageways and up a flight of stairs, to find the front door. Neither of them was surprised to hear the bell's chime playing *Rule Britannia*. When there was no answer, Bliss rapped his knuckles on the door, following up with a thump using the meat of his fist. Still no response. He peered through the letterbox, put his ear to it for a moment. He neither saw nor heard anything to warrant a hard entry.

'Can you hear cries for help or sounds of a disturbance inside, Sergeant?' Bliss said, raising his eyebrows at his partner.

'That depends, boss. If we crash our way in and find evidence but no bodies, our warrantless search will be challenged. We lose the decision, we lose the evidence. You want to risk that on what we have now? If so, then yes, there are clear cries and loud disturbances going on behind that door.'

Bliss heard what Chandler left unsaid. She thought they should wait until they had more than a name scrawled on a scrap of ketchup-smeared paper. He scowled but drew back, wanting to take the door off its hinges but knowing his DS was right.

After hanging around for a further ten minutes, Bliss decided to head back to HQ. He had no way of knowing where these interviews were leading, but he was keen to start looking at the Geraldine Price case. He asked Chandler to call Phillip Walker and arrange a suitable time for an interview. A short while later, having received no answer, she left a brief message on the voicemail.

Bliss remained contemplative as Chandler drove them back to Peterborough. Eventually, he and his team were going to have to dip a toe into the murky waters of the Geraldine Price investigation. Based on his own experiences, Bliss expected complications. The big push for computerisation within the service had come in the early seventies. In 1974, the Police National Computer system was established, with the first HOLMES database emerging over a decade later. However, police officers and detectives had been less than keen to use the computers available to them for anything other than intelligence searches, and were often uncomfortable entering data into a system they did not fully understand. This had led to paper-based recording systems being maintained for many years longer than they ought to have been, and the process of moving them across to a digital store was laborious and prone to human error. The PNC existed in a variety of forms for more than twenty years before it finally became a reliable case file storage system.

Currently when somebody was arrested, their details were fed into three main electronic records: the PNC, the national DNA system, and the IDENT1 fingerprint database. The three worked together seamlessly to maintain an overall profile of the arrestee.

Not all older case files had been transferred manually from micro-fiche, however, which was a problem cold case investigators often ran into. In addition, some records were inevitably lost or mis-placed during the transfer. With the Geraldine Price investigation having taken place early in 1994, Bliss was confident that at least a portion of the data he required would be missing. This always led to confusion, because you didn't know what you didn't know.

DNA was a less obvious route. The first British murder convic-tion to be based on DNA fingerprinting had happened just three years before Price had been murdered, and in 1994 it was still not standard procedure to obtain swabs, because no national database yet existed. Add to that the condition of the body by the time it was discovered, and Bliss was in little doubt that he would find no DNA evidence whatsoever.

By the time he got back to Thorpe Wood, Bliss had already decided to enlist the computer skills admirably demonstrated by DC Ansari. He'd have a chat with her, explain what he was thinking, outline the data he hoped to find, and leave her to it. Before doing so, however, he wanted to familiarise himself with the main players. The starting point – as ever – was the case file log.

The first thing he noticed was how little information the file itself contained. Modern case files held ample links to a complete range of information, but what he saw on the monitor as he sat in his office was extremely limited in scale and scope. Knowing the basics, as related by Conway himself, was a decent start, but the Super had spoken from memory, which was as prone to failure as any other storage device. Reading through the log, Bliss was pleasantly surprised to find the case and its evidence unfolded along the lines described.

He saw photos of the victim for the first time. Conway had called Geraldine Price a looker; if anything, he had understated her attractiveness. A stunning woman with blonde hair cut short into what Bliss imagined was a 'pixie' style, the array of images revealed close-ups of her face and wider-angle shots of her from a greater distance. Price was the full package, but Bliss's attention was caught more by her smile and bright eyes than any other features. The parted lips and even teeth spoke of confidence and enthusiasm, a lust for life and all it could offer. Beneath long and curving eyelashes, intelligence gleamed and passion burned. Until this point, the victim had been merely a name to Bliss. Now he saw the woman she was at the time of her death, and he was easily able to visualise the one she had hoped to be. Anger at her sudden and unnecessary murder swelled inside him.

Moving on to the crime scene photographs, Bliss heard himself gasp as the establishing shot came up on screen. Taken from above, it portrayed Price as she was found on a small patch of land off Wharf Road, alongside the canal basin. The plot was overgrown with dense hedgerow and tall grass, wild with neglected plantation and thick bushes, and she was not easy to spot. It had taken a passer-by leaning over the bridge wall to identify what the youth initially thought was a damaged mannequin. A keen photographer, he had pulled out his Nikon, replaced the standard lens with a zoom, and zeroed in on what he imagined would be a fun shot. In his statement, he told police he didn't think he would ever get over what he had seen through that lens.

As he scrolled through the photos, Bliss started to feel sick. This once beautiful woman had been rendered unrecognisable. Puffy and discoloured, her marbled and stained flesh had a wax-like sheen to it. The scenes of crime officers had done a fine job in distinguishing between bite marks and deliberately sliced sections of flesh, confirming Pete Conway's recollections. A great deal of attention had been paid to the area in and around her groin. Geraldine Price's pubic hair was matted with dried blood, her labia shredded in places, with ragged tears revealing the punishment she had endured. Bliss noted deep lacerations on both sides of the vulva, caused by a sharp blade. In two close-up shots, he saw what appeared to be indentations, which he thought had been caused by the hilt of a knife.

His mouth dry and sour, Bliss clicked away from the crime scene photographs. Unlike the amateur photographer who had discovered the body, he would recover from the impact of what he had seen; inured to such depravity, his thick skin was perhaps not entirely immune, but it was callused enough to prevent permanent damage. Though the graphic nature of the wounds left him feeling numb, he did not want his investigator's interest to become voyeuristic.

He searched for DNA but, as expected, found no evidence. Turning to the timeline section, Bliss followed the chronology on the screen at the same time as he replayed Conway's version of events in his head. They were a close enough match for him to nod approvingly at the Super's ability to not only draw on his memory, but also provide information in such a way as to create a vivid picture in the mind's eye.

Three pivotal moments captured Bliss's attention. The first was the window during which Price had been taken off the street. The first question to ask was whether she had willingly gone with somebody else, perhaps accepting a lift from a familiar face. If not – if she had been snatched – why had nobody noticed? It was the rush hour. There would have been vehicles and other pedestrians along her most likely route, all the way from the bus stop to the point at which she would have entered her housing estate. So was that where it had happened? Had she blundered into a street gang hanging around close to her flat? The evening would have been dark, the lighting in and around the area likely to range from dim to negligible. But was it possible for an abduction to have taken place without a single witness noticing or hearing her protest? Bliss thought it unlikely, believing instead that she had accepted a ride from somebody she knew.

The second critical juncture to consider was the dumping of the body. Although not a major thoroughfare, Wharf Road had always been well-travelled, as far as Bliss could recall. Often used as a rat-run between City Road and north Islington, bypassing the heavy traffic around the Angel tube station, it was busy enough for Bliss to speculate that the body dump had been carried out in the dead of night. Indeed, it was highly likely that her naked body had been tipped over the same bridge from which she had later been spotted.

In between the two time points, the living, breathing Geraldine Price had entered premises somewhere – probably in the same immediate vicinity – before being carried or dragged out to a waiting vehicle several days later. A van or estate car was Bliss's guess. Identifying the location in which she was held was critical, but something the original investigating team had been unable to do. Bliss had a shrewd idea that it would not have been someone's home, but a business property; somewhere out of the way, far from observant eyes and sharp ears.

Yet close by.

He was certain it would have to be near to where she had been both taken and returned. Why dump her in the same area several days later if not?

Bliss felt his stomach flip. He rushed out of his office and sped to the men's toilets at the far end of the corridor. He burst through the door and headed straight for one of the three sinks. For a good minute he leaned over it, hands gripping its stainless-steel rim. Cramps raced across his abdomen, and he felt a liquid burn at the back of his throat. When nothing came up and he'd choked back the bile, Bliss ran the cold tap, cupped his hands beneath the stream and brought the water up to his face. The coldness stung a little, but it felt good. He avoided looking into the mirror, not wanting to catch even a glimpse of what he knew must be a harrowing look on his face.

What had happened to Price was no longer a mystery. As for how it happened, where it happened, and who was responsible, there were still no answers a quarter of a century later. It wasn't a lot to go on, but it was all Bliss needed after seeing those photographs. Geraldine Price was now more than a case file to him. Her vicious, brutal murder had never been solved, but having seen her broken body, he was now stung by the reality of the situation. And he would not rest until he had answers.

SEVENTEEN

H E HAD NO IDEA how many hours or days had passed since he'd been taken, only that his future hung by the finest of threads. Death could not come soon enough for him, but he feared his own strength might enable him to survive another day or two. The thought chilled him so deeply he shook until his bones ached.

Since the loss of his left hand, shock had completely overwhelmed his body. Bathed beneath the midday sun and spotlit in its heat, he trembled and shuddered nonetheless. His mind was a confusion of images, and he wondered if he had hallucinated certain aspects of what he thought he had endured; he could not believe himself capable of withstanding such an onslaught.

While the masked figure punished him, his willpower fractured and unashamed tears spilled out, accompanied by pleading for the swift mercy of release. With the man gone once more, he was left consumed by pain, anger, bitterness, and a contempt for his own weakness. All too soon, however, he began preparing for the man's return, once more crushed beneath the weight of hopelessness and capitulation. Terror funnelled back in to fill the void where agony dissipated, and a dull throbbing rippled through his veins.

Throughout it all there were moments of lucidity. Minutes filled with the harsh reality of being some psychotic freak's captive, understanding there was no escape and nobody around to hear his screams. Now, as he waited once again for the man's return, he began to ponder his captor's motives for carrying out this degree of torture. The moment he realised it had to be personal, his thoughts turned to the figure's appearance.

Why wear the mask?

Was it for dramatic effect? Was its featureless design deliberately calculated to instil further terror? Or was the truth simpler than either of those explanations? Was the man hiding his face behind the ragged cloth because without it he'd be recognised? Was that it? Did he know this man? Had the two of them been enemies?

In those few idle moments when he was not being tortured, fearing torture, or anticipating the grim return of the creatures, Tommy Harrison reflected on how he had been abducted. These days he earned a crust fencing stolen items, and most of the time he worked out of a lock-up garage adjacent to a viaduct in Buckhurst Hill; for bigger jobs in the capital, he used one of his old haunts on the Isle of Dogs. On Saturday he had received a text message. The number was unknown to him, but since most of his new customers were friends of friends of friends, this was nothing unusual. He arranged a meeting with the caller in a supermarket car park close to Millwall outer dock later in the evening, indicating they should wait for him in the last available space at the far end, by the car wash. His policy was to meet people in person ahead of any transaction; if they had something of interest to him, he would then make the necessary reference calls prior to shaking hands on a deal. There was no risk involved at this point because neither cash nor goods were on offer during the initial meeting.

He rolled into the car park fifteen minutes after the appointed time. A blue Transit van was waiting in the assigned space, a lone figure behind the wheel. He parked up two bays down, and seconds later somebody wearing a sweatshirt with its hood pulled up climbed out of the van and ambled over, head bowed to avoid security cameras as Tommy had advised. As usual, he kept his doors locked but hit the button for the window on the passenger side. This ensured he and whoever he was doing business with remained at least an arm's length apart. It was an added precaution he had never previously required. But on this occasion, as the figure crouched, Tommy caught a bright flash of metal glinting in the fading sunlight. It was as if a camera's flash had gone off, momentarily blinding him. A second later, he felt a fierce cramp-like pain creep over his entire body. His muscles spasmed. He felt his body jerk around and his eyes begin to roll inside their sockets. Rearing back, he smashed his head against the window.

A swirling sensation followed by a slow submerging into darkness was the last thing he remembered until he woke up lashed to the wooden posts. He now realised he had been tasered, after which he'd been rendered unconscious by either a blow or being force-fed a strong sedative. It seemed like a long time ago now, though he knew less than three full days had passed. The man who had abducted him was without compassion. He was also patient and methodical as he went about slicing chunks of meat from Tommy's body. A number of wounds had been left untreated, depending on blood seepage. If the flow increased, out came the blowtorch, and the searing pain and nauseating stench of his own burnt flesh became hideously overpowering.

A sense of hopelessness squeezed his heart to the point of crushing it. Whatever this man wanted, it was not information. He had asked no questions; his actions were intended only to cause pain and terror. As for why he had removed the hand, Tommy had no clue. But the man had taken it away with him, carefully wrapped up in a carrier bag together with a couple of fragments of tissue sliced off with the smaller blade. At that point, Tommy had considered every remaining part of his body, the numerous sections so far untouched, the number of appendages and limbs left available for removal.

It all added up to a great deal more misery and agony to come. But why? He did not deserve this.

Tommy wept, sobbing as he had not done since early childhood. Alone and terrified. Not wishing for home, but for death to visit him – sooner rather than later.

EIGHTEEN

THE NEW OFFICES OF the *Peterborough Telegraph* were smaller than those in their previous building near the bus station, but infinitely more comfortable, and brighter by far. During the case in which Molly had created chaos for one of the city's most notorious drugs gangs, Bliss and Chandler had met with journalist Sandra Bannister and three senior editorial staff to discuss another case running in parallel; at the time, none of them could have known how important that meeting would later prove to be. On this occasion, it was just Bliss and Bannister thrust together in the conference room.

Bliss had been at his desk when his mobile rang, half an hour earlier. Bannister had called on three separate occasions since eight-thirty that morning. He'd let each one go to voicemail, but had not checked the messages. Three attempts to contact him in a single day was unusual, though, so this time he picked up.

'We need to talk,' Bannister said without preamble. Their relationship had returned to its original stilted, awkward state recently, and Bliss was unsurprised by her getting straight down to business.

'We do?'

'Yes, I think so. I believe I have information you'll be interested in.'

'Is that so? I didn't think we did this kind of thing any more.'

'Neither did I, but what I have for you today is important. Crucial, in fact.'

Bliss let that sink in for a few seconds. He sat upright, mind stirring. 'All right, you have my attention. Can you give me a clue?'

'I've been working on a story for a couple of weeks now. Judging by what I hear coming out of Tower Hill and your own media office, my story and your investigation appear to be crossing lines.'

That was something Bliss did not want to hear. He immediately understood the urgency. 'I'll be there in half an hour,' he said.

She had insisted he go alone. When he asked why, Bannister told him she didn't want DS Chandler jumping in and confusing the situation further with any official blowback after hearing what was said. Irritated by the request, but equally intrigued, Bliss agreed and left Thorpe Wood without saying a word to any of his team.

As close as he and Bannister had once been, a gulf now existed between them. Bliss understood why, and blamed himself. He had allowed their professional relationship to become a personal one, but when they were on the brink of becoming more than friends, he had pulled away. Despite his explanation, Sandra had not taken his decision as well as Emily had. They had spoken twice since, resulting in short, superficial conversations. The greeting they exchanged on this occasion was not entirely warm.

'You sounded concerned on the phone,' Bliss said, taking a seat at the central table. He thought she looked tired, puffy around the eyes. Pale and more slender than he remembered, Bannister did not present as the picture of health. He wondered what was bothering her.

She sat down at the opposite side of the table, as far from him as possible. 'I was. I am. The thing is, I'm not exactly sure what's cooking here, but I have a feeling we're about to reach a point where the overlap between your investigation and my own becomes impossible to navigate. Reluctantly, I now think it's time to share what I have with the police.'

'How about you tell me what it is you've been working on, and I'll give you my honest opinion?'

'That is my intention,' Bannister insisted. The worried look on her face deepened into something more troubled. 'I fought hard with my editors to bring this to you. My colleague and I have spent many hours on this project, and with no article yet posted there's a concern it will be time wasted.'

'You mean, once I hear what you have to say, I might ask you to sit on it.'

'Exactly. That's why I thought it best if Penny wasn't here with you. Despite our differences, I still feel you and I are capable of thrashing things out ahead of any formal decision. Plus – and I don't like to remind you of this, but I will – myself and my news-paper retain the right to publish, irrespective of what we discuss in this room.'

Bliss bristled, indignant at being given the official Fourth Estate line. 'Then why bring it to me at all?' he asked, with greater severity than he'd intended.

'Because it's the right thing to do,' she said simply. 'And yes, I learned that phrase from you.'

Bannister took a deep breath and launched into what she had to say. It had begun over two weeks earlier, she said, when she stum-bled across a brief online column in the *Huffington Post*, written by a freelance reporter. In the article, the author laid out the curious case of Benjamin Carlisle, a man in his fifties who had taken his two dogs for a walk and never returned. Both Staffordshire bull terriers were found three hours later, running free around a farmer's field nearby. Carlisle's wife reported her husband missing, but there were no suspicious circumstances and no witnesses to suggest that any criminal activity had taken place. In the final paragraph, the writer speculated as to whether the man's gangland past lay behind his disappearance.

'The item piqued my curiosity,' Bannister admitted. 'The article was not the best I've ever read, and journalistically weak – having referred to Carlisle's murky past, it failed to explore it further. Even so, I read it on a Friday, spent the weekend mulling it over, and on the Monday morning asked my editor if I could devote time to investigating the item thoroughly. She gave me a bit of leeway, I roped in a junior, and we began a deep dive into Ben Carlisle.'

Bliss had felt hairs springing erect on the nape of his neck the moment Bannister mentioned a gangland connection. 'I take it you discovered enough to keep you interested,' he said.

'You could say so. Carlisle is one sick and twisted individual. He's spent time in prison, but is thought to have committed far worse crimes than those of which he was convicted. Those crimes include malicious wounding, ABH, GBH, and murder. In fact, he was charged with all three during a four-year period back in the late eighties and early nineties, but each charge was eventually dropped due to lack of evidence, witnesses mysteriously withdrawing their statements or, in one case, disappearing altogether.'

'He sounds like a real sweetheart. But I have to say, Sandra, his name hasn't come up in my own investigation so far.'

After a lengthy pause during which her eyes never left his, she finally said, 'Do you know, that's the first time you've called me by my first name?'

He nodded. 'Given the circumstances, it felt like the right thing to do.'

'There was a time when I'd have been overjoyed. Now... I'm not so sure.'

Bliss wanted to shrug it off before he became too defensive. 'It's still your name, right? Let's not get hung up on it. Like I say, I'm not seeing where your Mr Carlisle fits in with our case.'

'I'm about to get to that. Once I got a sense of the kind of man he was, we went deeper still. Right back to his teenage years, following his reputation through the decades, until he all but disappeared from the news and rumour mills. It began to look as if our story had led us nowhere. Then two things came together in rapid succession. Both myself and my junior colleague were obviously aware of the find at the Bishop's Palace, and on Saturday we caught wind of the similar discovery in Wiltshire. By this stage we had carried out many interviews and completed dozens of hours of research, and after the news came in at the weekend, my junior happened to mention an idea he'd had.'

Bliss felt himself leaning forward, turning his better ear slightly towards her. 'Which was?'

'There are a couple of strands, so please bear with me.'

'I'll give it my best shot. I'm not used to this investigative lark.'

Bannister pouted. 'Do you want to hear what I have to say, or not?'

Bliss nodded amiably. 'It was a joke. Please, go on.'

'One of Ben Carlisle's fellow gangsters from way back was a man called Freddy Swift. His background was extremely interesting, and we discovered that he'd been interviewed in connection with an awful crime in the mid-nineties – a crime we'll come back to in a moment, but it's one I'm positive you'll be interested in. Also, we met with Carlisle's wife at their home, and although I didn't see it myself, while we were speaking to her my junior spotted a book on a shelf and it stuck in his head. He said he didn't think of it again until the report came in about the contents of the carrier bag in Wiltshire. He debated whether or not to mention it to me, but when he did, it stuck inside my head, too.'

'Which book?'

'It was called *Death By A Thousand Cuts*—'

'By Brook, Bourgon and Blue,' Bliss interrupted. 'I'm aware of it.'

Bannister seemed surprised. 'So you're also familiar with its subject matter?'

'Yes. And I can see why it stuck with you both. If I'm reading things correctly, you two decided to keep this to yourselves while you were still working on your story, but when a third discovery came into play, you felt you had to at least discuss the wider implications with me.'

Nodding, Bannister said, 'That's about the size of it, yes.'

All the interlinking parts snapped together inside Bliss's head. Infuriated and unable to contain his emotions, he leaned further forward and made slits of his eyes. 'Let me get this straight. Since before those scraps of flesh were discovered around the corner from here, you've been aware of this man having gone missing in mysterious circumstances. After we became involved, at which point you must have heard and seen our appeal for information in respect of a missing male adult – an appeal which, as I recall, your newspaper ran – you still kept all this to yourself until today, despite the second find becoming public on Saturday.'

'Yes. That sounds about right.'

'You withheld vital information you must have considered relevant from a police investigation?'

'Yes.'

'That is unacceptable!' Bliss snapped, slamming his fist down on the table. He shot to his feet and began pacing by his chair, his eyes burning into hers. 'What the hell were you thinking? I can understand why you might have failed to bring this to our attention when you first looked into it, but from the moment that slice of human flesh was discovered – what, twelve days ago now – you must have known there was every chance of it being connected to this Ben Carlisle bloke.'

'Please don't raise your voice at me, Inspector. I won't be intimidated by you.'

'Oh, so it's "Inspector" now, is it? You want to play it that way, do you? In that case, let me tell you, Ms Bannister, I have no intention of trying to intimidate you. My anger is both genuine and justified. You kept information from us, from an ongoing investigation. Why? To further your own narrow cause with a story?'

Bannister glared at him. 'My actions were not unacceptable, and your anger is not justified. I refute both of those statements. You want to know why I kept this from you until now?'

'Yes. Please do regale me with all of your meaningless journalistic platitudes. And try to make it sound different to the claptrap I've heard so many times before from you people.'

'There's no need to be quite so hostile.' Bannister stared up at him. There was anger in her eyes, but he saw that his venomous attack had wounded her.

Bliss reeled it back in, biting down on a retort. 'Okay. You win. Just tell me. Tell me why you held this information back.'

'Because it's my job. It's that simple. I am a journalist. I had a story. And I didn't know for sure if it had anything to do with the case you're working on until I heard about the second find on Saturday.'

'And yet today is Tuesday. What have you been doing for the past three days?'

Bannister planted her hands flat on the desk in front of her as she stood up. 'Haranguing my editors to get them to agree to this conversation, you bloody stubborn man.'

His breath coming in short, laboured pants, Bliss thought it through. Bannister keeping the story in-house until this point came as no real surprise. She made a living as an investigative reporter, and she was better at her job than most. She would not have wanted to come to him with anything less than clear evidence – if she approached him at all ahead of publication. He was not angry with her, despite his outburst. It was the situation he disliked, the rules allowing newspapers to keep the police in the dark if the story called for it. Bannister, however, clearly had more to say, and so he decided to give an inch.

'We're off the record as of now, right?' he said, raising his eyebrows.

'If you prefer.'

'I do. But I have to hear the words.'

'Very well. Off the record.'

They both retook their seats. Bliss calmed himself before speaking again. 'The whole Lingchi thing occurred to me, too. That's the proper name for the death by a thousand cuts, or slow slicing, in the book you mentioned. But it came to me after the third discovery, at Tower Hill. From the little I've read, I gather the art is in removing as many pieces of flesh as possible without killing the victim. However, major parts may also be removed when death is near, the challenge stepping up a notch as it approaches the end.'

Bannister shuddered. 'It's horrific. Barbaric.'

'We humans did enjoy indulging our baser instincts in those days. These days, too, it seems. So tell me, what eventually made you decide to bring me into this?'

'Well, now, this brings me back to Freddy Swift. One of the crimes he was interviewed about was particularly abhorrent. It involved the brutal rape and murder of a young wife and mother. When I read about the case, I noticed she was thought to have been tortured over a period of time before being dumped. Putting that together with the book in Carlisle's living room led me to wonder if both men may have had something to do with the murder. It seemed like a crazy coincidence otherwise. Of course, the similarities with the cases you were working on also struck me, but I couldn't see how they connected at all.'

'So what changed?'

'Only my perception of it. In the end, there were too many links for me to ignore between the men, your cases, and the old one I mentioned.'

'Geraldine Price,' Bliss muttered, his thoughts turning over quickly now.

Again the look of surprise. Bannister spread her hands. 'So you already know all of this? I'm telling you nothing new?'

Bliss shook his head. 'No, you are. I'm sure we would eventually have come up with the names of both Swift and Carlisle, but it would have taken longer. You can imagine what the record-keeping was like in the nineties, with computerisation and all that entailed. In fact, that's what I was looking into when you called. Many notes and statements will have failed to make it into those records, so at the moment we're relying on memory as much as anything else. You've saved us days of trawling through data. Did you know Conway, the SIO in Wiltshire, was on the Geraldine Price investigation?'

'No. That's news to me, I must admit. Our focus so far has mostly been on Carlisle's disappearance.'

'So, you argued the toss with your editors, and they stalled. But a third connected case, allied with your own findings, eventually tipped the balance in our favour.'

'Yes. With, I like to think, a little bit of persuasion from me.'

Bliss debated how much to reveal. Off the record or not, there were limits to what he felt comfortable discussing with a journalist. He trusted Bannister more than any other, but not enough to put his complete faith in her integrity. He opted not to tell her about the figures carved into the pieces of flesh, as this was a detail deliberately withheld from the media so far. It felt like the right card to hold back for a later date.

'There's still a great deal of confusion at the moment,' he said. 'We've locked into a joint task force, involving my team, a unit from

Swindon, and now the City of London police. A DI by the name of Max Riseborough is running things down there, and although the three of us have a professional overlap, we're not exactly sure how it all fits together, or even if it does at all. I'd be interested in hearing anything else you have, though.'

They talked for a further forty minutes, both having reeled in their emotions. Bliss apologised for his earlier outburst, and left with a promise from Bannister that she would send him all of her research, but no guarantee as to when her own article would appear either online or in print. They discussed the possibility of reaching an amicable agreement on a deadline, but he felt his own investigation wasn't sufficiently advanced to specify a date, and she did not want to be beholden to the police when it came to doing her job. This he accepted without complaint.

As he walked across the road to the car park, Bliss's thoughts vacillated between the information he had garnered from the meeting, and his sense of loss at letting Sandra Bannister's friendship slip away. Her fierce intelligence fascinated him, and he loved the way her mind worked. She had pulled together multiple strands of information and fashioned them into one stronger thread of knowledge. Doubting the implied coincidence, Bannister had instead focussed on one angle of approach, in much the same way he did when working a case.

Bliss admired her for that, but his veneration fell flat as the reality of their situation struck home. Theirs was a wholly professional arrangement once again, and if any genuine feelings had existed between them, they were now consigned to history. He suspected their corresponding interests in this case were not over, but he nevertheless felt terrible about causing the rift between them.

Another burden of guilt he would have to shoulder.

NINETEEN

'So what does it all mean?' DS Bishop asked after Bliss had thrown the two new names into the mix.

The team were gathered in the incident room, each updating their colleagues with whatever progress had been made since the morning briefing. JTFO teams from Gablecross and Bishopsgate took part via a secure videoconferencing link. Aware of the attention currently focussed on himself, Bliss was still mentally assembling the answer to his sergeant's question, straining to find a measure of significance. Their own case having stalled, this fresh impetus was exactly what they had needed; yet he sensed the mood in Major Crimes was more one of frustration than genuine pleasure at the renewed momentum.

'I'm still piecing it together myself,' Bliss admitted. 'Assuming these new findings are correct, of the two men, only Freddy Swift was interviewed in connection with the Geraldine Price murder. His friend Ben Carlisle, our man with the dodgy and highly pertinent book, was apparently not spoken to. How does that align with your own recollections, Superintendent Conway?'

Conway's image was sharp on the wall-mounted screen, now split fifty-fifty between Swindon and London. He paused for a moment before responding. 'I'm happy to have my team taking responsibility for digging back through the records, of course,' he said, 'but I'm struggling to recall either man, frankly.'

'Perhaps this Swift fellow was interviewed by other members of the squad at the time,' Riseborough suggested. The picture from London was grainy, but the DI's concern was apparent.

'That's always possible,' Conway conceded. 'But I would have studied the case files on many occasions, I'm sure, so if Swift was interviewed, it surprises me that I can't recall the name. I presume he was nowhere close to being a prime suspect – a passing interest at most. Still, provided we confirm the findings, this is a decent lead.'

'Do you think this represents a shift of emphasis for us?' Chandler asked.

Though it was not obvious from her tone, she was peeved that Bliss had taken the Bannister meeting alone. He glanced across in her direction, having shared his source only with her so far. 'In what way, Pen?'

'Well, we were split earlier, between this being an act of revenge or some fellow gangster covering his tracks. This new line of enquiry appears to be leading us down the track-covering route.'

Bliss had been thinking along the same lines, though nothing he had heard so far was sufficiently potent to pull him one way or the other. 'The way I see it, this Freddy Swift character being a suspect in the murder all those years ago is merely an extension of what we already knew: that Geraldine Price was likely killed by a handful of deviants who also happened to be villains. Swift being acquainted with Carlisle, a man who happens to own a book on an ancient form of Chinese torture reminiscent of our current cases, is an interesting point. However, it may not be a leading one. It steers us in that direction, I admit, but I don't want to get so sucked in that we become blinkered.'

'I tend to agree,' Conway said. Bliss noticed the female detective with whom he had spent Saturday evening nodding in the background. 'Tell me, Inspector, what kind of follow-up are you looking at?'

Bliss realised he had no option but to reveal his source. It was a risk, but he had already worked out a way to explain it if asked. 'My contact is a journalist who owed me a favour. She is sending me all the research she's gathered so far, and we'll want to interview both men – or certainly Swift and Mrs Carlisle, if her husband doesn't show. By that stage I'd expect us to have a clearer vision as to the direction our investigation is going in. With this fresh information, we can't ignore the strong possibility that the slice of flesh found at the Bishops' Palace may have come from Ben Carlisle.' He glanced around the room. 'Everybody okay with that?'

'We need to make the most of this change of gear, boss,' Bishop said. 'It's a welcome boost, but fillips alone won't achieve a thing. Your gut is usually a decent guide. What's it saying to you?'

Bliss shook his head and switched his attention to DC Gratton. 'No, we have Phil back with us, so let's hear from him. It wouldn't hurt to have a fresh opinion.'

'Boss?' Gratton spluttered. 'I… um… er…'

'Brilliant. We need a lot more of your sharp and creative thinking around here.'

Above the ripple of laughter spreading throughout the room, Gratton said, 'I'm sorry, boss, but I've been a bit out of the loop.'

'That's true. How have we managed without your searing intellect until now, Detective Constable?'

'I'm not sure, boss. Luck, maybe?'

Chuckling, Bliss turned back to Bishop. 'Why don't you let us in on your own thoughts, Bish? Say you were DI on this right now. Which way would you be leaning?'

Bishop was unusually circumspect for a big man. Often reserved, he kept his feelings to himself until he was certain the time was right to share them. The spotlight having fallen upon him, he gathered himself decisively. 'If I had to plump for a single line of investigation, I'd be looking harder at the revenge motive. We've heard how Geraldine's father was a bit of a rogue, and she also had a brother. Then there's her husband and children to consider. Any of them might want to treat these men like they treated her.'

'But why now?' Chandler asked. 'Why wait all these years?'

'Maybe there's a recent trigger we know nothing about. Something that set one of them off. Perhaps more than one.'

'But how would any of them track these men down?' Riseborough said. 'Their fellow villains, I can understand – somebody always knows somebody else in their line of business. But aside from the father, everyone else associated with Geraldine Price has a pretty normal background, from what I can tell.'

Bishop raked his eyes over a case summary he was holding. 'Her husband and son are both solicitors. Family business, criminal law. They'd likely have investigators sniffing around. Plus there's the father, who may be working with either or both. Between them, they'd find enough to obtain a list of names, I'm sure.'

Bliss took a breath before weighing in. 'What bothers me about that are the details not in the public domain. The suspicion that slices of flesh were removed from Geraldine's body before she died was never released to the media, nor to the family. I can understand the desire to replicate Geraldine's torture and murder on those who carried it out, but how would whoever is responsible know about the specifics?'

'Paid for it,' DC Ansari said flatly. She shrugged. 'We all know it happens. You pay the right amount of money to the right person, you acquire the right information.'

'That's true. Sadly. But I still think the more obvious answer is that whoever is doing this now was also responsible back then. Look, Bish asked me for my gut feeling. The truth is, I'm not sold either way. Both theories are entirely plausible. Which is why, for now at least, I'd prefer we followed both paths.'

'That will put added pressure on our resources,' Conway argued.

'I realise this represents a change of approach from me, but I think we have enough people on this to cope with two diverse strategies. For another day or so. We have to hope we don't tread water tomorrow.'

'In which case, how do you propose to divide us up?'

Bliss had been running through the permutations as he spoke. 'DS Bishop here is inclined towards the revenge angle, so he and DC Ansari can pay a visit to Andrew and Stephen Price – our two solicitors. As husband and son of Geraldine, either or both are decent candidates for this. One of the first things to find out, of course, is whether either of them was in a position to leave the bag at Tower Hill yesterday morning. We need to talk to them. Get a feel for them, and let's have statements from both as to their whereabouts during all three time windows – ours, Swindon's, and the one in London.'

'What about Geraldine's father and brother?' Riseborough asked. On screen, he looked dishevelled and weary, as if he'd been up all night. 'Will you and DS Chandler be taking them?'

Bliss shook his head. 'No – I'm leaving them to one of our DCs, Phil Gratton. He can take a uniform with him. Same deal as far as statements and alibis are concerned. DS Chandler and I will take Carlisle and Swift. Before we do, I need to know from Superintendent Conway if he has any further insight relating to the case. For instance, it would be nice to have a transcript of Swift's interview and a copy of his statement. I reviewed the case file, but I can't say I noticed his name anywhere in it. I'd also like to know where Carlisle slots in before we talk to his wife.'

'I'm wondering if I should join you, Inspector,' Riseborough said. 'I'll pull together whatever information we gather overnight at our end, but I'm thinking it would be best if we met up and planned a strategy together.'

On the screen, DSI Conway was nodding emphatically. 'That's not a bad idea, Max. I can push back anything I have arranged for tomorrow.'

'Are you looking to delay until the morning?' Bliss asked. He was concerned about the men whose body parts were now in evidence stores. He couldn't be certain if any of the three were still alive but, unlikely as it seemed, it remained a genuine possibility.

'You worried about our victims, Inspector?'

'Of course. If any of them are still with us, we can be sure they're not in great condition. Without wishing to state the obvious – the sooner we find them, the better chance they have of survival.'

'For what it's worth, I agree with DI Bliss,' Riseborough piped up. 'Locating these men must be our priority. That's been my position all along.'

'And I don't disagree,' Conway said. 'But if either Carlisle or Swift are involved somehow, the more we know about them before we go in, the better. Our questioning is likely to be different, plus deep background checks should help us identify those locations even sooner.'

'Which all takes time to gather,' Chandler said – grudgingly, Bliss thought. He spun the wheels. He was a fan of the phrase 'More haste, less speed', and he saw the merit in Conway's tactic. Going in blindly now was unlikely to provoke the kind of reaction they sought from either Mrs Carlisle or Freddy Swift, whereas a knowledgeable approach would likely garner insight as well as answers.

'All right, let's leave it until tomorrow morning,' he said. 'I want contact details and a summary on both men sent to all JTFO members overnight. I'll obtain addresses from Sandra Bannister. We'll start with Swift, and later move on to the wife of our missing gangster – she lives not far from our HQ.'

'Sounds perfect,' Conway said. 'I'll bring DS Baker with me.' Baker was the female detective with whom Bliss had spent his Saturday evening in Swindon.

Bliss drew in a deep breath. 'Ah, in retrospect, I'm not so sure that's a good idea,' he said. 'Sir, we have things covered at this end. With respect, you have your own case running down there, and I think it'd be better for you to concentrate on the finer details of the Price case. It'd be terrific if you could get the info I need relating to Swift and Carlisle over to me tonight or first thing in the morning. Whatever you can tell us about the case may help us establish current connections. Attending to these matters rather than taking time out to drive up here and shadow us would be the better option.'

Bliss knew Conway would be disappointed, but he couldn't let it sway him from doing the right thing for the investigation. After a slight pause, the Superintendent agreed to his suggestion, his reluctance obvious.

'I take it the same goes for me – in which case, what would you prefer we do?' Riseborough asked. He sounded glum, like a man shoved to the sidelines.

'Continue with the CCTV and see if you can follow our man any further,' Bliss said. 'It's an important lead, Max, and one we need running down as far as it will take us. Also, although we spoke with Vicki Harrison this morning, it'd be better if your focus remained on Tommy and his background. I'm sure the list of his associates is deeper than the one we currently have, especially in respect of his past. I'd be particularly interested in any possible connection with either Ben Carlisle or Freddy Swift.'

'Your wish is my command, Inspector.'

Bliss caught the sarcastic edge. 'I'm not trying to throw my weight around, Max. I just think it's a bit too early for us all to meet under the same roof again. We've yet to fully explore our own cases, which means there's further intelligence to gather. Another day could make all the difference. Please feel free to disagree with my judgement.'

Riseborough said nothing, seemingly pacified. Bliss moved on, reminding everybody of the media blackout regarding the names of their victims, in addition to the details that were deliberately being withheld. All statements were also to be vetted prior to release. He wanted press briefings to be short and on point, offering further details as soon as circumstances made them available.

Afterwards, Bliss spent time asking himself if there was anything he had missed. The thought of three men possibly clinging to life by a thread while he, his team, and members of the JTFO went home, had dinner, enjoyed a night in front of the box, and got a good eight hours of sleep, squirted something hot and irritating into his gut. The benefits of down time were obvious, but he seldom indulged himself. For him, there would be no relaxing overnight, yet no matter how stressful it became, it was nothing compared with the suffering of those men.

Assuming they were still alive.

TWENTY

B LISS BROUGHT HOME A bag of takeaway and went back over the case files while he scooped mouthfuls of lemon chicken and egg fried rice into his mouth with a spoon. He found it difficult to switch off at the best of times, but while three terribly wounded men were potentially struggling to stay alive, the op felt like a worm eating its way through his brain.

If he was wrong, and this investigation had nothing to do with torture, the men were assuredly already dead. But the hand removal convinced him he was right, because it had been severed from a living person. This made him suspect that Harrison, at least, was being kept alive. If the victims had only hours left, Bliss didn't want to waste them by watching TV or listening to music. He couldn't believe his search of the files would uncover anything he and his team didn't already know, but every so often the same information revealed itself differently; every so often, it was enough to see the slightest little detail out of context.

He barely tasted the food. It was fuel at best, not a meal to be enjoyed. He read the summary reports twice. The first time, he assumed the three men were the victims of revenge. On the second run, his mind came at it from the point of view of one of the original attackers going after everyone else who was either involved or knew who was. Bliss grew more frustrated the longer he thought about it; neither approach sparked fresh ideas. It was what he'd expected. None of the information or evidence they had gathered so far pointed to where these men were, or who their attacker was.

Bliss briefly contemplated calling in his team and ordering a late-night unannounced run at Geraldine Price's family. The list of possible suspects in her torture and murder was extensive, and almost certainly not yet fully known. But if revenge was the motive for this current spate of criminal activity, the number of possibilities reduced to the obvious four men: the woman's husband, son, father and brother. At a push, they might include Price's daughter as well, but these felt like crimes committed by a dominant male.

Time was when he would have gone ahead without further thought, but experience forced him to hit the pause button this time. If any of the men were involved, they were patient and they were clever, and unlikely to fold at the first hint of pressure. The task force would need solid evidence before going in hard. It was always better to already know the answers to the questions you asked. The urge to act was compelling, but Bliss saw sense in tapping the brake and taking the investigation where it led them rather than attempting to force it in a specific direction. Impatience was one of his faults, but it was a work in progress.

There was another solid reason to hold back, too: the Price family were, first and foremost, victims of a despicable crime back in 1994, and without demonstrable evidence implicating them in the current crimes, they deserved the benefit of the doubt.

As Bliss washed his dinner down with a bottle of Old Peculier, his thoughts turned to the signature aspect of the JTFO operation. Geraldine Price's abduction, in addition to the grotesque flesh-slicing prior to her death, steered the investigation towards her horrific ordeal being the original trigger. Looking back at that period, Bliss realised how much ground he had covered over the decades. He had been a detective for just shy of three years when Price was murdered. Tiny nuggets of memory rolled around inside his head, bumping up against his consciousness. Vague, fleeting glimpses into the past; he had been aware of the case, but working hard on his own.

It wasn't only his career he was focussing on at the time, either. Two months after the Price murder, he and Hazel married, following a four-year courtship. Although she, with her mother and his, had taken on most of the planning and arrangements, the prospect of becoming a husband and potentially going on to have his own family had occupied Bliss's thoughts to a significant degree. Life took over, and somehow the tragedy in Hoxton that February largely passed him by.

Stirring himself from his musing, Bliss found himself turning to look down the hallway and wondering about the stray lab. While his takeaway was being prepared, he'd popped into a local grocery shop, emerging with a tin of moist dog food and a pack of the dry stuff. He didn't know the animal's preference, but he wanted it to eat again if it was waiting for him. When he pulled up on his driveway, he wasn't sure if he was pleased or disappointed not to find the dog there, but he hoped its absence had a positive explanation rather than the one he feared. Before dishing up his own dinner, he'd taken a quick walk around the neighbourhood, checking out alleyways and passages, but he caught no sign of the animal. By the time he returned home, Bliss was asking himself why the lab had found its way under his skin. A question for which he had no answer.

Switching back to the job at hand, he noticed a mail from Conway waiting in his inbox. Its attachment contained the details he had requested, including Freddy Swift's statement from his questioning about Geraldine Price's murder. It took Bliss twenty minutes to go through it all, but although he made a few notes, he found nothing significant. By this time, Sandra Bannister had sent out the information she had promised him, and the list of actions was also available online. There was nothing else for Bliss to do.

He closed down his laptop, still dissatisfied. Forward momentum from a fresh lead was all very well, but it got them no further in identifying where these three men were or had been held. Bliss's thoughts strayed to the victims once again, and his chest tightened. He felt helpless, but he knew that if any of them were still alive, his feelings paled into insignificance by comparison.

One glance at his wristwatch told Bliss it was now gone 9.00pm. He'd intended to phone his friend, Lennie Kaplan, looking to arrange a curry night, but the uniformed Inspector had a family and it was past the cutoff point for calls. Instead he sent a text, realising he had finally given in to the demands of the modern world in which communication never ceased. Rather than expose himself to the chilly attitude of Sandra Bannister, he sent her a text as well, thanking her for sending him the addresses for Carlisle and Swift. He was considering what to do with the rest of his night when his phone rang. It was Bannister, getting back to him in person.

'Thanks for calling.' He kept his tone neutral, hoping she would do the same.

'No problem. Why the text? Did you think I was going to bite your head off?'

'More worried about frostbite, I think.'

'I thought perhaps it was something like that. I'm sorry, Jimmy. On reflection, I held it against you for far too long.'

'You had a right to be angry with me. But yes, I did think you would have been over it by now.'

Bannister chuckled. 'I was over you a long time ago, believe me. It was just the rejection I struggled with.'

'I think we came at it from different directions,' Bliss said gently. 'We'd not even been on a single date – not counting a brief lunch or two – so I thought it was best to nip it in the bud, before…'

'I understand. I understood at the time. But you took me by surprise when you asked me to dinner, Jimmy. And then your ex turned up unexpectedly and suddenly you didn't want to know me any more.'

'It wasn't quite the way you're painting it, though I understand why you'd feel that way. I'm sorry, Sandra. I had every intention of taking you to dinner after inviting you out. I'll be honest, I wasn't at all sure we were a good fit, but I admit I was keen to find out. I liked you. Still do. But Emily coming back into my life and being interested in me again felt more natural, and the history between us made a difference. But, if it helps, I ended up shutting her down as well, and life moved on.'

'What do you mean?'

'I finished things with Emily, too. More accurately, I prevented anything from starting up again in the first place.' Bliss realised he'd never fully explained this to Sandra before. He had ended whatever it was they had before the selfish side of him could begin a relationship that had no chance of going anywhere because of his illness. Without going into great detail, he quickly explained about the moment he'd had his vertigo attack as he was about to call Emily and ask her over.

'So you're on your own again?' Bannister said.

'I am.'

'I… suppose I assumed you were still with her.'

'No. As it happens, Penny tried to force us back together again only the other night. Our evening was pleasant and went smoothly, but I didn't have an attack, and nor was I called out to a job. It wasn't a fair test.'

'And you still believe those are two valid reasons not to enter into a long-term relationship?'

Bliss didn't even have to think about it. 'I do. I may not always enjoy coming home to an empty house, having nobody close to turn to – other than my colleagues – but it gives me peace of mind. This way I'm not inflicting my condition or my commitment to the job on anyone other than myself.'

'Then what you're saying is you don't trust me or Emily to accept the challenges that go with being part of your life.'

'No, that's not it at all. Irrespective of whether you'd chosen to go along with it, being in or out of a relationship was always my choice. I didn't want to be, and I still don't.'

'So you won't be seeing Emily again, even though you enjoyed your evening together?'

'Not quite. I'm unsure what to do next. We've agreed on a dinner. But seeing is one thing, being together quite another.'

'You're a strange and complex man, Jimmy Bliss,' Bannister said on a long exhalation.

Bliss made no reply. There was nothing to say.

He thought of giving Emily a call afterwards, to show there were no hard feelings about the ambush – he knew it hadn't been entirely Penny's doing – but decided it was too late. His eyes fell upon his laptop. One final look at the case file before bed. An hour; two, at most. He fetched himself another bottle of Old Peculier, but as he moved to sit down he heard a knock at his door. The sound jarred because it was so rare. Bliss frowned. The one person he could think of who would come over on the off-chance at this time of night was Chandler. Still carrying his beer, he went to the door and opened up.

'Hello, Jimmy.'

Bliss stood there silently for a moment, which stretched out so long Emily decided she needed to speak again.

'We decided you were being stupid about not having a full-time relationship with anyone because of your illness, but we'd still see each other on a part-time basis. Correct?'

Bliss cracked a weak smile. 'First of all, I don't think we agreed I was being stupid. Secondly, you decided for us, Emily.'

She shrugged. 'We can debate who decided what and when once we're inside. You are going to invite me in, aren't you?'

He shifted sideways, nonplussed by her appearance at his house. However light her tone, they certainly had not agreed on anything like this. He watched in bemusement as, instead of walking straight in, Emily first stooped to pick something up off the floor. When she eventually straightened, Bliss saw she was carrying an overnight bag. Emily seemed amused by the look he knew had to be spread across his face.

'I don't suppose you saw a dog out there, did you?' he asked. 'An old lab?'

Emily shook her head. 'No. Why?'

Bliss shrugged. 'It's not important. So, what are we doing here, Emily? What is this about?'

As she stepped across the threshold, Emily lightly brushed her fingers over his cheek and kissed him on the same spot. When she drew back, her eyes were warm and her wide smile was switched to full beam. 'One of us had to make this move, Jimmy,' she said. 'And we both knew it was never going to be you.'

TWENTY-ONE

FOLLOWING THE SECOND WORLD War, the exodus of Londoners from their bomb-blitzed homes into new towns like Harlow, Stevenage, Basildon and Hemel Hempstead resulted in a considerable expansion of the original developments. These moves were a means to an end during a time of mass rebuilding and housing shortage, particularly in the East End of London, around the docklands. Official new towns breathed life into the fringes of Greater London, while at the same time allowing for the regeneration of blitz-torn pockets of the capital.

Although Freddy Swift was not among those on the list provided by Vicki Harrison, his name came up several times in association with four of the men who were listed. Friends of friends. Men who ran together back in the old days. Yet Swift was into his seventies now, and the appearance of an older man among the broadening array of possible suspects caused Bliss some apprehension. From what he imagined of the crimes under investigation, it would be nigh on impossible for a man of Swift's age to pull this off on his own.

Nobody would realise it to look at the place, but the Mead Park industrial estate on the northern rim of Harlow was fast becoming the centre of the UK's porn industry. The nondescript single-storey unit leased by FS Film Productions was tiny compared with many of the vast warehouses and hangar-like units populating the estate. At the door, he and Chandler had to lean on a buzzer and show their warrant cards to a security camera perched high in one corner of the entrance porchway. A short and narrow corridor with toilets on either side led to a set of double doors. Bliss pushed his way through and waited for his partner. As they entered the main part of the structure together, a tall, upright man of advanced years was there to greet them.

'Freddy Swift,' he said, extending a hand. He wore a broad, confident smile. His clothes were casual, but expensive-looking; his short-sleeved shirt was designed to be worn untucked. The black tasselled loafers on his feet gleamed, in stark contrast to the man's beige socks. Despite his obvious age, Swift still had a healthy head of white hair, currently slicked back and hanging over his ears. He sported two heavy gold rings, both half-sovereigns with decorative bevels. His watch screamed money, but whispered taste.

Bliss introduced himself and Chandler, telling Swift they would like a few minutes of his time. The old lag gave a puzzled frown, but nodded and started walking deeper into the unit. He did not appear to be put out by their presence. Following Swift through another doorway, Bliss noticed a group of men gathered around a huge window that took up most of one wall, each of them peering into a brightly lit room in which a movie was clearly being filmed. A two-camera production, Bliss noticed; one establishing the long shots, another getting in close to the action. The set depicted a doctor's office; three naked bodies writhed on an examination bed.

'Take no notice of them,' Swift said over his shoulder. 'We always get the peepers and hangers-on in here on the days we shoot. There are some people for whom their computer screens just won't do.'

'You allow anybody in here when you're making a film?' Chandler asked, her revulsion evident in every word.

'No, no. These chaps are relatives or friends of crew or cast, invited in to hang around, but really just getting an eyeful of the action and hoping to cop off with one of the ladies.'

The hardcore story was obviously well under way, two women and a man going at it hot, hard and sweaty.

'I'd keep your eyes averted if I were you,' Swift said with a leery grin. 'That chap thrusting away between the mature woman's legs is called The Pole, and we don't call him that because of his nationality, believe me. You catch sight of it, you'll never look at your own equipment in quite the same way again.'

Bliss was paying greater attention to the girl who was dutifully squeezing the breasts of the woman being screwed. Her slender frame, the cut and colour of her hair, reminded him of Molly – the Molly he had first encountered, mid-teens and already with no control of her own life. This girl's face was twisted into what she hoped passed for excitement or passion, but her eyes were flat and lifeless. Her body was underdeveloped, and Bliss had to look away.

They entered an office. Swift was chuckling to himself as he walked across to a desk in the corner. 'No need for quiet on set today, either. Can you hear the racket those two are making? He squeals like he's been sucking helium, and she sounds like Barry White. Believe me, we'll be playing a lot of music over that footage.'

Bliss slammed the office door behind them, rage building inside. He turned on Swift, anger bubbling beneath the surface. He wanted answers.

'How old is that dark-haired kid back there?'

'Lola? Old enough, Inspector. Old enough.'

'Show me some evidence of that.'

'Evidence?'

'Yes. ID. Proof of age. Something to indicate the girl is legally able to consent.'

Swift nodded. 'Of course. You show me yours and I'll show you mine.'

Bliss felt his cheeks growing hot. He glared at the man, who laughed and said, 'You show me a search warrant, I'll show you my documentation. Besides, if she tells me she's eighteen, who am I to argue? My punters love a bit of dubious.'

Already horrified by what he had seen, Bliss reacted before he was able to talk himself out of it. He took two steps towards the man, grabbed him by the throat and marched him back a further two paces until Swift slammed up against the far wall.

'How. Old. Is. That. Girl?' Bliss spat the question out, each word accompanied by the dull thud of Swift's head thumping against the painted plasterboard. Behind him he heard Chandler mutter something like, 'Oh, shit! Here we go.'

Swift struggled gamely with Bliss's arms, trying to pull his hands away. His eyes narrowed, and a low snarl escaped the back of his throat. 'Did you make a point of coming here today to have a pop at me? I might be a decade or so older than you, pal, but this old dog still has some bite.'

Bliss fixed him with a crooked grin. 'I'm sure you do. Even if it is with false teeth.'

This time Chandler breathed the word 'Jesus' and he felt the palm of her hand on his shoulder. Bliss realised his partner might be feeling vulnerable. Freddy Swift's advanced age suggested he was no longer the imposing figure he had once been, but he'd still be able to pull the trigger on a gun if he happened to have one tucked away in his desk drawer. Bliss clawed back his fury and decided to lighten up. He loosened his grip and took a wary step back, prepared to fend off a violent response if necessary. Instead, Swift gave him daggers and smoothed down his wrinkled clothing in silence.

'Look, Mr Swift,' Bliss said after taking a deep breath, 'we didn't come here to give you a hard time. But I'm telling you now, if I find out that girl out there is under age, I'll have you for it.'

'Fuck you!' Freddy Swift shot back. 'Fuck you and the horse you rode in on, pal.' He regained his composure and took a seat behind the desk. 'You'd never have tried it on with me back in the day, squire.'

'I wouldn't take any odds on that,' Chandler said, now clasping Bliss's arm to prevent him having another go. 'And besides, my boss is right. We're going to need to see documentation, or have a word with the kid before we leave.'

'Whatever you say.' Swift settled back into the chair and made himself comfortable. 'I'll see what I can do. Now, tell me what you want, and we'll see how best to get you both to fuck off out of here.'

Bliss had steadied himself and was back in control. He glanced at his colleague and gave a nod of appreciation, before returning a wary gaze to Swift. 'What we want is to follow up on a meeting you had with a *Peterborough Telegraph* reporter, Sandra Bannister. We're looking into the disappearance of Ben Carlisle, and our feeling is that you may have more to offer us than you did the journalist.'

The pair had agreed upon the lie during the ride down the M11. They would change tack if necessary, depending where the conversation took them.

Swift scoffed by way of a response. 'I don't know why you'd think that. I told her everything I have to say on the matter.'

'Ms Bannister says she covered an old case during your chat. Something to do with the brutal murder and torture of a woman over in Hoxton.'

'Yeah. What about it?' Swift's bushy eyebrows rose on his gaunt face thick with creases, broken capillaries spreading like a rash from his nose out to the curves of both cheeks. Bliss noticed his fingers twitching as if seeking something familiar to do. Most likely an ex-smoker.

'It's of interest to us, Mr Swift,' Chandler said, taking over. 'We're wondering if it had anything to do with why we can't locate your friend, Ben.'

'Why would it? I was the one who got interviewed as a suspect at the time. Me, not him. And it was donkey's years ago.'

'Is that so?' Chandler pursed her lips as if this had come as a surprise. 'In which case, what can you tell us about it?'

'Exactly what I told your lot back in the day. I didn't know the girl, I didn't have anything to do with what happened to her, and neither did I know anybody who did.'

'Really?' Bliss said. 'She lived in your manor. Somebody snatched her off the streets in your manor, and later dumped her and left her to die with the vermin in your manor. So it stands to reason they also beat her, tortured her, and sliced her up in your manor. And you want us to believe all that happened without you knowing about it?'

Swift laughed, almost hacking up a lung as he coughed and spluttered until his face grew purple. 'Who the fuck d'you think I am – Reggie fucking Kray? Mate, a lot went down in and around where I lived that I knew fuck all about. Where I come from, you quickly learn to keep your nose out of other people's business. If it weren't you or yours doing it, you didn't want to know.'

Bliss nodded his understanding. 'Bad for your health, I imagine.'

'You got that right. And for your life expectancy.' Swift jabbed a finger at Bliss. 'You sound as if you lived through a bit of that yourself.'

Bliss told him about where he grew up.

'So, you know. You didn't take liberties, and you didn't involve yourself in things that were bugger all to do with you.'

'Why do you think you were a suspect in the first place?' Chandler asked.

Swift left it there unanswered for half a minute, churning it over before responding. He kneaded his knuckles throughout. 'Known associates is my best guess. You know the way it goes? If you move in the same circles as certain people, you're considered to be part of anything and everything they get themselves webbed up in. I dare say my name came up because of somebody I knew a dozen associates down the line. As I remember it, they were pulling in everyone with a pulse.'

'And yet not your mate Ben Carlisle.'

'All right, so I exaggerated a bit. He wasn't the only one of my mates not to get a tug. I'm just saying I was one of many. They threw out a wide net and I got caught up in it. I was let go, though. One interview. Short and sharp. Never called back, either.'

Bliss ran an eye over the posters and framed photos on the walls. The posed shots mostly featured Swift with his arm wrapped around a variety of women, a few of whom even wore clothes. The publicity posters for movies were lurid, each title a sexual pun based on a Hollywood blockbuster.

'Thinking back on it now, Mr Swift,' he said, 'did you or any of your pals have any clue as to who was involved? Mrs Price's horrific torture lasted several days, during which time she was also brutally raped and sliced up before being dumped and left for dead. It can't have gone unnoticed. Police swarmed all over the area after she was taken, and again after her body was discovered. I'm sure it was the talk of all the local boozers. If people didn't know, they must have speculated.'

Before Swift was able to reply, his phone rang. 'My PA,' he said, glancing down at the screen. He pressed a button and told the woman on the other end of the line not to disturb him again until he said so. 'Sorry, where were we again?'

Annoyed by the interruption, Bliss said, 'I was saying that even if people didn't know precisely what was going on at the time, they sure as hell speculated.'

Swift curled his lip and wrinkled his nose in distaste. 'Is this what you're reduced to? Digging into speculation after all these years? Surely you've got better things to do?'

Bliss opted to switch things up. He shifted closer to one group photo, feigning interest, as if his mind was focussed somewhere other than the casual interview. 'Of course. In truth, it was our current investigation that led us here, Mr Swift, not the old one. I'm perfectly happy to concentrate on current events. In fact, I'd like you to tell us a bit about Tommy Harrison. But before you do – were any of your mates, or his, black?'

Swift pushed back in his chair and frowned. 'You must be talking about Knocker. What do you want with him?'

Chandler glanced at Bliss, then turned back to Swift. 'Knocker?'

The elderly gangster chuckled, which set off his spluttering cough again. His rings sparkled as he hacked into a balled-up hand. 'Black as the ace of spades, darling,' he said, eyes dancing at some unspoken memory. 'Or black as Newgate's knocker, as the saying went.'

'I'm none the wiser,' Chandler told him.

'It's the heavy iron knocker on the door to Newgate prison in London,' Bliss said, watching Swift closely. 'Long gone, of course. Oscar Wilde was banged up there for a time, but generally it's thought of as a place of death because of the gallows.'

'You should let your partner do all the talking, sweetheart,' Swift said, his beady eyes fixed on Chandler. 'He knows his stuff. And if this coppering lark doesn't work out, I could maybe find room for you in one of my flicks. There's a few people out there who like a nice piece of mutton.'

Ignoring the barb and putting a hand on Bliss's arm to prevent him from reacting, Chandler said, 'So was this Knocker your only black friend?'

'As far as I can remember, yeah. I wouldn't say he was a mate, exactly. He hung around with us as a group. Not sure who he was closest to.'

Bliss considered that for a moment. 'What's this Knocker's actual name?'

'Dobson. Earl Dobson.'

Chandler made a note as Bliss continued. 'Mr Dobson may also be missing, though we'll need to confirm.'

Swift screwed up his face, his impatience seeping through. 'Look, what's all this about? You start off with a decades-old crime, you say you want to know about Tommy, and now you're banging on about Knocker. What's going on here?'

Ignoring him, Bliss said, 'Tell me, Mr Swift: either of them likely candidates for the Geraldine Price murder?'

'What? Look, instead of asking me stupid bloody questions, why aren't you out there looking for my mates?'

'So now Dobson is a mate, after all?'

Swift shifted awkwardly in his chair. Squinting at Bliss, his face remained creased into a scowl. He aimed a single bony finger. 'Don't fuck with me, old son. You caught me cold earlier, but you won't get that lucky again. I won't forget what you did to me. You took a right royal liberty, and I ain't standing for it. Listening to you two banging on about the past has been mildly amusing, but you're pissing me right off now.'

Bliss gave him a cool, hard stare. 'And that old-time gangster's rearing up inside you again, eh, Freddy? But all I see is a frail old man, a bit of a eunuch without your pals around you and a shooter in your hand.'

The two glared at each other. It was Swift who broke it off first. 'I want you two off my property. I think we're done here.'

Bliss had no intention of leaving until he was ready. He crossed the floor to stand at the desk, staring down at Swift. 'I'm sure you do, but aren't you interested in helping us out? I mean, you want us to find your friends, don't you?'

'Of course I do. But that ain't going to happen with you coming around here and having a pop at me in my own place of business. Time was I'd have…' He turned his head away, leaving the sentence unfinished.

'Yes, I think I know what you would have done once upon a time, Freddy. But I can see those days are long gone. Still, I'll tell you what: you help us out and I'll leave you be. How does that sound?'

'Help you out how?'

'To begin with, answer my question. If you had nothing to do with what happened to Mrs Price, do you think it's possible that either Harrison or Dobson did? Perhaps the pair of them together?'

'No. I don't.'

Chandler had leaned up against a filing cabinet, but now she stood upright and took a quick stride towards him. 'Would we get a different answer if we told you there's a chance Ben Carlisle's disappearance has something to do with the case?'

'No.'

Bliss thought differently. Swift's features altered each time one of them asked him a question, but whereas before his eyes had flitted between the two detectives, now they were cast downwards. 'I'm curious as to why you're not asking me about Ben, Mr Swift. For example, are you not interested to know why we think his disappearance may be linked to a cold case? I can't believe you have no interest, what with you and him being such good pals.'

'I don't know anything. I can't help. All I want is for you to leave me alone.'

'We will, soon enough. What can you tell me about a book your mate Ben has? It's all about an ancient Chinese method of torture. Ring any bells?'

'What the… I've no bloody idea what you're banging on about.'

'You think Tommy Harrison might be missing for the same reason, Freddy? You think him, Dobson and Ben have been taken because somebody other than us thinks they were involved in the torture and murder of Mrs Price?'

Swift's head jerked up, and this time his eyes were wild. Moist, too, though there was little gleam in them. 'I just told you – I don't know!'

Bliss allowed silence to add to the atmosphere. He'd been patiently building up the pressure; now it felt like the right time to push harder. 'But you do know something, Freddy. For instance, you knew Tommy was missing. We didn't tell you he was, and we've not released this information to the media as yet, but when I mentioned it just now you didn't bat an eyelid. How come?'

'Somebody must have told me.'

'Oh, I agree. What we want to know is: who?'

'I can't remember. I must've picked it up from somewhere.'

'I see. You realise if we end up making this little chat official, that answer isn't going to cut it.'

'Then I'll make no bloody comment at all. How's that suit you?'

Not wanting Swift to shut them down, Bliss softened his tone. 'All right, Freddy. Take it easy. Listen, you'll be doing yourself a big favour if you tell us where you were early on Monday morning.'

Swift's head jerked up. His eyes drilled into Bliss's. 'Why d'you want to know about Monday?'

'Because I asked you nicely.'

Swift continue to glare, but he was obviously thinking hard. There was a time for posture and a time to help yourself. If the police wanted to know where you were, they had many ways of going about finding out.

'Monday was an ordinary day. Got up, had breakfast, came to work.' Swift stopped and snapped his fingers. He ran a hand over his face. Licked his lips. 'As it happens, we had an early shoot. One of our girls was double-booked that day. She's popular right now, so rather than blow our chances of getting her on film, we started the session shortly before nine. I met her and her agent here at about eight. That do you?'

'They'll verify what you just told us, I take it?'

'Of course.'

'These girls have agents?' Chandler said.

'Sure. Well, the stars do. There are your low-level sorts, of course, the ones who do a bit of escorting on the side and some seedy amateur stuff and a bit of fluffing, but the top-tier birds can earn a fortune. The better the gig, the bigger the money, so yes, they have agents.'

Bliss nodded and started to move towards the door. They were done here. He did not offer to shake hands this time. 'Thanks for your eventual cooperation. You think you've not said a lot, but there's plenty to hear in the things you didn't say, too. Though I have to say, I'm surprised you're holding back on us, what with three of your old pals being missing.'

'Who says I'm holding anything back?'

'I do. But you claim you don't know anything, so clearly you can't help us. Now, back to the young girl out there.'

Twenty minutes later, they were outside in the car park. Swift had provided them with names and contact details for the porn actress and her agent. As expected, he had no documentation confirming the girl having sex on camera was of legal age; Bliss insisted on the filming being interrupted, allowing him and Chandler to talk to the kid. She came into the office with a towelling dressing gown wrapped around her, held tight to her throat, and declined to provide her real name. An Eastern European national, she spoke reasonable English and insisted she was sixteen. Up close, she did appear slightly older than Bliss had initially thought, so he decided not to push; any crime here was not hers. But he made a mental note to have the local police follow up on Swift's operation.

As they walked to the car, Chandler turned on him – as he had known she would. 'You were hard on him, Jimmy. Why did you keep pushing his buttons?'

'Because he was trying to play us and I wanted to keep him off balance. Plus, the girl's age was too close to call, or let go.'

'But did you have to smack his head against the wall like that?'

'I thought so. It seemed like a reasonable idea while I was doing it.'

'Five times?'

'Is that all? I must be slipping. Look, the man's a creep, and no way was he telling us everything.'

'He certainly knows more than he's letting on, I'll give you that.'

'Yep. But did you clock his face at the end there when I reminded him three of his mates were missing? That kind of reaction can't be faked, can it? He somehow knew Tommy was missing, but doesn't appear to have a clue about what happened to him afterwards. Nor the other two, for that matter. Which leaves him in the clear, at least.'

'As far as Harrison is concerned, yes. But he's wrapped up in this somehow.'

'Absolutely. Did you see his reaction when I mentioned Geraldine Price had been sliced up?'

Chandler nodded. 'I did. For a moment I thought you'd slipped up. Then I realised you'd put it out there deliberately.'

Bliss pinched the bridge of his nose, a headache starting to build between his eyes. 'Yeah. I know I took a chance releasing such a crucial piece of intelligence, but I thought it was worth the risk. We all agreed earlier to release that information to the media today anyway, and I was looking for something to provoke a reaction from him.'

'Well, you certainly did that.'

'Or rather, I didn't. For someone who shouldn't know the details of what happened to Geraldine Price, he was pretty unmoved by it.'

TWENTY-TWO

'I HAVE TO SAY, YOU seem pretty chipper today,' Chandler said as they dropped off the A1, hoping to speak with Mrs Carlisle before they returned to HQ for lunch. Bliss eased off the accelerator; if you yawned or blinked while driving through the tiny village of Glatton, you'd miss it entirely.

He turned his head briefly. 'Chipper? What happened, did you wake up in the 1920s? Have you become a flapper overnight, Pen?'

Alongside him, Chandler did her best impression of a moth, followed swiftly by a seated version of the Charleston. He laughed along. In truth, he was doing well, despite feeling as if he needed a shower after visiting Swift's seedy little empire.

'No, seriously,' she said. 'There's something different about you today. Other than wanting to take Swift's head off – which I completely understand – you seem relaxed. If I didn't know better, I'd say you got...' Chandler let her voice trail off, and her mouth formed an O as she shifted in her seat to face him. 'Oh. My. God. You did, didn't you? You went and got yourself laid?'

Bliss screwed his face up, feigning distaste. 'Oh, please,' he said. 'Is that any way to talk to your boss?'

She poked him in the ribs with her finger. 'No, but it is the way I talk to my friend. What happened? Who was it? I hope you used protection.'

Bliss snorted. 'Protection? Pen, my ball sack is so old and dry it contains mainly dust these days.'

Now it was her turn to pull a face; her disgust was genuine. She held up both hands. 'Okay, okay. Sorry I brought it up. Just please never say anything like that again in my presence. As it is, I'll need to scour my brain with acid and a wire brush to get rid of the mental image.'

'Serves you right. Hopefully that'll teach you not to pry.'

'Yeah, yeah. Come on, old man. Dish the dirt. Who was it? Please tell me it was the bone woman and not Lois Lane.'

He knew better than to keep trying to fend her off. Chandler was relentless in her own way. He thought back to the previous night, and told his partner a little of how it had panned out. But not all – not by a long way. Emily had taken him by surprise, and her unexpected arrival at his door was precisely what he'd needed, though he hadn't realised it until afterwards. No time for planning and looking to impress, no time for anxiety, no time to find a reason not to let it happen. She had dropped her bag on his hallway carpet, kissed him on the lips, and then led him upstairs to bed. Their first attempt was awkward and fumbling, as befitted a couple who had not slept together in fifteen years. Afterwards, they went back downstairs, where they sat together in his recliner and talked for hours, before moving up to the bedroom and trying again; they had far greater success the second time around.

His improved mood today wasn't solely due to the extra surge of oxytocin or dopamine in his system, either. The emotional reconnection meant far more to Bliss than the physical one. It conjured up many happy memories, of course, but it also gave him an insight into a future he had stopped imagining a long time ago. Emily somehow breached his defences, seeing him for all he was, all he could be. If she declared herself happy, he owed it to himself to consider the possibilities such a relationship offered. No commitment – at least, not immediately. Few expectations, and certainly none for which they were not fully prepared. He had imagined Emily would want more at this stage of her life, but had previously neglected to ask her. He'd turned his back at a time when he ought to have been opening up his heart. Now she was in his life once again, and the fit felt right. Comfortable.

'I'm thrilled for you,' Chandler told him, gently punching his arm. 'And it's about bloody time. I don't mean the… I mean you and Emily. Whatever you and Bannister had was never going to work out. You and our bone woman, however, are perfect for each other.'

Her reaction delighted him, but he was keen to play it down. 'Pen, don't go getting your hopes up and making it something it's not. There's no need to buy a hat. We've had one drink and one night together so far – that's all.'

'For the moment.'

Bliss nodded. 'Yeah. And the issue of my illness is still there. It hasn't gone away overnight.'

'I know that, Jimmy. But you've taken a step in the right direction. That has to be a positive thing.'

'It is. It was. Now, can we refocus and get back to the bloody investigation?'

The Carlisle property stood next to the village hall, directly opposite St Nicholas's church. A relatively new build, Bliss imagined the large two-storey house had not been an inexpensive purchase; ill-gotten gains, no doubt. As he gazed at it, he wondered if Carlisle was a man with only a past to gloss over, or if the present had subsequently intruded on his life and those of his family.

They found Lesley Carlisle at home, but after introducing themselves she told them she was due to leave for work shortly and could not afford to be late. A tall, slightly stooped woman who looked to be in her sixties, Ben Carlisle's wife had a slender build and suspicious eyes. They darted everywhere, imbued with doubt as they took in everything they fell upon. Bliss didn't think a lot slipped by this woman, but life had wearied her. She looked haggard, and the heavy makeup she had slathered on did little to conceal the lines of neglect.

'Whereabouts do you work?' Bliss asked, conversationally.

'The Addison pub. Here in the village, on the road out to Sawtry.'

Bliss knew the place; they had driven past it on their way in. 'I'm surprised you've not taken time off. With your husband missing, I'm sure your employers would make allowances.'

'I like to be busy. It helps keep my mind off other things.'

'That's perfectly understandable,' Chandler said. She smiled at the woman. 'May we come in, Mrs Carlisle? I understand if you have to shoot off soon, but we do have a few questions for you.'

'I have already spoken to the police.'

'Of course. But not to us.'

Carlisle sighed, turned and led them along a short passageway and into the kitchen. 'Nice place,' Bliss said, keeping it breezy. He felt the coolness of the stone floor through the soles of his shoes. The cabinets and appliances sparkled as if they were brand new.

'Yes, well, my Ben worked hard for his family.'

Bliss would have liked nothing more than to dispute her claim. Instead he said, 'You have children?'

'Two boys. Both adults now, of course. Making lives of their own.'

'How long since you moved up from London?'

'Twenty-odd years.'

'Big move. I should know. Still, I'm surprised you don't live nearer to your friends.'

'Friends? What friends?'

'Mr and Mrs Swift.'

The woman's mouth became a slit. She raised her eyebrows before responding. 'Freddy is Ben's mate. I barely know the man. And the little I do know, I don't care for.'

'I see. I thought all you London exiles stuck together. I naturally assumed you were close, considering you all came from the same area originally.'

'Like I say, they were Ben's friends, not mine. Listen, I don't mean to be rude, but what's this all about? Do you have news about my Ben or not?'

'No – sorry if we gave that impression,' Chandler replied. 'We came to ask if anything had changed over the past week or so. If you'd remembered anything else about the day your husband went missing.'

The woman sighed heavily and fussed around with a small flower arrangement on her kitchen counter. 'Don't you think I would have called you people if I had? Look, Ben went out for a walk with the dogs. He took the same route every day, up Denton Road and out onto the public bridleway. That's where Duke and Major were found.'

'Your two dogs, yes?'

'Yes.'

'Tell me something,' Bliss said. 'Your husband took the dogs out, and the dogs were later found running around in the field. What happened in between?'

'How d'you mean?'

'Well, as I understand it, they were discovered three hours or so after your husband left home. Were you not concerned about his absence before that?'

'Of course. It was me who got our neighbours involved search-ing for them. I called Ben's phone, but there was no answer. I went out, saw no sign of him. A couple of people noticed me, saw how frantic I was. I told them what had happened, and they helped me look. It was one of them who spotted the dogs.'

Bliss gave it some thought. He assumed whoever had taken Mrs Carlisle's statement had made a note of the number she had called and had sought to trace its activity. He made a mental note to request all relevant information from Huntingdon police.

'Tell me, Mrs Carlisle,' he said, 'what do you think happened to your husband?'

The woman bristled. 'I'm sure I have no idea. Now, I must be going.'

'We're trying to work with you here, but you seem more intent on getting away than you do in assisting us with our enquiries.'

Carlisle reached for her soft leather handbag, which was hanging on the kitchen door. 'I don't want to lose my job. I might need it now if… if Ben's not coming back.'

Nodding, Bliss said, 'Understood. I promise I won't take up a lot more of your time. But this is important. Clearly your husband didn't set out in the morning to leave you and walk away from his life. He didn't take anything with him, and I'm sure if he'd intended not coming home he would never have taken the dogs and allowed them to run loose. I had a couple of labs myself, and I know I wouldn't have left them on their own in a field. There was a major search of the area by police and volunteers later the same day and into the next, but nothing was found. No evidence either way, but certainly nothing to suggest your husband was still in the area, hurt or otherwise. So, did you ask yourself at any point whether his past might have caught up with him?'

This was the question he had been leading up to, and Bliss could see it had struck a nerve. Lesley Carlisle's cheek twitched as she bit down hard. Anger lit a flame in her eyes, but he saw it was half-hearted – more the kind of response she thought he was expecting than a true measure of how she felt.

'Come on, Mrs Carlisle,' he said, softer this time. 'You must have known we would eventually look into your husband's background.'

'It was all such a long time ago,' she snapped.

'As if time makes any difference at all. Either way, I'm sure you realise, as I do, that the kind of people your husband consorted with in those days have long memories. So let me ask you again: do you think his disappearance is a consequence of something he may once have been involved in?'

Mrs Carlisle tipped back her head and eased out a long sigh. She hooked her bag over one shoulder, then folded her arms beneath her chest and considered her next words with great care. 'Inspector Bliss, the truth is that while of course I've asked myself the same question, I have no idea as to the answer. Ben is Ben. He did what he did. Provided he kept it outside of our home and away from the kids, I didn't ask questions. When we left London, we left that life behind us.'

'That may not be the case. Just because Ben walked away doesn't mean he was forgotten about.'

'I'm starting to realise that.'

'So you do think it's possible?'

'Well, of course. I'd be foolish not to. What I am certain of is that Ben hasn't done anything to cause somebody to… to take him, hurt him… kill him… since we moved up here. So yes, if someone has done something to him, then it probably has links to his past.'

'Does the name Tommy Harrison ring a bell?' Chandler asked, stepping in as Bliss regrouped.

'No. Should it?'

'I'm not sure. How about Earl Dobson?'

'No. Nothing.'

'How about the Price family? Andy? Geraldine? Or Robert Naylor?'

Bliss saw recognition register in the woman's rigid features. She swayed, reaching out for the kitchen counter to steady herself. 'Are you telling me this has something to do with what happened to that Price woman a quarter of a bloody century ago?'

'You knew Geraldine?' Chandler pursued it, her face stern.

'I knew of her. Bob Naylor was a known face, and I heard about his daughter. It was tragic. That's as far as it goes.'

'Did Ben ever talk about them? Did he know any of them?'

'I don't know for certain. But I think he must have, because he lived on the same estate as the family. It was hard not to know your neighbours in those days. But what does Ben have to do with any of this?'

'We're not saying he does,' Bliss answered. 'However, Freddy Swift was interviewed under caution in relation to Mrs Price's murder, and someone else of interest to us in a current investigation was part of the same social scene. And in the middle of it all, your husband's name keeps cropping up.'

Carlisle hung her head. Deflated now, her strong will was spent. She had wilted under questioning. Yet Bliss sensed she was telling them the truth – or a pretty close approximation of it. He waited for her to look back up at them before continuing.

'Mrs Carlisle, may I have a quick look around your living room? I won't be a moment.'

Perplexed by this shift in emphasis and the odd request, the woman nodded and closed her eyes. Bliss went into the next room, found what he was looking for, and came straight back to join his partner. He held up the book he was carrying.

'Interesting subject,' he said. '*Death By A Thousand Cuts*. Is this your husband's book?'

Her eyes focussed on the cover for a moment, then she shook her head. 'No. Ben must have borrowed it from somebody.'

'Recently? This book was published ten or twelve years ago. I know because I came across it by chance when I was researching another subject. So if Ben did borrow it, you'd probably know who from.'

'I can't be sure – but I assume it would have to be Freddy. Ben and I have a group of friends, people we've met since we moved here, but nobody I can think of who'd own a book like that.'

'And you reckon Freddy would?'

'I think the likes of Freddy Swift are capable of just about anything.'

Bliss cracked the book open. It was a hardcover, not light, and there was no name written inside. But there was an unexpected barcode strip. And the strip told him something interesting. 'May I borrow this?' he asked.

'I suppose so. To be honest, I'd be glad to see it out of the house.' She shuddered involuntarily.

They left her to get off to work. As Bliss drove back towards Sawtry, the A1 stretching out not far beyond the village, he was quiet, and grateful to have a partner who knew him well enough to leave him to his thoughts until he was ready to speak. He turned the fresh evidence inside and out, getting a feel for it.

'She doesn't have a clue what happened to her old man, does she?' he said eventually.

Chandler grunted. 'I don't think so, no. On the other hand, she is definitely beside herself with worry. She knows there's every chance his past came back to bite him.'

'I think she knows he's not coming back. He's been gone for a fortnight, and not contacted her once. I think she believes he's dead.'

'And what do you believe?'

'I believe the chunk of flesh sitting in a freezer at the city mortuary belongs to Ben Carlisle. Forensics will have taken DNA samples during the original missing persons investigation by Huntingdon CID, so we can match them to our evidence. My guess is he's dead, but I'm as certain as I can be that he's our victim.'

'And what was with the book? Your eyes lit up like a bonfire. What did you find inside when you opened it up?'

'A barcode strip. One that didn't come with the book when it was published.'

'How can you tell?'

'Because it was marked with a name. It's a library book, Pen.'

'A library book?'

'Yes. A library is a big place with loads of books inside, which they loan out to people who can read.'

Chandler flipped him her usual two-fingered sign of defiance. 'I know that, boss. I'm just surprised you do.'

They reached the outskirts of the city, and as Bliss pulled onto the slip road, Chandler's phone pinged with a message. Moments later, her head jerked up from the screen. 'Oh, shit!' she said. 'Oh, shit, bugger, and balls!'

About to make a crack about his DS not visiting those kind of websites if she was going to be offended by them, Bliss noticed how rigid she had become. 'What is it?' he asked. 'What's wrong?'

'Breaking news on the *Daily Express* website. Gul sent me a link.'

'And?' he said, gesturing in a rolling motion with his hand.

'They ran a piece naming Harrison as our third victim. They also mentioned Ben Carlisle in connection with the first.'

'What!?' Bliss smashed a hand down on the steering wheel. A second later he drove his elbow into the side window, accompanied by a slew of swear words. 'How the hell do they have that?'

'It says "from a well-placed source inside the joint task force". And it doesn't end there, I'm afraid. They're also suggesting a connection between our body parts and the Geraldine Price murder.'

Bliss ground his teeth together and growled like a wild animal. He clenched one fist and left it raised in the gap between them. 'I'll have their bloody Jacobs for this. I'll hunt them down, I'll find them, I'll clip their knackers off, and stuff them down their bloody throat.'

Chandler made no reply at first. After a few seconds had passed, she said, 'And if it's a female officer?'

His lips curled into a sneer. 'I'll do whatever the female equivalent is.'

'I'm not sure there is one, boss. Not unless you're contemplating feeding them their own ovaries?'

Bliss realised what she was doing. He took a few deep breaths, gathering his wits. The next time he spoke his voice was even, though he felt tremors running the length of his body. 'Man or woman, whatever their rank, they'd better watch their back. I'll have him or her for this, Pen. I'll bloody well crush them.'

'I understand your anger, Jimmy, but we were releasing most of this information later today anyway. Is it such a big deal if somebody beat us to it?'

'Yes! It's a bloody massive deal. It tells us we have a leak, which can never be a good thing. And yes, while most of the information was in the formal statement due to go out later, not all of it was, by any means. The intention was to rattle a few cages, not destroy them completely. I especially wanted a lid kept on the Ben Carlisle connection, because he's not on anybody's radar as yet.'

'Other than Lois Lane's.' Chandler stared pointedly at him.

Shaking his head, Bliss said, 'Not a chance. Sandra wanted this story for herself. There's not a snowball in hell's chance of her turning it over to a rag like the *Express*.'

'What about the assistant you mentioned?'

'I don't see it. If he sticks with Sandra, he gets a byline credit on her story. This way he gets bunged a few quid. Anyhow, there are details in this story that Bannister didn't have. Remember, Harrison hasn't officially been named yet – not until the *Express* got a hold of it. Bloody hell, Pen. The timing is awful, and I'm not going to let whoever is responsible get away with it.'

'I'm with you all the way, boss. Just one thing?'

'What is it?'

'Is this a good time for me to tell you not to call me Pen?'

'Penny?' he said, turning his head towards her.

'Yes, boss?'

'Do bugger off.'

'Yes, boss.'

TWENTY-THREE

Upon their return to Thorpe Wood, Bliss spotted a uniform standing in the doorway leading into the custody area. Her name was Swanson, and she'd been at the station so long she was considered part of the fixtures and fittings. Bliss told Chandler to go on without him. He caught the uniform's attention and jerked his head, indicating he wanted a chat.

'What can I do for you, Inspector Bliss?' she asked. About his age, Swanson was thick-set and looked as if she could still handle herself if any of the more bullish idiots in custody decided to take out their aggression on her. She held a blue belt in judo, and until recently had taken part in national police tournaments.

'I just wondered if you'd had any word on Grealish recently?' Poor health had forced the long-serving sergeant to retire, and although he and Bliss had never exactly struck up a friendship, each had earned the other's respect. The look in Swanson's eyes told Bliss it wasn't good news.

'You heard he'd gone out to Cyprus to stay with his daughter?'

'Yeah. Inspector Kaplan told me.'

Swanson grimaced. 'Poor sod only lasted three weeks. Went in his sleep, at least.'

'Ah, shit. I never heard about a collection or anything.'

'He never wanted one. His daughter said he thought everybody here ought to keep their hard-earned money and raise a glass to him at some point.'

'He could be a bit of an arse at times, but I'll raise more than one.'

'You can be a bit of arse at times yourself, but you're welcome to raise them with me later if you like.' She must have caught the change in his expression, because she laughed and shook her head. 'No, I'm not trying to pull. A few of us are going for a couple after work, and rest assured my husband will be joining us.'

Bliss grinned. 'Shame – thought I was in there! If I get done early I might see you there. The Woodman?'

'Of course.'

Bliss trudged up the stairs. He and Grealish had clashed on more than one occasion, but had finally reached a point where they could tolerate each other. He'd wished the man a long and happy retirement, knowing it was unlikely but having no idea it would be cut quite so short. He didn't know how to feel, other than sympathetic for Grealish's family. He was surprised there had been no mention of it around the station, but maybe that's how it was. You walked away with people's best wishes ringing in your ears, and a couple of weeks later you were forgotten about. His mind was drawn to the labrador lying beneath his porch, and he wondered why he wasn't able to shake it off.

Before he made it into the squad room, Bliss's mobile went off and he was summoned to a senior leadership meeting, during which he brought Detective Superintendent Fletcher and DCI Warburton up to speed on what was now officially known as Operation Limestone; a handful of wags around the squad room were already calling it 'Tombstone'. After the short meeting was over, Fletcher asked him to stay behind. He eyed her warily, trying to recall if he had done anything recently to warrant a bollocking.

Marion Fletcher wore one of her better suits: a navy-blue skirt and jacket, with a fine pinstripe. Her blouse was shiny – silk, he thought. Always smart and neat, today she had taken greater care with her appearance; makeup applied with a deft touch, hair distressed to perfection. Bliss wondered if the rumours about her were true. She cleared her throat before speaking, hands placed flat on the desk in front of her.

'I won't keep you from your duties too much longer, Inspector. And it's nothing to concern yourself about. All I wanted to know was how you were coping with the JTFO. Unofficially.'

'Fine, ma'am – on or off the record. Unless you've heard otherwise.'

'Only positive things so far. And how would you say your team are shaping up?'

'Very well. I've always considered myself lucky to have strong detectives at the rank of sergeant. DC Hunt has no real desire to move on or up, content with the job he does and the level of responsibility that comes with it – every unit needs somebody like that. Gratton is destined for greater things, I'd say. And Gul Ansari will push hard for sergeant any time soon.'

'I'm glad to hear it. And those fine sergeants you mention?'

'Out of Bishop and Chandler, Bish is the one I fear losing most. By the way, he's still feeling the strain and I'm giving him a couple of weeks off after this case. His ambition is what bothers me, though. Penny is happy with her lot, no yearning there to step up. I'd say Bish is caught between wanting DI and needing the extra money that would come with a promotion, and the desire to remain where he is in the team, doing the job he loves.'

'I can't say I blame him. It's not always a straightforward decision to make. He has a family and he wants to do what's right for them. Equally, he still has a long career ahead of him; he must look to the future and wonder if he can possibly enjoy any of it if he moves up through the ranks.'

'I also think he doesn't want to let the rest of us down by moving on. He may be thinking of sticking with it until Gul is ready to make her first step up.'

'Losing Mia left a big hole in the team, didn't it?'

DS Mia Short had been gunned down on duty, losing her life and that of the baby she carried inside her. 'She was small, but she was mighty,' Bliss said wistfully. 'People say I'm a DCI in all but name, stuck in a DI's role, but Mia was a DI trapped as a DS and about to emerge from that stage of her career. Nobody is irreplaceable, ma'am, but Mia came pretty damn close.'

Fletcher looked up. 'You think you're not irreplaceable, Jimmy?'

Her use of his given name created a spark of alarm inside Bliss's head; he wondered where this conversation was going. 'I know I'm not,' he replied. 'Let's be straight, I'm no example to my team. Not in today's modern police service, at least. I'd love to think of somebody from my squad stepping into my shoes when I finally quit, but we both know the brass will take the opportunity to bring in a completely different kind of broom.'

'I can't speak for others, but that would not be my choice.' She gave herself a moment to filter what she wanted to say. 'Jimmy, at times you've tested even my patience, but nobody can argue with your intent. Nor your results. Major Crimes will be all the poorer for you not leading it.'

Bliss immediately pictured himself as an old hound lying beneath a porch, having perhaps been put out to pasture ahead of his time, no longer feeling attached to anyone or anything. His wrinkled, tired, and sagging face permanently forlorn. 'Have you heard something, ma'am?' he asked. 'Am I on my way out and you're trying to tell me without saying the words?'

Fletcher frowned, shaking her head abruptly. 'No, not at all. Nothing of the kind, Jimmy. Stop being so bloody paranoid. But having brought it up, when *do* you see yourself bowing out?'

Bliss didn't have to think about it. 'With the change in retirement rules, I have just under seven years before I have to step away. If my health holds up, I intend using up every single year of my time right here.'

'You'll end up as old and crusty as the cheese sandwiches in the canteen.'

'I'd rather be crusty than stale, ma'am. If that day comes, believe me – nobody will have to push me towards the exit door.'

'Have you thought about what you'll do afterwards?'

'Not as such. Wiltshire interests me. As a place to retire to, I mean.' Bliss paused, a question perched on his tongue. He decided to go for it. 'Permission to speak freely, ma'am?'

Fletcher raised an eyebrow. 'Since when did you feel the need to ask, Inspector?'

'Since it became personal.'

'Please, go ahead.'

'Ma'am, your desire to move on has not escaped our attention. Onwards and upwards, to be precise. So, given where this conversation has led us, I have to say you deserve it. Chief Super will be an excellent fit for you, no matter where you land. When the post came up for grabs here recently, we were hoping you would go for it. I will be disappointed, of course, because I've come to rely on your sound judgement and common sense. And I do worry about the cohesion of the place with you gone.'

The glimmer in her eye told Bliss he was right. The DSI was considering moving on, and was keenly aware of the impact her leaving would have on the team. 'No matter what happens to me, Jimmy, your new Chief Super will remain in position. That's where our leadership stems from.'

'With respect, ma'am, we both know that's not true. It may be early days, but he comes across as a results man. It's you who decides how we achieve them; you are the one DCI Edwards and Warburton look to for guidance. So what I want to mention is this: if you have a say in who replaces you, please do your best to make it somebody as much like you as possible.'

Fletcher regarded him curiously. 'That almost sounded like a compliment, Inspector.'

'It was meant to, ma'am.'

After a moment, she continued. 'I can't deny it, Jimmy. I am evaluating my position. I'm meeting with the Chief Super and Assistant Chief Constable later today, to examine my options. Clearly the jungle drums have been beating, but all I can say right now is that I haven't made up my mind about anything. In some ways, I'm like DS Bishop: caught between two schools of thought. The one thing I won't do is make a hasty decision. As for who takes my place, while I have no control over such matters, I will of course do my best to ensure this section gets the best DSI possible.'

A sharp rap on the door prevented Bliss from taking the conversation any further. Without pause, the new Detective Chief Superintendent, Sam Feeley, entered the room. He nodded at Fletcher. 'Sorry for barging in like this,' he said, his rich Lancastrian voice low but clear. 'I know we're due to meet later over at Hinchingbrooke, but I was in the area and I wanted a word with your Inspector here.'

Bliss was immediately concerned, wondering if Feeley had overheard any part of his conversation with Fletcher. He risked a sidelong glance at her, and her puzzled frown increased his anxiety; a Chief Superintendent never merely passed by an area's primary station.

The new man remained on his feet, but moved across to stand by Fletcher's desk, facing Bliss. Small in stature and ineffectual-looking, Feeley came with a reputation for commanding respect by being firm and forthright. This was the first time Bliss had laid eyes on him. In his early fifties, his hair appeared unnaturally dark, and his frameless spectacles were virtually invisible. Rumour had him down as a person not to be taken lightly based on first appearances.

'Unfortunate turn of events, this *Express* article,' Feeley said. He kept his hands behind his back, and Bliss wondered if it was to stop him gesticulating as he spoke. 'I don't suppose you happen to know who this "well-placed source" is, do you, Inspector Bliss?'

'Not yet, sir. I've not long been back in the office, so I haven't had time to discuss it with my team.'

'You think that wise? Discussing it with your team, I mean. After all, this unnamed source could well be one of them.'

Bliss bit down on his instinctive retort and settled for a glare. 'With respect, sir, what you're suggesting is not possible. I know my team, and talking to the press is not a game any of them play.'

'I imagine all bosses say similar things about their own team, Bliss. But some of them have to be wrong.'

'Well, it's not me. I can't vouch for the teams down in London or at Gablecross, but I can and will speak up for our own people. There is no way they shared this information with a reporter.'

Feeley pursed his lips. 'Time will tell, I imagine. And speaking of sharing information, I wanted to ask you about that, too. As you might imagine, Inspector, a major case like this, involving a joint task force between three large areas, requires a great deal of oversight. As such, I have my own people going over the case file updates and compiling reports for my attention. We wouldn't want anything falling through the cracks, am I right?'

Bliss kept his breathing in check, trying to work out where this was headed. 'I would agree, sir. It's the exact same principle we always work to.'

'Good. Then perhaps you can help by answering a query for me.'

'I'll do my level best, sir.'

'Excellent. So here's the problem, Bliss. We have all these threads and leads carefully chronicled in the case file – superb piece of work, by the way.' He mustered a smile, but Bliss saw through its insincerity. 'And yet, from what we can tell, there appears to be a slight gap. We don't seem to be able to find any record of how you linked Benjamin Carlisle's name with the find in Peterborough.'

Not for the first time, Bliss's ability to think quickly and clearly came in handy. 'Perhaps it was a simple omission on my part, sir. Naturally, one of the first things we did was to run a missing persons check based on the information we were able to obtain from pathology.'

Feeley seemed to bounce on the balls of his feet. 'Yes, that was our initial assumption. However, having checked the pathologist's report, we found no obvious indication of the victim's precise age. Gender, yes; not a child, either. But without being able to narrow the age range further, we were wondering how you managed to whittle it down to Carlisle.'

Bliss's thought process was rapid. He went through the sequence of events, looking for inconsistencies and tying it in with information he had discovered after talking to Sandra Bannister. Fraternising with the media was frowned upon. Exchanging information with them was potentially a sackable offence, though everybody knew it went on, and turned a blind eye provided it did not hurt investigations. Admitting such activity on the day a close source had fed critical details to a daily newspaper, however, was not something Bliss had any intention of doing.

'With respect once again, sir, nobody is suggesting we have identified Carlisle as our victim. We are concentrating our efforts on him, though – for two main reasons. First, I had a chat with Nancy Drinkwater in the mortuary on Monday morning. During our conversation, I was left with a rough estimation of age based on viewing the flesh one more time. Second, during our interview with Harrison's wife, she provided us with a list of acquaintances, and other than one name, it matched our own records. One of the names to appear on both lists was Ben Carlisle. From there, it wasn't a major leap for me to suggest looking hard at him as our victim, primarily because his home was ten or so miles away from where the flesh was found.'

He left it there. It would begin to look like an act of desperation on his part if he continued. In mentioning an impression of age related to the find, he had not implicated Drinkwater in any way. He doubted she would recall their conversation verbatim, so he thought he would be all right there. As for the second part of his explanation, it was all perfectly reasonable. Nonetheless, Feeley's direction was worrying. He wondered if the Chief Superintendent knew more than he was saying; had he been in touch with the *Telegraph* and somehow discovered the existence of Bannister's story? Bliss decided not to worry about it. He'd said his piece. Let Feeley shoot him down if he had the ammunition.

To his immense relief, the man let it go. Feeley's expression remained neutral, though Bliss thought there was a faint hint of suspicion in his eyes. Whatever the Chief Super was thinking, he obviously had no evidence with which to contradict Bliss's version of events.

Not yet, anyway.

TWENTY-FOUR

BLISS RELATED THE SALIENT portions of the conversation ten minutes later, his team alert to the potential impact of their superintendent's ambitions. He settled them down, insisting – as Fletcher had – that no immediate changes were planned. 'The Super is no different to me or any of you,' he said. 'We all reach a point where we consider the path ahead, and how we feel about taking it.'

'Last thing we need if you ask me,' Bishop said, setting his mouth into a tight slit.

'I agree, as it happens. But don't for one moment think that DSI Fletcher hasn't taken the impact on this unit into consideration. Team harmony will matter to her, of course, but this is the rest of her future we're talking about. I know you've wrestled with the same questions, Bish, just like I know you haven't yet reached a decision. Well, neither has she. So we go on. Speaking of which, somebody bring me up to speed.'

It was left to Chandler to provide an update. Bliss listened intently as his DS rattled off the situation as it stood. They now had a positive DNA report on Ben Carlisle; the sample taken from the portion of flesh found in the Knights' Chamber had been matched against items removed from the Carlisle property, and subsequently confirmed as his. Of the man himself there was still no sight or word – and the same went for Tommy Harrison and Earl Dobson. Dobson's records had arrived, and Chandler had been working her way through them when Bliss entered the Major Crimes area.

Talking about Carlisle reminded Bliss of Feeley's apparent fixation on how he had linked the man to the find. He began to second-guess himself. Would mentioning Bannister's role necessarily have been a negative thing? In this instance the information had gone only one way. However, questions might have been asked as to why a reporter would so willingly give up her story to Bliss. It was a tough call, but having had time to think about it in greater detail, he was content with the answers he had provided.

'Anything to give us a new direction or something positive to go on?' he asked.

Chandler linked her hands behind her head, supporting it in place. 'Nothing. Dobson's long-term partner reported him missing when he failed to come home on Wednesday last week. They live together in Devizes with their twenty-three-year-old daughter. Wiltshire police have the report logged. Other than that, we can confirm his association with Swift and Carlisle, but no obvious connection to any other persons of interest.'

Bliss winced. 'Which means very little. Could just be that he moved within their circles less than anyone else we're looking at. Did you follow up on the book?'

'Yes, boss. As you suspected, Phil Walker was the one who took the book out on loan. Ordered by him at North Weald library – which you noticed was printed on the barcode tag. I've tried calling him again, but no joy. We can either take another crack at him or ask the locals to pick him up.'

'Let me give it a stir when we're done here. I'm beginning to take a real interest in Walker, but let's clear the decks of everything else first. Any news from Swindon or London?'

'Nothing new,' Ansari said. She brushed away a few flecks of something from her plain green T-shirt. 'Superintendent Conway is going to try to track down some colleagues who worked the Price murder with him, see if they have anything to offer. Other than that, DI Riseborough appears to have run into a dead end regards CCTV. They traced our suspect on and back off the Tube, but at King's Cross he disappeared into a multi-storey car park and didn't come out again. They suspect he may have changed his appearance and either left in a vehicle or from one of a number of exits feeding into a shopping centre. He most likely had spare gear stuffed into the backpack he was carting around.'

Another potential lead taking them nowhere, Bliss thought. CCTV often saved their backsides when it came to incidents like the one at Tower Hill, but people's awareness of surveillance was as high as it had ever been. He accepted the situation for what it was and turned to DC Gratton.

'Nice to have you back in the fold full time, Phil. I forgot to ask, how was court?'

'Boring. I hung around most of the day, eventually got called in and was asked a single question. In and out inside five minutes.'

Bliss gave a 'what can you do?' shrug at the familiar story. 'At least you're swimming in the deep end with the rest of us now. What do you have for me on the two Price men?'

'I've set up an interview for tomorrow, boss. Neither of them are available today, but working with the father's PA we managed to find a slot when they are both free. I thought I'd get it actioned, but I wanted to run it by you first. I wasn't sure if you thought it was better to have a word with them individually, or speak to the two of them together.'

It was a good question. Both had their advantages and drawbacks. 'Let me come back to that,' Bliss said, running a hand across his chin. 'We'll see what else – if anything – we come up with beforehand. Whatever we discover may well dictate whether we go at them as bereaved family members or suspects.'

His thoughts turned to Tommy Harrison, Ben Carlisle and Earl Dobson. Were all three men now dead? Or were they being kept alive in separate locations, having slices of their flesh removed on a daily basis? If the latter, how feasible was it for a single perpetrator to keep such a mammoth task going? His mind strayed back to Andy and Stephen Price; husband and son of Geraldine. If the pair of them were engaged in an act of revenge, what had triggered their actions now? It was twenty-six years since her murder, so whatever it was must have been something seismic.

'Which of you has been looking into Geraldine Price's family?' he asked.

'We all have, boss,' Chandler said. 'We divvied up the jobs just to get them out of the way. Phil has been doing the leg work as far as the husband and son are concerned, but we've all contributed to the information pack.'

'Is Robert Naylor still around?' he asked. 'Geraldine's father?'

'No, boss.' This from Bishop. 'He died a number of years back. Her mother, too.'

'How about her brother?'

'We're still looking into him, boss. No records over the past few years, so he's a work in progress.'

'Fair enough. How about other children? Other than Stephen, I mean? Wasn't there a daughter in the picture?'

Gratton picked up on that. 'There was, yes. Her name's Valerie.'

Bliss nodded. 'Let's have a look at her, too. If we're taking this revenge motive seriously, I want to know why we're seeing a reaction now and not ten or twenty years ago.'

'I've been following up on Dobson, boss,' Ansari told him. 'Locals took a statement from his partner, Rachael Williams. Ms Williams claims Earl went fishing and never returned. A local patrol discovered his vehicle by a river known for angling, and Ms Williams confirmed it was one of Dobson's favourite spots. A couple of the anglers knew him to talk to, but hadn't seen him by the river at all that day.'

Her tone was listless, Bliss noticed. It had not taken long for the harsh reality of the job to dull all her initial bright-eyed optimism. This was a dangerous moment, the point in a career at which a detective either allowed the workload to grind them down, or pulled themselves together and gained a second wind. He made a mental note to have a word with the young DC before the case was over; Gul Ansari was too good a copper to be allowed to break.

'So whoever took Dobson did so as he arrived,' he said.

'It certainly looks that way, boss. His rod and tackle bag were in the boot of his vehicle, along with a pair of waders, which were dry.'

Bliss cursed. These men had disappeared far too easily for his liking, with no obvious signs of a struggle; whoever was responsible had to be somebody they knew. Once again, his mind flitted to Phil Walker and the library book. All manner of possibilities swam across his mind's eye, most of them drifting out of reach. Nothing made a great deal of sense to him, but a case over a quarter of a century old did not rear its head again without good reason. And that reason might provide the key to unlock the entire investigation for them.

'Right, before we draw this meeting to a conclusion, we need to discuss this leak to the *Daily Express*. Anybody have any thoughts on the matter before I say my piece?'

Nobody said a word.

'So be it. Let's get the obvious out in the open first of all. Our supreme leaders will follow protocol and suspect every member of every team. They will go through the motions by speaking to the reporter whose byline ran above the article, and they will get absolutely nowhere. They will sniff around all three teams comprising the JTFO. They will realise others outside the teams also had access to this knowledge, so will include forensics and admin staff. Again, they'll come up short. That's their end of the problem, and they are welcome to it.'

'But once again the stink attaches itself to all of us,' Bishop complained. Disgruntled, the big man threw down a pen he'd been holding. It bounced off the desk and ricocheted into a wastepaper basket. An ironic cheer went up around the room, and a couple of people awarded him three points.

'It does and it doesn't,' Bliss said. 'I've already had this out upstairs. I have something in mind, but there will be no massive witch-hunt. There'll be plenty of time for that when this is all over. And believe me, I have plans for whoever leaked this.'

'If it's a man, let's just say he's going to be speaking in a high-pitched voice afterwards,' Chandler said, desperate to laugh but nodding sternly instead.

Bliss gave her a disapproving look. 'Indeed. But, like I say, it can wait. My thoughts right now are on the damage this article may have done to our case. Giving away Tommy Harrison's name shouldn't be a killer blow; it beat us to the punch by a day at most, because we'd have had no choice but to release it anyway. A bigger deal is the article linking our case with Geraldine Price – that's something I'd rather had gone unnoticed for as long as possible. Whoever is responsible now knows we've made a connection, and they may well be worried about how close we are to them. For me, though, the biggest arse-ache is Ben Carlisle being named. Although they didn't go the whole hog and label him a victim, the implication was obvious.'

'Bastards!' Gratton said. He said it softly, but the sibilants echoed around the room. 'Whoever leaked it needs shooting.'

'I won't argue with you, Phil. Still, it could have been worse; I'm not sure how much longer we would have been able to keep such solid information to ourselves. Once again, the *Express* tucked us up on this to the tune of a day, so not all is lost.'

'But forewarned is still forearmed,' Ansari said, fussing with her top to the point of obsession. 'Now whoever is doing this knows we're coming.'

'Yes, they do.' Bliss nodded. 'But perhaps we can use that to our advantage.'

'How so, boss?'

'Off the top of my head, Gul, I'm not absolutely sure. But the circumstances on the ground have changed, and so we need to adapt our approach. Let's brainstorm it now and see what we can come up with.'

'Are you allowed to brainstorm any more, boss?' Chandler asked. 'Isn't that one of those terms you can no longer use?'

'Do you have a brain disorder, Pen?'

'Of course not.'

'We can agree to disagree on that. But, if you did, would my use of the word offend you?'

'I don't imagine so. But I'd probably have to have the brain disorder before I knew that for sure.'

'She's giving me a bloody headache, boss,' Bishop said, rolling his head like a newborn baby's. 'Does that count as a brain disorder?'

'How about we settle on calling it a thought shower?' Ansari suggested.

'I've heard of a golden shower,' Chandler said. 'Is that the same thing?'

Bliss said nothing as laughter erupted around him. Light relief was always welcome, and his team's thoughts would return to the darkness soon enough.

TWENTY-FIVE

Bliss reacquainted himself with Hoxton early on Thursday morning, cruising its streets shortly after dawn. He noted the unfamiliar – of which there was a great deal – as he spent thirty minutes breathing it all in and getting a feel for the place again. There was a time when he would have been able to navigate the area blindfolded, but not any more. Attempts at gentrification had completely changed its character, and not all for the better. The streets and pavements were in a general state of disrepair, and when Bliss looked out on the rows of shops, homes and office blocks, he noticed how little of it was bright and fresh or welcoming. Those few buildings that were stood out like acne on a Disney princess.

Had it always been this way? Or had he become jaundiced, time playing tricks on his mind? Whatever the answer, Bliss knew he would never move back here to live. These and many streets just like them had once been his playground, but now they seemed foreign to him. He would never belong here again.

Spotting the time on the dashboard clock, he pulled over to the kerb, took out his mobile and called Chandler.

'Morning, boss. You cadging another lift?' She sounded alert; clearly he had not woken her.

'Not today, Pen. I won't be in the office until this afternoon. I want you to sub for me. Find out all you can about Phil Walker. I tried his landline last night and got the voicemail message again. I also obtained a mobile number for him, but got the same deal there. I'm still keen on finding out more about him, though. I may yet drop in on him on my way back, but get everything you can for me in the meantime.'

'Okay, boss, will do… On your way back from where?'

Bliss could have kicked himself. He'd misspoken, and Chandler had been on it like a scrapyard dog hearing a chain rattle. He considered lying, but settled for telling the truth and dealing with the fallout later. 'I'm in London. I got an early start.'

'Doing what?'

'Looking up a few of the old faces who were around in 1994.'

'Sounds like a decent idea. But why are you doing it without me?'

'It's no big deal, Pen. Don't read anything into it. I need you to take the wheel for me today, is all. I'm also going to see Andy and Stephen Price later on.'

'Does Bish know?'

'If he doesn't, he soon will. I sent him a text when I decided to drive down here.'

'Okay, so how about this leak to the *Express*? What do you have in mind?'

'I've got a couple of ideas – leave them with me. We'll chew them over later.'

After a moment of silence, Chandler said, 'What's going on, Jimmy? Why are you cowboying this?'

'I'm not, and there's nothing going on. Look, this needs doing, but it doesn't require two of us this time. I need you lot to focus on other things while I'm taking care of one small part of the op. That's all there is to it.'

Bliss wrapped the call up quickly, but felt uncomfortable afterwards. In truth, he had not wanted the people he intended speaking to today to taint Chandler, and if he was already here, it made sense to save Bishop and Ansari a long drive at the same time. Not that Chandler couldn't cope with villains; she had encountered a great deal of ugliness in her career. Drug dealers, especially, were capable of any form of brutality you cared to mention. But in his time working organised crime cases, he had witnessed for himself the worst of humankind. He'd seen the sloppy remains of an entire family fed through an industrial meat grinder, bodies broken down by acid and flame, wounds in flesh caused by all manner of tools and devices, the decaying husks of men and a fair few women virtually unrecognisable as human. There was a certain finality to the work of a genuine, hardened gangster, and if Bliss had an opportunity to keep that dark energy from touching his partner and friend, he would.

In doing so, he recognised a familiar trait. His therapist, Jennifer Howey, had described it as his saviour complex. She believed his desire to save everyone was his way of making up for not being able to save one particular person: his wife. Naturally, he had argued the merits of her analysis, but had ultimately decided it didn't matter what label she put on it. He was protective of others, and would never regard this side of his nature as wrong. He was certain of one thing, however: if Chandler found out why he had benched her today, it was he who would need protecting.

As he continued his tour of the area, Bliss found himself becoming increasingly dejected. Despite the best efforts of investors, Hoxton was still a dangerous and derelict area of the capital. Loft-style living was chic, but an existence to be enjoyed mainly by those with sufficient money to secure their property against the barbarians at the gate. New developments stood cheek by jowl with dilapidated local authority estates, intimidating warrens in which the criminal element thrived and which the police largely avoided. Bliss had once dated a girl who lived on one of them.

Wenlock Street ran parallel to Murray Grove – the street on which the Price family had once resided – and it was here that Bliss hoped to find one of the most notorious women ever to have survived the clutches of the Doyle family. Her flat was on the third tier of a five-storey block built from bricks the colour of red clay. He tried the lift, but its floor was swimming in the sticky remains of whatever toxic mixture of alcohol, vomit and urine had been left behind overnight. He decided the stairs would be better for his health in more ways than one.

After receiving no response to his first two rattles of the letterbox, Bliss tried again. This time the door was yanked open – almost off its hinges. The woman who stood before him was on the wrong side of fifty, but beyond the bed hair and lack of makeup, it was obvious she took care of herself. She wore a short, flimsy dressing gown over an even shorter, flimsier nightdress. Bliss thought of Freddy Swift, wondering how many of his movies had opened this way.

'What the fuck do you want?' the woman barked at him. Her eyes were red-rimmed and swollen.

'Mrs Daley?' he said. 'Siobhan Daley?'

'Who wants to know?' She folded her arms as if challenging him to ruin her day.

'Police. I'd like a quiet word inside if possible. I can show you my warrant card if you like… but it would be better if you invited me in so your neighbours aren't aware.'

'Pull the other one, shit-for-brains.' She went to close the door on him, but Bliss leaned in to prevent her moving it. He dipped into his pocket to fish out his credentials.

Daley gazed at his card and said, 'What the fuck do you want?'

Bliss scratched his head. 'I just had déjà vu,' he said. 'It's almost as if we've had this exact same conversation before.'

'Okay, so you're a joker. I'm happy for you. So, what the fuck do you want?'

'I want to come inside. And I think you're going to want me to come inside, too.'

She looked him up and down, chewing it over. Bliss let the silence work its magic. He was allowed to enter, but not before Daley had rolled her eyes and huffed her irritation. She led him into a narrow kitchen and sat down at a small breakfast bar, where she already had a hot drink and a cigarette on the go. As she perched on a padded wooden stool, she crossed one leg over the other, and Bliss's attention was caught by a large expanse of thigh. His mind drifted back to Swift, and the thought teased a smile out of him.

Daley had a sip of her drink and took a drag from her cigarette, releasing smoke from the corner of her mouth after savouring it for a couple of seconds. 'What's so funny?'

Bliss was about to brush it off, but it occurred to him that the story would make a decent ice-breaker. Without naming Swift, he told her about the porn baron and the clichéd scene he'd thought of when she first opened the door. He laughed and shrugged when he was done, as if to say it was one of those stupid isolated thoughts and maybe you had to have been there.

By way of a response, Siobhan Daley stretched out her evenly tanned bare legs, angling them slightly as if appraising their appeal. 'You a leg man, Inspector?' she asked.

Her calves were firm and nicely shaped. Both ankles were marbled with heavy veins, but they were lean and strong-looking, and her toenails were manicured and painted a cherry red. He gave a stiff nod of approval. 'I'm a great admirer.'

She cupped her small breasts over her gown. 'Really? What's wrong with boobs?'

'Nothing at all. I'm in favour of them as well, generally speaking. But legs are my thing.'

Bliss felt her eyes on him, and he was sure he saw them soften. Eventually her lips curled into a delicate smile. She moved both hands to her lap. 'I'm sure they are. But we all know what you prefer, don't we?'

Daley was playing him. Hers was either an attempt to entice so as to establish control, or to belittle for precisely the same reason. He had the authority, but they were on her home ground and she had the allure of experience on her side. It was probably her best card, given the life she'd had. But Bliss was not about to let her have things all her own way.

'May I call you Siobhan?' he asked.

'You can, darling. And you can call me anytime.' The fluttering eyelashes on this occasion were unnecessary and sad. She was trying too hard, and Bliss saw through the pretence.

'Siobhan, I realise you opted out of the Doyle family when you ended your marriage to Patrick. From what I understand, walking out on a Doyle was unheard of at the time, and many people regarded you as either the bravest woman in this manor or the most foolish. The Doyles gave you a hard time, I believe?'

Bliss saw all thoughts of sultry flirting fleeing from her eyes. The hardening of her face was immediate, the sneer she now wore filled with resentment. 'A dog would have been treated better,' she said, her voice now low and reflective. 'I was spat at, slapped, punched, kicked. And that was only by the women in the family. Pat slashed me with a knife, cut me somewhere even I wouldn't show you. His brother, Colm, put me in hospital for two weeks, after throwing me down a flight of concrete stairs. Pat cheered him on as he did it.'

Bliss hung his head and let out a long gasp, hissing between his teeth. 'But you stuck to your guns. You made it through.'

'Oh, yeah. I did that. I'd never let them bully me into moving out of the area, either. This place is my home, and it always will be. It's not been good for my sex life, though, that's for sure. What bloke in his right mind is going to try it on with Patrick Doyle's ex-missus? Most of the family moved away, into their big houses and their fancy lives, but there's enough of them and their friends around to make sure nobody dare have a crack at me.'

'You think tongues will be wagging right now if anyone saw me coming inside?'

'I wouldn't bet against it.'

One of the reasons Bliss had chosen to come without Chandler was that he thought he'd get a better response on his own. Now, having recognised the issue of perception when it came to male visitors, he wished he'd chosen differently. 'I'll be as quick as I can.'

'Aw... I just got done telling you how hard it is for me to have a man in my life, so I was rather hoping you'd take your time with me, sweetheart.'

Bliss saw through Daley's playful brassiness and chose not to play along with her little game; he let her know it with one look. 'I understand I'm never going to get anything out of the Doyles themselves, but I thought a chat with you might be worth a shot, Siobhan.'

'About what?' She drained her mug and took one final drag of her cigarette before stubbing it out in a pottery ashtray that looked as if a child had made it.

'Geraldine Price,' Bliss said.

Daley blew out her lips. 'Now, there's a blast from the past. I haven't heard her name spoken in many a year. What do you want to know about Geraldine?'

'Did you know her?'

'No. Should I have?'

He shrugged. 'Hoxton is a decent-sized place, but it's a pretty small community.'

'If you mean we were all in and out of each other's houses, you're right – but around these parts, there are friends of the Doyles and then there's everybody else. Pat's parents and his brothers still lived in Clerkenwell when me and Pat got hitched. He and I moved over this way, which caused a bit of friction at the time.'

'But who's going to say a word to him, right?'

'Too bloody true. Of course, there were a few faces who stood up to the Doyles, but they didn't last long. Probably supporting flyovers somewhere, if you ask me. Most locals talked a better fight than they gave, but it was the sane thing to do if your enemy was a Doyle.'

Bliss thought she was right about that. He wondered what her life had been like since becoming an outcast in her own neighbourhood. From the limited information he'd been able to gather, the Daley family were no angels, and Siobhan was known to have been involved in criminal activity since she was old enough to bear children. Assault, theft, robbery, and running brothels and a blue movie theatre in nearby Shoreditch all formed part of her arrest record. Yet she had never been charged, often because her victims were either unable or unwilling to provide evidence against her. He had no doubt this woman could be vicious if she were so inclined, but her life had clearly become an existence to be endured over time. He tried to muster up sympathy for her predicament, but failed. Some people regarded Siobhan Daley as a victim herself, but Bliss believed she was rotten to the core.

'Back to Mrs Price,' he said. 'You say you didn't know her, but you knew of her, yes? Do you mean in respect of what happened to her?'

'Of course. As you pointed out, the walls are both close and thin along these streets. Not much goes on around here that you don't get to hear about. And something so awful... the stink never goes away.'

'I can imagine. But the thing is, we now have a renewed interest in the case, Siobhan. At the time of the original investigation, police decided no locals were involved. Instead, they believed a group of men, ultimately passing through but perhaps staying locally for a week or so, tortured and murdered Geraldine, then dumped her beside the canal and drove away without a backward glance.'

'And, what…? You're now saying that's not the case?'

'I'm saying we're looking at it again from a different perspective. Although none of the conversations in question appear on any official records, we know that members of the Doyle family were spoken to by detectives investigating the murder. Basically, there were two theories: either they were involved, or they knew who was.'

Daley snorted, folding her arms once again. 'I can imagine how they reacted.'

'It's fair to say they were not particularly forthcoming. But you were still part of the family at the time. Within their inner circle, as it were. I have to wonder if you remember hearing anything. Any mention of it at all, a slip of the tongue, maybe?'

'A confession, you mean?' She shook her head and puckered her lips. 'Not a chance, Inspector… Bliss, was it?'

'That's right. Okay, so nobody in the family coughed to taking part in her abduction, torture, murder, or dumping. But this was a serious crime right on their doorstep – it would have drawn a lot of unwelcome attention, both from us and the media. If they had nothing to do with the murder, I'm sure Pat and the others must have been steaming about that. You must have heard something, Siobhan. Even if it was just speculation.'

Huffing through her nostrils, Daley lowered her eyes. She lit another cigarette and took a long draw on it, resting one elbow on her cupped hand. 'I can remember one thing. I'll tell you about it, but then you have to go. I overheard Colm having a rant about it one day. He was looking for information, and he'd put the word out on the street. You're right – the filth flooded this area for days after she was taken, and longer still once her body turned up. I think if Colm and Pat ever had proof as to who was responsible, they would have acted on it.'

'Okay. So, no proof, perhaps. How about rumour? A name?'

'I was getting to that. Look, it's probably nothing, pure guesswork on my part, but I remember hearing the Walkers being discussed.'

Bliss was instantly alert. It was not a name he had expected to hear. 'Would Phil Walker be one of them?'

Daley nodded, and took another drag before adding to the smoke coiling in a lazy cloud that nudged the ceiling. 'There were three of them. The old man and two sons. Phil was the youngest, and by far the worst. On his own, he was a match for any of the Doyles. The Walker gang was small, but they drew other people in. The thing I most remember is, they were organised before "organised" became an actual thing around here. I never heard of any of them getting their hands dirty, you know? But they ran things. No question about it.'

'And their name was mentioned in connection with what happened to Geraldine Price? You're sure about that?'

'Yes. Colm and Pat were totally hacked off about it.'

There was nothing sexual about the woman now. She'd played her role out, and dropped it when he refused to play along. This was the real Siobhan Daley, and she was all business.

Intrigued, Bliss reeled off the other names on his mental list, asking Daley if she knew any of them in connection with the Walker crew. She recognised them all, with the exception of Earl Dobson. He felt a tingle of excitement work its way down his spine, like a trail of cold sweat on a hot day. It was electric.

Phil Walker.

The one name on Vicki Harrison's list of known acquaintances that did not appear on police records. Dobson was the second victim, Harrison the third. With Ben Carlisle now confirmed as the first, where did Phil Walker fit in? As the next victim? Or the man responsible for slicing pieces off his fellow gangsters?

While they were talking, Bliss had noticed Daley glancing nervously at her phone. At first he thought she was waiting for a call or text message, but then realised she was checking the time.

'Are you expecting somebody?' he asked, nodding towards her phone.

Daley shook her head. 'Not expecting. But if you *were* seen coming in, those same people will be wondering why you're still here. They'll think the worst, of course. They'll be earwigging to see if they can hear the sound of my headboard bashing the bedroom wall.'

'You reckon they'd come banging on the door?'

'No. But they might tell someone else to do it.'

'Has my coming here this morning made trouble for you, Siobhan?' Bliss asked.

Daley wrapped both arms around herself in a tight hug. 'I hope not.'

'Let me see what I can do,' he said, getting to his feet.

Back outside on the landing, Bliss told her to slam the door behind him. He made a meal of it, raising his voice, venting his spleen about people no longer wanting to help the police and telling her she could go to hell along with the rest of them. Anybody observing would hopefully no longer suspect her of having had a man in her bed.

As he drove away, Bliss found it hard to imagine living life the way she had to. Judging by the few minutes they had spent together, Siobhan Daley was no longer the woman she had once been; all her pride and dignity had been stripped away. The price she had paid for her own sins as well as those of the person she'd chosen to marry.

TWENTY-SIX

BLISS'S SECOND UNANNOUNCED VISIT in Hoxton was a complete washout. One of his old informants had lived there, but Bliss hadn't been in touch with the man since leaving London for Peterborough the first time around. There was always the chance he had moved home – but if so, he would not have gone far, and Bliss was confident of tracking him down. He was ultimately disappointed, though not at all surprised, to discover his snitch had been a decade in the ground due to complications arising from liver disease. His crutch had always been hard booze of dubious quality, and it had eventually seen him off. But in any case, perhaps it would have been a mistake to expect the man's alcohol-sodden mind to conjure up any worthwhile memories.

The setback left Bliss with time on his hands, which he spent browsing Chapel Street in Islington. The hustle and bustle and cacophony of voices and music jarred at first, but it didn't take him long to acclimatise. The smells of the street market were completely different from those of his childhood. In those days it had been all fried onions from burger vans; now the deep-rooted odours were a heady mixture of spices. Today's stallholders were of all creeds and colours, their wares ranging from bright rolls of cloth to fruit and vegetables, from household goods to banks of clothing on wire hangers. From a stall selling music in a variety of media, Bliss bought a Stevie Ray Vaughan live album in mint condition, and a Little River Band CD. Satisfied with his haul, he set off for the short drive to Old Street and parked up a short walk away from the building in which Andy and Stephen Price had their law practice.

Bliss carried his suit jacket hanging over the crook of one arm, the top button of his shirt undone, sleeves rolled up. A cooling breeze took the edge off the heat. All along the pavements his fellow pedestrians seemed less burdened by life, as if the pleasant weather alleviated stress and provided a calming influence. People even looked up from their phones occasionally, smiling awkwardly as they passed one another. Nose to tail, the seething mass of gleaming traffic rumbled by, basslines thumping from windows, e-cigarette vapour scenting the air. Bliss enjoyed the short walk, feeling invigorated as he mentally prepared for what he expected to be a difficult meeting.

Price & Son Solicitors had a suite of offices located on the ground floor of a shared building a hundred yards or so from Old Street station. Andy Price was in his late fifties, but looked a decade younger. The man was of average height and build, but Bliss could tell he worked out. His grip was firm as they shook hands, and he filled out his sharp suit across the chest and arms. By contrast, his son Stephen looked older than Bliss knew him to be. Pale, with ill-fitting clothes and a soft centre, he looked nothing like his father; not that he bore any discernible resemblance to his late mother, either. Both men eyed him with overt suspicion.

The room they used was compact with a high ceiling. Shelves ranged across one wall held weighty tomes, many of them referencing cases in which precedents were set, while others related to current law. Bliss knew they were mostly for show, given the wealth of information available online. He noticed a wide range of framed certificates littering the walls, and wondered if they were meant to impress the clients or the Prices themselves.

As the three men took their seats and Andy Price ordered a round of coffees from an assistant, Bliss weighed up the situation and decided to change his play. It was a tough call; potentially, he had one stab at this, and if he approached it the wrong way, it might leave the investigation further behind by putting the victim's family at odds with the lead detective. Having initially intended to come at them aggressively, he softened his eyes and unburdened his shoulders.

'Thank you for agreeing to meet with me,' he said. 'I realise this is the last thing either of you wishes to do. Raking up the past can be a fraught process, and in your case I understand how delicate the matter is.'

'To be perfectly honest with you, Chief Inspector Bliss, I'm not at all sure you do.' Andy Price spoke with a local accent that had been strangled from trying to appeal to a more refined clientele. 'If you did, I don't think you would be here.'

Bliss was prepared for some pushback. 'It's just Inspector, sir. And this will go a whole lot easier if you hold off on your judgement until you've heard me out.'

Price senior accepted the mild rebuke with a shrug. 'In that case, please let's get it over with.'

A young man wearing a snazzy red bowtie brought their drinks in on a tray, which also held cookies fanned out on a plate. Hungry though he was, Bliss ignored the biscuits but sipped his black coffee before breaking the news.

'Gentlemen, I have to tell you this is not a courtesy call. I'm not merely ticking a box on an unsolved case file.'

'Just tell us what you *are* doing here,' Stephen demanded. The flesh was drawn tight across his face, cheeks bordering on the concave. He sat back with one leg hooked over the other, the dangling foot jerking fitfully.

Bliss looked both men in the eyes before making his announcement. 'We are reinvestigating the murder of Geraldine Price. I imagine you've heard about the severed hand found at Tower Hill on Monday?' Father and son flashed sidelong glances at each other, the look enough to convince Bliss they were fully aware of the findings so far. 'Good. Then you'll probably also know there are three separate cases we believe are connected: one involves a man by the name of Earl Dobson, another is Tommy Harrison, while the third case relates to a Ben Carlisle. I'm sure at least one of those names will be familiar to you, but I suspect the others are, too.'

Andy Price reacted first. 'Tommy Harrison was a person of interest in connection to the murder of my wife at one point. I have a vague recollection of the other two as names from the past, but that's about as far as it goes.'

Usually, Bliss focussed on whoever was speaking, while Chandler concentrated on the reactions of others. Without his partner by his side, however, he was having to cover both men. He had seen a flicker of interest in Stephen's eyes when Harrison's name was mentioned. The gleam lingered, so he was unable to tell whether the other names meant anything to him. Bliss appraised the Prices with what he hoped was a degree of subtlety. Despite his age, the father certainly had the build and strength to tackle any of the three victims; Stephen, on the other hand, looked as if he'd struggle to tear his way through a wad of wet tissue paper.

'Our current strategy in all three cases,' Bliss said, continuing to eye both men alternately, 'is built around the belief that they have their roots in the murder of Mrs Price.'

Once again it was the older man who was the first to respond, his voice charged with emotion. 'In what way? Are you suggesting all three were somehow responsible for what happened to my wife?'

Bliss nodded. 'It's certainly a theory of serious interest to us. We believe it's entirely possible that one of the men involved in your wife's murder is now reacting against the others for some reason.'

A deep wedge appeared across Andy Price's forehead. 'I don't understand. From what I have been able to glean, your investigations amount to little more than finding some pieces of flesh and a hand. I don't see how they have anything to do with what happened to Geraldine, other than belonging to three men who admittedly lived in the same area as us when she was murdered. I'm not seeing the connection, Inspector. And I do this sort of thing for a living, remember.'

Bliss began to filter the conversation he was about to get into. If either or both of these two men were responsible for the current spate of mutilations, he could not afford to have them suspect the true purpose of his visit.

'Mr Price,' he said. 'As I'm sure you're aware, in certain investigations – and especially in cases of murder – the police may hold back specific pieces of information. This is true of your wife's case, sir; there is information the police would not have shared with you. It's also true of the three ongoing cases. We believe the link lies within those unreleased details. Please, trust me when I tell you the connection is valid. I wouldn't be sitting here otherwise.'

Andy Price appeared to relax, his posture losing its rigidity. His son continued to show signs of apprehension, though Bliss saw nothing untoward. Speaking with the police about such outrages was a difficult experience, and anxiety levels often went through the roof. Bliss thought the time was right to poke at them just a little.

'I have to be honest,' he said after finishing his drink, 'I'm not sure either of you can help me. However, it would be absurd of me to run an operation like this and not speak to the people who were the most affected by Mrs Price's murder. And given your occupation,

I'm sure you understand I have to ask certain questions. Formalities, mainly, but asking them often provokes a negative response.'

'You want us to provide alibis,' Price senior said. His expression did not change, but his body tensed.

'For the current investigations, yes. Actually, for the time being I think we can settle on the one, and let's see where we go from there.'

'Please, go ahead. We understand you have a job to do.' The man spoke for his son, though this time he did not glance across at him.

'Thank you, sir. So, let's look at earlier in the week. Where were you both between the hours of, say, seven and nine on Monday morning?'

For the first time since Bliss had entered the room, Andy Price smiled. 'That's an easy one. We were both in Manchester. We travelled up on Sunday after lunch, came home late on Monday evening. We were in chambers all day, meeting with Queen's Counsel. I can vouch for our entire day, but during the specific time window you mentioned we were enjoying an early breakfast with the QC himself. And three other people.'

Bliss smiled as he nodded. It helped if they thought this was the answer he had been hoping for. If they were no longer suspects – as now seemed obvious, at least in respect of dumping the bag at Tower Hill – he wanted to keep the Prices on his side and feeling comfortable in his presence. There was a fair way to go before he'd be willing to dismiss either man as a potential suspect, however; they clearly had the means to pay for somebody else to carry out the physical aspects of the crimes.

'Excellent,' he said. 'I love it when things are so clear cut. Makes our job easier all round. Obviously, I'll need to have one of my team follow up on this with you, Mr Price. Obtain details and contact names, perhaps briefly discuss the other two finds and their less precise timeframes. But at least now that's out of the way we can move on – although, in this instance, that also requires us to look back.'

They spent the next half hour in much the same way: Bliss asking questions, the father answering them before responding with a few of his own. Stephen Price chipped in if spoken to directly, but otherwise sat fidgeting and seemingly distancing himself. Bliss understood: twenty-six years had passed, but still they were discussing the man's mother, her sadistic torture and brutal murder. There would never be a time when enduring those horrific memories would not be agonising.

From what he remembered of the original case file, Andy Price's current verbal account matched in all critical aspects. The last time he had seen his wife alive was when she left for work on the morning of Friday 4 February 1994. He had since remarried and raised a second family. He spoke about the moment he first became aware that one of his neighbours, Tommy Harrison, had been interviewed as a suspect. Emotions were running high at the time, and every name mentioned in connection with his wife's murder had turned Andy's grief into white-hot fury. He had always believed no locals were involved, simply because there were too many eyes, ears and mouths on every estate for such a terrible secret to remain undiscovered. His wife's father, Robert Naylor, had convinced him of this after the man had personally interrogated every able soul in the district.

'And now?' Bliss asked when they reached that point in the conversation. 'With Harrison, Carlisle and Dobson falling victim to whatever is being done to them?'

'You're forgetting, Inspector Bliss: you know something I don't. I can't change my mind if I don't know what it is that connects those men to Geraldine. I'm having to trust in your theory, but I'm doing so while blindfolded. Without being privy to the information you have, I still think the murder of my wife was the work of outsiders.'

If he was guilty, he was the best Bliss had ever seen. But the man was intelligent, calm, and completely rational. He could just be that good. His son, on the other hand, was a bundle of nervous energy, and clearly in the room under sufferance. Yet both of them had what appeared to be solid alibis for Monday morning, and Bliss had to weigh the evidence against anything his instincts were telling him.

They spoke further about the initial investigations – first the abduction, then the subsequent murder. Both men found it difficult, Stephen Price coming close to tears as he revealed how numb he had felt during the entire time from hearing his mother was missing to the point at which she was laid to rest. He admitted he had switched off; Bliss didn't think the man had ever flicked the switch to restart. Married, with a son and daughter of his own, Stephen had followed his father into law on the back of obtaining no justice in his mother's case. Bliss thought it was as good a reason as any to start a career, and better than most.

Throughout the entire meeting, Bliss picked up mixed signals, and wasn't at all sure what to make of them. On the surface, he was neither seeing nor hearing anything to elevate either man to the status of prime suspect, but an unidentified feeling in his gut made him reluctant to rule them out. As he cleared his thoughts to form the next question, something else popped into his head.

'Believe me, I'm sorry to have to do this,' he said, shrugging and spreading his hands. 'But just as I've had to ask you two gentlemen some awkward questions, so I will also need to speak to your daughter, Mr Price – Valerie. We've attempted to track her down, but so far without luck. I was hoping you would be able to provide me with her contact details.'

Andy Price's eyes became pained and angry in an instant. 'You need to do your homework,' he said, barely able to look at Bliss this time. 'Val took her own life eight weeks ago. If you're wondering why my son and I are not exactly welcoming this reinvestigation of yours with open arms, Inspector, it's because it's too damned little, too damned late.' His voice cracked, then softened. 'She left us a note. All about the severe depression she'd suffered ever since her mother's body was found. My daughter became an addict, Inspector. Drink and drugs. It was a habit she was never able to kick, despite our many attempts to find her some peace of mind. She eventually found a way to achieve that for herself.'

Horrified, Bliss apologised for the misstep. The sympathy he expressed was genuine, but his nerves jangled as a result of what he had learned. If he and his team were looking for a single recent event that may have triggered the crimes they were investigating, he had just discovered a massively significant one.

TWENTY-SEVEN

MORE THAN TWENTY-FOUR HOURS after his run-in with the police, Freddy Swift was still feeling queasy, as if adrenaline continued to pump through his veins at high pressure. He'd barely been able to eat since the two cops from Peterborough had interviewed him, his subsequent thoughts consumed not only by the attitude of the senior detective, Bliss, but also the reason for their presence at his place of business. Despite the fuss they had kicked up about the shoot, their interest went way beyond the young girl he was using. They had far worse on their minds, and he felt completely entangled in the web they had spun.

Since leaving his office the previous evening and booking himself into a hotel under a false name that matched the credit card he was able to produce, he had practically lashed himself to the TV, devouring the news cycle on multiple channels. Following confirmation that the body part discovered at Tower Hill belonged to Tommy Harrison, the names of two additional missing men had been formally released to the public by the police; they were thought to have come to significant harm. Swift was beside himself with worry at how quickly the investigation was moving, and he needed to do something about it.

The alibi he had provided was good for all of the five minutes it would take the police to speak with the star attraction he had boasted of meeting on Monday morning; one short conversation and they would be back, sniffing around him again. He wouldn't risk going home, not even to empty his bedroom safe of cash. For all he knew, his lie had already been exposed, though he hoped the police had not yet verified his responses. Alternately scratching his head and clasping his hands together, he paced the narrow strip of carpet at the end of the bed.

He had to find a way out of this nightmare. The call he had made earlier would go part of the way to achieving that, but his stress levels remained dangerously high. He felt ill. He wasn't built to cope with this extreme level of anxiety, and he was acutely aware of how close he was to falling apart completely. He had this one move left, but if it proved unsuccessful his entire future would be in the lap of the gods. There was no way he'd handle a second police interview.

Swift checked his watch for the twentieth time, gathered up his things and left the hotel. He kept his head down, covered with a shapeless grey hoodie, unaware of any security cameras but knowing there must be some around. From the cool shade of the entrance porch, he surveyed every inch of the car park. There were no obvious signs of occupation, none of the vehicles belching exhaust or windows misting with exhaled breaths. A couple of cars entered, and their occupants retrieved luggage before booking into the hotel. A number of people exited, went to their cars, got in and drove away. Nothing out of the ordinary. Still feverishly checking his watch, Swift gave it all the time he could spare before making his own move.

The small Epping Forest car park off the A104 was familiar to him, as were the roads leading to it. He drove a circuitous route, within the speed limit, checking all the while for any sign he was being followed. By the time he felt comfortable enough to pull in and stop, he was ten minutes late. Enclosed on three sides by trees, the car park spawned four paths leading away into the forest itself. A row of wooden picnic tables and seating lay to one side, waste bins overflowing with wrappers and plastic bottles, several of which glinted in the sunlight on the ground beneath. There was one other vehicle parked up; he didn't recognise it, but had not expected to. He saw nobody else. The arrangement was for him to take the path to the right and keep walking until he was met. With mixed feelings, Swift eventually climbed out of his car and followed the instructions.

In spite of the clandestine meeting and a heart hammering so loudly he thought people an entire county away would be able to hear it, Swift began to relax. He started to feel safer, secure in his anonymity here. His aim was to avoid the police, and there was no chance of them being in on this as part of a sting operation. This was about old-school loyalty, which was something you did not screw around with.

The deeper into the forest he walked, the less the sound of traffic intruded, replaced by the gentler sounds of nature. He brushed against dense undergrowth to the side of the dirt path, heels kicking up miniature clouds of baked, dusty soil. He felt a smile crawl across his mouth; this was a moment to enjoy. Just him and the forest he remembered exploring as a child.

And the person he had come to meet.

He'd walked the length of two football pitches into the forest before he heard the sound of leather scuffing hardened soil up ahead. Swift hesitated, fight-or-flight instincts rearing up inside him. A brief moment of panic… and a familiar figure came into view, walking slowly towards him. Freddy Swift blew out a deep sigh of relief.

Only to suck it back in again as his eyes zeroed in on what the man held in his right hand.

TWENTY-EIGHT

A NGEL SPICE, IN THE village of Stilton, was Bliss's favourite Indian restaurant. Ideally located directly opposite the Bell Inn, it was possible to stumble from one to the other without doing any real damage to yourself – provided you looked both ways as North Street broke seamlessly into the High Street. On the drive north he had called Chandler and arranged to meet her for a late lunch; by the time he arrived, she was already tucking into a serving of thin and crispy poppadums. The place smelled great, and his stomach let out a gurgle of anticipation.

'Bit early in the day for something this heavy,' Chandler said as he pulled out a chair. She chomped down on her starter, crumbs spreading out across the white table linen like the final remnants of a landslide.

'I have a horrible taste in my mouth,' he told her. 'I need to nuke it away, and sometimes only a Ruby will do. Besides, I won't go crazy. I needed refuelling and thought I'd rather have tasty than tasteless.'

They ordered, Bliss adding a bottle of Cobra beer to his. Chandler stuck with the sparkling water already on the table. Bliss grabbed a couple of poppadums and started tucking in. He was hungrier than he'd realised.

'Where did you get to with Walker?' he asked.

'Ah, yes, Mr Dark Horse.' Chandler waggled her eyebrows suggestively. 'I'm willing to bet that twenty or thirty years ago, Phil Walker was one of those behind-the-scenes villains. You know the kind: doesn't ever let the ugly side come anywhere near him, has no obvious source of income, but still drives around in a Roller and lives in a big fuck-off mock-Tudor house.'

'I have a feeling you may be right,' Bliss said. He paused as the waiter came over with his drink. It wasn't as cold as he would have liked, but he took a long pull anyway and cuffed the foam away from his lips. 'But go ahead and tell me what you found out.'

'To all outward appearances, Walker runs a thriving import and export business. And despite the economic climate, it's somehow seeing substantial growth, with plenty of new clients sniffing around. Which, in and of itself, is no big deal, yet he seems to have financed his company a decade ago with hardly any startup capital. Nor can I find any evidence of him ever having a pot to piss in beforehand.'

'So, bad money, then? The type you keep under your mattress?'

'Only if your mattress is made of steel and comes with a biometric lock. But yes, clearly he had seed assets the taxman knew nothing about. I would assume he'd try to pass it off as a loan from a friend, but this man stinks of organised crime.'

'A man with fingers in many pies, by all accounts. One too many, is my guess.'

'I'd say so. His business springs up about six months after he's laid up by a stroke, at which point he starts buying in stock from abroad and trading it here, and vice versa. But this is not a small trader by any means – we're not just talking about a vanload of knock-offs. The numbers I've seen run into tens of millions. We ran a credit check and went deep on those finances, and although he does have a few major companies on board, for the most part they're small outfits that seem to trade well above their profile. I'm still digging around, but I'd say most of them are not legit.'

'So he's also laundering.'

'That's what I was thinking. The flat we have as his address is almost certainly a front, providing him with a strategic base. He passes himself off as a pillar of the community, involved with all manner of business enterprises, including the local chamber of commerce. There's also mention of him being the next big thing in local politics.'

'Family?' Bliss asked. 'Is he married? Can we find a way in there?'

'Divorced, one son. The ex and the son both live in Greece, and have done for a number of years.'

'I get the feeling Walker is bad news all around.' Bliss told his partner about his meeting with Siobhan Daley. His impressions of the woman herself were not important, but he'd valued what she'd had to say. Chandler was impressed at how neatly it tied in with everything she had discovered.

'We need to double our efforts to find him,' Bliss said firmly. 'Because either he's wiping his old mates off the map, or he's due to be wiped.'

'Which way are you leaning?'

'I'm on the fence with this one, Pen. If I had to guess, I'd say he's our man. If he's seriously looking at a run for local elections, and he realises he'll come under closer scrutiny from the authorities, he may be tidying up behind him so nobody can pull the rug from under his feet.'

Their food came to the table sizzling and crackling; the mix of spices smelled divine. His mouth watering, Bliss poured all three dishes onto a plate and mixed it all together with a fork. Chandler, he noted, ate from each individual bowl. She broke off a piece of naan and appeared to think of something she couldn't wait to say.

'I think I've been patient enough. When are you going to tell me why you went to London on your own this morning?' She popped the bread into her mouth afterwards so as not to talk around it.

Bliss did his best to look innocent. 'I thought I already had.'

Chandler finished chewing and swallowed with some difficulty. 'I don't think so. You told me what you thought you'd get away with telling me. I doubt there was a lot of truth in it.'

'In which case, what exactly do you think I left out?'

'To begin with, I think you were unsure of what was waiting for you down there. Meeting with a woman who used to be married to one of these psycho Doyle brothers you and Conway mentioned – what was it, Jimmy? Were you worried you might not be able to handle yourself if it all kicked off? Or do you think I can't?'

Bliss ate a portion of his food, allowing himself time to form a suitable response. 'Neither. I just didn't see any advantage in putting us both in the same awkward position.'

'You didn't see the benefit in having backup?'

'Pen, with these people, if you need backup it has to come by way of a Chieftain tank. No offence, but your entire nine stone, even in Rottweiler mode, would not have been a deterrent if things had turned to crap.'

'Why not go mob-handed, then, if you knew it could go side-ways? Why does it always have to be you fronting up on your own?'

Bliss held a hand up. Her voice had risen somewhat, and he wanted to calm her down. 'You're exaggerating. Look, I needed to slip in and out of there, on the QT. I thought it was something best managed on my own, leaving you to bring another aspect of the case further along while I was gone. We both achieved what we set out to as far as I can see, so all is well.'

'We both got the same end result, more or less,' Chandler said sharply. 'And I didn't have to move away from my desk.'

'Yes, but this way we now have confirmation. Two separate sources, which can never be a bad thing.'

'Not unless one of those sources happens to be surrounded by a bunch of lunatics who, when they spot a copper on his own, are willing and able to make sure that copper never makes it home again.'

Bliss set his fork down. 'You're giving me heartburn. Seriously. Stop nagging and eat. What's done is done. We need to make sense of what we've learned, and we start by having words with Phil Walker.'

They ate in silence for a few minutes. Whenever she was angry or frustrated with him, Chandler needed time to compartmentalise her feelings before continuing as if nothing was wrong. She excelled at it, too. If she entertained grudges, they were held in abeyance until disintegrating entirely at some point in the future .

Bliss took two calls during the meal. In Chandler's absence from the office, Bishop was nominally leading the case from HQ. Superintendent Conway, he told Bliss, had provided an update on the situation at his end. His report contained a minor link between Earl Dobson and Tommy Harrison; both men had been questioned in connection with a raid on a brothel in the late eighties, witness statements putting the pair together at the same time on several occasions inside a house being used by prostitutes. The fresh information was enough for Bliss; he was now convinced Dobson was an occasional member of the same gang as Harrison, Carlisle and Swift. Which essentially also tied him to Phil Walker.

That name again.

The second call was from Harlow police station. Uniformed officers had visited Walker's address on two further occasions, but had so far been unable to make contact. They had questioned neighbours living on the same floor as Walker's flat, but the one person who admitted knowing him had no insight as to where the man might be. The last known sighting was a month ago. Bliss thanked the officer, and asked for the visits to continue whenever crews were in the area until Walker was finally spoken to.

When he was finished with the calls, Chandler was waiting for him with a question. 'So, let's talk about the leak. I take it you have something in mind?'

Bliss took a quick pull from his glass. 'Yes, and I'm going to need everybody to support me on this. So, when we get back to HQ, I need you to tell the team to follow my play, irrespective of what they hear. We have to narrow it down. That's the first thing. Easiest way is to feed different intel to Conway and Riseborough.'

Chandler looked up from her plate. 'Risky. Lying to a superior comes with all manner of consequences, no matter how well-intentioned. Conway isn't going to like it, Jimmy.'

'Well, he's going to have to lump it. It's the right call. Besides, I won't be lying to a more senior officer if I feed *him* the correct information.'

'Okay. And the next step?'

'Is a bigger risk. Which is why you're staying out of it.'

Chandler put her fork down with a clatter. 'What is it with you? When will you ever learn to trust people? Me, especially.'

'No, it's not that,' Bliss said abruptly. 'This has nothing to do with trust. I'm protecting you. If what I have in mind goes pear-shaped, it's me who gets taken down for it. There's no need to involve you or anybody else, so I'm not going to. And there's no point in arguing the toss with me, because my mind is made up.'

His DS slipped into silence once again, and Bliss took the moment to make a call of his own. He asked DC Gratton to run a PNC check on any vehicles belonging to Walker, and to flag them as possibly being driven by a person of interest in their investigation; if any ANPR cameras recorded the licence plate, police would be alerted. He also asked Gratton to instigate a search on any mobile phones owned by the man, and to obtain authorisation to run a trace on them and gain access to their records. Bliss would love to have listened to the voicemails or read any messages which might offer clues as to Walker's whereabouts, but these were out of bounds. His final request was for a search of the land registry to see if Phil Walker owned another home.

'You want me to verify the Prices' alibi?' Chandler asked when he finally put his phone down on the table.

Bliss knew this signified their spat was over, though not forgotten. 'Yes, please. It seemed legit enough, but let's run it down anyway.'

'They could just as easily have hired somebody to do the hard graft for them.'

'I know. That same thought occurred to me at the time. But one of the compelling arguments for the revenge motive is how personal these mutilations are. I can't see either the father or son paying somebody else to inflict them – it seems to me they would want to do it themselves.'

'Was that before or after they dropped the bombshell about Valerie Price killing herself?'

It was a valid point, which Bliss acknowledged with a shrug. 'Before. So yes, we can't ignore how significant her suicide may have been in triggering either or both men. It would have made 1994 seem like yesterday all over again, and this fresh loss must have made an impact. Tell you what – let's get into their financials, Pen. If they're shelling out for someone else to do this on their behalf, it's not going to be cheap. Unless they happened to have a cash stash prior to these events, it's going to be hard for them to hide a transaction of this magnitude.'

Chandler took a notebook from her bag and scribbled something on a fresh page. Bliss wondered if his partner was aware that she had taken over Mia Short's proclivity for making copious notes during an investigation. At least she hadn't gone as far as to continually tap her pen on the pad; that particular habit of Mia's had driven Bliss crazy at times. He winced at the stab of pain from the memory. There was nothing he would not give to still be suffering at her hands.

'How's Shrek?' he asked, looking to steer the conversation away from work for the final few minutes of their break.

'He's terrific, thanks. Why'd you ask?'

'No particular reason. You like him, don't you?'

'I do. We're having a nice time together, and we make each other happy.'

'That's always a good sign. He seems like a decent enough bloke.'

She narrowed her eyes. 'What, no warning lecture? No insisting he may be too good to be true?'

'Nope. Pen, if you and I can't sum a person up inside one or two meetings, we don't deserve to be doing this job. Shrek may or may not turn out to be the man of your dreams, but he's not a wrong'un. He won't feature in your nightmares.'

Bliss had already run a background check on the man she was dating, though he had not told her about it. She would regard the move as one protective and intrusive step too far, so it was best she never found out. It had made him feel better about the relationship, though, and meant he could relax knowing Chandler was in safe hands.

'What's the latest from Anna?' he asked. 'Any plans to meet up?'

'I'm due off this weekend, so we're having lunch together on Saturday and spending the afternoon shopping in Cambridge. Unless I'm needed for the op, of course.'

Bliss popped a mint into his mouth, nudging it to one side with his tongue. 'Screw that. Take your days off and enjoy time with your daughter, Pen. You missed out on enough as it is. Besides, we'll get by without you.' He shook his head. 'I'm still utterly amazed how well you two have fitted together again after all those years apart.'

'I know. It's still so horribly sad that I missed out on all those years, all those firsts, birthdays and Christmases, her growing up, graduating school. But I also missed out on the terrible teens, that parental fear of her living her own life. In truth, I don't feel quite how I always imagined I would with a daughter. I suppose in some ways it's more like we're friends who are related, having to grow into a deeper relationship over time. So it's awkward sometimes, but I'm grateful for every moment I get to spend with her.'

Bliss stretched out a hand across the table to grasp hers. Her small and thin fingers were warm. 'The fact that she gave herself up to you so completely tells me she couldn't be happier to have you in her life. Sure, having not been with you since she was two is bound to make things a bit strained at times. But you're still her mother. She's still your daughter. The time you spent apart can't negate a connection like that. In time, I'm sure it'll be as if those intervening years never existed.'

Chandler flashed a wide smile and gave a nod of appreciation. 'Thank you, Jimmy. You always know what to say.'

'Either that, or I know what you need to hear.'

'Same thing.'

'Let's hope so. But I'm right. I genuinely believe that.'

'So, what's your next plan of attack, boss?' she said, freeing her hand from his to signify their personal time was at an end. 'Any inclination to drive back down to London again without me?'

Bliss groaned inwardly. He'd been right – she had not forgotten. 'Not at the moment, Pen. To tell the truth, I feel at a bit of a loss. We're making progress, but there's nothing moving us closer to locating Harrison, Carlisle or Dobson. I have my doubts as to whether any of them are still alive, but they might be. And in my view, that's worse than the alternative, especially if we don't find them soon. However, right now I think our way to them is through Phil Walker or Freddy Swift.'

'Because neither of them has been touched,' Chandler said.

'Precisely. Because neither of them has been touched.'

TWENTY-NINE

B LISS WAS MEETING WITH DCIs Warburton and Edwards when DS Bishop rushed into the room to interrupt. Warburton had asked for an update as she was unable to attend the evening briefing; his previous boss, Alicia Edwards, elected to sit in at the last minute. He'd outlined the day's events in the same way as he had to Chandler, assuring both Chief Inspectors that irrespective of however slow their progress to date, there was now momentum and several clear investigative paths for them to follow. Edwards was the first to respond, agreeing with him but moving swiftly on to the issue of his trip to London.

'Skipping your morning briefing and taking these interviews on your own was a little extreme, don't you think?'

'I'm not quite sure what you mean?' Bliss frowned as if bemused.

Edwards widened her expression. 'And you can cut that look out, Inspector. I've seen it before, and it won't wash this time. Feigning innocence is not your particular forte. Let me put it another way, one you might understand better: what do you think Jennifer Howey's reaction would be to your decision?'

Using the service therapist against him was a low blow. Howey was his Kryptonite, having seen through him with dispiritingly regular ease. 'I'm guessing she wouldn't be overly happy,' Bliss admitted. 'On the other hand, she may assign motives to my decision that don't exist in reality. Just as you appear to be doing.'

'So you didn't go down there on your own expressly to protect your DS from the potential dangers of consorting with the ex-wife of one of the nastiest villains to run an empire in London since the sixties?'

'Not exactly, no.'

'Bliss?'

When DCI Edwards used his surname, he knew he was pushing it too far. He looked to Warburton for support, but she stared back at him in silence. 'Okay… well, not entirely. Look, boss, you know how it is when you have something in common with people and others don't. Penny is a superb detective with a great head on her shoulders, and she's as stoic and unruffled as they come. But there are times when like opens up to like; that's the plain and simple truth. I thought if I spoke face to face with Siobhan Daley as a fellow Londoner, someone who knew the score the way she did, I'd get more out of her. Yes, I also realised my visit might stir up a trickle of animosity among the locals, and yes, it's true that I didn't want any of that shit to rain down on my colleague. I've already had a bollocking from her, which was more than enough punishment for one day, believe me.'

'I rather think that's my decision,' Warburton said. She took a deep breath, her expression grim. 'Jimmy, we can't keep going down this same road without changes being made.'

'Do I not score any points for delegating? Howey was always banging on about my iffy delegation skills, and by conducting those interviews myself I left Chandler and Bishop to run the ship between them.'

Warburton bounced clasped hands on the desk, her thumbs steepled. 'Nice try, Inspector, but that isn't going to cut it. This ought not to be a vicious cycle. Your entire team accepts your ways – for now. But if you constantly pour doubt on their ability to do the job properly, eventually their loyalty towards you may start to dissipate. Do you understand what I'm telling you?'

Bliss edged forward on his chair, forcing himself not to fold his arms. 'I do. If they stop trusting me, I lose my effectiveness. I get that. But at the time, when I'm making those decisions, I admit I don't view things in the same light. It's only afterwards, when I reflect or when I'm pulled up on it like I am now, that I realise my choices may be misinterpreted as doubting my colleagues' ability. You have to know that genuinely is not the case.'

'I do, Jimmy. But do they?'

She had made her point; they both had. Although Warburton was his direct line manager, the fact remained that Edwards was his superior too, and as such he had to suck it up. He knew he was in the wrong, yet still he felt the urge to defend his actions. Knowing it would make no difference here and now, he held his tongue. Warburton shifted gears, keen to learn which new investigative lead he favoured. He'd just finished telling both women of his inclination towards Phil Walker being his chief suspect, when Bishop started rapping his knuckles on the door. Warburton beckoned him in and asked what was so urgent that it couldn't wait until the meeting was over.

'Sorry, boss. Ma'am. Ma'am,' he said, looking between them. 'But we just got word of another find and I thought you'd want to know as soon as. This time it's the man we've been trying to get hold of – Phil Walker. Or part of him, at least.'

The news struck like a solid kick to the gut, but Bliss recovered swiftly. 'If it's only just been discovered, how do we know it's Walker?'

'It's not a hundred percent until DNA comes through, but the hand they found this time had a distinctive tattoo on the back.

Penny ran a check on the records for both Walker and Swift, and under distinguishing marks, Walker has the exact same ink.'

Bliss lowered his head for a moment, regrouping. The timing was spectacularly awful, but it would have come as a blow at any time. This did more than put a major dent in his theory; it tore it apart at the seams and scattered its contents to the four corners. He stood and looked down at Warburton. 'Are we finished here, boss? I want to get into this right away.'

His DCI gestured towards the open door. 'Of course. Do what needs to be done. Keep me briefed, Inspector. I'll keep DCI Edwards and DSI Fletcher up to speed.'

'I cannot believe this,' Bliss said to Bishop as they walked to the incident room. His jaw was set so firmly he barely got the words out. 'I've just this second finished telling the boss Walker was our main suspect.'

'I bet you're feeling like a bit of a tit right now, then.'

'Yes, thank you for pointing that out, Sergeant.'

Bishop grinned and winked at him. 'He was an obvious candidate, boss. The Price men may have had motive and a serious trigger to kick all this off, but they also have the best of alibis. Which, by the way, Gul confirmed a few minutes ago.'

'Oh, bloody hell! So if it's not them and it's not Walker, where does that leave us? Who does it leave us with? Freddy Swift?'

'Or somebody entirely unknown to us.'

Bliss grimaced. He'd gone into the meeting believing the way forward had narrowed. Yet all it had taken was one alibi and one new find to put their investigation on its widest track yet – so wide, Bliss was unable to see either side. He was sure Swift was not their man, but they would have to interview him again, here at HQ this time, with a solicitor alongside him.

The mood inside the room was solemn. Every member of the team knew what the fresh find meant to their case. Bliss clapped his hands together to gain their attention, walking to the front to stand beside the whiteboards. He wasn't in the right frame of mind to deliver words of optimism, but he was still their leader.

'Okay, listen up. Obviously, this comes as a serious blow. Walker looked good for it, but now he's another victim. The Prices have a strong alibi. But we can't allow this news to demolish our operation – there are still jobs to do. Bish, at the conclusion of this briefing I want you to go and bring Freddy Swift in for questioning. Arrest him if you have to. Get him here under false pretences if need be. Say we want to discuss his use of underage girls in his mucky movies. The kid me and Pen saw happened to be legal, but not all of them will have been. He's the type.'

'And other than Swift?' Bishop asked.

'I'm afraid we're going to have to start all over again. I'll have a chat with DSI Conway and DI Riseborough. We'll see if between us we can come up with any other decent leads. Otherwise, we'll have to trawl through those names we do have, make a list of all known acquaintances, and go through them one by one.' Bliss held a hand up in the air to quell the sudden hubbub of disquiet among his team. 'I know, I know. It's going to be a tough old grind from this point on unless we get a lucky break. A thankless task. But it's the job. Now, somebody talk to me about this latest find.'

Chandler, who was also on her feet by one of the room's two windows, outlined what they had so far. 'The hand was found inside a white carrier bag at something called the Redoubt Fort in North Weald, which is the village where our victim, Phil Walker, lives. Lived. Whatever. Apparently, the fort is an old defence relic, now derelict.'

'Another historical site,' Bliss remarked. 'Any engravings?'

'No. Not this time.'

'I wouldn't have expected any. Whoever did this gave us all he needed to with the first three deposits. By now he knows we're following up on the Geraldine Price murder, so there's no need for further markings. And mentioning Price brings me back to Freddy Swift. Both Pen and I got the distinct impression he already knew about the slices removed from Geraldine's body before she was dumped. If our suspicions don't exactly make him our offender, he's most definitely in the frame for something… Pen, if you've not already done so, get hold of the porn star Swift said he'd met with on Monday morning. And her agent. Confirm his story, but make sure they both understand we'll be wanting written statements. That may spook one of them if they're covering for him.'

Everybody swung into gear. Two uniforms new to the team that morning were given actions to run down, their contributions to the investigation far greater than standing guard outside an address or lifting tape for detectives. Bliss appreciated their presence on his operations. They were superb at chasing down leads and running ad hoc interviews, and were always on hand whenever Bliss and his team carried out arrests. He and his fellow suits were so often bathed in the narrow glare of attention, but he valued the unsung heroes. He also looked to them for potential future recruits.

With Phil Walker now a victim rather than a suspect, Bliss regarded the latest find as a step backwards. He'd drive down to visit the scene, but his own responsibilities in this case were now clear. The answers, he believed, lay buried in the 1994 murder investigation. Which was where he would start digging, as soon as he was finished in North Weald.

THIRTY

Aᴜɴɪꜰᴏʀᴍᴇᴅ ꜱᴇʀɢᴇᴀɴᴛ ɢᴜɪᴅᴇᴅ ᴛʜᴇᴍ along a narrow dirt track before striking out across a field of unkempt grass that lapped against their thighs as they pushed through it. Bliss was glad he had dressed casually, though he could have done with sturdier footwear than trainers. On the far side of the open land, they followed the officer through a gap in a section of half-hearted fencing where the original steel panels had been replaced with chain-link, which had in turn been clipped and pulled back to create a wide enough opening for people to enter grounds belonging to the Ministry of Defence. Their route within the compound took them through thick woodland that felt preternaturally cold and gloomy in the fading sunlight, an eerie silence seeming to press down on them from within the canopy of branches above.

Emerging from the woods into dense undergrowth, they came across a dome-like shape, its metallic skin stained green by time and exposure. 'What the bloody hell is that thing?' Chandler asked as they tramped through fallen branches and leaves that turned to dust beneath their feet. 'It looks like a Dalek buried up to its neck.'

'A pill box,' the sergeant replied over his shoulder. His name was Wallace, his demeanour courteous rather than friendly. 'Machine guns would have been mounted inside. If you look beyond, you can see the entrance passage – it's remained open ever since the fort was built.'

Bliss had known what it was the moment he laid eyes on it, but was astonished by its size. The top hatch was still in place but ajar, the side panel missing altogether. He tried and failed to imagine how unbearably cramped and noisy it must have been for whoever had to man the guns. Given the location, he doubted they had ever been used for anything other than practice sessions.

'Daleks don't have necks,' Bliss whispered from one side of his mouth, shaking his head at Chandler.

'Yes, they do,' Chandler hissed. 'It's that three-ring grille thing.'

'Are you sure? I thought that was part of the head.'

'It's a neck, now shut up about it.'

Bliss shook his head again. 'Bloody nerd.'

'This place had to be guarded at all times,' Wallace went on. 'It was the first mobilisation centre built as part of the London defence system. Many tons of weapons and ammunition were stored here for the batteries and infantry.'

'It must have been enormous,' Bliss said.

'It still is. It's dilapidated now, of course, but most of the structure is still solid enough. It has to be all of five hundred feet across, and it's built in a rather odd semicircular shape. Plenty of people in this area will tell you the fort is haunted, but I can't say I've ever seen or heard anything.'

'You're local, then,' Chandler said conversationally.

'Oh, yes. Born and bred. I know these parts like the back of my hand.'

'I'm glad we had a guide.'

Bliss nodded; Chandler was echoing his own thoughts. The woods were not deep, but the fort they were heading towards was built below ground, so would not have been easy to find alone.

They emerged into a clearing and he saw the first concrete ridge appear in the earth in front of them. A question had been niggling away at Bliss since the location had first been divulged, but as soon as they reached the lip, exposing a wide corridor of land between the crest and the construction itself, he had his answer.

'I get it now,' he muttered.

Chandler caught it. 'Get what?'

'The other finds were all in areas where the carrier bags would be readily discovered. This place is old MoD property, tucked away behind fencing, in the middle of the woods… I didn't understand that aspect at all.'

She looked at the low building beneath them, then back to Bliss. 'And now you do?'

'Yep. Look at all the graffiti. Some of the tagging is still shiny. I bet kids come here every day.'

Wallace eyed him with renewed interest as he shortened his stride. 'You're spot on, Inspector,' he said. 'We send in a presence a couple of times a week, but rarely catch the little buggers at it. During the winter and spring we don't have to worry about it, because these tunnels get flooded out. Not enough to ward off your hardened ghost-hunters, but no self-respecting tagger is going to wade through this place just to spray a can of paint.'

They located a set of concrete steps which they began to descend, Wallace leading them along the wide-open ditch past two entrances. Ahead and above the far wall, Bliss spotted a couple of brick-built houses whose innards had been completely gutted, along with the roofs and windows. He guessed they had been administration offices, perhaps living quarters. A chill ran between his shoulder blades as he thought of all the people now long gone who had once filled this fort with discordant noise and bustle. At the third entrance – a short tunnel leading into the heart of the main storage area itself – Wallace came to a complete halt. He gestured towards the inside. 'Over there is where the bag was found.'

Bliss immediately became aware of the absence of movement. There were no other police officers, no local detectives, nor any sign of a forensics team. 'Where the bloody hell is everybody?' he asked.

Wallace raised his eyebrows. 'You just said it yourself, Inspector. This is MoD property. We have an agreement to patrol and enter the grounds in order to keep the place as clear as possible, but we have no remit to carry out an investigation here without their authorisation. They haven't given us the nod to do so yet. By rights, I shouldn't even be showing you two around.'

Bliss scratched the back of his neck. His MI5 contact would be able to open up that particular door if necessary – but judging by the condition of the place, he did not foresee even the best of CSI managers obtaining any worthwhile forensics here. The mass of evidence would surely confuse matters further still. Then something else occurred to him.

'Hold on. If that's the case, who has the bag? Who has the hand?'

The sergeant turned to him, smiling for the first time. 'Oh, I made sure my officers removed it, Inspector. I wouldn't have trusted the MoD not to turn up and pilfer it for themselves. It's currently being biked up to your forensics lab in Huntingdon. You must have passed it on your drive down.'

Bliss thanked him; it was a good move on the man's part. He'd met plenty of coppers, including fellow detectives, who would have balked at messing with the MoD, so removing the find had been smart and courageous thinking on Wallace's part.

Meanwhile, Chandler was rubbing her arms through her light-weight jacket. 'No wonder people say the place is haunted,' she said. 'It's downright creepy.'

Bliss nodded. 'Yeah, all those buried Daleks are enough to give anyone the willies.'

Chandler screwed her face up and saluted him with the usual two digits. Wallace ignored them both. 'Locals tell me their kids have reported hearing footsteps, orders being shouted out. Nothing official, mind – just pub chatter. I tell them their kids shouldn't be close enough to the fort to be able to hear anything, which usually shuts them up. I've been here more times than I care to remember and never heard a thing out of place. As for the imagination, we're dealing with another thing entirely, I reckon.'

Bliss's attention was on the tagging at the entrance to the tunnel. None of it looked as if it was still drying out. He turned to Wallace once again. 'I assume it was one of your local graffiti artists who reported it?'

'Bound to be. Anonymous call from a phone box outside the railway station, down the road from here.'

It made sense. A kid – or more likely a gang of them – came to demonstrate their artistic flair and instead discovered a severed hand. Enough to send them scarpering before they even managed to uncap their spray cans. But at least one of them must have had a conscience.

There was one thing still bothering him. The relevance of the location had been explained: historical, and with every chance of the bag being found within a day. But this was no easy place to find. It was certainly not a tourist trap, nor widely known about, as far as he was aware. He'd lived in London for decades, and had never heard of it, though it was at most a twenty-five-mile drive from Mile End. So how had their man known about this vestige of war in the small village where Phil Walker lived?

He shuddered; whether it was the thought of the man they were hunting, the horrors he was inflicting on other men, or the chilling effect of this cold and miserable place, Bliss was not sure. He knew only one thing with absolute certainty: he wanted to leave, and he hoped never to return.

THIRTY-ONE

T HEY BARELY SPOKE DURING the drive into London the following
morning. Chandler hadn't slept well and kept dozing off, mut-
tering to herself every so often. Bliss, who felt he functioned better
on small amounts of sleep than on a solid eight hours, watched
the countryside flash by in a blur and concentrated on the case.

Following their visit to North Weald the previous evening, Bliss
had spoken to Bishop, requesting a warrant to enter and search
Walker's flat and any of his vehicles and garages. He'd turned to
Chandler afterwards, suggesting they spend the night at a local hotel
and save themselves a couple of lengthy drives. Bliss convinced her
Warburton would stump up part of the budget in order to keep her
detectives fresh. Chandler had given in without a fight.

He and his faithful companion ate dinner at a chain pub, discussing their experience of the old fort and the unease it had elicited,
as well as making plans for the next day. In the boot of his car they
each had an overnight bag containing clothes and basic toiletries;
something Bliss had always insisted they carry. After dinner they
had one final drink at the bar before Bliss called it a day. He had
brought his work laptop with him, and he wanted to dig into the

case files again. In addition, he hadn't caught up with either Conway or Riseborough all day, and he owed them both an update.

Those conversations had not gone as well as he had hoped. Conway was annoyed at being left out in the cold for virtually an entire day, and when Bliss related the news about the fresh discovery, his frustration became vocal and loud. Quietly soothing the DSI's bruised ego, Bliss said he would call for a face-to-face meeting as soon as he returned to Thorpe Wood. Given his unique connection to the case, Conway had no choice but to accept Bliss's apology and strategy, but he made his feelings quite clear.

They agreed that Gablecross should focus their efforts more precisely on Earl Dobson; Conway claimed the individual task of tracking down local journalists who worked the original case, to see how many of them knew more than they should, and whether those details had somehow leaked out at the time. Bliss realised he was putting a lot of emphasis on what he and Chandler believed Freddy Swift did or did not know, and was keen to rule out common knowledge as a factor.

Max Riseborough was a different matter altogether. Bliss changed one crucial fact when discussing the recent find with him; he said the victim had yet to be identified, but that he was expecting an update within the next twenty-four hours. Riseborough took in the new intel, but immediately complained about his team being grossly underused since their CCTV trail had gone cold. Other than drilling down into Tommy Harrison's background, they had been allocated little in the way of caseload. Bliss accepted the rebuke and gave his apologies; he would have felt the same in Riseborough's shoes, but the man was making a big deal out of nothing. He attempted to pacify the DI by explaining how difficult it was to include a team unknown to him and based so far away – but, thinking quickly, offered up Freddy Swift as an olive branch.

'I was going to have his sorry arse dragged into Thorpe Wood to interview,' he explained. 'But DS Bishop was unsuccessful in tracking him down. Swift also failed to show up at work today, which suggests we spooked him. He's all yours if you want him, Max.'

Riseborough did. 'Anything specific you'd like me to push him on once we have him?'

Bliss admired the DI's confidence. Thinking in terms of 'when' rather than 'if' was the sign of a fine leader. It gave him pause. 'Yes, there is. For my money, he knew more than he should have when we spoke to him – especially about the Geraldine Price case. I mentioned the slicing of flesh and he reacted as if he was familiar with it, though it was never revealed at the time by the media. To be honest with you, Max, I still don't see him as our doer, and neither did Penny when we met him, but he's either involved with the cold case or he knows somebody who was.'

In truth, he was keen to keep both Riseborough and Conway working the edges; the meat and drink would go to his own team until he was told otherwise. He had nothing against either man or their units, but Conway had a reputation to maintain, and Bliss did not want to be misled either by an act of self-preservation or a simple lapse of memory on his part. More to the point, he did not wish to confuse the two. As for Riseborough, he seemed decent, both as a man and a copper, but he had also worked closely with Conway in the past. Bliss wanted to take any misplaced loyalty off the board.

Before turning in, Bliss had sent a text message, and the request he made applied a layer of guilt all over his skin. Providing different information to both Conway and Riseborough was an act both men would undoubtedly frown upon, but Bliss knew they would eventually understand why he'd done it; this latest move, however necessary he believed it to be, would create a lasting storm of controversy. As he started drifting off, his phone stirred, and when he checked the message, Bliss knew he was in for a sleepless night.

He recalled those conversations and message exchanges as he took the slip road onto the Woodford New Road towards Whipps Cross. He'd spent the night tossing and turning, but by dawn he had made peace with his decision. Now he had to forget about it and move on. He hung a left at a junction that had once been a sizeable roundabout. Chandler stirred from her slumber as he drove past the hospital, which was opposite a leisure spot known as Hollow Pond. Bliss had fond memories of boating out on its lake and splashing around at the lido – now long gone, covered over so well it might never have existed – with his friends. The Leyton Flats was a green area of suburbia in which families congregated during sweltering summer months. When the ponds and the outdoor swimming pool were too overcrowded, wide open spaces lay nearby on which you could kick a ball around or play a game of cricket.

It was another bright day, warm but overcast, but the small car park was virtually empty as they passed. As Chandler blinked the fog of sleep away and stretched out her arms, Bliss felt nostalgia wash over him. Rather than drip from his body, it clung, seeping into his pores. His childhood had been one of simple pleasures, days filled with laughter and action and a few minor transgressions along the way. He wondered where the local kids were now – sitting at home playing video games, or out earning their colours by stabbing some unsuspecting innocent. It was a radically different world from the one he had grown up in; if this was progress, Bliss did not want any part of it.

'What the hell did you just experience?' Chandler asked.

Bliss glanced across to his left. Her stare was a curious mix of intrigue and concern. 'What d'you mean?'

'You had this distant smile on your face. As if you were reliving a wonderful experience inside your head… but all at once your smile turned upside down and something dark passed across your face.'

He didn't think he could explain. Not in any meaningful way. He guessed she had experienced her own childhood pleasures, but the tumble from joyful reminiscence to deep melancholy was harder to appreciate. It was not a place he wanted to take his friend.

'Sorry,' he said. 'I don't know where I was. Drifted off, I suppose.'

'That's not at all comforting considering you're the one behind the wheel, old man.' Chandler added a smile, but Bliss saw his lapse had disturbed her.

All of the properties were on the right-hand side of the road. Bliss eyed the car's navigation system; the moving image told him the house they wanted was less than fifty yards away. One of many similar three- and four-storey houses along Whipps Cross Road, the home belonging to ex-DCI Drayton had been significantly modernised. From what Bliss could see of the other houses on the same stretch, Drayton's was the only one not to have been converted into either flats or a B&B.

Bliss had arranged via text for DC Ansari to call ahead and make arrangements, preparing Drayton for their visit. He'd suggested Bliss park on the driveway, but then head across to the large field opposite the house, where Drayton would be watching a five-a-side football tournament. Ansari had given the former detective chief inspector a vague idea of the subject matter, and within a few minutes of shaking hands Bliss and Chandler found themselves standing with him by the side of an unmarked pitch with collapsible goalposts at either end.

'My grandson is playing,' Drayton explained. He pointed towards a tall, skinny kid wearing a bright yellow training bib. 'The one with his socks rolled down, despite my protestations.'

The two detectives watched the game with him for a few minutes. The team wearing blue bibs were the dominant force, but Drayton's grandson was playing a blinder.

'He's pretty good,' Bliss acknowledged, shortly after the boy had robbed an opponent of the ball and sent a slide rule pass down the left-hand channel between two players.

'You like the game?' Drayton said over his shoulder.

'Oh, yeah. Chelsea supporter since I was a nipper.'

The man pulled a face as if he'd bitten into something rotten. 'Owned by a Russian oligarch. Do you ever consider how he made his fortune when they splash out their millions?'

Bliss hiked his shoulders. 'For all I know, he earns his money legitimately. Do you know otherwise?'

This time Drayton turned fully. He smiled and said, 'Is it possible to earn so many billions legitimately in Russia?'

'Oil is oil.'

'And Putin is Putin. Nice to have friends like that.'

'I wouldn't know. I don't move in those kinds of circles.'

'Right. And you didn't drive all the way here to listen to me rant about money ruining the game I love. Besides, your partner's looking bored. Football not your game, DS Chandler?'

'Not so's you'd notice. I'm not into sports in general.'

Bliss and Drayton exchanged bewildered looks, reaching a shared understanding: people who didn't like sport were somehow lacking. The moment seemed to thaw a little of the ice Bliss felt had been building up.

The blue team scored and immediately the referee blew for half-time. Drayton gave his grandson a clap and a few words of encouragement. When he returned, he led Bliss and Chandler out of earshot of the players and coaches. 'Fire away,' he said. 'Though I warn you now, I don't see how I'm going to be of any help.'

Drayton was a man of average height, and the sag of his skin told Bliss he had lost weight recently. Liver spots covered his mostly bald head like a spray of freckles, his bare arms and hands not escaping the markings time left behind. He had not aged well. Bliss thanked him and took up the offer. 'You were a DS working under Pete Conway back in 1994, is that right, Morris?' The ex-detective had asked them to use his first name.

'I was. He'd not long been made up to inspector. I was asked to partner up with him to add some experience.'

'Did you think he was too inexperienced to run the Geraldine Price investigation?'

Drayton moistened his lips and shifted on his feet, clearing his throat before he responded. 'When it came to major and serious crimes, you cut your teeth early in those days. I'm sure you'd agree, Inspector Bliss. I bet your first cases were no cakewalks.'

Bliss remembered them well. Especially the first. He nodded. 'I was as green as they come. Did my time in uniform, of course, but working CID was a different matter. Landed my first big one after a few weeks. We were after a couple of brothers for several armed robberies. They were originally into wage snatches, but when that game dried up they turned to safes and armoured vans. I was thrown in at the deep end, undercover with a bunch of blaggers. I got roped in as their new safe man, which was fine because we were working hand-in-hand with the warehouse they were going to hit, so we had all the inside information we needed. It was one of those ops where nothing could go wrong... until it did. That first break might easily have been my last. So, yes, I understand why Pete was given such a high-profile case.'

'He was nervous about it,' Drayton said. 'But he remained composed at all times, and had some bloody good ideas when things didn't quite go our way. It wasn't his fault we never got a result; nobody would have in that place. The scum of the earth came together as a community, all right – not to find out who murdered one of their own, though, oh no. They formed a wall of silence and left us grasping at straws.'

'You still sound bitter about it,' Chandler observed.

He looked up. 'You're damned right I am. They all knew Price was a normal woman trying to make her way in life. They knew she'd been dumped and left for dead, and word soon got around about her being sexually abused. But instead of reaching out to us for answers, they pulled their doors together and slammed them tight. Nobody wanted to know, and any who did kept it to themselves.'

Bliss picked up on something. 'You say word got around. That's one of the things we're keen to find out about. How much leaked, Morris? That you're aware of?'

'You mean the stuff we opted to keep from the media? Nothing, so far as I know.'

'No information passed on to reporters for a decent backhander?'

Drayton shrugged. 'I can't be certain. I mean, anything's possible. All I can say is that to my knowledge it never appeared in the papers or on the news. I never heard a whisper about it. Usually, you'd get a journo call you up and ask you to confirm something they'd heard via a reputable source – you know the kind of thing – but not this time. You have to remember, this was as ugly as they come, and Mrs Price wasn't one of your usual toerags. To those of us on the case, she seemed like a lovely, beautiful woman doing her best for her family and trying to live her life. It was one of those cases that got its hooks into you.'

Bliss understood. You got used to seeing a lot of villain-on-villain crime, and although you did your job, you didn't break your back trying to solve it. And if there was money to be made, you dropped a hint or three to journalists looking for the inside word. Then along came a more meaningful investigation, everybody stepped up their game, and lips remained firmly pressed together.

The notion of operational silence and integrity was unspoken, but every uniform and suit involved became aware of the stakes.

'I've had several chats with Pete,' Bliss said. 'He'd like to be working it again, but he also understands he's too close. If what happened to Geraldine Price lit the fuse for what we're facing now, he's man enough to stand aside and allow us to get on with whatever we have to do. If that means asking awkward questions, so be it. He wants honest answers in the same way we do.'

'I understand you, Inspector. And in the spirit of full disclosure, I admit I called Pete first thing this morning. I didn't feel entirely happy having this conversation about him without first speaking with the man himself. Please don't misconstrue that as my attempting to obtain any kind of party line from him.'

'Of course not. How did he respond?'

'Much as you'd expect. He cut me short, refused to discuss the case with me, and insisted I should be forthcoming with you.'

'Good for him,' Chandler said. 'So why am I detecting reticence on your part?'

Bliss flashed her a look. He'd felt it, too, but was surprised she had gone for the jugular so soon. He hoped it wouldn't backfire on them.

Morris Drayton was smiling, but Bliss thought his face looked sad, perhaps something like his own countenance earlier as he'd driven past Hollow Ponds. The ex-DCI took a deep breath before speaking. 'You have to understand something. Pete and I were a fairly new team at the time. We became great friends as well as colleagues, but our partnership was in its infancy back then. I've already told you I liked his reaction when we hit a brick wall, but he also made errors of judgement. As did I.'

'And they were?' Bliss asked. 'His first, then yours, please.'

'I felt Pete should have fought harder against the idea of involving the Doyle brothers. Our Superintendent at the time – a man few of the team really trusted – suggested the idea. There were rumours of him taking payoffs for tips on raids, providing information. I told Pete the Doyle family were bad news and far too likely to be involved in some way for us to go begging. In my opinion, it gave the wrong impression. It felt as if we were telling them they ruled the streets, that they were in charge and not us.'

'He disagreed?'

'No. That's just it. He felt the same way. But he was eager to please, didn't know the Super the way we did, and so he caved. The fact that Mrs Price's body turned up a few days later – that it was more than likely dumped the same day we spoke to the Doyles – told me our suspicions about them were right.'

'And your errors?' Bliss asked. So far he had heard little more than he'd already guessed, and he put no blame on Conway for buckling beneath the weight of pressure from his superiors.

'I took it a stage further. In truth, I may have been pissed off at the decision and throwing my toys out of the pram. Whatever the reason, I took the same story and offered the same deal outside of the Doyle family. I'd not been instructed to do so, but neither had it been expressly forbidden. I took it as implied permission. At least, that's what I told myself.'

'So you approached other gangs in Hoxton and Islington. Asked them for their help in return for a blind eye turned at some point in the future?'

'Clerkenwell, too. But yes. And I didn't mention it to my guv'nor. Not until afterwards, at any rate.'

Bliss's head was buzzing. The area would have been on high alert, the local faces desperate to get the police off their streets and estates. One name in particular scratched at the back of his mind.

'Tell me something, Morris,' he said slowly, betraying no sign of the mounting excitement building inside him. 'Was one of those gangs you approached run by the Walker family?'

The man's eyes narrowed. 'Yes, it was.'

'That's interesting. And one last thing; this may be equally important. Did you ever inform Geraldine's husband? Did you tell him what you were doing or had done?'

Drayton swallowed and took his time to reply. When he did, his nod was apologetic, the voice softer and less assured. 'I did,' he said. 'And I'll always regret it.'

Bliss thought he knew the answer to his next question, but he asked it anyway. 'Why's that, Morris?'

'Because I saw in his eyes that all I had done was reignite his imagination, his pain and his anger.'

'What you told him affected him, then?'

'Yes. Yes, it did. More than I could ever have imagined.'

THIRTY-TWO

T HE RICKETY STABLES STOOD within a huge swathe of Wiltshire
land that had belonged to various members of the horseracing
fraternity for almost one hundred and sixty years. For much of
that time, local riders rented out the individual units, but as the
care of racehorses developed and technological advances began
to address their health and welfare, the original wooden stable
area became obsolete and was left to stand as a monument to its
creators – though not a memorial any of the dozen owners of
the five-thousand-acre estate had ever thought to maintain. In its
existing neglected condition, the structure built to house twenty
horses sat abandoned in the foothills of a ridge far from humanity,
no longer ridden or tended by ground staff. This made it ideal for
keeping a man strung up, no matter how loud or how often he
screamed.

Earl Dobson was dying. There was no doubt about it any more.
Weakened beyond all endurance by pain and misery, lack of food
and water, and exposure to the elements and the hunger of creatures,
he willed his body to tick away its final minutes like an unwound
clock and stop dead. He was done weeping, done asking why him,
done wondering why anybody.

As for the horror, the sheer terror of the past few days, it had all fused together somehow, existing in his mind as someone else's tall story. Someone else's imagined torment. Someone else's memory revealed as a dark nightmare. During rare moments of clarity he understood he would never see his family or friends again, nor his girlfriend or daughter. But he had long since accepted that as part of the overall deal. His suffering would eventually become their grief, and so the cycle went on.

His mind in a whirl and conjuring all manner of things that could not possibly be, Dobson heard the growl of an engine working its way towards the stables. His stomach lurched, already anticipating the next stage of his humiliation; he had soiled himself on several occasions and now had to live with the foul odours of his own effluence coating his legs and feet.

By now, the routine of his ordeal was familiar to him. A slight groan of brakes still a fair way off in the distance. Engine off. Door creaking open on uncertain hinges, then closed firmly. Repeated for a second door – collecting from the back seat, no doubt, the bag containing water, a solitary sandwich, and the tools wrapped in cloth. After a while, the sound of footsteps scratching their way across a gravel and stone courtyard directly outside the stable door. As they grew louder this time, he turned his head to witness the approach of his tormentor, determined not to show the merest hint of fear …

… and knew today was the day he would die.

For the first time, the man who had visited such outrage upon him, wore no sackcloth to mask his appearance. It meant only one thing. Dobson's vision was hazy and blurred from dehydration and fever, so it wasn't until the figure stood directly in front of him that the man's features coalesced into a face he recognised.

'You,' he croaked in a dry whisper.

The man said nothing. Instead he set down his backpack and slid a zip from one side to the other, opening up the large central section. This was the point at which he usually withdrew a bottle of water and a limp sandwich, followed by a cloth roll of various sharp tools and weapons.

But not today.

Today it was the axe alone, still smeared with dried blood and flecks of foul-smelling tissue.

The axe, but no butane blowtorch.

Dobson swallowed with difficulty.

Today there would be no cauterising of flesh rent asunder by the axe.

Today there would be nothing more than the chopping and cleaving of limbs.

'Why?' he asked with one of his final breaths.

When no response came, he managed to utter two further syllables: 'Thank you.'

The man appeared to study him for a moment. He parted his lips as if to respond, but instead of speaking, he nodded once and raised the axe.

THIRTY-THREE

Bliss fell silent as they drove away from an area that had been so familiar to him for such a large part of his life. A Pink Floyd lyric popped into his head; it spoke of grass being greener, lights brighter, and friends surrounding in nights of wonder. Which was exactly how he remembered his youth. He wondered if life only seemed better in retrospect as you peered back at it through the prism of time, or if in fact it had been a better world entirely? When the time came for him to take his last sigh, would he reflect on the present time as his halcyon days? Or was a golden age any but the one you were living in? Bliss thought he would never know the answer, and it bothered him.

Chandler must have sensed his low mood, cajoling him into discussing what they had learned from Morris Drayton, and how his information tied in with everything their case had thrown at them so far. Bliss admitted he was stumped, uncomfortably unde-cided. He had favoured Phil Walker as their prime suspect, but now the man was just another victim. If not for their alibis, either Andy Price or his son, Stephen, would be next up in the crosshairs; they fit the alternative theory perfectly. Either, or both – especially after Drayton had revealed his mistake of telling Andy Price about his efforts to reach out to the underworld. But to Bliss it still only worked if they carried out the ugly crimes themselves; the slicing revealed either a psychopathy characteristic of the old-time gangsters, or emotions stemming from injustice and loss. He saw nothing in between.

'Everything points towards the Prices,' he said. 'Except that we know they were elsewhere when Tommy Harrison's hand was dropped at Tower Hill, and I have a feeling we'll eventually discover they have alibis for the other time windows as well.'

'Which in itself would surely be a mark against them,' Chandler said. 'Nobody ever has an alibi for everything. Law of averages would be against it.'

'True. So they may not be able to provide evidence or witnesses to the first two finds, but we know they didn't drop the carrier bag off on Monday. Neither could they have removed the hand, because they were both in Manchester.'

'Which brings us back to them employing somebody else to do it.'

'Of course. But does it feel right to you? If it were me – if that had happened to my wife or mother, and then my daughter or sister spiralled into depression and addiction, and killed herself – I'd want to get hands-on with the bastards that caused it. I'd want them staring into my eyes while I hurt them, and I'd want to be inflicting all kinds of pain and misery on them myself, not farming it out to some mercenary.'

Bliss felt Chandler's eyes boring into him. He turned his head. 'What?'

'Do you hear yourself, Jimmy? Do you hear the raging psycho inside you trying desperately to get out?'

He scoffed. 'I don't mean *me*. Not literally me. I mean if I am them. If I'm them, that's how I'd want it to go down.'

'If you say so. Only… it didn't come across like that.'

'I put myself in their shoes. That's all.'

He didn't sound convincing, and in truth he wasn't sure how much of what he'd said stemmed from the darkest regions of his own heart. The beating he had given the fellow cop who murdered his wife, Hazel, was in no way similar to these current attacks, but he remembered how he'd felt as he administered blow after blow; or rather, the lack of feeling. He had not rejoiced at the sound of bones breaking, but neither had it repulsed him. It lasted a few minutes at most, but a sense of detachment had consumed him throughout. As if he were looking at someone else exacting their revenge in the most primitive of ways. No empathy, no remorse. Both classic markers of a psychopathic mind.

Chandler wasn't about to let go of it. 'Maybe you could do with a few sessions with your shrink,' she said. 'Iron out a few of those kinks you've built up lately.'

'Oh, behave yourself, Pen. I'm fine and we need to concentrate on the case. Look, we've not focussed on the drop locations in a wider sense. Forget the historical connection for the time being, because I think that's part of our man's MO. It's who he is and what he is, a preference is all, and the sites are irrelevant. Let's start at the beginning. We have Ben Carlisle, whose slice of flesh was left ten or fifteen miles from where he lived and close to where he was taken. Then there's Earl Dobson, whose flesh was found close to where he lived… no way of knowing where he was taken, but it's fair to assume it was locally because he had no need to be out of the area at the time. Phil Walker's hand couldn't have been left much closer to his home.'

'Which means?'

'It's a definite pattern – for those three victims. But when we look at Harrison, it changes. Lives in Theydon Bois but his hand is found by the Thames. Why the discrepancy?'

Chandler drew her hands down her face and let out a soft groan. 'You know what, Jimmy? I don't have a bloody clue. My head aches, my stomach is growling, I'm not sleeping well, and my focus is definitely not what it ought to be at the moment.'

'I hear you. This case has been gruelling. So, because Harrison doesn't fit the pattern, for the moment let's ignore where they lived and accept it has nothing to do with where their parts were found. In which case, we're left with where they were taken, or where they are or were being held. Nobody is going to cart chunks of flesh around for too long. If we go by the first two, I'm willing to bet Tommy Harrison was in London when he was taken. If I'm right, then I say he's still there.'

'Okay. I'm hearing a nice neat theory. But again, even if we accept everything you say as true, how does it help?'

Bliss was ready to counter her question. 'To keep a person for any length of time requires solitude plus easy and fairly regular access. There must be hundreds of suitable places around us, and down in Wiltshire. In North Weald, you've got the whole of Epping Forest and plenty of open land and farmyards to choose from. But Tower Hill is a different matter entirely. It's an anomaly. It may be nothing, but I don't think we can afford to ignore it.'

'What do you suggest?'

'I'm going to have a word with DI Riseborough, ask if he can think of anywhere within a fifteen- to thirty-minute drive of Tower Hill that meets the conditions. I imagine it'd be damned hard to find somewhere out of earshot and out of sight anywhere nearby, but he may have one or two bright ideas. There was a time when I would've suggested the docklands, but you can't move for hipsters and vegan cafes around there these days.'

'And if he has no idea?'

'Perhaps the Super will stump up some cash for a chopper and we can fly around and take a look for ourselves.'

Chandler choked back a laugh behind her fist. 'Yeah, good luck with that. But seriously, while I think it's a fine idea to change our focus, we'd have to cast a wide net, boss.'

Bliss agreed. It was hopeful at best, and he had never been a fan of hope.

His mind itching for additional intelligence and consumed by the lack of progress, Bliss pulled off the motorway at Epping and found a parking bay on the high street. He had Chandler check the *Daily Express* website. Without a word, she handed over her smartphone to show him the result. He read the piece with mounting anger and resentment.

'So it's Max's team,' Chandler said. She gave a small nod. 'You were right, it does at least narrow things down.'

Having hoped to be wrong, Bliss now sighed, considering the implications. 'Now all we have to do is manage the situation. I'll need to speak to the boss when we get back. And Pete Conway, of course.'

They had a bite to eat and a coffee at Subway, after which Bliss wandered back and forth along the pavement making a string of phone calls. The first of them lasted less than twenty seconds; Bliss asked one simple question, to which there was an equally direct response. He closed his eyes and took several deep breaths afterwards. The answer was one he had anticipated, but hearing it came as a blow.

Keeping his anger in check, he next spoke to Riseborough about intensifying the hunt for Harrison by searching for specific locations. The DI enthused over the positive move and said he'd pull in his team to thrash out some ideas. Bliss suggested an evening briefing for the JTFO senior team members – to take place in person rather than via videoconferencing. Having actively sought greater input, Riseborough was in no position to refuse.

Next up was Superintendent Conway. Bliss first mentioned the briefing, to which Conway readily agreed. Bliss swallowed; the next part was going to be far more difficult. 'Pete,' he said, 'some news on the leak. It came from Riseborough's team. In fact, from Max himself.'

'What? Are you positive?'

'I know you two were friends, but yes, I'm certain.'

'How?'

'With respect, I'd rather leave the details for the time being. I'll explain when I see you. There's an update in the *Express* online, so if Max contacts you about it, you need to go along with it. The article says we have yet to make a positive ID, so it contradicts the information I gave you about Phil Walker. That's how I knew it was his team, because I gave the incorrect intel to him.'

'Which he would have fed back to his team.'

Bliss understood Conway's desire to clutch at straws. The stench of betrayal was foul, and the DSI was bound to be taking the news badly. 'I agree,' he said. 'Which was why I also put in play a way to narrow it down further. I'm sorry, Pete, but it's definitely him.'

His final call was to DS Bishop. Freddy Swift had yet to be located, something both men agreed was a major concern.

Bliss made a rapid decision. 'I don't think we can hang around any longer, Bish. There's every possibility Penny and I tipped him with our visit and he's now on the run. I did give the job of pulling him in to Riseborough's team, but I don't want to wait. Apply for RIPA access to his phones. Let's trace him and see what surfaces. ANPR on his vehicles, too.'

The Regulation of Investigatory Powers Act governed covert surveillance, including access to all digital devices. Bliss accepted the need for the requirement – introduced at the start of the millennium – though he and his team understood how to manipulate the language required for authorisation. It was a game police authorities and their employees had to play, and Bliss always made sure his team knew the rules and how to take advantage of them.

'You think Swift is our man, boss?' Bishop asked.

'As it happens, I don't. But if it's not him, then I think he may know who it is, because if he's not running from us, he may be running from somebody else. By the way, did you rustle up that warrant I asked for?'

'I did.'

'Good man. In that case, would you call Harlow nick for me? Send a copy of the warrant to them and have a couple of uniforms meet me and Chandler there with it. We're only ten or fifteen minutes away.'

'On it now, boss.'

Bliss thanked his sergeant. With his calls out of the way and actions implemented, he and Chandler got back on the road, heading into North Weald once again.

THIRTY-FOUR

A LOCKSMITH FROM CHIPPING ONGAR with a sour disposition and the delicate hands of a Swiss watchmaker picked the lock on Phil Walker's front door rather than drilling it. Bliss had the two local uniforms wait outside while he and Chandler conducted a search of the premises. He wasn't sure what he hoped to find, but Walker was the only single victim so far. With no family to question, if they were going to gather answers, they would do so inside the suspect's flat.

As the pair had noted the first time they'd tried reaching Walker, the man's home bore none of the hallmarks of a successful business-man – from the outside. The interior, however, told a completely different story. It reeked of money and good taste. The fixtures and fittings were sleek and looked brand new. It was crisp and clean, everything in its place and positioned just so.

Though not large, the kitchen was beautifully equipped. Bliss checked out the cabinets and noticed a sticker affixed inside one of the drawers. He knew the name; a high-end company whose expert joiners individually designed and built the units. The company was based in Devizes – where Earl Dobson lived. Bliss wondered if that was another fluke, deciding it most likely was. A bulky Smeg cooking range dominated the room, still with its showroom sparkle. It was impossible to tell if a single meal had been cooked on it.

In the long narrow living room, Bliss admired the hi-fi system. Chandler must have noticed his eyes light up as he crouched down to run his appreciative gaze over the separate units. 'You boys and your toys,' she said, with a shake of her head.

Bliss kept his focus. 'Some toys. There's not far short of ten grand's worth here.' He stood upright, knees cracking like pistol shots. A shelf adjacent to the hi-fi overflowed with books, albums, and CDs. 'Hmm, our Mr Walker is a swing jazz man by the look of it. Big band stuff. Nice collection, too.'

Moving on to the books, Bliss immediately noticed the assortment he had fully expected to find. Lined up in a group were a dozen or so hardback books on the subject of torture, including ancient, medieval and modern. Several philosophical studies of the topic stood out, while a few appeared to be more exploitative. Some of the glossy illustrations were extreme in nature, with beheadings and disembowelling seemingly popular subjects. Among the grotesquery, Bliss recognised portrayals of Dante's *Inferno*. He wasn't sure what the pieces said about Phil Walker's state of mind, but given the work was so familiar, he also had to question his own psychological makeup.

Among the many collected works were books investigating historical and legendary spots around the United Kingdom. Bliss noted two devoted to myths associated with standing stones, and a few others about 'haunted' monuments and disused sites. Intrigued, he began to work through an idea.

In the bedroom he came upon something even more disturbing. Ranged along the wall opposite the bed hung a number of framed prints, each of which portrayed crucifixion scenes. Two of them were named: *The Martyrdom of St Andrew*, by Antonio del Castillo y Saavedra, and Francken's *Crucifixion of St Andrew*. Bliss didn't notice Chandler walk into the room, but he heard her low mutter of revulsion as she came up behind him.

'Phil Walker is one sick puppy,' she said. 'Fancy going to sleep at night with all that ugly shit staring down at you.'

'He probably got off on it.'

'Ugh! Don't.'

'I'm not joking.' He glanced back over his shoulder and jerked his thumb towards the bedside cabinet. 'Our man keeps two boxes of tissues and a large bottle of baby oil handy.'

Chandler closed her eyes, but he knew she would carry the mental image around with her for the rest of the day. When he looked at the prints again, he noticed something peculiar. 'Check out the crucifixes,' he said. 'They're not the usual T shape.'

'Yes, I noticed that. I've never seen those X-shaped ones before.'

Bliss peered closely at the print farthest from the door. It caught the light spilling in from the lone window, almost as if the sun had wanted to attract them to it. 'Look at this one. It's not St Andrew. This poor sod is strung between two of those X-shaped crucifixes. And see what's being done to him, Pen.'

Chandler stepped up in front of the print. The original painting had skimped on detail when it came to facial features, but there was no disguising the activity portrayed. Around the bound figure, whose mouth was an open black smudge, one man was hacking away at his stomach, while two others gleefully held aloft bloody chunks of his body.

'This is ghastly,' she said, cringing as if in pain herself.

'Yeah. It's awful stuff. I don't know about you, Pen, but I put all this together with those books about legends and historical sites, and even though we now know Walker is a victim, this tells its own story. Whoever took him, sliced him up and removed his hand, based their method on the man's own horrible appetites. They also got the idea of where to leave the bags from his interest in legend and ancient locations. That tells me they knew each other well. To me, it says our man's ultimate target was Walker, and he built his entire sordid plan around Walker's taste for the macabre.'

They spent just under an hour searching Walker's flat before asking for it to be sealed. They found no evidence other than the books and paintings, but as they left and headed back to the motorway, Bliss thought he now understood the man better. Although circumstantial, the specific subject matter revealed by the textbooks and artwork convinced him Walker was the final victim. It also squared the circle, confirming links between the torture victims and the murder of Geraldine Price; there were no coincidences to be found in those connections.

Northbound traffic was heavy around Stansted airport and the A14 junction, but they were soon in the outside lane, hovering just over the speed limit. Bliss enjoyed driving. Usually it helped clear his mind, but today his thoughts were flapping around inside his head like clothes in a tumble dryer.

'You know,' he said as they reached Alconbury, 'it occurs to me that none of what we've seen or heard in recent days slams a door on either of our two main theories. But if one of our old gangsters is topping those who were involved in Price's murder, we're fast running out of suspects. Equally, if it's out of vengeance, who exactly is seeking justice? Geraldine's father is dead, the husband and son have strong alibis. Are we missing somebody? Did Geraldine's brother check out in the end?'

Chandler took out her phone and logged into the case file. She scrolled down, jabbed a link and read what came up on her screen. 'He did.' she said. 'Oddly enough, he suffers from Ménière's. He's married with one child, and currently living in Canada. Phil spoke to him at his home address, and his passport hasn't been used in three years.'

'Didn't come home after Valerie died, then?'

'It's a long way, boss.'

'True.' He fell into silent thought again for a few moments. 'In which case, I wonder if Geraldine Price was having an affair. A love affair, I mean, involving actual love and not just sex. If she was, perhaps whoever loved her at the time is now on some kind of crusade.'

'But why wait until now? And why involve Conway? Why carve the case file reference into the flesh?'

'I've always thought the Conway angle cuts both ways – no pun intended. If it's a gang member, we can assume he's mocking Pete. You know the sort of thing I mean – *you couldn't catch me before and you're not going to now, either*. And if it's not that but a question of revenge, highlighting Conway is a different type of taunt. *You couldn't catch them and make them pay, but I can.*'

'Yeah, I can buy that. But do you honestly think she could ever have been so close to another man that all these years later he would decide to take on a bunch of old-time gangsters? And I keep coming back to it: why now? Why wait all this time? If he exists, what's *his* trigger?'

Acknowledging the comment with a shrug, Bliss felt himself running out of steam. Not so long ago he'd been convinced their man was Phil Walker, yet now they knew he was a victim along with Harrison, Carlisle and Dobson. His gut told him Swift was running not from the police but from whoever was slicing chunks off his friends. Valerie Price killing herself may have been a substantial enough trigger for Stephen or Andy Price to have snapped and sworn vengeance on these men; yet, despite the obvious conclusion, evidence suggested this was not entirely the case.

But it had to be one or the other. A cover-up or revenge. If it was the former, he was wrong about the acts being so personal they could only be committed by somebody close. Could he have got it so badly wrong? Was somebody once tentatively attached to the gangsters now taking them out one by one? Or a different type of killer doing so on behalf of the Prices, whether paid for or otherwise? Neither felt right to Bliss, because it put distance between the doer and the motive, but unless the perpetrator was someone they knew absolutely nothing about, his gut had to be wrong.

'The Price financials didn't throw up a single question mark, right?' he said, seeking confirmation of what he thought he knew.

'Not a thing. We checked business and personal accounts.'

Bliss concentrated harder still.

One or the other.

The phrase stuck in his mind as he went through it all one last time with his partner. 'Tell me what you think,' he said when he was done. 'Honest opinion. I'm tying myself up in knots here, and I may not be seeing any of it clearly any more. I can't seem to take a step back, so I need you to do it for me.'

'Rationally speaking,' Chandler said after a few moments, 'I think Andy and Stephen Price have the greater motive. Put them together with the recent trigger of losing Valerie and we'd have little reason to look beyond them if it weren't for their alibi. Remove that, and they'd both be in for questioning right now.'

'But we can't ignore the alibis. We can be certain of two things: neither of them deposited the bag on Monday morning, and the condition of the hand inside it also tells us neither of them removed it. None of which entirely rules out their involvement, so perhaps we shouldn't be allowing the alibi to cloud our judgement. They have motive, they have the trigger. I don't like the distancing factor, but them paying for somebody to do this on their behalf may be a plausible explanation; I have to accept that, though it doesn't mean I have to believe it. And from there, it's reasonable to assume they also told their man to kill the victims in this precise way.'

Bliss was nodding to himself as he spoke. He paused briefly before continuing. 'Which leaves us with Freddy Swift as our only viable suspect. Now, does he seem right to you?'

'No. No, he doesn't. But right or wrong, we can't ignore the Prices and we can't ignore our porn king.'

'I know. I'd like to speak with the pair of them again, but I don't know the best way to handle it. What I really want to do is bring them in for interview and statements.'

'Then let's do that.'

He shook his head. 'No – they're both savvy solicitors. They know they're under no obligation to speak to us, so they won't. They'll insist on being arrested, which puts us on the clock. With what we have on them we'll get twenty-four hours, eight of which will be set aside for sleep, a few hours for legal chats and comfort breaks. No, we don't go near them unless we're either desperate or have something more solid to tackle them with. On the other hand, we can arrest Freddy Swift on sight. If we manage to break him, he may lead us to their door.'

Chandler glanced out of her window for a few moments, the scenery switching from rural open fields and distant housing developments to a vast industrial background; a sure sign they were closing in on the city. 'You're right, though, boss. The circumstances seem to fit, and at the same time not quite fit, both theories. The sole thread binding them together is the victims.'

Something about Chandler's flat statement tugged at him. She was absolutely right. The victims were the common denominator, but only if they were involved in Geraldine's murder – a theory for which the police had absolutely no evidence. But just because the shared connection between the Prices and the victims lay in the past, it didn't mean there were no links in the present. Andy and Stephen Price were solicitors, often advocating for the defence; Freddy Swift was the one current suspect who was also a previous suspect. Given his proclivities, was it so outrageous to imagine that either Andy or Stephen Price might have acted on Swift's behalf in the recent past?

'One or the other,' Bliss muttered, adrenaline now hammering through his veins like rocket fuel. The phrase repeated itself, but this time he recognised it for what it was.

'Did you say something?' Chandler asked, absently.

'I keep thinking it has to be one or the other – either the gangsters or the Prices. But what if I'm wrong, Pen?'

'In what way?'

'What if it's not one or the other at all? What if it's both?'

THIRTY-FIVE

B LISS BEGAN THE BRIEFING by informing those seated around him of his conversation with ex-DCI Morris Drayton. That interview seemed so long ago now, as if days rather than hours had passed. He also went into detail relating to the warranted search of Phil Walker's home. Everyone listened intently, captivated by Bliss's gentle unravelling of intelligence and logical speculation. Keeping a surreptitious eye on DI Riseborough, Bliss noticed the man's brow furrowing every so often, though he did not speak out at the time.

DSI Fletcher was the first to put voice to her thoughts after Bliss stopped talking. 'That's an awful lot of work to get through in such a short period of time, Inspector. You and DS Chandler did well. I'm particularly drawn to your own impressions regarding Walker's involvement.'

Bliss felt fatigue wrestling with his thoughts. He was bone weary, but up for this encounter. 'I took photos on my phone, ma'am. I arranged for a full forensic sweep, but for now we can go over my own snaps if you like. But if you'd been there you would have seen it more clearly. It all fits. The man we're looking for is close enough to Walker to know his sickening tastes, and to physically exploit those preferences in order to punish the crew who raped, tortured, and murdered Geraldine Price. I now believe Walker to be his final victim. With him, the desire for revenge dies. All of which tells me one or both of the Price men is involved, and they are working with another man.'

'Presumably this Freddy Swift character,' Conway said. Today he carried his weight poorly, looking uncomfortable and ill-prepared for what lay ahead. He understood a great deal of scrutiny would later come his way.

Bliss's features contorted into a brief grimace. 'I doubt it. I admit I was wrong about Andy or Stephen Price – perhaps about both of them – but on reflection I can see how either man could have snapped and may now be capable of doing something unimaginable. No matter how many times I try to do the same with Swift, however, I don't see it.'

'Not that you have any real evidence against Andy or Stephen Price,' Fletcher reminded him. 'I can certainly see the merit in your argument, Inspector. The pieces do appear to fit quite neatly. But you're going to need a great deal more before we can proceed along those lines.'

'I realise that, ma'am. All I'm doing here is outlining my theory. I'm as certain as I can be about so much of it, but it's those final aspects I'm not quite sure of, and if you agree with me then those will be our main area of focus from this point on.'

He had been waiting for Riseborough to speak up. When the DI finally did, he asked the exact question Bliss had been expecting. 'I'm sorry if I seem more confused than usual. I assume wires have become crossed. But am I the only one at this table who was under the impression the severed hand found at North Weald had not yet been identified?' He cast an accusatory glare in Bliss's direction, folding his arms defensively.

'You are the one person in this room who believes that to be the case, yes,' Bliss confessed. 'Because you're the only person in this room who was given that information. Deliberately so.'

Bewildered, Riseborough looked around the table. Bliss thought the wild gleam of panic in the man's eyes suggested he realised all was not well, but had not yet formed an opinion as to precisely why. 'I'm sorry,' he said, 'but you're going to have to explain that to me, Bliss.'

'I intend to, Max. Let's start right there. I decided the leak to the *Daily Express* had to have come from either your team or Gablecross.' Bliss held up a hand to forestall any argument at this point. 'I gave the correct intel to Superintendent Conway, the incorrect version to you. When the newspaper's online presence ran an update stating the new victim had yet to be identified, with police expecting to name him within a day, I knew the leak had to be at your end.'

Riseborough shot to his feet. 'This is an outrage! How dare you not tell me what you had planned? I'm a leading figure in this joint task force, and as such I ought to have been informed!'

Bliss leaned back in his chair and stared the man down. 'I dared because I couldn't take the risk. I don't know you well enough, Max. You could have told your team everything on the off-chance that one of your people was the leak, perhaps having decided to prevent it from happening again rather than root them out.'

'And you consider that an acceptable way to behave? To con one of your colleagues? You have no right to question my own actions, let alone perpetrate this… this… scam on me and my team.' He looked around for support, his face crimson. 'Are you all okay with this? You think this is professional behaviour?'

'Please retake your seat, Inspector Riseborough.' DSI Fletcher nodded towards his chair. 'DI Bliss is not quite finished.'

'Oh, really? What else does he have in store?'

'Now, that I can't tell you, because none of us know. DI Bliss chose to inform us all at the same time, so we are as much in the dark about this development as you. Now, please, Max, sit yourself down and listen along with the rest of us.'

Bliss took the time to compose himself. The others had agreed to him holding back the most telling information, but he was expecting uproar irrespective of the result of his own investigation.

'Thank you, ma'am,' he began. 'And let me be clear: no other member of my team is aware of what I am about to tell you. They had no clue as to my intentions, so whatever your reaction, I'd be grateful if you would aim it at the two people involved and nobody else.'

'This is all starting to sound terribly ominous,' DCI Warburton said.

Her eyes met his and asked the question. Bliss shrugged and got on with it. 'Having created the strategy for identifying which team had the leak, I went a stage further. Initially my intention was to eliminate two of my colleagues, so that I could bring them both into the next phase of my plan to isolate the culprit – though I did wonder if it might have the opposite effect.'

The room became quiet and still. Bliss understood the consequences of his actions, but there was no turning back. 'The step I took – alone – was to monitor four mobile phones and two internal switchboard extension numbers, with the specific intention of identifying communication between the users of these devices and the *Daily Express* reporter whose byline sat beneath the leaked information. If the latest leak appeared online without any apparent contact between these individuals, it wouldn't have ruled them out entirely, but it would have given me greater confidence in their trustworthiness.'

'You said four mobiles,' Conway pointed out.

'Yes. A personal and a work device for each of the two individuals. I was ninety percent sure this monitoring would produce no results, but unfortunately, that was not the case. Between the time I provided the information about Walker to both DSI Conway and DI Riseborough, and the time of the update article appearing on the *Express* website, a call was made to the reporter from one of those devices.'

All heads turned now to face both men, who sat together opposite Bliss. He looked up and saw anticipation on each face, together with a kind of fascinated dread at the secret about to be divulged.

'The device in question belonged to Detective Inspector Riseborough,' Bliss said. 'He used his personal mobile phone to make the call to the journalist.'

This time there was no explosion of fury, no dramatic propulsion from the chair. Riseborough sat in silence, eyes downcast, no longer full of bluff and vitriol, attempting neither to deny the allegation nor to explain it away.

DSI Fletcher edged forward in her chair. The blaze in her eyes was not for Riseborough alone, Bliss assumed. 'What do you have to say for yourself, Max?' she asked calmly.

For a second or two, Bliss thought the City of London DI would refuse to answer. But when Riseborough spoke, the look he gave Fletcher was one of stubborn defiance. 'A case based on an illegal, unauthorised trap on any communication device, never mind one attached to a personal contract, doesn't stand a chance of making it to court. Whatever the rights or wrongs of what I did, you will never bring charges against me.'

Fletcher's cheeks pinched. 'I wouldn't be so sure of that if I were you. Let's not forget that the *Express*'s article contained incorrect information. They may have fired the shot, but it was off target. Persuading the owners to have their staff member cooperate with us may not prove to be as difficult as you imagine.'

Riseborough's lips curled into a tight sneer. 'Perhaps you're right. But you risk exposing the illegal actions of one of your own senior detectives. I don't envisage that going down well back at county headquarters.'

'If you believe I wouldn't hesitate to throw Bliss to the wolves, Inspector, you are sorely mistaken. However, as I'm sure you are well aware, there are many other ways by which we can compel you to walk away from this. You're right in thinking we wouldn't relish a scandal, which gives you leverage. But only to a certain degree. You're done, as far as your career is concerned. And for what? Why would you leak to the press?'

The mass of contempt ripping across Riseborough's face created hard ridges of flesh. 'Oh, please. Let's be adults here for a minute, shall we? I doubt there's anybody in this room who hasn't provided the media with information at one time or another. Not for personal gain, perhaps, but for reasons we felt were right at the time.'

'But the intelligence you shared with the first leak could have undone a great deal of good work. Don't you see the difference?'

'I was angry!' Riseborough snapped, pointing across the table. 'With him. Bliss. The arrogance of the man. Gave us all the piddling little jobs while he swanned around breaking new ground. I wasn't about to stand for it. So yes, I called my contact at the newspaper and yes, I included more intel than I'd intended to. But your man's decisions forced me to act. It's Bliss you want to be looking at when all this is done, not me.'

There was stunned disbelief around the table. Nobody quite knew where to look or what to say. Bliss chose not to respond to the accusation, leaving Fletcher and Riseborough glaring at each other. Nothing was said for a couple of seconds, and Conway took the opportunity to speak up.

'I'm not sure we're going to get anywhere if this turns into a shouting match with fingers pointing all over the place. That will do more harm than good. Clearly there's still a great deal to discuss, but at this juncture I suggest we take a ten-minute break, and that when we reconvene, we do so without either of our Inspectors in the room.'

'If I'm not under arrest, I would like to go home,' Riseborough said, his tone muted now. 'You people say what you have to say, but please remember I've done nothing you haven't all done yourselves at one point or another.'

'I think it best if you do leave us,' Fletcher told him. 'Consider yourself on informal suspension. By that, I mean you don't go near your office and you don't discuss this meeting or the operation any further with your colleagues until further notice. Understand?'

'Isn't that a decision for my own senior leadership team to make?'

'You are a member of this task force, and as such I am your direct superior at this moment. Believe me, your bosses and I will be having a conversation.'

Riseborough gave no further response. He eased himself up out of the chair and took one last look around the table before marching briskly from the room.

'I'll make myself scarce as well, ma'am,' Bliss said, standing and buttoning his suit jacket. 'Am I also under informal suspension?'

'I haven't made up my mind about that,' Fletcher said brusquely. 'You and DCI Warburton will meet with me tomorrow morning at eight sharp – by which time I will have calmed down and had time to weigh up all my options.'

Bliss agreed and left the room. Riseborough was nowhere to be seen, and he assumed the man had not lingered. He knew he should leave the building, but he hadn't been forbidden to speak to his team first. He imagined the break and meeting in the conference room would give him at least half an hour. It was all he needed.

Down in Major Crimes, he gathered together his colleagues and spoke about the case itself, ignoring Chandler's eyes pleading with him for an update on the outcome of the meeting. In his opinion, he told them, Phil Walker was most likely still alive, but in a bad way and fading fast. The Tower Hill evidence was still relatively fresh as well, so there was a chance Tommy Harrison had not yet been killed, though death from blood loss or cardiac arrest was a distinct possibility. Survival was less likely in Earl Dobson's case, he thought, but still conceivable. As for Carlisle, Bliss now considered their own case as a search for a body. But irrespective of what state these men were in, none of the three teams involved had any idea where they were, and this remained a source of intense frustration to all.

Bliss remembered to tell his team about the large number of officers out scouring potential sites within a fifteen-minute drive of Tower Hill. The plan was for the search radius to expand to thirty minutes if necessary. The City of London team had already identified plenty of undeveloped plots of dead ground within the circle.

Having liaised with Gablecross during Bliss's absence, Bishop reported his own news. Conway's dig into the archives had apparently proved fruitless. Plenty of names had come up during the search, and his team had two distinct lists. The first identified everybody who had been spoken to in connection with Geraldine Price's murder; the second highlighted other known faces in the area at the time. One by one the names were being eliminated or retained. The retained list had two sections: men known to be prone to violence, and those who had convictions or charges relating to aggravated crimes. The number of names amounted to three figures in all.

For the next ten minutes, everybody listened in respectful silence to Bliss's theory. If Andy and Stephen Price really were working with Freddy Swift, he told them, there was nothing by way of evidence to suggest who was doing what, let alone verify the involvement of these three specific individuals. DS Bishop concurred, but made a point of saying it was a valid idea that they should follow up on.

Bliss thanked him, relieved to have somebody on his side. 'Look, I know it's a stretch,' he said. 'The next action we need to take is to look at Swift's record to see if either of the Prices ever represented him. Having spent time with the man, I found Swift to be as seedy and pathetic as you'd expect of somebody who earns his living in the sex industry by exploiting others, but I don't see him as our killer. We may discover he has a lesser role to play. I'm also convinced the slicing is born of personal animosity, which again rules him out, unless he had a closer connection to Geraldine Price than we currently understand to be the case. Having said all that, any connection at all between the three men will be a lead worth running down.'

DC Gratton had been listening intently, but now sought clarification. 'So you're suggesting Swift abducted the victims, and also deposited the carrier bags during times when the Prices had concrete alibis. You're also saying one or both of the Price men carried out the actual torture. Is that a fair assessment?'

'It is. It works. It fits – with the exception of Harrison, to a large extent. Either of the Price men could have tortured him, but at the time his hand was removed they were both still in Manchester. Which means that if Swift is the man working with them, he must have severed it as well as leaving it for us.'

'That's not an unreasonable hypothesis, is it, boss?'

Bliss ran a thumb over his scar. He hated getting bogged down in theories he wasn't entirely convinced of, but he was as capable of being wrong as anyone else and had to admit to the logic of the premise.

'Not at all. It's perfectly valid. However, I met all three men, talked at length with them, and I never once got any kind of gut feeling they were involved. But both Andy and Stephen Price are solicitors, which means they're intelligent and trained to be guarded. Either one could pull it off. I do keep coming back to Freddy Swift, though. Sleazy though he may be, my gut tells me he's wrong for this. But if we look at our initial group of men, he is the last one standing.'

It was hardly compelling evidence, and Bliss knew he had not hit his mark. He realised he was not completely in the room nor in the moment. Elsewhere, his future was being discussed, and those conversations would not be flattering. He sensed a change in the direction the wind was blowing, and he feared the outcome of DSI Fletcher's ruminations. He hoped she would agree to one additional day before tossing him and the Peterborough Major Crimes unit off the case. That would give his team twenty-four hours to achieve a result.

THIRTY-SIX

B LISS QUICKLY LEFT THE station after the meeting in the squad room. He was desperate to avoid another confrontation with Fletcher before she'd had the chance to reflect on his actions and decide on his punishment. He stopped off for a drink in the Woodman with the team before slipping away, collecting a pizza from Domino's, and driving to the marina at Orton Mere.

Bliss seldom made use of the yacht club facilities, though he paid the same annual subscription as everyone else for the privilege of mooring his boat by the lock. The cost did not include either ownership or lease of one of the dozens of wooden huts dotted along the towpath, but he had everything he needed on board the *Mourinho*.

He'd first bought the fifteen-foot cruiser in 2004, shortly after Jose Mourinho had taken over as manager of Chelsea football club. A lifelong supporter, Bliss had purchased the boat on a whim because of its gleaming royal-blue finish, and named it with the same lack of foresight. He sold it when he left the city, but repurchased it again a year or so after his return. Many people had suggested he change the name, but he was happy to stick with it. His resolve had been sorely tested when Mourinho moved to

Chelsea's arch-rivals, Tottenham, but the truth was Bliss couldn't be bothered to re-register the paperwork.

By the time he climbed aboard the boat, Bliss had lost his appetite, and he left the pizza box unopened. Dazed by the events of the past forty-eight hours, he sat at the stern, drinking and staring down at the river, feet overhanging the small swim platform. As he sipped his third beer, Bliss thought back to the briefing and marvelled at how rapidly two careers had unwound within the space of a few minutes. It often took decades to build respect, yet a single decision was capable of blasting it apart as if it had never existed. But he had not wandered blindly into the minefield. The moment he requested the phone monitoring he knew his days might be numbered, but he had not allowed that near-certainty to deter him.

As leader, you had to take one for the team every now and again. He would not stand idly by while the leaking of potentially critical information diminished his team's progress. Exposing Riseborough had been a necessary act, and Bliss was not going to second-guess himself now. It was a decision he would have to live with, no matter what the consequence. He felt like a hypocrite when he thought about his many conversations with Sandra Bannister – the DI had been right to rant about that – yet his conscience was clear in terms of how potentially damaging anything he had given the local reporter had been.

As he twisted the cap off the fourth of six bottles tucked by his side, he became aware of movement nearby. There was nothing unusual about people walking around the area, because boat owners came and went at all hours. But Bliss knew thieves operated locally, so he immediately felt his defensive hackles rising.

'Permission to come aboard, skipper?' a voice called out.

Chandler.

Bliss took a swig of his beer. 'No, bugger off. Why aren't you at home, curled up on the sofa with Shrek?'

His partner pulled herself up onto the boat and joined him at the stern. The small boat rocked as she sat down. 'Other than when I'm with Anna in Cambridge on Saturday, he and I will be spending the weekend together, remember. Unless you need me to change my shift around?'

Bliss took a bottle out of the pack and passed it over. 'I'd forgotten. But no, you stick to your plans. Bish is on duty, and Hunt is due back from his holiday. We'll manage.'

Chandler didn't argue. She took two long swallows, then sighed gratefully. 'I thought I'd pop over to see how you were,' she said, stifling a gentle belch.

'And why would you do that?'

'Because of how the briefing went – and because you sneaked out of the pub without a word. You had that disgruntled look you've perfected over the years. I guessed you were coming down to the boat, and I decided I'd better make sure you weren't thinking of throwing yourself into the mere.'

Bliss laughed. 'Right. My bet is your fridge was empty and you knew where to come to cadge a free drink.'

She gave an easy shrug. 'Yeah, let's not go with that. I prefer my version of events.'

'So, you still think you're right?' he asked. 'About my idea being way off target?'

'I don't think Bish and I are wrong. It's a long shot at best, boss. You admitted as much yourself.'

'True. But I'd hoped for a bit more enthusiasm.'

'I think we may be focussed on the victims. Perhaps we're not seeing around the edges the way you do.'

'And I'm not thinking about the victims?'

'Not in the same way.' Chandler shook her head, her ponytail slapping against her back. 'You think they're dead – if not all of them, most likely the first two, and probably three. You also know exactly what kind of men they are, so although you have some basic concerns for their welfare, you're not overly bothered about them as people. Your internal focus is on whoever did this to them, so you see it differently to everyone else.'

Bliss turned his friend's observation over for a while. He drank his beer, wondering what it said about him if Chandler was right.

'I don't say it like it's a bad thing, boss,' Chandler explained. 'I know you care. I know you don't want these men to suffer, no matter what they've done. And I know if it ever came down to a choice between saving them or nailing their torturer, you'd choose the former.'

'But...? Come on, Pen, I know there's more.'

'Okay. But... you think finding our man will lead us to his victims, not the other way around. And you feel driven towards that angle because you don't believe they'll survive.'

'You think I'm wrong?'

'No. But I don't know if you're right, either.'

This was precisely why he appreciated her. Chandler could always be relied upon to be honest with him, even if being forthright meant getting on the wrong side of him. The thought brought an unbidden memory to the forefront of his mind. Not long ago, he'd been out in Ireland visiting his mother. One night as they sat out in the garden, the two had discussed his career, perhaps in greater detail than ever before. When he was through talking about himself, his mother remarked upon how often he had mentioned Chandler.

'Penny is the part of you that makes you whole,' she told him.

'I don't know about that,' he'd argued. 'I did okay for myself when I was with the NCA, and the Met before that.'

'Of course you did, Jimmy. But doing okay is a far cry from what you've achieved with her alongside you.'

It was true. He hadn't needed his mother to convince him of it. He drifted back to their early days together, the support Chandler had given him when he'd struggled to settle in to his new life away from London. She had later come back into the team because he was leading it again, after more than a decade of making few strides in what felt like heavy water. The NCA's focus on organised crime was wearing because it never let up; no matter how many bad guys you put away, there were always a dozen more ready and able to take their places. Heading up the MCU in Peterborough was more of a critical role, one with an immediate and obvious impact. He had never regretted returning to the post, and realised how fortunate he was to have Chandler along for the ride.

Many people had made the mistake of believing the two were romantically linked. In his more reflective moments, Bliss would admit he had felt the appeal. Attractive without being obvious, Chandler's character revealed itself to him every day they worked together. Here she was once again, thinking of him and not taking the rest she was due. It was another of the traits he loved about her. Occasionally he thought of what might have been, but always ended up accepting that any romantic involvement would have put an end to their friendship – and their partnership. This way he got the best of both worlds, and he was content.

'So what's your own sense?' he asked.

Her reply was instantaneous. 'The truth is, Jimmy, I don't know if I have one. No matter what they did in the past, I want to find these men alive, and I hate to think of them suffering in the meantime. But I'm finding it increasingly difficult to drum up an ounce of sympathy for anybody involved in this horrible mess.'

'Apart from Geraldine Price.' Bliss inclined his head as Chandler reacted with a sad smile. 'I feel the same way you do, Pen, but she is likely to be the one true victim in all this. I cling to that thought because, like you, I have to find something to believe in. If things don't improve soon, the idea of finding a semblance of justice for her may be the only thing that keeps me going.'

'You surprise me, Jimmy. I thought you didn't believe in true justice any more.'

'I don't, not especially. I think it's a myth, for the most part. But every now and then a case crops up to make me reconsider.'

'You mean, it gives you hope?'

Bliss gave an awkward grin. 'I wouldn't go that far. But Geraldine deserved more, and I'd like to think we can still give her something.'

Chandler tipped the neck of her bottle towards him. 'I'll drink to that.'

They clinked beers and both took a hit, savouring the moment in silence.

'You seeing Emily over the weekend?' Chandler said after a slight pause. 'You're having a meal together, aren't you?'

Bliss realised his colleague was trying to steer his thoughts elsewhere, hoping to prevent him from becoming morose. Right now it was an easy ride to take. The thought of Geraldine Price's murder remaining unsolved burned a hole in his stomach, so he appreciated his friend's efforts. 'Supposedly. Of course, I don't know where I'm going to be with this bloody case, so we'll have to see.'

'Let me cover for you. It's not a problem.'

Bliss shook his head abruptly. 'No way. It's your weekend off the clock. Emily is familiar with how my job works. Either we'll get together or we won't. It's no big deal.'

'To you, maybe.'

'Pen, Emily and I went through all of this the other night. I told you, we came to an arrangement.'

'Yes, I know. But just because a woman says she understands and is happy to go along, doesn't mean she understands and is happy to go along. Now who's the teacher and who's the grasshopper?'

Draining his bottle and sprinkling the dregs over the side into the calm waters of the Nene, Bliss huffed a sigh and peered down into the river. He didn't think he'd ever understand women, even if he lived to be a hundred. It was easier to bore deep into the warped and twisted psyche of a serial killer than fully comprehend the workings of the female mind.

'Come on, Jimmy. You know I'm right. I don't care what Emily says now – this understanding will not last the test of time, not when she looks in the mirror one day and tells herself she deserves better. She's with you now because she thinks she can change you. Not today, nor tomorrow, but soon. She wants a relationship she can have faith in, one she can buy into. We all do, eventually.'

The sun was setting upstream, bathing his partner in a crimson-purple hue that for a moment made her look like an oil painting. Soft, warm ridges of light kissed the water behind her, framing her outline perfectly. 'Isn't that a bridge we jump off when we get to it?' he said. 'Pen, I could not have made myself clearer with her. Either this is how it works, or we don't go forward with it. In the life-versus-work balance, I've always had my thumb on the work end of the scale. It's always been my priority, even when I was with Hazel. I'm not about to change, unless it's on my terms.'

'Why not?' Chandler leaned forward, peering up at him.

'Because I never want to resent her. If she manipulates me against my will and I lose my edge at work, I'll know it and I'll always feel aggrieved. But if she wants to stick along for the ride until I hand in my warrant card, that'd be great. I have feelings for her – strong feelings – but she has to wait until I am ready. That might sound selfish, it may well be selfish, but that's how it has to be. It's the only way she and I will ever work in the long run.'

After a moment of silence interrupted only by the gentle bobbing of the boat and the scrape of a rubber protective float against the wooden dock, Chandler said, 'And that's what you want, is it? The long run, with Emily?'

He did not have to pause before replying. 'I do. Despite all previous appearances to the contrary, I have no great desire to live out my days alone. I'm comfortable in my own skin, however, which has always made a big difference. I enjoy being around the people I like, the people I love, but I don't mope around when they're not with me. I don't… I don't miss people in the way I know I'm supposed to. The same way other people seem to. I switch it off, block it out, somehow prevent myself from dwelling on what I don't have and instead focus on what I do. The one constant is the job, Pen. And I believe you understand that better than most.'

The pair chatted amiably for a while longer. They avoided talking about the case, the distraction reminding Bliss of something he'd meant to ask Chandler.

'Did you know about Grealish? About him passing away?'

'Of course.'

'I only just found out. Why didn't you say anything?'

'I assumed you knew.'

Bliss breathed heavily through his nose. 'Poor sod. All those years in the job and life can't even give him a few years to enjoy his well-earned retirement.'

'Yeah. It's a shame.'

'It's more than that. Doesn't it make you question your choices? Don't you ever wonder how your life might have turned out if you hadn't become a copper?'

'Nope. Not even once. I've made a difference, and our lives aren't all about us. How we live them, the effect we have on others, that's all part of it.'

'And then you hand in your papers and walk straight into your grave.'

Chandler laughed, as if what he had said was absurd. 'Some people do, Jimmy. From all walks of life. But not all, by any means. Jesus, you can be a maudlin bugger at times. If you're feeling your mortality these days, that's just part of getting older. And you should be grateful for that. The way I see it, you got this far – far enough for your end days to seem closer. Think about all the people who never even make it to that stage.'

Bliss knew she was right: getting old was better than the alternative. 'Sorry,' he said, patting her bare arm. 'My outlook can be pretty bleak at times. It's my Irish heritage. The Irish love to enjoy themselves, but a few pints in and they all seem to relish talking about death. You want to hear my mother tolling the iron bell when she's got a few sherbets inside her.'

'One of these days I'm going to have to meet the esteemed Mrs Bliss. I have so many questions.'

'Oh, she'd love you, Pen. She's heard all about you, of course. I tell her what a dead weight you are. The millstone around my neck. I think she knows I mean quite the reverse. She's pretty insightful that way.'

Chandler raised her bottle. 'To Mrs Bliss,' she said. 'And to Sergeant Grealish. May he have found some peace.'

Bliss tipped his own drink but said nothing. He was not averse to melancholy, but knew how often the black dog was following close behind. He had fought against it all his life, and had no intention of inviting it in now.

When Chandler left, shortly after sunset, Bliss immediately felt her absence, the night becoming less appealing as the minutes ticked away. He'd had too many beers to drive home, and he decided he was not up to the short walk. It was a warm night, so he moved into the pilot area, reclined the cream leather seat as far back as it would go, wrapped his jacket over himself, and stared up at the sky as darkness fell and the night exploded with stars.

THIRTY-SEVEN

SATURDAY MORNING BRIEFING WAS a relatively quiet affair, though Bliss was surprised to find both DCI Warburton and Superintendent Fletcher in attendance. He had expected to meet with them afterwards, so their presence in the room unnerved him. He wasn't sure if it was a good or a bad thing, but chose not to speculate; one way or another, he'd be apprised of his immediate fate before the day was out. To a team lacking both Chandler and Gratton he provided an update and case status, concluding the session by asking Olly Bishop to bring DC Hunt fully up to speed upon his return from holiday. There were no questions or last-minute surprises, so after Bliss had said his piece he traipsed upstairs with his two superiors.

DSI Fletcher remained on her feet while he and Warburton took a seat at her desk. She gazed out of the window, hands on hips. She had the same view of the scrubland at the back of the building as Bliss often sought out from the stairway landing, and although it wasn't particularly enticing, the open spaces were an improvement on the road system and industrial units at the entrance to Thorpe Wood. Bliss hoped she was struggling with the best way to tell him what his punishment was, rather than still debating it and settling for a snap decision. She had entered the briefing room earlier without offering a nod in his direction, and her face had been a rigid frown of concentration throughout. He was relieved when she turned to face him, though his heart lurched in anticipation.

'You and I have largely been on the same page since you were posted back to Thorpe Wood, wouldn't you agree, Inspector Bliss?'

Bliss pulled moisture into his mouth before replying. 'Yes, ma'am. I would.'

'And you've found me to be frank but fair, yes?'

'Yes, ma'am.'

'You respect me, respect the position, respect my authority?'

'Again, yes, ma'am.' Less enthusiasm this time; Bliss was not a fan of preamble.

'That being the case, why would you not come to me with this phone tapping idea before going ahead with it?'

Fletcher was bowling him easy deliveries so far. 'Two reasons, ma'am. First of all, to distance you from the ramifications if I was proved right. And secondly, because I assumed you would say no.'

The DSI hooked one leg behind the other and folded her arms. 'You get no marks for honesty at this stage, Bliss. That ship has sailed, I'm afraid. Let me ask you this, then: having gone ahead with your rash and illegal plan, why did you not warn me about the results ahead of yesterday evening's briefing?'

'Because I thought you'd stop me saying what I had to say – not because you would have wanted to spare Riseborough, but because you would have wanted to save me.'

'And what of my own reputation? How do you think that came across yesterday? Not only can I not control my Major Crimes DI, but he doesn't trust me enough to take me into his confidence.'

'I didn't consider it to be an issue, ma'am; the opposite, in fact. I thought the more distance I put between us, the better it would be for everybody. I didn't warn you, I didn't warn DCI Warburton, and I didn't warn my team. Not even Penny Chandler.'

'But you told somebody, Bliss.'

'Ma'am?' He looked up, surprised by the comment.

Fletcher unfolded her arms, pulled out her chair and dropped into it with a heavy sigh. Her eyes remained on his the whole time as she leaned forward. 'You must have told whoever ran the trace for you.'

Bliss had been prepared for this line of questioning from the start. 'That's not the case, ma'am. It was all my own work.'

'Inspector, while you may not receive marks for being honest with me, I do frown upon dishonesty.'

'I'm telling you the truth.'

'Rubbish! We're both well aware you lack the technical know-how to pull this off. Nor do you have access to all the relevant numbers you put a trace on.'

'Ma'am, these days having a degree in tech is not a requirement. A simple app will do the job, and I obtained the numbers I needed by making a few well-placed calls of my own, none of which alluded to how I intended to use them. It isn't difficult.'

'I don't believe you, Bliss. You're covering for somebody, most likely from our own tech division.'

He was, but he wasn't going to admit it. Instead, he shrugged. 'With the greatest of respect, I can't be held responsible for what you choose to believe or disbelieve. I freely own up to running those traces myself, but I'm telling you nobody else was involved. That's where we are. Ma'am.'

Fletcher studied him for several seconds, before squinting at him and shaking her head. 'No, no, no. You've come up with a terrific story, Bliss. Excellent, in fact. I especially like the part about why you failed to warn me ahead of the meeting. But it's not the complete answer. How about you tell me the truth now? And be convincing this time; your future here may depend on it.'

Bliss licked his lips and thought it through. In his head, he'd delivered everything as intended, but somehow Fletcher had seen through it. He had to give her credit; she was better than he'd realised.

'Okay. You're right. It wasn't you I was concerned about. I knew if I came to you before the meeting with what I had on Riseborough, you'd feel obliged to take it higher up the ladder. They're the ones I was afraid would prevent me from going ahead.'

'Why were you so certain?'

'Because by that stage internal politics would have kicked in – just as it always does, ma'am. Chief Superintendent Feeley would have squashed it. Riseborough ends up being shifted sideways or eased out with a nice juicy pension, and nobody is any the wiser. That's how it goes.'

'And you didn't think that was by far the best way to handle this matter? The thought never occurred to you at all?'

'No. Because it wasn't. It isn't. It might make a few people feel better about themselves to sweep it all under the carpet, but the truth is the dirt doesn't stay there. It seeps out and sticks to the heels of everybody involved.'

This drew a frown from Fletcher. 'How so?'

'Because instead of identifying the one true culprit and nailing them for it, we all remain potential suspects in the minds of those who know there was a leak. I know you have plans, ma'am, and I'm guessing DCI Warburton imagines herself sitting in your chair one day. Then there's my team and their careers. All of you tainted by suspicion if the person responsible isn't named and shamed. No matter where you all go, it will follow you, and your new colleagues will always wonder if you were the one who leaked critical information to the press. I couldn't risk that happening. I had to tell my story in a meeting I knew would be minuted. I had to be sure Feeley didn't get the chance to do or say anything to prevent the truth coming out.'

'That's still Chief Superintendent Feeley to you, Bliss,' Fletcher said smartly.

'Yes, ma'am. Of course. But my point remains.'

Clearly still infuriated with him, Fletcher hissed through her teeth and gave a nod in Warburton's direction for her to speak up. 'Inspector Bliss,' his DCI said softly, 'last night the Superintendent and I spent a great deal of time discussing every single aspect of this case. Our conclusion was that up until yesterday, the JTFO had run smoothly enough, and clearly you had made advances. DI Riseborough was both right and wrong. Talking to the media as he did is not something we can tolerate, though we all know it goes on. The price he will pay is for getting caught, not for what he did, specifically. A formal inquiry will examine the consequences of his actions, but I am quietly confident that being forced to leave the job will be punishment enough.'

'For what it's worth, boss,' Bliss said. 'I agree.'

'I wish your opinion was valued right now, Inspector. Because Max Riseborough's contract of termination is going to be festooned with all manner of caveats – one of which will be to ensure he does not come after your blood, now or in the future. He's likely to want you charged, Inspector; if he were to go down that road, he would get his way, because your own lapse was worse than his. You committed an illegal act, and by rights you'd be off the job sooner than he will be.'

Bliss reached around to the back of his neck to rub a pressure point as a sharp stab of pain ground its way through the cervical part of his spine. He had thought it was the result of spending too much time in the car recently, but now he recognised it as stress. He regretted disappointing these two women, but now he needed to know how badly he had screwed up.

'Just get it over with,' he said. 'Please. I want to know where I stand.'

Warburton continued where she'd left off. 'The reason you're sitting here now, as opposed to being on suspension, is because what you did was not for personal gain. We spoke to Superintendent Conway first thing this morning and persuaded him that our own internal inquiry can wait until this case is over. He's an honourable man, and though he was hugely disappointed in both you and Max, he accepts your motives were pure. Therefore, as far as Operation Limestone is concerned, you and your team have been given extra rope.'

Bliss exhaled his relief. 'Thank you. Thank you both. I know it can't have been an easy decision for either of you to make.'

'No, it wasn't,' Fletcher said, her voice clipped. 'And don't go thinking this gets you off the hook, Inspector. There will have to be consequences for what you did, but we believe it's in the best interests of the case for you to carry on with it for the time being. To that end, are we absolutely clear as to where the operation stands?'

'I think we covered everything earlier,' he said. 'If it didn't arise in the briefing, then it's on the boards.'

'In which case, I think we're both up to speed, Inspector,' Warburton said. 'You believe the best way to the victims is via the suspects, and your strategy is to apply pressure to them?'

'That's precisely my line of thinking, boss. Despite what my gut says.'

'And what is it telling you?'

'That we're already too late. Walker has a chance because he's the most recent. Having said that, we don't know when he was taken, and if we work on the basis that the hand left for us on Thursday was not the first significant piece of flesh removed from his body, I realise now there must be some doubt about him being alive. Additionally, I can't help but wonder how long our man can keep up the whole slow slicing method. At some point he's going to decide enough is enough, at which time he'll kill whoever is still alive. For all we know, he already has.'

'What about our suspects? How firmly are you behind your theory of a deal between one of the Prices and this Swift character?'

Bliss took his time before responding. The truth came easy to him, though he wasn't sure how well either of his superiors would take it. He decided to tell it like it was and play the hand he'd been dealt.

'I do have a strong sense that one of the Prices is involved – perhaps even both of them. I believe at least one of them is responsible for the flesh slicing. They might be taking it in turns, for all I know. But if that's the case, their alibis mean they are not working alone, and given the list of potential suspects is becoming a list of victims, Freddy Swift has to be considered a strong candidate. Put simply, we've had three teams looking back at the Geraldine Price case, and nobody else stands out as an obvious suspect who might also easily be a victim. As you know, I was willing to throw my weight behind Phil Walker being our doer, only to see my theory fall flat when his hand was discovered.'

'So you're looking at Swift as much by default as anything overt?' the DSI said.

'We are, ma'am. My logic tells me it's not him, but my common sense says it has to be.'

Fletcher stood and brushed down her beige skirt. Both women were dressed casually, which told Bliss they were off duty. He hoped the Super would support him for a while longer. She gave him a stern look and cleared her throat. 'Your full explanation of why you did not inform me about DI Riseborough's guilt ahead of the meeting was very *you*, Inspector – frustrating and admirable in equal measures. But I haven't quite decided how I feel about your phone-tapping nonsense, so I suggest you do nothing else to try my patience. Understood?'

'Yes, ma'am.'

'Very well. You're on notice. Let's meet again on Monday afternoon, ahead of the evening briefing. All three of us, yes?'

'I'm sorry,' Bliss said. Having aimed the apology at Fletcher, he turned to Warburton. 'Both of you, please know I truly am sorry. I won't attempt to make excuses for my actions, because there aren't any. I meant what I said yesterday – I hoped to rule out both men so that all three of us could put our heads together and come up with a plan to find the leak. But, yes, I did also have a terrible suspicion that in doing so I might expose one of them. Ultimately, I wanted the leak, I found the leak.'

'Another example of how the end justifies the means where you're concerned,' Warburton said.

'I suppose I can't argue with your assessment.'

'No. And if you're capable of listening to advice, I suggest you wrap this up by Monday evening's briefing, Inspector. I'm not saying a win will help your cause, but it will put us in a better mood when we're considering your fate. That's all, thank you.'

Bliss blew out a long sigh of relief as he stood up to leave. Warburton had remained reasonably neutral, perhaps waiting for Fletcher to show her colours; either that, or they had already made a decision ahead of the meeting. Whatever the reason, he'd been given latitude to carry on for at least the next two days. It was longer than he had expected, but it needed to be enough. They simply had to get a break between now and then.

DS Bishop was waiting for him in the corridor. The big man leaned back against a wall, head down, a grim look on his face. He looked up as Bliss emerged from Fletcher's office. 'Sorry, boss. I didn't want to interrupt this time. Thought it best to wait for you to leave before speaking up.'

Bliss nodded, curious as to why Bishop had held back.

'I'm glad you're not the type to shoot the messenger, boss,' Bishop said. His features weary with fatigue, the usually gregarious DS looked as crestfallen as Bliss had ever seen him.

'That doesn't sound good, Bish.'

'No. It isn't. Thing is, on Thursday when I told you Phil Walker was no longer a suspect because he was now a victim, you'd only just got done informing the big cheeses he was our man.'

'I'm not liking where this is headed.'

'I'm so sorry, boss. I can't quite believe I'm doing this to you for a second time. And I thought you were right about Swift, despite the fact you kept saying you weren't convinced about him.'

'He's turned up, I take it?'

'He has. Though not in one piece. Several, in fact. Boss, Swift is our fifth victim.'

Bliss cupped both hands over his mouth, recirculating air while the case he had built tumbled all around him as though caught in the path of an avalanche.

'Boss… there's more.'

He looked back up at his sergeant, feeling every one of his years in the painful bones and aching muscles of his body. 'And when you say there's more, I take it you mean there's worse?'

Bishop nodded. 'TOD is estimated to have been between 10.00am and noon yesterday.'

The implications were immediately obvious to Bliss. 'Where?' he asked.

'Epping Forest.'

The beginnings of another headache jabbed a barb the size of a railway spike into the base of Bliss's skull. In utter despair he punched the wall. 'Which means this time, *I* am Andy and Stephen Price's alibi.'

THIRTY-EIGHT

I T WAS A LITTLE over eighty miles from Thorpe Wood to the Sunshine Plain visitors' area off the Epping New Road. This time Bliss
took the A1, headed clockwise on the M25 motorway and left it
at junction 26, signposted Waltham Abbey. From there it was a
short run on quiet roads. After he and Bishop pulled up in the
car park, Bliss got out and arched his back until he felt something
click into place.

'I wouldn't like to guess how many miles I've travelled this past
week or so,' he said over the roof of the car, stretching out his arms
and rolling his neck. 'The sooner boffins get around to solving the
problem of instant travel the better.'

'Yep. Beam us here, Scotty. Beam us there, Scotty.'

Bliss smiled at the comment; Olly Bishop wasn't usually one
for quoting popular TV or movie references. As he went through
his contortions, Bliss noticed a young man engaged in a heated
exchange with the officer guarding the scene. The voices of both
men grew louder, encouraging Bliss to walk over and investigate.

'This gentleman is demanding access to the paths we have
cordoned off, sir,' the young constable said. 'Says he has special

permission and that if he doesn't get in there soon he'll have wasted a month of work.'

The uniform was burning up in the sunlight, the heat perhaps agitating him more than usual. Bliss gave him the benefit of the doubt. He nodded and carefully regarded the other man, who carried a backpack over one shoulder.

'What's your story?' he asked.

'I just got done explaining to this… officer, but he seems to think his job description allows him to behave like a fascist and deny me right of way.'

Bliss prickled. He turned fully to stand square on to the man. 'Right. I'm giving you a second chance to present your case. You can either continue to be rude and annoyed and puffed up about it, or you can explain to me why you should be allowed beyond the tape. Your choice. I have better things to be doing with my time.'

The man took a beat to compose himself. Full of youth and himself, he clearly had disdain for authority, yet he seemed bright enough to know when and how to back down. The next time he spoke, he was contrite. 'Okay. Sorry. Thank you. As I just explained to the constable, I work for the Wildlife Trust. My department has a grant to monitor animal movement in these woodlands. I need to get to my hides to change the camera batteries. If they stop working, there'll be a gap in our captures, and all the work we've done so far will be utterly meaningless.'

Bliss allowed himself to enjoy the immediate shot of adrenaline. His initial thought when he had spotted the altercation was to wonder if they had lucked into a witness; now he knew the man might be about to provide so much more than recollections. Turning to the uniform, he said, 'Is this all you aspire to, constable? Lifting tape, lowering tape, writing names and numberplates on your clipboard? Pissing off members of the public?'

'Sir, I—'

Bliss made a zipping motion across his own mouth. 'That may be part of your problem – speaking rather than listening. Consider this a teachable moment, officer. Listen to me now and maybe, just maybe, you won't still be on this kind of duty a year from now because it's the only job you're suitable for.'

'Yes, sir.' The young man swallowed thickly and lines of tension bracketed his jaw.

'Good. But tell me something: did you hear what this gentleman had to say? I don't mean did you listen – I mean did you *hear*? Because if you had, you'd have put what he said together with what happened in those woods. And rather than turning him away, you might have brought him to my attention and earned yourself a gold star and a lollipop.'

The constable continued to stare at him in mute bemusement.

Bliss rolled his eyes and shook his head. 'The man is here to feed life in the form of battery power into his cameras which are, I'm guessing, motion-activated. Constable, as I'm sure even you must realise, motion is not restricted to woodland creatures; yet somehow it never crossed your mind that those same cameras were just as likely to be triggered by our victim and his killer.'

Light dawned slowly somewhere within the officer's dim eyes. Tension ebbed away, resulting in a shoulder slump of dramatic proportions. Bliss ignored him and turned his attention back to the man from the Wildlife Trust. 'Sir, when this officer lifts the tape for you, please walk over to that man there.' Bliss pointed across to Bishop. 'Tell him what you told me. Then tell him exactly where your cameras are. I can't allow you onto our crime scene, but if you give your batteries to my sergeant he will make sure they get swapped for the dying ones. Okay?'

He did not wait for a response from either man. Instead, he turned and walked across to a small gathering of suits and uniforms. 'Is one of you DCI Kerry Ansolem?' he asked.

The lone woman in the group turned to face him. 'Take a wild guess,' she said, throwing out her arms and grinning. She was friendly enough, though seemed somewhat guarded.

'My apologies,' Bliss said. 'Can't be too careful these days. If I assume you're a woman and it turns out you're a man in a skirt, I'm in all kinds of deep shit.' He held out his hand. 'DI Bliss. Peterborough. Running the JTFO with London and Swindon.'

'Pleased to meet you, Inspector.'

Her hand was small but warm in his as they shook. 'Likewise. So, what do you have for me?'

'Victim is one Frederick Swift. He had ID on him. Correction – in fact, he had two separate sets of ID, but when we ran his prints he came back as Swift. His name also popped up with your arrest warrant flag. Unfortunately, our cuffs are useless, what with his remains being scattered over a small area of our finest Essex woodland. Our scene manager tells me a few parts may be missing, but it's impossible to be certain at this stage. If any fail to show up, it could be they were carried off by animals, or perhaps removed from the scene by whoever carved him up. Judging by your case, I assume the latter is a distinct possibility.'

'Most likely, yes,' Bliss agreed. If first impressions were anything to go by, he was going to like this woman. His thoughts turned to the camera hides – had the investigation finally caught a break by having the murder, or at least the killer, captured on video? Although he knew neither Andy nor Stephen Price could be directly responsible, either could still have been working with somebody else – but the devastating scene here blew apart his notion of that person being Freddy Swift. Bliss had no idea where to turn next.

'Nasty old business,' Ansolem said, shuddering reflexively. 'Nothing I haven't seen before, but this looks like a vicious attack.'

'I'll want to take a look for myself.'

'Of course. We're waiting for the crime scene manager to create a safe pathway for us. He wasn't happy with us for taking a quick look when we arrived, and as he's pals with the Chief Super we decided to accept the bollocking and wait in the wings.'

Bliss laughed. 'Sounds familiar. CSI managers can be such drama queens at times. The head of our forensics team calls me a cowboy. Always complaining about me. Tells me I have no respect for his profession.'

'And do you?'

She asked the question in a way that suggested he was being judged on his answer. He nodded. 'I do, as it happens, though I'd never let on. We rely on them for prosecuting these scumbags. It's just… because their job is meticulous, they're often so busy it can take hours for them to respond, and I'm too bloody impatient to hang around doing nothing.'

It was Ansolem's turn to laugh. 'Sounds like we were separated at birth.'

They chatted for a few minutes, at which point Bishop came bustling over, a backpack hooked over one shoulder. He and the DCI exchanged greetings before he turned to Bliss. 'Boss, the man has a dozen cameras in hides close by. We're pretty sure a few of them are pointing at the trail going towards our crime scene. Most are tucked away at low level, but others are mounted in trees. If we're lucky, our man is now a film star.'

Bliss filled Ansolem in on the confrontation in the car park, and saw her anticipation ratchet up several notches – as had his own. In carving Swift up and depositing the pieces along the woodland path, their man had, in Bliss's view, reached saturation point. Perhaps Swift was the last of them and he had decided to go out in style. Either way, their perpetrator was finished with the game and unravelling fast.

What was still unclear in Bliss's mind was where the Prices came into the picture – if they did at all. And the deviation from the usual method of torture bothered him. Why treat Swift differently? Why break the pattern now? If the desire for personal revenge had overtaken Andy or Stephen Price, either or both men taking their time with their victims, enjoying their pain, why had they not finished their campaign in the same way? He suspected it was because they were not involved in this murder. It was looking increasingly likely that the man who had abducted the old gangsters and deposited the bags of their flesh had been talked into taking the last one off the map quickly. And – worst of all – with such precise timing as to put both men in the clear.

'So, do you know where the cameras are?' he asked Bishop.

His DS pulled a scrap of paper from his breast pocket. 'The bloke drew us a sketch. Approximate locations. When I told him what we needed and why, he quietened down a bit. And he gave me a dozen new SD cards. As soon as we're allowed entry, I'll swap out the batteries and cards and take the footage from all twelve cameras with us.'

Bliss nodded. 'Good thinking, Bish.' He glanced across at DCI Ansolem. 'I'm sorry. I'm taking a lot for granted here. This is your scene.'

'No, no, no. I understood what we had here. Basically, I just babysat the scene for you. Now you're on site, so it's all yours, Inspector Bliss.'

'Cheers. I do appreciate it. The wrangling we sometimes have to do with colleagues in different areas pisses me off. I'm grateful for your understanding.'

'It may sound trite, but I don't give a flying fart provided the bastard responsible for this mess is nailed to the wall for what he did. I hope at least one of those cameras exposes him for you.'

'For all of us,' Bliss said, casting his eyes over the trail and spotting movement. White protective suits were coming their way. 'Looks like we're up next.'

THIRTY-NINE

THE FIND THIS TIME was exponentially more grisly; no single white carrier bag was going to contain the result. Freddy Swift had been unmercifully sliced and diced, appendages and limbs hacked off and scattered along the wooded pathway. His head and neck remained attached to the torso, but virtually every expanse of flesh had been deeply lacerated or excised. The person responsible either had a deep hatred for the man, or had fully emerged from their psychotic pupal state at the onset of this killing.

Bliss made arrangements with DCI Ansolem for all forensic and investigative exhibits to be transported up to the Hinchingbrooke divisional headquarters as soon as they had been gathered, tagged and recorded. The body parts would go to Nancy Drinkwater at the Peterborough city mortuary. After offering his thanks to the various Essex teams, he and Bishop drove back to Thorpe Wood with a stash of twelve SD cards secured in static-free packaging. The station's in-house tech division had recently been swallowed up by the more comprehensive unit in Huntingdon, but DC Ansari had received a bag of electronic goodies from the IT techs on the day they left. Bliss felt sure she would have the necessary cables and digital readers to hand.

Less than ten minutes after he and Bishop arrived back at HQ, the vastly reduced team sat in the incident room and watched closely as Ansari flicked through the footage on card after card. On several occasions she paused a clip – the camera in question having picked up foot and leg movement – made a note of the SD card's serial number, and logged it into evidence. They were four cards in when the breakthrough they were looking for appeared on screen.

The figure was unaware of the hidden cameras, but walked with a stoop and wore a navy blue sweatshirt with its hood pulled up, so none of the viewers were able to get a clear picture of the wearer's face. Whoever it was had a rucksack on their back, and their gait suggested the load they carried was a heavy one. Bliss thought the figure had the build and shape of a man, and got nods of agreement from his team when he voiced that opinion.

He watched the screen without daring to blink. Irritated at not being able to see his features, Bliss's gaze took in the physical stamp of the man; the way he moved, the bodily shifts and tics. At one point he frowned; an alert was going off inside his head, though he was unable to pinpoint why. His subconscious told him he had seen something of note, but it was short on specifics. For some unaccountable reason, he thought it tied in with something Chandler had said, but the sheer volume of information they had exchanged in recent days prevented him from picking it out.

They moved on through the other cards. In all, three of them held footage of note, including one stark piece showing the hooded figure distributing body parts and slices of human flesh as though scattering rose petals at a wedding. At no point was the team able to get a clear picture of the killer, but there were ample opportunities to gain a lasting impression. The third card retained had the best view of all, and when it was finished, Bliss asked to see it again.

He watched in silence. When it was done, he told Ansari to run it through one last time. Still alarm bells jangled, red flags snapping in a stiff breeze, springing up and bouncing around inside his brain. There was little to see on the screen beyond the overall dimensions and movements of the figure, yet some base instinct insisted he was missing a detail relevant to identifying the killer.

Bliss blew out a laboured breath. He felt the eyes of his team upon him. The video feed had ended again and they were now staring at a black screen. Ansari asked if he wanted her to run it one last time, but Bliss shook his head. He closed his eyes and replayed it for himself.

And this time he saw it.

Having suffered with Ménière's disease for over a decade, Bliss knew all about imbalance. Since his diagnosis he had altered the way he moved, allowing for the sudden, often minute shifts that originated from his brain when it misconstrued the signals from his eyes and ears. He captured the figure in his mind's eye and held it there as it crept along the wooded pathway. In doing so, he observed the occasional lurch to one side. He drew a bead on the ungainly movement and asked himself why this man was struggling with his balance.

The uncertain movements suggested the instability was new to him; that something had occurred recently, resulting in a loss of equilibrium and a need to alter the mechanics of movement after a lifetime of familiarity. A blow to the head? A loss of hearing, perhaps an infection? As the vision took root inside his head, Bliss noticed one specific motion occurring every few steps. And when it happened, the man's arms came out to steady himself.

Bliss leapt to his feet. 'Gul, are you able to splice together all of the relevant clips, or will you have to send it all off to Huntingdon?'

'To do it properly, it's best we hand it over to the experts, boss.'

He nodded, grateful for her honesty. 'Okay. If you have a way to copy the crucial footage to disk, please do so. But please get it all over to the techs.'

'You got something, boss?' Bishop was squinting at him.

'I'm not sure, Bish. Give me a few minutes, will you?'

At his desk, Bliss pulled up the operation files. His lips were as dry as soil baked in the summer sun, and his heartbeat had kicked up a notch or two. Annoyed with himself that he was unable to put whatever it was Chandler had said to him together with the video footage, he thought the case files might jog his memory. He navigated his way through a series of pages before landing on a document containing individual records and photos. He cycled through them until he came to the name that had surfaced while he had looked within himself for answers. Initially satisfied that the person whose record he was checking out and the figure in Epping Forest might feasibly be the same person, he shifted to Google and began running searches using specific keywords.

As he searched, Bliss told himself he had lost it this time. This person could not be their killer. It was an impossibility – as their own investigative records proved – yet for some reason he was unable to see past it. Ten minutes later, an article popped up on the page that caused Bliss to push back in his chair and question everything he thought he knew about this case.

FORTY

ANDY PRICE'S TWO-STOREY VICTORIAN end-terrace house had retained its original brick exterior and wooden sash frames in the upper and lower bay windows, but a new roof and a recent paint job gave it both a new and deliberately distressed appearance. It was an upmarket location for a man who had made his way in the world. The solicitor was not at home, but his wife told Bliss and Bishop where to find him. The Wray Crescent cricket pitches in neighbouring Finsbury Park were not far away. Bliss knew the area well, having lived there himself for a while during his marriage.

He found the irregular circular fields easily and parked on a nearby street where vehicles stood tight together like sardines in a can. Price was standing with a small group of spectators, watching a cricket match in full flow. A loud appeal went up, followed by groans of disappointment as the umpire judged the batsman to be not out. As he joined in with the playful jeering at the bowler, Price spotted Bliss and Bishop approaching and broke away from his companions. The look on his face suggested he was not entirely happy to see the two men about to disrupt his day.

'I hope you have a good reason for being here,' Price said in place of a greeting. He kept his voice low and even, but there was grit in it.

'I think you'll find we have, Mr Price,' Bliss said. He introduced Bishop but was not surprised when Price failed to offer his hand.

'Let's hear it, Inspector Bliss. I make no apology for my demeanour. Your visit the other day was unsettling, to say the least.'

Bliss feigned surprise. 'How so?'

'My son and I felt it was duplicitous. On the surface you were there to inform us of the reopening of my wife's murder case, but I've been in this business too long not to recognise a fishing expedition when I see one.'

Keeping up the pretence, Bliss said, 'I'm sorry you took it that way, sir. I assure you it was not my intention. Perhaps a clash of styles. That said, I'm bringing you good news today.'

Price gave a lengthy sigh. 'The one piece of good news you could possibly bring me is that you've apprehended those responsible for torturing and murdering my wife. That, or they're all dead. In fact, the latter may be preferable, given how few years most of them would have left to serve for what they did.'

'It's the former,' Bliss told him. 'Perhaps a bit of both.'

Now he had the man's full attention.

'What did you say?'

'Let me explain, Mr Price.' Bliss started walking slowly into an open area of the field, away from the pitch. Price kept pace, Bishop having fallen in a step behind. 'We haven't grabbed up anybody as yet, but we do now know who we're looking for and where to find him. He is certainly one of the men responsible for what happened to your wife. As for the others, if they are alive you can be sure they are in a rough old state. I'm confident we'll obtain their locations from the culprit. We'll find them, whether dead or alive.'

'Why are you telling me this now?' Price asked. 'Why didn't you wait until you had this man in custody?'

Bliss slapped a pained expression on his face. 'Mr Price, I came here to tell you in person because I didn't want you to hear through the grapevine or from reporters knocking on your front door. I felt we owed you, having taken twenty-six years or thereabouts to solve the case.'

Price hung his head for a moment, and Bliss watched his reaction keenly. Bishop stood directly behind the man, barring any attempt to run should things go awry. When he looked up, Andy Price's face was tear-streaked. He wasn't sobbing, nor crying aloud – merely giving in to a kind of silent weeping befitting a grief so deep it could not be fathomed. Bliss felt an immediate surge of sympathy for the man who had lost his wife in such an horrific fashion. Nobody deserved such a fate. And if he had chosen to exact revenge after all these years, who was Bliss to condemn him for it?

The police, he told himself silently. *It's your job.*

If Andy Price was guilty of anything.

'We were about to drive over to Dartmouth Park to inform your son,' Bliss said gently. 'I'm still happy to do so, but if you'd rather attend to that yourself…'

'Yes. Yes, I would.' Price wiped away his tears and drew himself upright.

'We'll be in touch, sir.' Bliss turned to leave. 'Soon. Later today, I imagine. Tomorrow at the latest.'

'Inspector… can you… are you able to give me a name? Can you tell me who killed my wife?'

'I suspect you already know a few of those names, Mr Price.' Bliss met the man's gaze full on. 'I'm sure you've been keeping up with recent events, and will be familiar with some of the recent victims. As for the man we are about to arrest – no, I'm afraid I can't tell you who he is. I'm sure you understand my reasons, given your profession.'

The two detectives left Price nodding to himself and reaching for his mobile phone. Bliss took out his own and punched in

Superintendent Conway's number. 'We're done here, sir,' he said. 'Price is calling his son as we speak.'

Sitting in an unmarked saloon opposite the Highgate Road chapel, fifty yards from the house in which Stephen Price lived with his family, Conway said, 'We've got eyes on his home, and he's inside. If he makes a call, we have ears on. If he moves, the Met have five additional mobile followers, including two bikes.'

'We're similarly equipped,' Bliss said.

'Are you sure we were right to hand this part of the job over to the Met?'

'I know you're concerned, but this is their turf, sir. They know these streets like the backs of their hands, so in addition to following they can also anticipate and get ahead of the game. In my experience, outside of counterterrorism, these are the best surveillance officers around. We're lucky to have them at such short notice.'

Luck had played no part in their fortune; Bliss had called in a couple of favours. He was sure his team were up to the task, but had felt that a brief expecting them to watch two men and follow their every movement was too broad for the JTFO alone. If his time working for the Met had been tainted, his years with the NCA and the inevitable overlap with them had turned the situation around. It had gained him new friendships, and renewed others.

As they left the playing fields and hit the pavement heading back to the car, Bliss detected something in Bishop's manner. The big man was thinking hard, which always made him look as if he were in pain. 'Something on your mind, Bish?' he asked casually.

'Actually, boss, there is.'

'Spit it out, then.'

'I realise it's probably not the time or the place, but I can't help noticing DI Riseborough's absence from this part of the op. None of his team are involved, either.'

Bliss stopped walking and turned to face his sergeant. 'You're right. This is neither the time nor the place. If you're wondering if it has something to do with the newspaper leak, you're right to wonder. That's all I can or will say at the moment. Plenty of time for recriminations after we've put this to bed. You all right with that?'

Bishop nodded. 'Yes, boss. Whatever you say. But speaking of putting things to bed, are you sure this is going to work?'

The two started walking again, allowing Bliss a few seconds to consider his plan. As they reached the car, Bliss popped the locks and said, 'To be brutally honest with you, Bish, no, I'm not. But if I'm Andy or Stephen Price, I'm going to panic right about now. I'm going to want to cut the one remaining tie to our victims, and I'm going to want to do it as soon as I possibly can. This may provide us with our one clear opening, our last chance to find some answers. Whether we succeed or fail, we have an opportunity, and we can't afford to waste it.'

FORTY-ONE

CHIGWELL PROVIDED EASY ACCESS to both London and the motorway grid. That afternoon, several different police units converged on a lake adjacent to the river Roding and the line of railway tracks between Roding Valley and Chigwell stations. The precise location for the meeting had been mentioned during one of the phone conversations being monitored by the comms team. This gave Bliss the opportunity to post his various JTFO colleagues close by. Because of this piece of timely good fortune, everybody was concealed in place long before the appointed time, and ready for what was about to go down.

The sun was low on the western horizon, but a bloodshot sky provided sufficient lighting for clear visuals. The day's heat had faded, but still the JTFO personnel felt sticky and sweaty as they readied themselves for what lay ahead. Every few minutes or so, Bliss offered words of encouragement, soothing their natural fears. At this point of any operation, stress levels always went through the roof, and he did his best to keep everybody calm. Having an edge was a positive asset, but it had to be finely honed.

Stephen Price was the first of their suspects to arrive. According to the team following him, he had taken no obvious countersurveillance measures; evidently he suspected nothing as he drove through Seven Sisters, past the Walthamstow reservoirs and Woodford on his way to the rendezvous point. Having left his vehicle a couple of streets away, he stooped to pass through an opening in a long stretch of chain-link fencing, and hurried across the railway tracks, accompanied by the gentle crunch and shift of stones beneath his weight.

Less than five minutes after Stephen's arrival, his father parked up in another street close by and used the same method of accessing the grounds beyond the fence. Bliss found himself tensing in eager anticipation, worry causing him to chew on his bottom lip. From his position, he now had a clear view of both men, and their arrival had amped up the pressure tenfold.

Father and son huddled close together. They spoke in low voices, the sound almost obscured by the serenade of crickets from the tall grass along the treeline. The younger man shifted from foot to foot, and Bliss noticed the fingers of both his hands flexing. He was by far the more anxious of the two, his father standing stoically by his side.

In Bliss's ear a faint voice said, 'Vehicle approaching.'

He did not have to utter a word. Everybody had heard the same announcement. This was the stage at which the sluice gates opened up fully, pumping adrenaline through the body and flooding it with enough stimulus to cause a respiration overload. Bliss had every confidence in the training of his own team, and extended the same respect to those officers he did not know. But experience told him this was the most dangerous moment of any stakeout. A solitary unfamiliar sound, a discordant reaction to something said or done, any sudden reactive movement at all, and everything might yet go terribly wrong. Bliss felt his own heart thumping away behind his ribs, and wondered how his colleagues were handling themselves.

'Vehicle stopped. Lights off, engine off. Possible suspect exiting vehicle and heading towards the railway line.'

And so it went on.

The surveillance officer ideally positioned to observe all ingress and egress to the location relayed the man's every laboured movement right up until he joined Andy and Stephen Price in a small clearing between a field and the ring of trees surrounding the lake. The moment he walked into view of Bliss's team, each of them sucked in a lungful of air and released it slowly. It was as if until this moment they had not believed in the man's identity, in spite of their DI's conviction.

Phil Walker.

Their fourth victim.

FORTY-TWO

OLLY BISHOP, STANDING TWO yards away from Bliss, turned to face him. He said nothing, but gave a single respectful nod. Bliss returned it with one of his own. He was unable to stop his body from shaking, such was his excitement at laying eyes on Phil Walker for the first time. He was right about the man's involvement, but there was still an enormous amount to learn about the relationship between him and the Prices.

'What the bloody hell is going on, Stephen?' the newcomer demanded. His voice was urgent, laced with tension.

Andy Price stepped forward and held up both hands to fend the man off. 'Take it easy, Phil. We want to know if our loose ends have all been tied off. That's all.'

'What, and you couldn't have asked me that over the blower?'

'I don't trust the phone. I want this over and done with, so please tell me your part is now finished.'

'Yeah, as agreed.' Walker turned to face the younger man. 'I visited every site and did exactly as you asked. I clocked the state of those unlucky bastards, too. You didn't mess about with them, that's for sure.'

Stephen Price spat on the ground. 'I wish they'd suffered more. For longer.'

'Yeah, well, judging by the mess you made of them, they went through quite enough as it was. Ben was long gone. By days, I'd say. The others needed taking care of. But I did the business, and nobody's ever going to find them – trust me on that. So what now?'

'Now we go our separate ways.'

Walker gave a satisfied nod, but stood his ground. He hunched deeper into his lightweight jacket. 'That's fine by me. But don't go thinking this is a well you can keep drawing from. I don't ever want to hear from either of you again.'

Andy Price snorted. 'Believe me, the feeling is mutual. But the fact is, we have no need to.'

'Fair enough. I think we both got a pukka deal out of this. You had your revenge after all these years, and I made sure nobody was ever going to talk about what happened to your wife. In the end, they got what they deserved, so fuck 'em. Me and you two now have our own cold war going on. Both got our own nuclear deterrent, so to speak. But don't get any bold ideas about taking me out, either of you. It's never going to happen.'

'We wouldn't dream of it, Phil. Like you say, my Geraldine can finally be at peace; Val too, I hope. As for those evil bastards, I'd say they've had this coming for a bloody long time.'

That was enough for Bliss. 'Move in,' he said, taking his first step before he'd finished giving the order.

The response was instantaneous and loud. Police officers exploded from their concealment, surrounding the three men in a flurry of arms and legs, a cacophony of warning cries telling them to stand still and raise their hands. To the fore, officers armed with tasers, their odd-looking yellow guns extended. A canine unit had been standing by barely half a mile away, and Bliss called them in now in case anyone tried to make a break for it across open ground.

Ignoring the instruction to stand still, Andy Price dropped to his knees and clasped both hands together over his head. His son froze in place, but Walker reacted with surprising speed and agility. He stepped behind Stephen Price and wrapped his truncated left arm around the man's chest. His right hand now gripped a long, machete-type blade; it came around smoothly to rest directly over Price's throat.

'Stand back!' Walker called out, his voice deep and powerful. 'I mean it. You come any closer and I'll drop this fucker where he stands.'

As one, the ring of officers halted their forward momentum. Bliss swore beneath his breath, realising Walker must have been carrying the weapon underneath his jacket. He sized up the situation immediately and took charge of proceedings. 'You do that and you lose your leverage, Walker,' he said. His voice carried well as he inched closer. He and his team had tucked themselves away behind the closest thicket of trees; now out in the open, their advance slowed but did not stop entirely.

'And if I don't release him, how long do you think you can keep this standoff going?'

Bliss held up a hand, palm out. 'Haven't you just outlined your own problem? Either you kill him now and we grab you up, or you keep the knife to his throat and eventually you'll get tired and give up anyway. There's no way out of this for any of you, and threatening to kill Stephen Price is no threat at all, is it?'

Walker threw his head back and howled his rage into the darkening sky like an animal. 'How the fuck did you know?' he spat, wild eyes bulging from their sockets.

'We've had surveillance on Andy and Stephen since we informed them we were about to make an arrest.'

'You lied to them? You lied to them and these dozy bloody idiots bought it?'

Bliss shook his head, his eyes darting everywhere. 'We didn't lie, Walker. We *are* about to make an arrest. Three, in fact.'

After a moment, in a smaller, calmer voice, Walker said, 'Who were you expecting to turn up to meet them?'

'You.'

'That's bollocks! After I gave up my hand you must have had me down as a victim.'

'We did at first. And then we didn't. The truth is, you screwed up: a couple of cameras caught you when you took out Freddy Swift.' As he spoke, Bliss's feet continued to slide forward.

'What the... you got me on film?'

'Yep. Starring role in your own horror movie.' Bliss wet his lips and thought about how to keep Walker's mind racing. 'Tell me, why did you do that to him, Walker? Why carve him up and toss his body parts around like confetti? Your last instruction was just to kill him, I'm guessing. I doubt you were told to eviscerate the man.'

Walker glared back, snarling. His eyes bulged and a thick cord arced across his forehead. 'Fuck him! And fuck you, too! Fuck all of you! Freddy Swift was a fucking nonce. He deserved everything he got.'

Bliss thought back to the young girl at Swift's porn factory; it wasn't a stretch to imagine the man taking part in a few private sessions of his own. His gaze drifted across to the man kneeling on the ground. Andy Price was completely focussed on his son and the fierce-looking blade at his throat. Bliss saw tension rippling the lines on his face.

'Don't even think about doing anything stupid, Andy,' he called out, catching his attention. 'Walker has nowhere to go. And he has no reason to finish the job on your son.'

'No reason not to, either,' Walker said, a crooked smile plastered across his face. He looked deranged. In fact, Bliss thought the man may now be so far beyond the edge there was no pulling him back. He had to take a risk.

'That's not true,' he said. He took a step closer, both hands now raised in supplication. 'We know all you did before you butchered Freddy Swift was abduct your old mates and drop off a few carrier bags.'

Bliss left out the part where Walker had severed Harrison's hand, hoping he would believe the police had little on him other than conspiracy prior to the killing in Epping Forest. To explain that away, he would have to concoct one hell of a story, but if he thought he had wriggle room he might just take the bait.

That hope died in Bliss a short moment later.

'You think I didn't know what this crazy bastard was doing with them?' Walker yanked back on Price's chest. His left arm, swathed in bandages at the wrist, still managed to apply impressive strength. 'He wanted to pay them back in kind for what they did to his old lady. Told me killing them was too good for them, and way too quick. Oh, and let's not forget my having to sever Tommy's hand before I took it to Tower Hill, just to give these wankers an alibi. Besides, I don't care what you say… it's not going to make any difference now after what I did to Freddy.'

Bliss sensed an opportunity. 'It may do if you tell me where they all are. The more you say now, the more we can do for you when it comes to sentencing. And you're right about Swift, too. Who cares about a paedo?'

Walker shook his head. His hand was trembling and mucus dribbled from both nostrils. Sweat poured from his hairline. 'It's too late. They're all dead. Burned and buried. All four of them are where they belong, roasting in Hell.'

Bliss eyed his colleagues. Those carrying tasers were not in range of Walker, though at least two of them appeared to be edging closer. He needed to buy them some time. 'All of which makes you the clean-up man on top of what we already know. It was Stephen who took his time with them.'

'You're bloody right I did!' Price cried, pulling against Walker in defiance, attempting to shrug out of his tight grip. 'Those men debased my mother, butchered her and tossed her away like she was a piece of garbage. We had to live with that knowledge. Me, my dad, my sister. But it all got too much for Val. It wore her down. She gave it her best shot, but in the end it won. *They* fucking won.'

'I'm sorry for everything you and your family went through, Stephen,' Bliss said. 'And there's not a man or woman here who doesn't sympathise with you. Many of us, me included, can also understand why you did what you did to those men. It's human nature, and people are going to understand that.'

He neglected to mention the part about none of it mattering, that ends so depraved were never justified by even the most harrowing of beginnings. But he didn't have to utter the words for Stephen Price to realise the consequences of his own actions; the man didn't need to be a solicitor to be aware of the hefty punishment coming his way.

The thought snapped Bliss's head up to full alert. He opened his mouth to call out a warning, but he was too late.

Because, at the exact same moment, Price's hands came up to wrap around the long blade of the machete. He gripped the sharpened steel and in a single movement dragged it violently across his throat and around to the side of his neck, opening up the flesh in a deep and unforgiving gash. Blood first gurgled from the wound and then began to surge freely, spurting rhythmically with the beat of the man's heart. Walker gasped in horror and recoiled, releasing his captive as he took a hurried step back. He stood blinking Stephen Price's blood away from his eyes, his face and clothes already smothered in arterial spray.

Experience and training kicked in immediately as officers swept forward to take charge of the rapidly escalating situation. Andy

Price had leapt to his feet, reaching for his son, a cry of terror pouring from his lips. It took three men to pull him off and secure him where he stood, his mouth wide open as if he were screaming at a pitch none of them could hear.

Four members of the local team crowded around Stephen Price, whose bleeding decreased with each fresh eruption. They forced him to the ground and flipped him over onto his back, at which point two officers compressed the gaping wound in his neck with their hands. A third stripped off his shirt, bundled it up and pushed it hard against the slick and tattered flesh. Urgency was manifest in every raised voice and stern command.

Meanwhile, Walker had reacted with that innate instinct for survival his predatory kind always have; with everybody's attention diverted, he'd made a desperate bid to escape. Bliss's own focus had become split, but he caught the man's movement from the corner of his eye and reacted to it in an instant. Walker's feet initially struggled to gain purchase, but he managed to stagger upright and started to run. He headed into the field, the one area Bliss had not been able to populate with officers. After a dozen or so strides, he angled left and headed for the railway line.

Bliss responded swiftly, setting off in pursuit. He looked beyond the fleeing figure of Walker and spotted a train heading in their direction. Summoning up whatever his tired body still had, he immediately realised that if Walker made it across the tracks ahead of the train and nobody else did, it might be enough to buy him all the time and distance he needed to get away.

'Get those dogs here!' he cried out. 'Get those bloody dogs here!'

His legs pounding up and down like rusty pistons, Bliss called out across comms to the team of surveillance officers who had observed all three suspects entering the plot. If Walker evaded his own chase, maybe they would be able to head him off.

Up ahead, he saw Walker labouring just as much as he was. The man was lean and fit for his age, but the years were against him in this situation. Fear would be constricting his windpipe, and he'd be struggling to draw in deep enough breaths to keep up the pace he'd set. Bliss could tell he was gaining on the man, but still Walker was closer to the rails and the train pounding towards them.

He wasted no breath demanding that Walker stop; the man was locked on escape and only physical force could prevent it from happening. Bliss felt a jagged spike of pain in his sides, and his own breathing became ragged. It was laughable; two ageing men attempting to recapture their youth.

Now only twenty yards from the tracks, Walker closed in on an embankment whose steep incline would slow him further. The train had curved around into the long straight length of track and was now bearing down on them, but Bliss thought their suspect would make it across the line before two hundred tons of thrashing steel and glass became a temporary barrier. For one awful moment, Bliss pictured himself, Walker and the train reaching the same spot on the tracks at precisely the same instant.

Desperate now, he called upon his last reserves of strength and energy and put in one final burst. Walker was slowing all the while, and Bliss was gaining on him with every stride. The clattering of the train wheels over joins in the track was impossibly loud, and Bliss imagined he could feel the beast's heat. Walker's feet started to slither on gravel rather than turf as he reached the plateau, which told Bliss time was up: if he wanted to stop Walker escaping, it was now or never. In a last desperate bid, he lunged forward and dived, arms outstretched. He felt one sweeping hand connect with something solid. When he saw Walker stumble, he realised he'd grasped the man's shoe but the foot had popped right out of it.

Now Bliss was down, but Walker was somehow managing to carry on scurrying away even as he fought to regain his stability. As

Bliss's chest hit the gravel with a thump that knocked the remaining air from his lungs, his face smashed into the small, sharp stones. Bright starbursts of light exploded like fireworks in his eyes, obscuring his vision. He felt rapid movement on both sides of his prostrate body, and a second later he looked up to see Gul Ansari rush by in a blur of arms and legs, closely followed by a uniformed officer. DC Ansari moved with astonishing speed across the large stones and hurled herself at Walker like a missile, grabbing him by the waist and bringing him down in a spray of stones and pebbles barely a split second before the passing train thundered past, three feet from his head.

Bliss raised himself up on his elbows, coughing up stones and dirt and dust. Walker wasn't done attempting to wrestle himself free, but he was no match for Ansari and the uniformed man as they swarmed all over him. Within seconds they had their suspect's arms pinned to his back, and Walker let out a yelp of pain and bitter frustration. By now the dogs had reached them and were jumping around and growling, adding to the mayhem. Bliss forced out a sigh of relief when he saw handcuffs glimmering softly in the fading light. The chase was over. He slumped to the ground once more, panting and gasping.

By the time he had struggled to his feet on unsteady legs, Walker was being led away. Bliss's remaining colleagues had caught up and now surrounded him, throwing all kinds of questions at him. After reassuring them that he was only winded, he turned to survey the scene they had left behind. Secured by four officers, a sobbing Andy Price had been allowed to remain close by while they fought for his son's life.

Bliss felt a rush of heat swarm over his chest, into his throat and up to his face. He blinked away the giddiness and focussed on the man now receiving emergency first aid. He had not anticipated Stephen Price's ultimate capitulation; the man who was in many ways both victim and perpetrator settling for a quick death rather than a lengthy jail sentence. That possibility had never entered the equation, not during any stage of the planning.

'You're going to need some first aid, boss,' Ansari said, her eyes narrowed as she walked by with her prisoner. 'Some of that gravel opened you up.'

'I'm fine,' Bliss insisted, though he felt anything but. He waved away her obvious distress and brushed himself down, feeling the nagging after-effects of the chase spreading an ache throughout his body in a single concussive wave. He tried pulling in deeper breaths, but each one felt like a punch to his chest.

'Gul!' he called out, looking up. When she turned, he raised a thumb and gave a single nod of congratulations.

Ansari broke into a wide grin and she nodded back at him. By her side, Walker dragged his feet, head bowed, the fight driven from him. Bliss looked on, pride swelling inside him over his young DC's heroics.

Then Bishop stepped into his line of vision, concern in his eyes. 'You still need to get yourself checked out, boss. You hit the ground hard, and you're bleeding.'

Bliss shook his head, more at the scene they had left behind than in response to his DS. 'What a bloody mess,' he said, his voice a harsh rasp.

'You couldn't have known,' Bishop said in his ear, little more than a whisper.

Bliss continued to focus his attention straight ahead. There was nothing they could do now but look on and ask themselves how it had gone so badly wrong.

'No, I couldn't, Bish,' Bliss said eventually. 'But that doesn't change a damn thing.'

FORTY-THREE

IT WAS SHORTLY AFTER midnight when the task force next met, and at that point they agreed to postpone the planned interrogations. Their decision meant the investigation would have no issues with PACE, while at the same time allowing everyone involved to regroup. Their prisoners had subsequently been given time to eat and rest, to be checked and cleared by a doctor, and offered legal representation.

Bliss was feeling the benefit of the delay, having had time to get cleaned up and change his clothes. After holding off and observing while others went hard at both men, getting nowhere with either one, finally it was his turn. He'd been happy enough to take a back seat so far throughout the morning, but having keenly watched the interviews he realised the odds were stacked against him.

Bliss went with Walker first, hoping to elicit information he could later use against Andy Price, but he didn't rate his chances. Neither Warburton nor Conway had budged Walker since the arrest, his implacable stare and disinclination to speak grating on Bliss's raw nerve endings.

To everyone's surprise, Walker had not demanded a solicitor. Bliss couldn't decide if the decision was a sign of overconfidence, if the man was wary of allowing the depths of his depravity to be known by an outsider, or if he had merely accepted the magnitude of his crimes and the likely consequences. His expression gave nothing away as Bliss and Chandler entered the interview room and sat down at a small table pressed up against the wall opposite the door. The dull green tiles seemed not to reflect anything from the recessed tube lighting in the ceiling.

Bliss began by outlining the salient information he and the JTFO had gleaned so far. He opened up with the murder of Geraldine Price and then walked the case through, including everything the police had overheard by the lake the day before; he ended his opening salvo with the man's unsolicited confessions. Walker eyed him throughout, tilting his head this way and that as if studying his inquisitor in the hope of picking up his own read. He said nothing. Bliss got no further when it came to questioning him. Judging by Phil Walker's previous form and the lack of charges brought against him, his man-of-stone performance was no act.

After forty minutes of spinning plates and seeing them all crash to the floor one after the other, Bliss took his final shot. 'I have to say I'm surprised you don't want to drop Andy Price in it up to his neck. We suspect him of being both an advocate and an accomplice to everything you and his son did, but with what we have on him at the moment, he stands every chance of walking away from this with barely a scratch on his reputation. It'll all fall on his son's shoulders. And yours. Surely that's got to hurt?'

Walker's expression altered slightly; reflected in his eyes, sculpted by a shift in his body. He continued to stare back mutely, but although the change had been subtle, Bliss thought he had an idea regarding the man's refusal to talk.

'He's suffered enough, right?' Bliss said. 'Andy Price. Lost his wife all those years ago, then his daughter, and now his son. His entire family ripped away from him. You're thinking he'll be punished enough because he'll never escape those demons.'

Still no response.

'As for you, Walker, I'm willing to bet that whatever happened to Geraldine Price, you were mainly on the periphery – not directly involved, but I'm guessing you helped out in the cover-up afterwards because those men were useful to you. So now you're looking to give Price the break you think he deserves, knowing his mind will create a prison cell for him anyway. As evil as you are, you have respect for everything the Price family endured, and for Andy in particular. Keeping schtum now is not even any kind of penance on your part, because it costs you so little.'

Bliss gave it a moment, then smiled. 'You do know they were there to murder you, don't you? Stephen Price had two penknives in his trouser pockets, each with a four-inch blade. The Prices were never going to allow you to walk out of there last night. I can't believe you're going to let that go.'

'Save your breath,' Walker said at last. 'It won't do you any good.'

Bliss shook his head, energised by having got the man to talk at last. 'No, I don't think I will. I'll have my say. Stop me when I mention anything you know to be untrue. See, I'm guessing Stephen had something on you and applied pressure you couldn't wriggle out of. Something which, if it became widely known, would scupper all your plans for making a mint with your new business venture, and halt your political ambitions in their tracks. I'm pretty sure he had a decent grasp of the role you played, and how he could make it work in his favour. I'm guessing you agreed partly because of the blackmail, but also because you realised those same men were capable of dropping you in it in exchange for shorter sentences if Price instead went to the police with what he knew.'

Silence hung like a veil across the table. The prisoner glanced around at the walls, seemingly unmoved. Bliss absorbed every tic of his cheek, each flicker of those cold, hard eyes, and the small but telling twitch of his lips. He read Walker and understood this was a story whose ending he would never learn.

'Come on, Walker,' he said. 'It was a win-win for you, surely. After all, yours was the easy part. No getting your hands too dirty. What you did to Tommy Harrison was under orders… But then we come to Freddy Swift, of course. I'm betting he lost his nerve and saw the writing on the wall. He worked out he was next and came to you for help, having no clue he was meeting with the man he should have feared most. With Price's little game winding down, you saw your opportunity and offed Freddy while you had the chance.'

Something pulsed along Walker's jawline, but still he kept his mouth closed. The pattern of his breathing altered on several occasions, but he never once showed signs of panic. Bliss accepted this man was never going to tell them anything. He'd said enough back in that field, the meeting recorded by a forensic team videographer brought in by Bliss to film the entire takedown. This would prove invaluable when it came to the prosecution, but from the man himself they would get nothing further. Bliss did not bother to glance at Chandler to see if she had questions of her own. There was no point. Phil Walker had nothing to gain by speaking to them. Bliss finished the interview and they took a ten-minute break before moving on to Price.

As he had done ahead of the previous interview, Bliss entered all relevant details into the digital recording device's touchscreen keyboard and popped two writeable discs into their respective slots. When it came to using the electronic notepad, however, he gave Chandler the dubious pleasure of interacting with the casefile information. She was a quicker and better typist, and had far more patience with the often glitchy software system than he did.

After offering his condolences, Bliss began the second interview in the same way as the first. He outlined the police case so far, embellishing this time by adding excerpts from the suggestions he had thrown at Walker, making statements of them as if the man himself had given them up.

'Anything to say before I continue?' Bliss asked, expecting nothing in return. Price was also unrepresented, though in his case the reason was obvious. A shake of the head was all he offered before Bliss went on. 'If you refuse to talk to us about your own role in these events, perhaps you'll be happier discussing precisely how Walker was conscripted. You should tell us about that particular aspect, Mr Price, provided we're able to think of a way of doing so that doesn't involve you admitting to your own role. Let's see if we can work out a way for you to do that.'

This time, Bliss thought he saw interest flicker in the man's nerveless gaze. 'Mr Price,' he said, 'for the moment, let's concentrate on how Walker first became involved in this prolonged act of revenge. Our records suggest it happened when *your* son represented *his* son in a legal matter, is that correct?'

Bliss watched as the question churned inside the man's head. Mentally seeking traps and finding none, Price eventually nodded. 'Yes. Phil Walker's son was charged with committing an act of fraud. Stephen was asked to represent him.'

'By Phil Walker himself?'

'Yes. My son's speciality was white-collar crime. He was one of the best in the area.'

'Did your son know who and what Walker was at the time?'

'He knew Walker was an old-time villain who was out of the game. That was about it.'

'And it didn't bother him?'

'Most of the people we represent are guilty. We tend not to hold it against them.'

Bliss rubbed his forefinger and thumb together. 'A lucrative business in that part of London.'

'Yes, it is. I make no apology for the way we earn a living. Everybody is entitled to legal representation.'

'Speaking of which, I note you don't have anybody yourself.'

'I don't need anyone. Not at this stage. I know how the game is played.'

'Of course. So, getting back to Stephen. You say he knew of Walker's background, but he had no clue the man was involved in protecting the gang who murdered your wife?'

'No, he did not.'

'And yet I get the impression you did.'

Another pause. Bliss wondered if Price was going to clam up.

He was delighted when the man started nodding. 'I had an idea, yes. I once represented an ex-cop turned rogue; I won't give you his name. He worked out of Islington nick around that time, and in part payment for the work I did on his behalf, he gave me the names of the men who were rumoured to have murdered my wife. I should tell you that he had not come by that knowledge as a cop. You know what kind of people lived in the area in those days, Inspector. On the estates themselves, people knew but didn't know the truth. Rumours spread, and there was plenty of gossip, but according to my source the same names kept cropping up in reference to my wife.'

'And you never discussed any of this with your son?'

'I knew how Stephen would react. Plus, I didn't see what benefit it would bring. You may think it was a constant topic of conversation between us, but that's not the case; we never spoke of it. It was a taboo subject when my kids were growing up, because of the effect it had on Valerie in particular, and it stayed like that long after she moved out.'

Bliss was not unsympathetic. He tried to think around the subject. He desperately wanted confirmation that Phil Walker had been blackmailed into taking part in the revenge attacks, but he saw no way of compelling Price to admit to any of it, because doing so would implicate either him or his son. Nevertheless, he made one more plea.

'Mr Price. If I'm reading this right, after your daughter took her own life you saw that Stephen was triggered by her death, and you were afraid he'd choose the same exit door. You thought one way of preventing him from spiralling out of control would be to gain revenge on the men responsible for Geraldine's death – or, more accurately, for Stephen to do so. The kind of hands-on revenge that can sometimes pull a man back from the brink. But you also realised he needed help, because he was incapable of dealing with such men on his own. That's when Walker's name first came to you, I suspect. You gave it some thought and eventually decided on a way to use what you knew about him. You also realised how easily he'd be able to get close to his old mates, because he knew how they operated. And, of course, you considered the issue of alibis, right?'

'What do you expect me to say to any of that?'

'Nothing. You're not denying it, which is in itself revealing. But tell me this, because in doing so you admit to nothing: why involve Conway? Why carve out the case file number at all?'

'Seriously, Inspector? Do you really expect me to answer that?'

Bliss snapped his fingers. 'Tell you what, why don't you tell me your theory? You're an intelligent, articulate man. Speculate as to why somebody looking for revenge might also want to do that?'

Price sat back, breathing out heavily as his gaze first rose to the ceiling and then fell back on the two detectives. 'Hypothetically, if I were involved, I might decide to include Conway in order to prove to the man who'd investigated my wife's murder that his job was finally being done for him. In my own small way I'd be demonstrating his incompetence; shoving it in his face, knowing he could do absolutely nothing about it but sit back and watch in horror as it all unfolded around him.'

The explanation fed directly into Bliss's own thoughts on the matter. Involving the police who had failed to convict a single person for Geraldine Price's murder brought added satisfaction to the act of revenge.

'Sticking to the purely hypothetical,' Bliss said. 'Why do you imagine somebody might go to such lengths as to kill their enemies slowly by slicing pieces of their flesh off? Who would come up with such an idea?'

'You mean other than the ancient Chinese?' Price locked eyes with Bliss. 'Oh, I don't know. This hypothetical somebody may have been looking for a way to inflict a slow, painful and lingering death. Similar to an ordeal that somebody close to him, perhaps, had been subjected to in the past. Then along comes a man who has an idea based on, say, something he once read in a book…'

Walker.

Walker's book.

Andy Price was giving it all up, but also telling them absolutely nothing at the same time. Bliss glanced over at Chandler, who was busy tapping away on the notepad's grimy screen. She looked up and nodded for him to continue.

'Are you certain you don't want to unburden yourself, Mr Price?' Bliss asked. 'I, for one, can sympathise. I understand why you and your son did what you did.'

'But it wouldn't stop you charging me if I admitted to that level of complicity, correct? And neither will it prevent you from telling the full story to the media, allowing them to hang my son out to dry before I'm able to say my final goodbyes to him.'

'I suspect the media will hear all of that anyway. I don't doubt they will be given one side of the story: the side we choose to present. You do have the opportunity to provide a different perspective.'

'Whatever statement you feed to the media, it will contain few facts. It will be mostly conjecture and snatches of overheard conversations. What it won't be is confirmed. And you will never, ever get that from me. Not even when my case comes to court. I'll make sure there is always room for doubt.'

'I think you're playing it all wrong,' Bliss told him. He turned to one side and crossed one leg over the other, arm slung over the back of his chair. 'People have a tendency to side with the underdog. In your son's case, he reacted against dangerous and violent men in the only language people like that truly understand. He reacted to what they did to his mother. He reacted to them being the reason his sister killed herself. The way I see it, a fine young man snapped, briefly became somebody unrecognisable even to himself while taking revenge on monsters. I'd buy that. And you could sell it, Mr Price. Certainly to the media, and possibly to a jury as well.'

After a moment, Price looked at him with red-rimmed eyes and said, 'And what good does it do my son now?'

'It would preserve his reputation to a certain degree, both as a solicitor and as a husband and father. Not to mention a son.'

'Well, if that's what you genuinely believe, why don't you sell him to the media that way, Inspector?'

'Because it's not my job.'

'Then whose job is it?'

Bliss, who had been absently drumming his fingers on the table, stopped and regarded Price with compassion. 'I'd say it was his father's.'

Price met his steady gaze for a few seconds, before turning away. 'You should go about your business,' he said. 'We're done here.'

Bliss rose without argument. About to turn and walk away, he paused. 'Just tell me this. Was it Phil Walker's idea to remove his own hand?'

'Are you asking me to speculate once again, Inspector?'

'If you like.'

'In that case, yes, I'd guess it was his idea. I imagine he would consider it useless to him these days, so better to put it to some worthwhile purpose. Perhaps he thought that removing the hand would make you regard him as another victim, which in turn might steer you in a different direction.'

'He was right about that. And did he remove it, or did your son?'

Price smiled at him and shook his head. 'Nice try. No, Phil seems to me like the kind of man who would know a different kind of man, able to carry out that type of surgery professionally. I don't know what you know about him, Inspector, but do you genuinely believe his kind would risk a quick chop and burn?'

Bliss had been speculating as to how Walker had gone about it, assuming the job must have been done with precision and care, and with medication to handle the pain and prevent infection. Part of him admired the man for taking matters to such extremes, and it had nearly worked.

Price's last response told Bliss he knew the precise fate of each victim. Another facet also seemed clear to him now: Andy Price had largely sat back and cheered his son on from the sidelines. Quite what the two of them had had in mind for Walker was another matter – one Bliss decided to revisit.

'I have to say, Mr Price, although I do believe you and your son met with Walker to conclude your business with him, I'm not convinced you were planning to let him walk away unscathed.'

Price regarded him with interest. 'Is that so? Why do you say that?'

'Because Stephen was armed, for one thing. I'm betting he would have liked to finish the job he started. I don't see him letting Walker off so lightly.'

'You think my son intended him harm?'

'No. I think your son intended to kill him.'

'You saw the two of them, Inspector. Even with just the one hand, Walker had the drop on my boy physically. If Stephen had a weapon on him like you say, I'm not sure he would ever have had the opportunity to use it.'

Bliss had already thought it through. 'You're right. Stephen alone might not have been able to handle Walker. The pair of you could have, though. Even without the knives, there was a lake close by, not to mention the railway tracks he almost made it across.'

Andy Price stared up at Bliss and put a finger to his lips.

The gesture irritated Bliss. 'What does it matter if you tell us now? We were there. We had you surrounded, remember? We heard every single thing Walker admitted to, and also what he said about your son torturing those men. By the time we're done piecing those exchanges together, we'll have everything we need.'

'If that were true, you wouldn't still be trying to wring out the last few drops from me.'

'It's my job,' Bliss told him.

Price's eyes gleamed and he stuck out his chin. 'And mine is to protect my son.'

Bliss stared at the man for a moment. 'Yeah, and what a great job you did of that.'

Bypassing the pain inflicted by Bliss's words, Price snapped back. 'You think I had any idea what he was going to do to himself? I admit I failed with Valerie. I saw it coming for years and could do nothing to stop it, no matter how hard I tried. Stephen was a kind and gentle soul, but I didn't lose him yesterday. I lost him when his mother was murdered by those sick bastards. And again when Val…' Price whipped his head away, nostrils flaring. 'Ah, what would you know?'

'More than you realise,' Bliss said quietly. 'But you allowed your son to go on the rampage, Mr Price. More than that, you helped him keep it going. It takes a lot of rage and a twisted mind to pervert yourself the way he did. You didn't turn your back, but you did turn away. You shut your eyes to it. You knew what he had become, and you did nothing to prevent it. All because you thought he would come back to you once it was out of his system. You never once stopped to consider what might happen if it took him further the other way. That's not protection in my book.'

'No? What is it, then?'

Bliss regarded the man with contempt. 'I would call it abandonment.'

This time, Price turned away and clamped his lips together. Bliss knew they were done.

FORTY-FOUR

N THE MAJOR CRIMES area, shortly after ending the interview with Price, Bliss immediately noticed a lack of the usual euphoria that resulted from solving a case. Instead, the team were edgy, simmering rather than boiling over. They had most of the answers they'd sought, and those who were not dead were in custody. Despite these wins, Bliss understood the mood; Stephen Price taking his own life had cast an ugly pall over the entire investigation, leaving everyone involved with a sense of unfinished business and deep regret.

He took a few minutes to address his team as a unit, before speaking with each of them individually. He had barely enough focus to keep his own thoughts in order, but it was vital for him to temper the overwhelming feeling of failure by pointing out their group successes. The operation had ended unsatisfactorily – but it had ended. There would be no more body parts, no further killings. Not every investigation wound up with a glossy finish. He made sure his colleagues felt more upbeat by the time he was done with them, before taking his own advice and leaving for home.

As he drove out of Thorpe Wood, Bliss noticed Sandra Bannister standing outside chatting with fellow journalists, a number of TV news crews close by. This was going to be a big story, and he wanted no part in it. Like ants at a picnic table they swarmed around his vehicle, shouting out their inane questions. Photographers snapped away, and the experienced camera crews were finding the right spots from which to shoot. Bannister appeared to hold back the moment she saw who was behind the wheel. For that reason alone, Bliss waved her forward. He motioned for her to join him inside the car, which she did, amidst howling protests from the crowd.

Bliss drove to the Woodman, parked up and killed the engine, but remained in his seat behind the wheel. When he eventually turned to Bannister, he noticed how fatigued she looked. The reporter had clearly not been sleeping well, and he thought he knew why. Nodding to himself, he said, 'Go on. One free shot. Any question you like. If you're the person I think you are, I already have the answer for you.'

Her smile was half-hearted and insincere. 'There are so many I could and probably should be asking, but if you're reducing me to just the one, I'll have to give it some thought.'

'No, you won't,' he said. 'Not if I'm right about you, Sandra.'

Her lips puffed out in annoyance. 'You are such a frustrating man, Jimmy Bliss. All those times I asked you to call me by my first name, and now here you are doing it willingly yet again when it doesn't count.'

'I think it does. I think we have professional fences to mend, even if our personal ones are beyond repair.'

He let his observation sit with her for a few seconds. Finally, she turned to him, and the earnest look she gave him told Bliss he had been right all along. 'Okay – one question. Did my holding back information for my story cost lives?'

Bliss's shake of the head was firm. 'No.'

'How can you be so certain?'

'That's a second question, but I'll make allowances and continue to answer the first one. Believe it or not, amidst all the crud coming my way over these past few days, I did take time out to consider the same question. I asked myself if I could have done more, done what I did any sooner. And I started to reflect on how and when information had come to my attention.'

'And what conclusion did you arrive at?' Bannister went rigid, and Bliss could tell she was anxious about his answer.

He gave it to her straight. 'If I'm remembering the sequence of events correctly, you and your colleague did wonder if the slice of flesh left for us here in Peterborough had anything to do with Ben Carlisle – mainly because of the book your colleague noticed when you were in his home. And in fact, it was the one real lead to come from that source, because Mrs Carlisle was unable to give us anything to go on. So, yes, if I'd known about the book earlier I would have looked at it sooner, which in turn would have led me to Phil Walker ahead of when we finally figured out his involvement.'

'Phil Walker? The man you arrested yesterday? What did it have to do with him?'

Bliss told her about the library barcode he'd discovered. He also mentioned Walker's influence regarding the method Stephen Price had used to inflict his own form of torture on his mother's killers.

Bannister loosened off a low whistle. 'So, the book wasn't merely happenstance after all.'

'It doesn't look like it, no. I mean, Price said so without saying anything, if you get my drift. If there was a stroke of luck, I suppose it was that Ben Carlisle borrowed it from Walker and never bothered to return it. Not that it would have made a huge difference either way. Eventually, we would have entered Walker's home and found the book there if it had never been loaned to Carlisle.'

'Not necessarily. It was a library book. If Carlisle had given it back, it might have already been returned to the library.'

Bliss knew she was looking for something that wasn't there. 'That's not the case. I checked it out. The book was three years overdue, and the library has closed down. Don't go searching for the fatalistic, or looking too hard at all the ifs, buts and maybes. That way leads to madness. Believe me, I've been there. Better to concentrate your efforts on the things we know transpired, rather than dwell on what might have been.'

He waited while her brain scanned all the information and began reassembling it to provide a larger, clearer picture of the whole thing. After a moment, she seemed to reach the same conclusion as Bliss. 'I suppose I'm trying to make sense of the nonsensical. There will always be aspects we never fully understand, which is something I need to accept.'

'That's true enough. You're carrying a weight around with you and you're not sure if it's justified. But I'm confident that by the time the first bag was left for us, Walker had already quit his home and taken himself off the grid. I genuinely don't believe we would have put all those pieces together in time to have helped or saved anybody had you come forward earlier.'

The look of relief on her face was all the reward he needed, but he asked for more anyway. 'I can see knowing the truth means a great deal,' he said. 'So I'm going to ask a favour in return.'

'Name it.'

'Thank you. Sandra, if in the coming days and weeks you find you can't take it easy on me, please don't go especially hard on me, either.'

'You? But you were the one who put an end to all the mayhem, weren't you?'

'Yes and no. I think it had run its course by the time we wrapped things up. Plus we still have three dead men out there somewhere, unaccounted for. Somebody will have to pay for us not getting a complete result.'

'And you'll be their scapegoat. How can that be fair?'

'It's not about fairness or otherwise. I ran the joint task force. There's nobody else to blame. Just – please don't speculate. There's a major debriefing tomorrow morning. What I'm asking you to do is follow the official statements and not add anything. I'll feed you what I can if I think something important has been omitted.'

'I can't believe they'd come after you again, Jimmy. No matter how things finished up, it's over now. Why can't they be happy with achieving a perfectly respectable result?'

'And I can't believe you have to ask.'

'What does *that* mean?'

'Because you lot won't be satisfied. You never are. You'll probe and you'll dig and you'll hypothesise and you'll print or say things that will have two plus two making five – not you, specifically, but reporters in general. Others. They'll spot weaknesses and tear into them like a pack of hyenas.'

'Says a lot for my chosen profession.'

'And we both know your chosen profession is not what it used to be. Standards have declined. You're up against bloggers, social media, YouTube… and they have absolutely no professional standards to play by. We both know there are plenty of people willing to believe whatever you tell them and repeat it all over the internet. On this occasion, it'd be nice to have our local newspaper on my side. And if your editors won't agree, at least convince them to let you stand on neutral territory and not come for my throat, teeth bared.'

'I won't do that. I promise you. You were honest with me just now, and it meant a great deal. I'll concentrate on the official statements, but I'll also be guided by anything you have to say as well. No matter what our differences, I won't bury you, Jimmy. You don't deserve that, and I hope you know I'm not that kind of journalist anyway.'

'I do. I also don't expect it from your newspaper, but these are tough times and hysterical headlines are great clickbait. I said at the beginning I was asking for a favour, but in reality all I want is a fair shake.'

'I can guarantee you'll get that – from us, at least.'

It was all he could ask for. Bannister had taken a cab to the police station, so after reaching their agreement, Bliss drove her back to the *Telegraph* building in the city centre. As she unbuckled her seatbelt, she turned to him and said, 'Jimmy, I'm sure this will work itself out. It always has in the past, and you've been in worse situations before.'

Bliss knew this was the case. In truth, he wasn't overly worried. And that, ironically, bothered him more than the threat of having the finger of blame pointing in his direction.

FORTY-FIVE

THE POST-OP DEBRIEFING TOOK place on Monday morning at nine o'clock. In attendance at Thorpe Wood were every available officer and detective from the station who had worked on the case, plus all relevant senior personnel, including those from London and Wiltshire – DI Max Riseborough excluded. The tables and chairs in Major Incident Room One had been arranged into a large rectangle, with no head of table; this was not an inquiry, though everyone there knew otherwise. However, Chief Superintendent Feeley had been invited to chair the meeting, which did not augur well.

It was standing room only as Bliss eyed the clock above the whiteboards. Fifty minutes in, and they were fast approaching the events of Saturday afternoon and evening. His contributions thus far had been succinct, mostly to clarify specific points arising from the sharing of information. He knew things were about to change dramatically; he was going to become the subject of in-depth questioning. He took several deep breaths, telling himself he had nothing to worry about.

Bliss batted away the initial volley of questions with ease, confidently outlining the process that had led them to Epping Forest, the collection of SD cards, and the subsequent viewing of the footage they held. There was a sudden shift in atmosphere as Feeley zeroed in on the final moments prior to him leaving the room on Saturday.

'Now, Inspector. It's evident that at some point during the viewing of the footage, something significant occurred to you – something you felt required individual examination ahead of bringing it to the attention of your team. Would you elaborate on that for us, please?'

Bliss took a sip of water, not wanting his voice to become brittle. 'Of course. As we watched the unidentified figure in the woods, I became aware of some kind of subliminal message in the footage that was not immediately apparent. I asked for the film to be replayed a few times, though I can't recall precisely how many. Afterwards, I realised the subject's movements were speaking to me, specifically in the way he appeared to stagger every other step or so. As many people in this room are aware, I am intimately familiar with the effects of imbalance, and I recognised the particular gait of somebody recently exposed to that condition.'

'And this tied in with Walker how, Inspector Bliss?'

'Well, at first my thoughts turned to Geraldine Price's brother. We'd checked him out, but as far as we knew he was in Toronto, and records suggested he had not left there during this period. He has Ménière's disease, the same condition I have, and that's what drew me to him. But I couldn't see how he had managed to be here in the UK while his passport suggested he had never left Canada. I had also spotted another reason for the imbalance. Or, rather, saw something I believed strongly indicated it.'

'Which was?'

'His left arm. Its movements were not natural. At first, I couldn't quite make out why, but later on I realised it was possibly disabled, or at the very least incapacitated.'

'But we're talking about a man whose left hand was removed entirely. Surely that must have been apparent to everybody.'

Bliss shook his head. 'The angles provided by the cameras were not ideal, and at no point did we get a clear view of the man's lower extremities. We saw perhaps down to his elbows or just beneath, but it was impossible to see the complete picture. However, as soon as I considered the possibility of him being disabled in or around the arm, my mind immediately went to his hand and whether it was missing.'

'That's a bit of a leap, wouldn't you say?'

'No, sir. I wouldn't. If we were working any other case, I would agree with you – but this one already included two severed hands. I would have considered it an oversight not to have at least asked myself the question.'

At this point, DSI Conway interjected. 'And from this you immediately began to suspect Mr Walker?' He asked the question as if doubting the logical pathway Bliss was mapping out for them.

'Not quite. We of course knew Harrison's and Walker's hands had been removed, because they were in our possession. But just because we hadn't been left the hands of either Ben Carlisle or Earl Dobson, didn't mean they had not been removed. So, at the point at which I realised we were looking at one of the victims, the only person I knew it couldn't be was Freddy Swift.'

Feeley had taken the opportunity to polish his spectacles on a small black square of cloth. 'So how did you eventually arrive at the conclusion that, of the four possible victims, the figure in the forest had to be Walker?' he asked.

'The first thing I did was go through the information we had obtained in relation to Andy and Stephen Price's clients. I found a couple of connections; one to Walker and another to Swift. Stephen Price had represented Walker's son, while Andy had acted on behalf of Swift himself on a number of occasions in connection to his porn empire. I then ran a general search on Walker, looking into his online presence over the past couple of decades. Given that he had once been a notorious gangster, and was now running a lucrative business which was currently fighting hard for contracts across Europe, the US and the Middle East, there were a lot of articles to wade through.'

His glasses back in place, Feeley blinked rapidly to adjust his vision. 'And you did not consider bringing your team in to help at that point?'

'Had my search gone on longer, then yes, I would have roped them in to assist. But I happened to hit upon a piece in the *Daily Mail* from 2017. It referred to Phil Walker having partially recovered from a severe stroke, and I recalled DS Chandler mentioning this to me previously while we were discussing his background. I had my suspicions as to why it was deemed a partial recovery, and in reading further I found I was correct. He had, in fact, suffered irreversible nerve damage and lost the use of his left hand. That knowledge sparked an idea I couldn't let go of.'

Bliss took a longer sip from his glass, looking around at the faces staring back at him. He coughed up a choked laugh. 'Now I have some idea of what it must be like to be a prize exhibit in a zoo,' he said.

Amid the polite laughter, Bliss sought out DCI Warburton, whose smile and nod of encouragement boosted his confidence. The feeble joke seemed to have lifted the oppressive anticipation inside the room. Buoyed by this, he continued. 'Those of you closest to the operation will already know I originally had Walker down as my chief suspect. But no sooner had I put him in the frame than his hand was left for us to find, and he immediately turned from suspect to victim.'

'It does seem like a logical assumption to have made,' Superintendent Fletcher offered encouragingly, nodding at her colleagues.

'Yes, ma'am. I never liked Swift as a suspect, and we were always of the opinion that either Andy or Stephen Price, or both, were involved. But after finding Walker's hand, we were left with Freddy Swift as the accomplice – well, either him or someone who hadn't yet been picked up by our radar. Of course, what we encountered in Epping Forest on Saturday put paid to any notion of it being Swift.'

'Naturally,' Conway conceded, as if the issue required no explanation.

Bliss was about to let it pass, but felt he should at least offer up an alternative line of thinking; it was reasonable to assume every conversation would eventually have to appear on a statement. He cleared his throat and said, 'Except… I briefly toyed with the idea that Swift might still be our man, and that perhaps one of his victims had escaped and paid him back in spades. It was a reasonable theory. Swift could have been the person who took care of the abductions and bag drops, with one of the Prices – or both – carrying out most of the butchery. In which case it was also possible one of the men managed to free himself, lured Swift into a trap and took care of him. But I couldn't get past my feelings about Swift. The man was a poor excuse for a human being, and it looks increasingly likely that he was involved somehow in Geraldine Price's abduction, torture, and murder. In the end, I truly couldn't imagine any of his victims recovering sufficiently from such awful mutilation to take their own revenge so quickly.'

Chief Superintendent Feeley snorted. 'You thought it more likely that Walker either chopped his own hand off or allowed it to be removed, to throw us off the scent?' he said. 'I find such an admission extraordinary, Inspector Bliss.'

'Extraordinary or not, it was also entirely possible,' Bliss shot back. 'The stroke was severe enough to render his hand useless. The way I viewed it, he felt the pressure of our investigation and saw an opportunity to remove himself from our thoughts entirely. No, that's not right – in fact, what it did was force us to regard him as a fresh victim. All he had to do was lose an appendage which was of no use to him anyway. In many ways, it was a perfect strategy. So yes, I thought it possible. Not probable, perhaps not even likely. But possible.'

Feeley moved them on. 'Which was when you came up with the idea of feeding information to the Prices and waiting for them to give themselves away.'

'Them and, hopefully, the third party. By this time, I'd dismissed Freddy Swift as the accomplice, which left Walker as the most likely candidate. I was confident phone calls would be made following our chat with Andy Price. I thought either he or his son would seek out our man and attempt to silence him. I admit I was surprised by the meeting they arranged, but it worked in our favour because it gave us time to put people in the right positions to end it that same day.'

'Which leads us neatly on to the final moments, Inspector. Please tell us, in your own words, what happened.'

Bliss swallowed. This was it. The moment it either all fell apart or he clawed it back.

FORTY-SIX

'I BELIEVED WE WERE IN control of the situation,' Bliss said, feeding off the memory. 'We watched all three men enter the plot, and there was no sign of any trouble. We were alert to the possibility, of course, but we were close at hand if the Prices decided to take out Walker there and then. The three of them talked for a while, and as soon as I felt we'd heard enough I gave the word to go.'

'Which is where things began to unwind, yes?'

To give him his due, Feeley did not appear to relish the statement. For him it was a simple matter of pointing out the true state of the operation at the time. Bliss did not hold that against him, though he was starting to feel boxed in.

'Yes,' he admitted. 'What happened next came as a huge shock to us all. But even after Walker reacted by grabbing hold of Stephen Price and putting a blade to his throat, I still felt we were in charge. It was the exact opposite of how we'd anticipated things would go, of course, but no matter how many times I run it through my head, I'm convinced I'd managed to talk Walker out of any action he may have been looking to take.'

'Excuse the interruption, but I'd like to go on record as saying right now that I agree with DI Bliss.' All eyes turned to DSI Conway.

'I apologise for breaking the flow,' he continued, 'but I didn't want this salient point to get lost. My recollection of the confrontation is clear, and I'm with DI Bliss when he says we were still in charge at that point. It may not seem like it in retrospect, but Walker was not a man determined to have one final kill. If anything, he was looking for a way out.'

'Thank you for your input, Superintendent Conway,' Feeley said, his tone remaining flat and neutral. 'You will have every opportunity to have your say.' His eyes snapped back to Bliss. 'Do go on, Inspector.'

Nodding his thanks at Conway, Bliss said, 'At the beginning of this meeting you read from a couple of statements, one from the local police and the other from a Met surveillance team. Both of them attested to my response in real time. And remember, that's how it all happened – not with the benefit of hindsight or in slow motion. In my judgement, there was no reason for Walker to injure or kill Price. Him grabbing Stephen and pulling the blade was an unexpected move, but I took it to be nothing more than a bluff. We had armed officers on scene who initially drew tasers, and Walker obviously realised his predicament pretty quickly. I spoke to him calmly, led him through the permutations, all of which looked bleak for him. I saw the changes in his demeanour. He was going to back down, exactly as DSI Conway indicated a few moments ago. Other officers will attest to the same belief.'

'Yet something changed. You had the situation under control, and then you didn't.'

Bliss closed his eyes for a moment, reliving the awful moment of realisation when he saw Price's hands tugging at the blade. 'That's correct. In my opinion, the reason Price ended up taking his own life was because we did have the situation under control. Quite simply, he killed himself the moment he realised Walker wasn't going to do it for him.'

Feeley leaned forward, setting down a pen with which he had been scribbling copious notes. 'Even if we accept what you say as true, Inspector Bliss, upon reflection over the past day or so, do you still not believe it would have been possible to intervene quickly enough to prevent the suicide?'

'No, sir. If Walker pulling the blade came as a surprise, Price using it on himself was a complete shock. I don't think any of us could have predicted what happened based on what we knew and what we were seeing at the time.'

'So, in your opinion the armed officers could not have acted sooner?'

Bliss realised the Chief Superintendent was prising a door open for him. All he had to do was slip through the gap... and the blame was neatly avoided and passed along the ranks. He swallowed thickly and met Feeley's stern gaze. 'They couldn't have, sir. And that's not an opinion, it's a fact. I think about it now and it still takes me aback.'

Feeley recovered quickly from having to slam the door shut again. 'Do you have an opinion as to why Stephen Price did what he did?'

'I think there were two primary reasons. First, he knew he was caught and his future consisted of nothing but a hefty prison sentence. But second, he was heavily traumatised by what happened to his mother, and again many years later when his sister took her own life. By that stage he was incapable of thinking straight any more. I'm convinced Stephen Price took his revenge on the men who murdered his mother, with the knowledge and full support of his father and the help of Phil Walker. In those final moments, he also assumed Walker would be severely punished for what he had done to Freddy Swift, which in some ways made amends for his covering for the men a quarter of a century ago. In one sense it freed Stephen from all the angst he had built up over the years, but in another it meant the past had no further claim on him, and clearly he came to the conclusion that he wanted no part of whatever future lay ahead. Obviously, though, I'm not him, so I may be completely wrong.'

After a lengthy pause, DSI Fletcher spoke up for the first time. 'Questions are already being asked by the media. We've informed them they will have a statement from us today, but I think we all know where they will take this. How did we allow it to happen? Why did we not have greater control of the situation on the ground? Then there's the fact that three victims are still unaccounted for.'

They had little leverage in their attempts to persuade Walker into giving up the locations of the victims. He would live out the rest of his life behind bars, so it was hard to see what they might offer him in order to plead down his sentence. Bliss knew the only cards they had to play were in dictating where Walker ended up being imprisoned; life could be made easier for his family in terms of logistics if he was willing to tell them where his fellow gangsters were, but thus far he appeared uninterested in the offer. Time – as ever – would tell.

'What works for us is that all of these men either carried out or were involved in hideous crimes,' Bliss said. 'We eventually have to prove it, but for now we can at least steer the conversation along those lines. We feed the media the story we want to tell, the one we believe to be true. We continue the search for the remains of Harrison, Dobson and Carlisle. Andy Price is saying nothing on their whereabouts, and I don't think he will. Not just because he won't want to put himself in the frame; I'm equally sure he'll do everything he can to paint his son as the victim somehow. Frankly, I'm not entirely convinced he knows where those men are, anyhow.'

'So our statement will say…?'

'That the one-time notorious gangster Phil Walker abducted three men, severed Tommy Harrison's hand, and distributed the carrier bags containing body parts and chunks of flesh from the victims. That Stephen Price seriously wounded the abducted men at best, murdered them at worst. That Walker then murdered Freddy Swift and finished off the other victims to ensure their silence, leaving himself as the last man standing. That all five gangsters were involved in the murder of Geraldine Price. That Stephen Price began planning his revenge the moment he heard about his sister's suicide, eventually co-opting Walker into his scheme. And that his father was complicit in everything he did.'

'Which sounds like an awful lot to prove with so little evidence,' Feeley said.

'That's true, sir. And we won't succeed in doing so in a number of instances. My belief, however, is that we have enough to push for convictions on all counts. We have the word of every officer who overheard the conversation on Saturday evening; we have the meeting itself and the recording we made. Remember, Walker said something about Ben Carlisle already being gone – from that, we can infer Stephen Price's guilt, making him a murderer. We now have their phones, which will conclusively prove these men were in touch before and during these events. We have the camera footage from Epping Forest. We still have both Walker and Andy Price in custody and going nowhere anytime soon. Plus, with neither of them willing to offer up their own statements, we don't have to offer proof when we tell our story. That comes later.'

This time Feeley shifted uneasily in his chair. He put an elbow on the desk, chin in the palm of his hand, fingers curling up towards his mouth. 'Everything you listed is circumstantial, Inspector, other than the sworn testimony of our officers and the recording. But Walker's entire confession was made before his arrest, so he had not been read his rights at the time. The recording will help, but the CPS will demand more.'

'Which is why we have to start building our case,' Bliss said evenly. 'We've all been here before. The hard work doesn't stop when we nail the bastards; that's just where it begins. We dig deeper into what we know, deeper still into what we can only surmise. We apply pressure on both Walker and Price.' Bliss hiked his shoulders. 'In short... we do our jobs.'

After the debriefing, Bliss was asked to remain behind with DCI Warburton, Superintendent Fletcher, and Chief Superintendent Feeley. He swallowed hard; it was not a good sign. When the room had emptied out and the four of them were left alone, Feeley broke the news.

'Inspector Bliss. We've decided that, for the time being at least, it's better for all concerned if we place you on temporary administrative leave.'

Bliss felt the full force of his rage rear up. It had been brewing; he'd known all along what they were planning. 'You cowards,' he said, his lips barely moving. 'You bloody cowards.'

'Jimmy!' Fletcher spoke his name like a warning.

'I'll put your outburst down to the pressure of the situation,' Feeley said, though his squint suggested he was throttling down on his own anger. 'Just this once.'

'I don't give a damn what you put it down to,' Bliss said, turning on him. 'The three of you have not spoken since you asked for the room to be cleared out – which tells me you'd already made up your minds about putting me on leave before you set one foot inside the door. This is about the phone tracing, isn't it? It didn't matter what you heard in the debriefing, you were always going to do this to me.'

'You think we needed a debriefing, Bliss?' Feeley regarded him with a contempt he did nothing to disguise. 'Forget the phone tracing. That's for another day. A man cut his own throat on your watch. Right in front of you. I'm sure you believe the fact that you closed the case means none of that ugliness taints you, but it does.

And by rights it should. And yes, of course your previous actions regarding the phone traces are also being taken into consideration. But ask yourself, what is it that we've done to you, Inspector? Administrative leave means you receive full pay and benefits. It means your HR record will be swelled by a single sheet of paper. You are not being suspended – a decision we were well within our rights to make.'

'Jimmy,' Warburton said to him softly. 'I'm sure when you reflect on this you'll realise it's nothing more than a slap on the wrist. What it also means is that none of us here is assigning fault to you or your operation – and I do mean none of us. It's a temporary measure, designed to remove you from the firing line at a time when the media will be at their most enthusiastic.'

'And with the greatest of respect, boss,' Bliss said, feeling the weight of betrayal in his chest, 'I've been here before. I know what so-called administrative leave is all about. It's not supposed to put a stain on my record – but it will be there, all the same. It's not supposed to last long, but it will drag on. It's not supposed to be held against me in the future, but I fully expect it will be. I've been held to account like this before, and I still carry the stink of it around with me. Also, there is one message the media will take from this decision, which is that the blame is being laid squarely on my shoulders. So please, spare me the banalities. Don't pretend this is anything other than what it is: a knife in the back, and each of you with one hand on the shaft.'

In a remote voice, Feeley said, 'Inspector Bliss, that is quite enough. More than enough, in fact. You and I have had few dealings so far during my time here, but I can already see the stories I've heard about you are true. This reaction is fairly typical, from what I understand. Or, at least, it has been until now.'

'What's *that* supposed to mean?'

'It means either your attitude changes before you leave this room, or your career with this or any other police service is in dire jeopardy.'

Bliss shot to his feet. He leaned forward, placed his hands palms down on the table in front of him. He regarded all three senior officers in turn, ending with Feeley. 'Is that so? Well, Chief Superintendent, you may consider what you just said to be a threat. But for me, it's the final straw. My methods may be questionable at times, but I get results. And before you chime in again, no, of course this case did not end as I would have liked, and in fact I don't consider it to be over. But I'm damned if I'm going to be mauled to pieces over it, either. You say my career is at risk if I don't change my attitude? What of it? My so-called career means less and less to me every single day. And if what you're really telling me is that it's already over bar the paperwork, I'd say: go tell someone who gives a shit.'

FORTY-SEVEN

BEFORE LEAVING THORPE WOOD for the day – possibly for the last time – Bliss gathered his team together in the incident room. He made no mention of the meeting he had stormed out of. Reeling in his outrage, he instead made his feelings clear about the investigation.

'I do feel sympathy towards Andy and Stephen Price, losing both Geraldine and Valerie like that. Such terrible grief is something nobody should have to endure.'

'It's unimaginable,' DC Gratton said. 'Enough to make anyone flip out.'

'I agree. I can understand either or both men wanting justice and exacting some form of revenge for what those sick bastards did to her and, ultimately, her daughter as well. But I'm not shedding any tears over what Price did to himself on Saturday evening. You shouldn't, either.'

'What makes you say that, boss?' Bishop asked.

Bliss composed his thoughts before replying. 'Because he made a conscious choice to butcher those men the way he did. He stepped over a line that can't be re-crossed. Having done so, he was set free from whatever mental and emotional hell he'd found himself in – only to realise he was about to be imprisoned again, this time with real walls, real bars, real guards and real fellow cons. For him, that was no way to end his story. So he made that ultimate choice as well. Ultimately, we'd failed him and he took the easier way out.'

'If there were failures, boss,' Chandler said, 'they occurred during the original investigation.'

'A failure to provide justice, perhaps. I'm not sure there was an investigative failure, though. Conway and his team would have been up against it. The community threw up a wall of silence, closing ranks and never allowing the police in. I'm surprised they got as far as they did.'

'So it'll be us who takes the blame,' Bishop said, miserably.

Bliss considered mentioning the conversation he'd had upstairs, but once again thought better of it. 'To a certain degree, yes. Which ultimately means me. A man killed himself right in front of us. We were unable to prevent it, and four other men are dead, three of the bodies still missing. Somebody is bound to get it in the neck for that. And if the journos do their job, then I'm sorry to say, but Superintendent Conway will be at risk as well. He was involved in both cases, let's not forget, so I think they'll go after him first. Then me, because I led Saturday's op as well as the JTFO.'

'I don't see either the DCI or DSI unloading on you, boss,' Ansari said. 'They understand the bigger picture.'

Bliss nodded, thinking about how neither had ridden to his rescue. 'You may be right, Gul. This team will not escape censure, but it'll blow over in time. Not that we should be patting ourselves on the back any time soon – the men are all still dead. And you can ignore the initial debriefing, because that was a show for the box-tickers. The upper echelons are not happy with how this turned out.'

Bishop fidgeted in his chair, running fingers around the neck of his shirt collar. 'What did they have to say to you afterwards, boss?'

For a third time, Bliss decided not to mention his administrative leave. 'Let's leave the finer details for another day,' he said dismissively. 'The real investigation into how this all unravelled begins and ends with us. I want you all to re-examine everything we did: every detail and every decision. Without any thought of recrimination, I want the team as a whole to front up to whatever mistakes were made. *If* they were made. If we learn from this, then something positive will have come out of it.'

'You shouldn't be so hard on yourself,' Chandler reminded him. 'We do have two men in custody. It may have taken us a while, but we followed the evidence and we got there in the end.'

Bliss ran a hand across his chin. 'We did? Where exactly did we get, Pen? Given what we now know, there was only going to be one further victim anyway, which was Walker. So ultimately, we saved him but lost Stephen Price in the process. Four other men lost their lives. Whatever kind of spin we try to put on it, that's a net loss after we got involved. We didn't end this. Not in any positive or satisfactory way that I can see.'

'That's the way it goes sometimes. You don't always get to solve everything and tie it all up in a neat bow. Isn't that what you always remind us when things don't go our way?'

'Yes. And it's still as true today as it was when I first learned that harsh lesson for myself. But let's not pretend it was any great victory, either.'

Bliss raised a hand to silence any retort, calling for a calm and methodical approach to piecing together the evidence package for the CPS. 'However I or anybody else judges the outcome, I'm proud of the way you all went about your business. This was a tough case, one we might never have made any ground on. But you all stuck to it, you all did your jobs, and you can all hold your heads up high.'

'We will if you will, boss,' Bishop said. His implacable face told Bliss his DS did not intend to change his stance. 'You led from the front as always. We're a reflection of the hard graft you put in every single day. We either all win or we all lose, but whatever the result, we do it together.'

Bliss was grateful for his colleague's kind words, but he knew togetherness could only reach so far. He had no doubt that Bishop's statement was from the heart, and to a certain degree it was accurate. But not when viewed from above; to them, a win was one for the team, a defeat a loss for its leader. Whatever this was, Bliss alone would be left to pick up the pieces. He thanked Bishop, told his team once again how grateful he was for their efforts, then said he was going home and didn't want to be disturbed by phone calls. He bid his goodbyes as if it were any other day.

As he drove away from Thorpe Wood, without once looking in his rear-view mirror, Bliss asked himself where all the understanding and acceptance he'd given his team had been earlier. His outburst at Feeley had been unforgivable, though he remained furious with the decision to place him on leave. The Chief Superintendent's intransigence proved everything he had ever felt about the brass, and the whole encounter left him feeling nauseated. But so did his reaction to it. He had shifted like lightning from smouldering to molten in half a second, and his characteristic lack of filter had almost certainly talked him into a worse punishment than he might otherwise have expected to receive.

Worse still, he had insulted two fine women he respected. For that, there was no excuse.

FORTY-EIGHT

RATHER THAN HEAD HOME to either the garden or his music – his usual preferences for clearing his head – Bliss decided to find his centre again on the boat. The sky was dense with cloud cover, which left the day warm and sticky, but at least he would not burn. The city was in need of a storm to freshen the air and flush away the grime, and Bliss hoped it would come soon. He parked the car and trudged along the towpath, realising with every step that his was the tread of a man in despair. He felt it gather at his throat, almost choking him.

In the boat's tiny fridge he had two bottles of beer left. He uncapped one and sat in the pilot's chair, attempting to reassemble his thoughts. When DCI Warburton called, he sent it to voicemail; minutes later, he did the same to Fletcher. There was nothing left to say – not today. If he was sorry, an apology was surely already too late. But Bliss wasn't even sure how repentant he was. Reacting the way he had, branding the three of them as cowards, was wrong, unprofessional; he accepted that. As for being remorseful about it, especially where Feeley was concerned, the notion required greater thought. And a lot more beer.

As Bliss got into the second bottle, his mind drifted. He didn't know where it had taken him, but when he blinked to moisten his eyes, it came as no surprise to see Chandler walking along the towpath towards the *Mourinho*. Bliss helped her aboard and she virtually fell into the chair beside him.

'Sorry I have nothing to offer you,' he told her, waggling the bottle. 'This is my last one, and my need is greater than yours.'

'I wouldn't be quite so sure about that,' Chandler said. Her voice was small and anxious. 'I've just come from a short but illuminating meeting with DCI Warburton.'

'Ah. She told you, did she?'

'She said you'd been placed on temporary administrative leave. About which I made my feelings clear. I told her I thought the decision was outrageous. To her credit, the DCI agreed. She suggested I tell you that when I saw you, and to also let you know Fletcher feels the same way. Feeley, however, is adamant about there being repercussions.'

'The man's a fool.'

'Quite. But from what I'm told, it looks as if that's where it would've ended had you not erupted and branded them all cowards. That did not go down well, Jimmy.'

'I don't imagine it did. So, are you here to tell me my admin leave has been upgraded to suspension or dismissal?'

'I wouldn't know about that. There would have to be a disciplinary panel, and Diane didn't know if Feeley was up for the fight. She and Fletcher tried to stamp out the fire, but they don't know how successful they were. You pissed the man off and embarrassed him, Jimmy. And you did it in right front of two less senior officers. This time you might have brought about your own downfall.'

Bliss waved a careless hand. 'So what? Fuck them. I'm sick of the bullshit, Pen. I'm tired of playing their game. I'm bored with it.'

'So, what? That's you done? Out of Major Crimes? Out of HQ? Out of the job? Is that what you want, Jimmy?'

He breathed out slowly. 'Right at this moment I'm not sure what I want any more. The job keeps me awake at night, but it also keeps me sane. I hate it sometimes, but I love it most of the time. And sanity is overrated. On the one hand, I get to work with fantastic people like you and the rest of the team, but I also have to put up with snidey little pricks like Feeley who've forgotten what it's like to run an investigation. Besides, after what I just did and said, I doubt my future lies in my own hands. Sometimes you dig a hole too deep to fill.'

'Give it time. You left a few open wounds back at Thorpe Wood, and they'll have to heal before those affected reflect more clearly.'

'Hark at you, oh wise one.'

Chandler gave a self-deprecating laugh. 'I'm not so sure about wise. I certainly don't feel competent enough to put together a prosecutable case against Andy Price. Not even with Bish's help.'

'Then let DCI Warburton step up. She's earned her rank – let her prove it to you.'

'But you're the one with the insight as well as the know-how. Besides, I thought you didn't like leaving loose ends.'

Bliss took his time to think about it. He realised Chandler was already attempting to lure him back in. Finally, he said, 'I don't. But this one doesn't feel important enough for me to get bent out of shape about, so I'm happy to let it go.'

Chandler sighed and shuffled over between the two chairs towards him, perching herself on their padded arm rests. She leaned across, inviting him to wrap an arm around her shoulders, snuggling into him when he did. Bliss smiled to himself and closed his eyes. His friend felt warm tucked up in there. She felt right. Bliss could smell the fragrance she wore, the light citrus of her shampoo. Both familiar to him. Both comforting in their own way. He handed her the bottle, a quarter of its contents still inside. She took a sip and gave a raspy sigh of pleasure.

As they gazed up river, a voice came from behind. 'You know, if I were the jealous type, this little scene might be worrying.'

They both jumped, startled out of the cosy embrace, and turned. Emily stood there with a huge grin spread across her face, one hand resting on her hip. 'Fortunately,' she continued, 'I know how close you two are, and I don't feel at all threatened.'

'Nor should you be,' Chandler said, pulling away from Bliss and clambering up out of the chair. 'I'm way too good for him, and he's way too old for me. So he's all yours, Emily. Perhaps you'll be able to talk some sense into him.'

Bliss was now also on his feet, and looked between the two women. 'You've already spoken to Emily,' he said, the accusation ringing hollow.

'Of course I have. Told her what a stupid bugger you are and how I don't want to be breaking in a new boss.'

He rolled his eyes. 'And you knew she was on her way over?'

'I did. That's how I knew the cuddle was safe.' Chandler winked at him, which made Bliss smile.

He pointed back along the track. 'Get your bony arse shifting in the direction of home. You're a born troublemaker, and we don't take kindly to your sort around here.'

As was her custom, Chandler flipped him two fingers, then she embraced Emily for a couple of seconds and marched off down the towpath back to her car without another word.

'She'll be the death of me,' Bliss said, watching her go.

'If not her, then definitely me,' Emily responded. 'What the bloody hell have you done now, Jimmy?'

About to explain himself, Bliss was saved by his ringtone. This time he answered gladly. 'Hey, Molly. How are you doing? Enjoying your new phone privileges?'

'Of course.'

'Glad to hear it. So, to what do I owe this honour? Did you call me just to chat, or was there something specific?'

'Both. I've been watching stuff about you on the telly, Jimbo.'

'I see. Look, don't worry yourself about any of that old cobblers. It's all over now. We got the bad guys.'

'No, it's not that. I figured you would. I just wanted to tell you something. See, it got me thinking about when I was doing all that crazy shit. I never once thought about how it affected your lot. We were always taught to hate you coppers, to think of you all as barely human scum who just wanted to get us off the streets. But once I got to know you and Penny and Bish and the others, I realised you're all just people. The things you see, the douchebags you have to deal with – it must be hard on you.'

Her insight took him by surprise. 'Well, I'm not going to deny it. But we're trained to deal with all kinds of situations and all types of people. We're experienced, and we have the law on our side. It's not such a big deal.'

'That's just you being modest. I heard all about what's been going on with these body parts and shit, and, like, I can't imagine how that stuff must screw with your head.'

Bliss laughed it off. 'Molly, I'm way past it screwing with me in any way. It doesn't get to me any more.'

'You sure?'

'Sure I'm sure. But thank you for caring.'

'Of course. Like I wouldn't. So, when are you coming to see me again?'

'I don't know about that. I'm due a bit of a break, so it might be sooner than you expected. Only this time I may bring somebody with me.'

'For real? You mean, like, a woman?'

'No, not *like* a woman. A woman.'

He could almost hear Molly's eyes rolling in their sockets. 'That'd be okay. It's not Penny, is it?'

'No, it's not.' Bliss chuckled at her enthusiasm. 'Would you like to see her again?'

'Yeah, of course I would. I still think you two have got something going on, even though you're an old man and it'd be so gross.'

'Thank you for that little pearl of wisdom. Okay, well let's wait and see. I have one or two things to tie up first. Perhaps I'll bring two women with me. Because that's just the way I roll these days.'

'Two women? Wow! Jimmy B, cruising with his hoes!'

This time Bliss's laughter echoed around the marina, his stomach aching by the time he was done.

'All well in Molly's world?' Emily asked, after Bliss had hung up.

'Yep. She's great. But I think she just called you my "ho".'

'I wondered what made you laugh so hard. How sweet.'

'If it's any consolation, Penny's one as well, apparently.'

Smiling, Emily said, 'It isn't.' She patted the seat beside her and held out her arms.

The two sat together in the boat, watching the sun struggle its way through the clouds to add colour and life to the still waters of the river. She cajoled him through his version of the morning meetings, but this time when he spoke about his reaction, he felt no tightening of his chest.

'What do you think it means?' he asked her. 'Why did I go off on one so badly?'

Emily rubbed his bare arm, running her fingers through the fine hairs. 'I'm not sure, Jimmy. Perhaps you genuinely don't care what happens any more.'

He nodded. 'That's what I thought. And I don't know how to feel about it. My mind keeps coming back to that stupid bloody dog under my porch, the lab I told you about the other night. Honestly, it looked as if it had given up and was waiting to not exist any longer. I got the feeling it sensed I was going to keep on feeding it and giving it something to drink, which forced it to stir and slope off rather than prolong its time. I can't explain it, Emily, but I think it had given all it had to give and then had no idea what to do next other than roll over and die.'

'A random dog is not you, Jimmy. It was just a stray. You're reading more into it than it deserves.'

'Yeah, that's what Pen said as well. I understand what you both mean, but… like I say, I don't know how I feel about either the damned dog or my job and the crap I just took all over it.'

'You don't have to feel anything right now. Give it time. It's not as if you don't have any to spare.'

'All the time in the world, I expect. I don't think they'd have me back now even if it was what I wanted.'

'Perhaps that's how things were meant to be. But Jimmy, don't kid yourself. You feel this way now, and you may feel the same way tomorrow and even the next day. But I give it a week before you're busting a gut to get back to it.'

'Am I so obvious?'

'It's not just what you do, Jimmy. It's who you are.'

'If true, how sad is that?'

Emily looked at him for a long time. Then she leaned in and kissed him on the lips. 'It's not sad at all,' she said. 'In many ways, I think it's noble.'

He laughed, but cut it off quickly. 'Nobility is not usually a trait people would list among my attributes.'

Both arms wrapped around him now, Emily looked deep into his eyes and said, 'I think you're wrong. I think they would say that about you. And if they didn't, it would only be because they don't know you.'

'And you do?'

'I wouldn't say that, exactly. But I'd like to, Jimmy. I really would.'

Bliss nodded as Emily rested her head on his shoulder. 'Yeah,' he whispered. 'I think I'd like that, too.'

AUTHOR'S NOTE

REGULAR READERS WILL NOTE that I've gone for something slightly different again with this one. Although the 1994 unsolved murder case lies buried within the main plot, *Slow Slicing* really only features a single storyline. I kept it this way because I felt it was complex enough. Having a major sub-plot would have added word count and made the book unwieldy overall. For me, doing something different, even if it's only slightly, keeps it fresh.

The entire story began inside my head with that opening chapter. Can you imagine all that imagery stuffed inside my brain waiting to come out? Initially, I saw it as the start of a whole new series, but Jimmy Bliss is seldom far from my thoughts. I began editing this book just as COVID-19 took us all in its grip, and I debated long and hard as to how I would approach such a worldwide event. In the end I decided to ignore it altogether. This *is* a work of fiction, after all, and although I usually prefer my fictional world to have an authentic feel, I didn't feel like trying to entertain by mentioning real suffering and misery.

I've dedicated this book to the key workers who allowed the rest of us to get on with our own lives as best we could, and of course I mourn the lives lost to this terrible pandemic. The year 2020 will be one so many of us will want to forget, but if my work has brought even the tiniest drop of comfort to some, then believe me it's my honour and, as always a privilege.

ACKNOWLEDGEMENTS

THIS BEING MY SECOND self-published novel, I stuck with the exact same wonderful team as I used for my first. So, once again I am delighted to offer my deepest gratitude to Alison Birch for improving this book no end with her edit, Cherie Foxley for another magnificent cover, Sarah Hardy for putting together a wonderful list of bloggers for the tour, and to Caroline Vincent for the beguiling promotions.

The members of my 'Forder and Friends' Facebook group kept me going with their uplifting support whenever I got down. The bloggers and reviewers who were so kind to me at the release of *Endless Silent Scream* inspired me to work through the complications this new book threw up – believe me, the timeline surrounding who knew what when and how, almost drove me insane.

I hope those of you who yearned for Emily and Jimmy to get together are pleased with what you read. I wouldn't get carried away thinking about wedding bells if I were you, because knowing Jimmy Bliss there are a few bumps in the road ahead. But for now his life has turned a corner – personally, if not professionally. And if you're wondering how he's going to get out of this latest little fix, believe me… so am I. But I do have an idea that brought a smile to my lips when it occurred to me.

I couldn't help but bring Molly back, albeit as a peripheral figure in this one. I'm still not quite sure why she wormed her way into my heart, but she's there now and I'm not about to let her go. I hope you approve.

As ever, I want to thank each and every one of you, my readers. I don't know where you all came from, nor what exactly it is about these characters and stories that keeps you coming back for more, but I could not be happier nor more grateful that you do.

Finally, please don't dwell too long on the dusty contents of Jimmy's ball sack. He wouldn't want that to be your abiding memory of this book.

If you would like to keep up with news, offers and releases, please visit the Contact page on my website at www.tonyjforder.com and sign up to my newsletter. Finally, if you enjoyed this book, please take five minutes if you can spare it to write a review on Amazon (preferably) or Goodreads. Many thanks.

Best wishes – Tony (June 2020)

Printed in Great Britain
by Amazon